I0763507

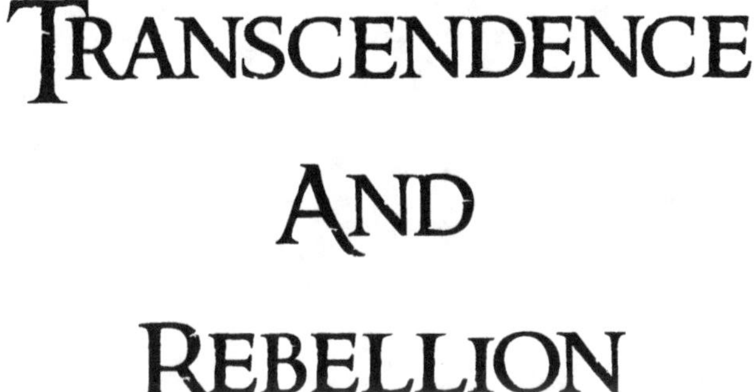

THE RIVEN GATES
VOLUME THREE

BY

MICHAEL G. MANNING

Cover by Amalia Chitulescu
Map Artwork by Maxime Plasse
Editing by Keri Karandrakis

Printed in the United States of America

ISBN: 978-1-943481-30-9

For more information about the Mageborn series check out the author's Facebook page:

https://www.facebook.com/MagebornAuthor

or visit the website:

http://www.magebornbooks.com/

THE WORLD OF MAGEBORN
Western Ocean
N
W
E
S
Graysparrow River
Iverly
Rellito
Sterling
Is
G
Wyvern Marsh
Turlingtor
L
Cantley
Surrey River
Verningham

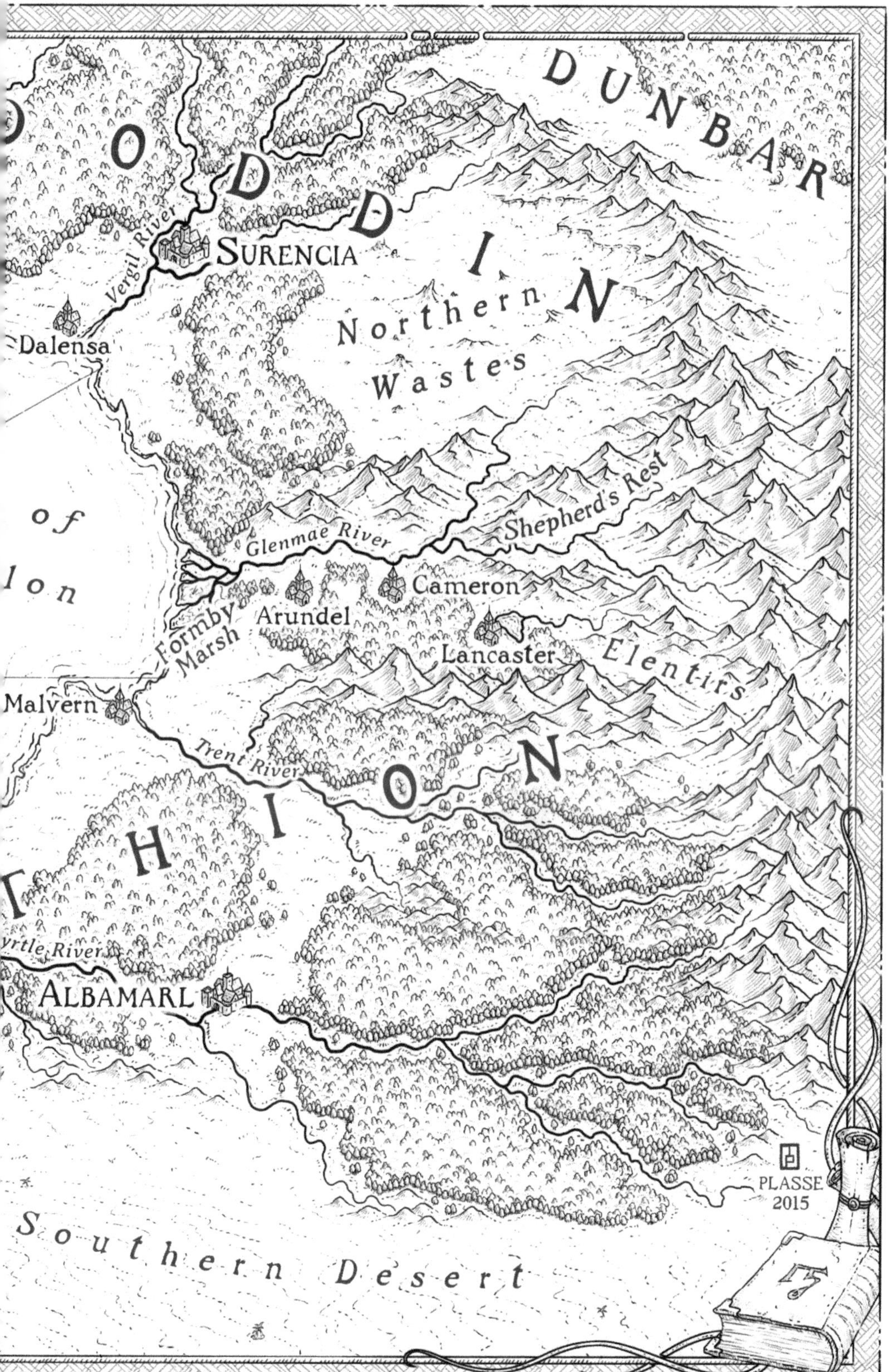

DUNBAR
O D D I N
SURENCIA
Vergil River
Dalensa
Northern Wastes
of
lon
Glenmae River
Shepherd's Rest
Cameron
Arundel
Formby Marsh
Lancaster
Elentirs
Malvern
Trent River
I H I O N
yrtle River
ALBAMARL
PLASSE 2015
Southern Desert

CHAPTER 1

The guards nodded as Tyrion stepped past them to enter the Queen's chambers. In the front room he encountered Conall, the boy who had been a constant nuisance for the past two weeks. "Her Majesty is changing," said the young man. "You'll have to wait."

"I think you know better than that, Lord Cameron," said Tyrion, putting extra emphasis on Conall's new title. "She sent for me, and she's changing—for me."

Conall looked distinctly unhappy, and before Tyrion could try to push past him, he knocked on the door to the next room. "Lord Illeniel is here, Your Majesty. Should I have him wai—"

"Send him in, Conall," came the Queen's response, cutting off his question.

Frowning, Conall opened the door, but after Tyrion passed, he followed the man in. The next room was a more private sitting room with several doors leading out, one of which being a door to the Queen's bedchamber. Ariadne stood in that doorway, dressed in a light gown that was so sheer as to be almost see-through.

The Queen smiled at Tyrion before turning a disapproving stare on her champion. "Did you need something, Lord Cameron? I don't recall giving you permission to enter."

Conall was blushing slightly and struggling to keep his eyes away from things that he knew he shouldn't see. "My apologies, Your Majesty, but you shouldn't be alone with—"

"Outside, Conall," snapped Ariadne. "And I don't mean the front room. If you insist on wasting your time like this, you can do it in the hall with the other guards."

"But…"

"Now!"

Conall left, and Tyrion smirked at his back before turning to take in the Queen's sultry attire. "It has been a while since you called for me, Your Majesty," he said mildly.

Ariadne cast a hungry look in his direction. "Far too long," she muttered. "Recent events have kept me busy."

Amused, Tyrion responded, "You don't think the boy will talk?"

She shook her head. "Conall's a good lad. He isn't given to gossip, though I am certain he doesn't approve."

Tyrion went to a sideboard and found a glass. All he needed now was wine to fill it with, but Ariadne interrupted, "How long are you going to leave me standing here, Lord Illeniel?"

He glanced up. "Does my Queen have need of me?"

"I require your service," she replied smokily.

Tyrion put the glass down and crossed the room, his stride swift and confident. When he reached the Queen, he only slowed slightly, using his momentum to sweep her off her feet and catch her in his arms. Then he lifted her up and took her to the bed, using his power to shut and lock the door behind him as he went.

He tossed her down and then studied her with the hungry gaze of a man standing before a feast table, but Ariadne wasn't in a mood to wait. Reaching up, she grabbed his shirt front and pulled him down until his lips met hers.

"Where's your necklace?" he asked when she finally let him come up for air.

Ariadne waved her hand toward the dressing table. "Over there."

Tyrion gave her a look of disapproval. "I told you to keep it on."

She frowned. "You sound like Mordecai."

"It's a well-crafted protection," observed Tyrion. "My grandson was wise to give it to you. Make sure you wear it whenever you leave. Ideally you'd never take it off."

The Queen gave him a mischievous look. "Do I need protection?"

"Always," said Tyrion without hesitation.

"Even from you?" she added.

"Especially from me." Tyrion's hands went to her legs and began to slide her nightgown up her thighs.

She shook her head. "No. Don't take it off like that. Show me your ferocity."

"This is getting expensive, Your Majesty," he told her, but her eyes told him that she didn't care. Reaching for her neckline, he ripped the fabric open. The Queen was a woman of stern control in public, but in her private chambers she was perhaps even more wild than he preferred.

He was willing to make the sacrifice, though.

They didn't talk for several minutes, as their appetites grew more out of control, until Ariadne whispered in his ear, "Use your magic."

Tyrion grew still. "I've told you before, I don't like doing that."

"But it feels *wonderful*," breathed Ariadne. "You have a gift. Share it with me." Looking up at him she saw a shadow cross his face. "Why don't you like using it?"

"Bad memories," he said quietly.

She put her hands behind his neck and pulled him closer. "Then let's make new ones."

In the end, he relented, giving her not just himself, but the artificial pleasure she desired as well, until the Queen's cries grew so loud he feared her guards might burst in to save her. When he finally released her, Ariadne's exhaustion was such that she fell asleep within minutes, leaving him alone with his thoughts.

Why do I keep thinking of her? he wondered. In the past, he often found himself remembering Kate's green eyes, but lately his dreams had been haunted by eyes of blue. *Probably because I want to kill her so badly,* he told himself.

He considered leaving. He wasn't tired enough for sleep, nor was his passion fully sated. Ariadne's appetite for magic had left her satisfied while he felt empty. *When she wakes, I'll remedy that problem,* he thought, running one hand over the Queen's soft curves.

Bored, he used his magesight to study her body. Ariadne had been married for many years, but she still had borne no children. Looking within, he found something that might be a cause. The tube-like fingers of flesh that led from her uterus had been damaged at some point and had healed improperly. Scar tissue blocked them. *That's easy enough to fix,* he thought.

It only took a few minutes to make the correction, but the strange sensations caused Ariadne to stir. Her eyes opened, and her hand went to her stomach, where she felt an odd warmth.

Tyrion wrapped one hand around her knee and turned her over to face him. "You're awake."

She smiled drowsily. "Barely."

"That's enough," said Tyrion, lifting her hands and pinning them above her head. "I'm still hungry. You've left me in quite a state."

Ariadne chuckled. "I'm too tired now. You'll have to petition me when I hold court tomorrow if you seek redress of any perceived wrongs."

"You can redress after I've finished wronging you," he replied, using his knee to tease her legs apart.

She bit his ear, then whispered, "You seem to have an urgent petition, my lord."

"An impassioned plea for justice, Your Majesty," he responded throatily. Then he presented his case.

Returning to his room a short while later, Tyrion felt one of his knees buckle, almost causing him to fall. He caught himself, placing one hand against the wall to help him balance while the other leg took his weight. The pain was intense. *This body won't last much longer. It has almost been three months. I need to return,* he thought.

One of the krytek was standing guard beside the door to his room. Most residents in the palace didn't have personal guards, but Tyrion wasn't one to take chances anymore. He made sure one of his guardians was close by at all times. His experience after Mordecai's trial had been a stern reminder.

"Send for the dormon," he commanded the guardian. "I need to return to the Wester Isle."

The krytek left to do as he bid, but it also sent another to take its place until it returned. Tyrion went to his room and gathered a few personal things and then sat down to wait. *I hope Lyralliantha has finished. It's been long enough.*

A knock at the door disturbed his reverie. "Sir Conall is here to see you, milord," announced his new guard.

"It's Lord Cameron now," shouted Tyrion. "Don't make me remind you again. Let him in." The stupidity of his krytek annoyed him. They were born with the knowledge they needed, but their other attributes varied considerably, according to what he wanted when he made them. At the moment, he was wishing he had made them smarter. These had trouble adjusting to new information, such as the fact that Conall was now a landed lord, rather than simply a knight.

The door opened and Conall stepped inside. His face spoke of barely suppressed anger. "Your Grace, I'm here to talk to you about—"

"The Queen," interrupted Tyrion. "As if it were any business of yours."

"It's my duty to protect her," said Conall stiffly. "Your behavior is a danger to her."

Tyrion stood and took two strides, crossing the room and putting himself nearly nose to nose with the young lord. "You are her champion, Conall, not her moral guardian. Who the Queen decides to fuck is none of your concern. Or are you upset that it wasn't you she chose?"

Conall's face colored. "She's my cousin!"

"Twice removed," said Tyrion. "Which is the same as a second cousin. She could marry you if she wanted. Have I struck a nerve?"

"No!" protested Conall, feeling off balance. "I'm worried about rumors. Her husband has just been murdered…"

"By your father," reminded Tyrion. "Your position is looking more and more confusing from my perspective. Perhaps you should be happier that she's moved on so quickly."

"I don't believe it was him," said Conall. "I heard the testimony. Only a fool would believe what the girl said at the end. It was almost certainly Leomund's servant, Vander."

Tyrion smiled maliciously, then went to a small cupboard and took out a bottle of wine and two glasses. Opening it, he filled both halfway and offered one to the young man. "It's a shame the judge didn't agree. Your father has been convicted, whether he did it or not. He's a wanted man. It's our duty to bring him to justice."

"Executing an innocent man isn't justice," insisted Conall.

Tyrion sat down and leaned back, crossing his legs. "I don't give a damn what you call it. I intend to kill the man when I see him next. Call it duty, call it justice, call it revenge, it makes no matter to me."

Conall frowned, staring at the glass of wine in his hand, but didn't drink.

"The question, Lord Cameron," continued Tyrion, "is what will you do? Will you support the Queen and betray your father, or commit treason?"

Conall lifted his glass and swallowed the contents in a single gulp. "I am loyal to the Queen, but I won't lift my hand against my father."

Tyrion began to laugh. "We'll see if fate is kind enough to save you from such a choice. I highly doubt it. You owe your current title to his misfortune. I suggest you accept your good luck and move on. Children have to cut ties with their parents eventually."

"Independence is one thing," said Conall, "but I will always honor my father."

"Really?" said Tyrion, raising one brow. Then he reached behind himself and patted his back. "I can still feel it sometimes, the blade my daughter stuck in me. My children were more than happy to murder me to get me out of the way."

Conall said nothing, staring at his empty glass.

"Don't be so sullen," said Tyrion. "I don't blame my daughter. She did the right thing. I was sick with the need for violence back then. I've forgiven her and moved on. A few thousand years as a tree does wonders for one's perspective."

"I would never do something like that," said Conall at last.

Tyrion leaned forward and refilled both their glasses. "We'll see. Your father reminds me of one of my sons, Gabriel. Did I ever tell you what happened to him?"

"I've heard the story, but I forget some of the names," answered Conall.

Tyrion nodded amiably. "He was one of the first to die. He couldn't kill his sister. He was too kind, so she slew him instead."

"What's your point?" asked Conall irritably.

"Don't be like Gabriel. Don't be like your father, or it will end badly for you," said Tyrion. "If Gabriel had killed her, it would have ended the bloodshed sooner, but he was weak. Instead, my daughter Brigid had to finish the task for him. I lost two children instead of one. Your father's weakness could cost a lot of people their lives. Your faintness of heart could do the same."

"You're sick," observed Conall. "Why are you here? I don't understand your motivation in all of this. Why did you come back?"

Tyrion sipped his wine. "You wouldn't believe me."

"Try me."

The archmage stared at him for several seconds, then answered, "Fine. I was quite content to stay a tree. It's a damn sight more pleasant than being human. I don't really care about restoring the She'Har either, but my hatred for them has dulled with time."

"So, what do you want? Power?"

"Power?" grunted Tyrion. "What a joke! I have as much of that as I desire. Power is merely a tool. I was happier dreaming away eternity, but when your father woke me I began to take notice of the world. Over time I realized that things were happening again. The world my children created in my absence is an interesting place, but the people in it, such as your father, lack the will to do what is necessary to protect it. ANSIS will destroy you.

"No, I don't want power. I came back to save the world from the weak," finished Tyrion.

Conall emptied his second glass but declined to let Tyrion fill it again. He was ready to leave. "I can't decide if you're an obsessed megalomaniac or simply a deluded idealist, but either way you don't sound like a savior."

Tyrion's eyes narrowed. "Watch your tone, boy," he warned, but after a second he relaxed. "You can think whatever you like, but I'll tell you a secret. Saviors are never people with noble intentions or higher ideals. People claiming those are either fools or conmen. I would put your father in the first group. No, true saviors are men who aren't afraid to do what is necessary, men who are willing to get blood on their hands.

"In the end, I don't care what people think of me. I will eliminate ANSIS and every other threat to this world, and when I am done, I'll go back to my island, and leave the rest for the fools to fight over. I care nothing for titles or crowns. In the meantime, be careful, young lord, lest you get on the wrong side of me. Until I retire from the field, I will destroy anyone or anything that interferes with my goal," said Tyrion.

The door opened and one of the krytek stepped in. "The dormon is ready, my lord."

Standing up, Tyrion gave Conall a small nod. "You'll have to excuse me, Lord Cameron. I must return to my land for a short time. I'll be happy to continue our discussion another time."

CHAPTER 2

"Come here," commanded Moira Illeniel.

The krytek guard walked over, stopping in front of her. It had been a week since the Queen and Tyrion had left it and the others to keep watch over her and the house. She had worked slowly, subtly, suborning their loyalty and free will, but they were now hers, completely and utterly. It was time to begin the real work.

"Lower your shield and open your mind," she told it.

The krytek did as she bid, releasing its protective shield and giving her free access to its mind.

Moira smiled. "This will hurt. Don't resist me and it will be over quickly."

"Yes, milady," answered the krytek.

Her power lashed out, boring into the krytek's mind, but not for the purpose of altering its personality any further. She invaded the creature and ripped its mind asunder, until it was nothing more than a living shell, then she replaced it with a new mind. "What is your name?" she asked the krytek.

The krytek smiled. "Moira Illeniel," said the creature, then it frowned. "Wait, no, I'm the copy, aren't I?"

Moira nodded. "How do you feel in that body?"

The creature frowned. "Strange, powerful, and sad."

"It should have enough power to allow you to do whatever is necessary," said Moira. "The sadness I can't do anything about."

"I have less than a month to live," said the krytek. "Unless…"

"Unless you turn rogue," finished Moira. "I'm hoping you're brave enough to do the right thing."

The krytek studied its hands, and then it met her gaze again. "You're willing to sacrifice yourself for this—so am I."

"I'm glad to hear it," said Moira. "Remember, when you go back…"

The krytek held up a hand impatiently. "I know, go slow. I'll be careful."

"A copy of a copy is more unstable. If even a single one goes rogue, it could mean disaster so don't…"

"I won't," said the krytek. "I'll make sure the spell-twins all stay within the third or fourth order of the original, just to be safe."

After her first spell-twin had left to return to Albamarl Moira moved on to her other guards. She repeated the process with the remaining nine krytek, killing their minds and replacing them with spell-twins. The human guards she left alive, making only final adjustments to ensure their absolute loyalty. They would never be completely the same afterward, but at least they could go on to live relatively normal lives someday, once she released them.

It still isn't right, she thought. *But they haven't given me much choice, have they?*

She returned to her room to rest for a while. Making spell-twins wasn't as tiring as creating a spellbeast from scratch, and when the host body was that of a mage, she didn't even need to use much of her own aythar. Her fatigue wasn't so much mental or physical as it was moral. She hadn't wanted to do what she had done.

Myra was sitting on the bed, petting the dog, Humphrey, when she entered. "Finished?" asked her first and oldest spell-twin. Myra didn't have a physical body. She was a creature of pure aythar, and because of that she was dependent on regular infusions of power from Moira to keep her going.

Moira nodded. "Yeah. I'm thinking about taking a bath."

"I still don't see why you didn't let me have one of them," said Myra. "Then you wouldn't have to keep replenishing me."

"You're too old," said Moira. "It's been so long since you were created that we really aren't twins anymore."

Myra pursed her lips in annoyance. "I don't think we've diverged that much. Are you starting to mistrust me?"

"You know that's not the case," said Moira. *Not that I really trust anyone completely anymore, least of all myself.* "But you've become a true sister to me. What I'm sending those krytek to do is dangerous. I couldn't bear to lose you."

Myra rolled Humphrey onto his back and began to give him an intense belly rub. "Well, I suppose I should be glad to know that you want to protect me, but I'm *bored*!" She picked up Humphrey and held him in front of her with his paws in her hands. "Think about poor little Humphrey here. I've been petting him so much he's going to go bald." The dog promptly licked her face.

Moira smiled. "I think he's enjoyed all the attention. Besides, I'm stuck here too. It's just as boring for me. I'm going to be lonely once you leave."

Myra perked up. "I'm leaving?"

"Someone has to check on Matthew and Irene. Now that the guards are all firmly under my control, we need to find out what's happened to them. You're the logical choice to send. If I'm not here when Tyrion or the Queen come to check on me, they'll know something is afoot," explained Moira.

Myra put Humphrey down and spun in a small circle, then stopped. "What if it takes too long? Even if you put everything you have in me, I'll only last a week or so. You aren't planning to use one of the human guards, are you?"

Myra required not only aythar to survive, but more specifically, her creator's aythar. The only way around that would be for her to take possession of a living aystrylin. That was what Moira's recent spell-twins had done with the krytek. A normal human would work as well, although the aystrylin of a normal person would leave Myra with very little extra aythar to spend, aside from what she needed to stay alive.

It was also murder. The body of the host lived, but the mind and soul were destroyed.

Moira blanched. "No! I'm not that bad, yet." She went to her wardrobe and pulled out a wooden jewelry box. Inside was a silver ring set with a large sapphire. Runes were engraved around the band, and the stone glowed with power to Myra's magesight. "I've been saving aythar for a rainy day. You can take this with you."

"I can't take that. Your mother gave you that ring," protested Myra.

"*Our* mother," corrected Moira. "Take it. You may need it if anything delays your return. There's enough aythar in it to keep you alive for at least an extra week or two. We don't know if they're checking the boundary or not, so it might be a while before anyone notices you."

Myra nodded, accepting the ring. "When do you want me to go?"

"There's no one watching us any longer, so now is fine. Don't stay any longer than necessary, though. Return as soon as you talk to them. I need to know what they're doing, and I'm sure they want to know what's going on here," said Moira.

After a short goodbye, Myra left and Moira went to take her bath, but no amount of water and soap could make her feel clean after what she had done to her guards.

***

Matthew Illeniel stared out from the battlements of Castle Lancaster. The field that stretched out before him was littered with wreckage. Over the past week, the attacks on the castle had increased in frequency and intensity, but it wasn't ogres and spiders they worried about anymore. Those had vanished days ago, replaced by a more sinister foe.

The machines had come.

It had been small flyers in the beginning. Chad Grayson had shot the one that flew over the castle out of the air with an enchanted arrow, but soon after that they had become too numerous for their limited supply of such weapons. Karen, Elaine, Lynaralla, and Irene had taken over then, bringing the swarms of flying machines down with bursts of fire, lightning, and beams of channeled force.

Unfortunately, Castle Lancaster didn't have an enchanted shield the way that Castle Cameron did, so they had no defense that could give them a respite. The young wizards were forced to work in shifts to keep their attackers at bay.

Cyhan, Gram, and Alyssa hadn't had much to do. They had been forced to watch helplessly while the mages took care of the majority of the defense. Normal arrows were largely ineffective against the metal flyers. That had soon changed, though, when the crawlers had appeared.

Crawlers, that had been the best name they could come up with for the six-legged machines that had come swarming across the field. They were the size of large dogs with razor sharp claws at the end of spindly metal legs. Those that had evaded the wizards attacks hadn't paused at the moat; they had gone straight into the water and come up the other side without hesitation, climbing the walls with a speed that rivaled the spiders that had so recently been trying to sneak in.

They had almost overwhelmed the men-at-arms who guarded the walls. The machines' metal bodies were difficult to damage with normal weapons, and their claws tore into the soldiers with deadly ease. Cyhan, Gram, and Alyssa had been busy then, trying to prevent them from overwhelming the defenders.

Even with the help of so many wizards, it had been a close fight. And through it all, Matthew had kept himself apart, watching from one of the towers and engaging only those that came close to his observation point.

Karen had stayed with him through most of it, providing the bulk of the magical support for that corner of the walls and occasionally relaying his instructions to the others. Her ability to teleport anywhere at a moment's notice made her invaluable for carrying warnings to the others or stopping surprise attacks.

And there had been plenty of surprises. The enemy had used intense attacks on one side to draw defenders away from other areas, only to send hundreds of previously unseen crawlers up the wall in the section that was least defended. The moat had worked against them in that regard. Their enemy didn't need to breathe and could hide beneath the water for extended periods of time before emerging suddenly.

Yet, Matthew had anticipated every ploy the enemy used.

Karen had just teleported back to his side. She was breathing hard from her latest exertions. Magic was just as tiring as swinging a sword, more so in some ways. A warrior didn't have to worry about swinging his sword so many times that his body died of simple exhaustion, but that wasn't the case for wizards.

Karen's exhaustion had reached a level she hadn't known was possible. She had used so much power that she felt as though she would collapse at any moment. And yet there was still more power in her. Power she had to be careful not to use, lest she use so much her body could no longer keep her heart and lungs working. That was the danger of magic. Unlike physical exercise, the human body had no natural protections to prevent the user from going too far and killing herself from overuse.

And still Matthew refused to use his power to assist. He was standing next to one of the merlons, staring outward with eyes that seemed to see everything and nothing at the same time. Karen stared at him worriedly. He was so still that if it weren't for the wind stirring his hair, she might have thought him a statue, and the light reflected from the lake on that side of the castle made his blue eyes appear silver.

"I can't do much more," she told him. "I'm almost done, and the others are just as tired. If they keep this up, we'll be overrun."

She wasn't sure he had even heard her, but after half a minute, Matthew answered, "Just a little longer, Karen. They're almost here."

Karen looked at him in alarm. "They? What do you mean?"

"The main force," said Matthew, his voice dead and emotionless. "This was all to soften us up, to wear us down so we wouldn't damage their most valuable assets."

"Well, it's worked!" said Karen, her voice rising to a higher pitch as she struggled to contain her panic. "We can't take anymore, and now you're saying this was just the warmup."

A cry went up from the north wall, and Karen saw the crawlers were swarming again. Only a few guards were left there, and as she looked on she saw two of them eviscerated by shining claws as the crawlers came up in numbers too great to stop. She started to teleport, but Matthew chose that moment to speak. “Don’t.”

Another man died as she hesitated. “What do you mean? Don’t? They’re dying!”

“That’s the last feint,” said Matthew. “Gram can handle it. The losses will be heavy, but he will clean up the last of them before it gets out of control. I need the last of your power.”

“How do you know that? They’re dying! I can help them,” she argued.

Matthew turned to look at her, fixing her with eyes that were pools of molten silver. “If you do, we all die. There’s a larger group behind the tree line to the east. They’ll come through the hole in the wall if they aren’t destroyed.”

“What hole?” she asked.

“Another minute,” said Matthew. “When I give the word, I want you to take me to the trees on the west side. After that leave me and come back for the dragons, Cyhan, and Alyssa. Take them to the same point on the east side. Leave Gram here to finish the ones coming over the wall.”

“What about the wizards?”

“They stay. They’ve done enough. If you take any of them, they’ll die,” he told her.

Karen blinked, feeling tears of frustration beginning to well up in her eyes. “What about me? I’m not sure I have enough left to make that many trips.”

“You do,” he said confidently. “Once for me, twice more for the Zephyr, Cyhan and Alyssa, and one last teleport to bring yourself back here. You can rest then.”

“Can’t Zephyr just fly them over there?” she pointed out.

Matthew shook his head. “No, they’ll lose the element of surprise.” Then he stopped, tilting his head to one side with an odd expression on his face. “Get ready. I need you to take me in about fifteen seconds.”

“You’re insane,” she said. “Where is this coming from?”

“Karen,” said Matthew. His eyes changed back to blue suddenly, and his face grew serious. “After you take me and then teleport the others, you have to come back. When you do, go to the dungeon.”

“Why?”

“Most of the castle will be safe, but I can’t be certain where the attacks will hit. There are too many variables still. The dungeon will be safe. Anywhere else and you might die,” he explained. Then he held out his hand. “Now.”

Exhausted, frustrated, and angry, she took it. Karen wanted to refuse, but over the past few days she had seen his predictions come true too often to ignore his words. Gritting her teeth, she summoned a portion of her nearly depleted aythar and teleported him to the tree line to the west.

Matthew released her hand immediately after they arrived. "Go," he commanded. "You have less than a minute to get the others to the east side."

She struggled to marshal the necessary power to teleport back. Ordinarily it took little more than a thought to be wherever she wished, but now it was a test of will. After a few seconds she felt her aythar begin to move, but just before she teleported she saw the trees in front of them collapse, revealing a host of massive metal monsters. Then she was gone.

Matthew stared at his three-legged adversaries. He had faced them before; they were known as tortuses back on Karen's homeworld. They were a type of military machine that carried two main weapons, one a powerful gatling gun that could destroy people and small buildings with ease, the other a specialized type of artillery called a railgun. The railgun was slow to fire and reload, but its firepower was great enough to destroy castle walls, dragons, or pretty much anything else that got in its way.

There were at least a hundred of them amassed there, a classic example of overkill. It would only take two or three to level Castle Lancaster if they were allowed to bombard the castle over a period of several minutes. This many could destroy everything with a single volley.

Matthew walked forward, raising his metal fist as he went.

The ground behind him exploded as high-velocity projectiles tore through the space he had been standing in, accompanied by the high-pitched whine and roar of gatling guns. He didn't have a shield up to protect himself—it would have been pointless, the firepower present was such that a shield would merely have made him a target, and rendered him helpless when it soon collapsed under the withering fire.

The tortuses were close, and he moved among them, using their bulk against them. Those farther away couldn't target him because their line of fire was obscured by those closest to him. Even so, several managed to find clear lines of attack, and they fired with the perfect precision that only intelligent machines could accomplish.

And yet, they missed.

Just before every attack began, he moved, slipping into the shadow of a different tortus to avoid the blazing hail of bullets. In the open field, it would have been physically impossible. Each tortus could target and move with a speed that even his precognitive danger sense would have been useless, but in close among them, he was able to avoid them—barely.

Shrapnel and ricochets made it even more difficult and at moments he was forced to accept minor injuries to avoid serious ones, but as he moved a long metal staff grew from his fist. It extended until it reached a length of six feet and then he gave the command to activate it, *"Bree talto, eilen kon, sadeen lin. Amyrtus!"*

It was a complex activation sequence that set the parameters for the Fool's Tesseract as it came into existence. In an instant, Matthew was surrounded by six planes of dimensional force that acted as one-way portals to a temporary dimension. Within the cube he was untouchable, while outside of it, air, dust, and weapons fire were all sucked inward as though gale-force winds had suddenly appeared—winds that all converged on a single point, the Fool's Tesseract.

The machines recognized his enchanted construct. They had seen it before on Karen's world, and they began to scatter, moving to put as much distance between them and the black cube as possible.

Within the dark interior, Matthew smiled. They didn't have time to get far enough away. The Fool's Tesseract only needed a few seconds to draw in enough matter to do what he needed. The interior dimension that had been accepting mass was very small, and depending on how much matter was within it, the result when it was expelled could range from explosively impressive to catastrophic. Given a small enough interior dimension and enough time and matter, it could potentially destroy the world.

But not today, thought Matthew grimly. Then he voiced the command to invert the enchantment, *"Rextalyet, amyrtus!"* The result was an explosion powerful enough to cause the ground to buck beneath his feet, and as he was still safe within the cube that was the only part of the explosion he could sense.

Outside, however, the tortuses were tossed and thrown into the air by a concussive blast so powerful it flattened the trees within fifty yards. The closest tortuses were torn apart, while those farther away were either damaged or sent tumbling if they were lucky.

Matthew uttered a new activation command, changing the Fool's Tesseract to a three-plane configuration. He now had a black plane above his head and two in front of him. The three square planes converged to form a pyramidal structure that protected him from attacks that might come from above or from the front and sides.

He took the staff that anchored the Fool's Tesseract into his other hand and then lifted his metal fist again, this time summoning two pieces of triangular metal that began to spin as soon as they appeared. With a thought he sent them away, and as they flew, black planes of dimensional force grew from them until each of the spinning weapons appeared to be a black circle.

Desperate, the tortuses that had recovered began to fire on him once more, heedless of whether their attacks might damage one another. They knew, with perfect machine logic, that unless he died soon, they were all lost.

But Matthew knew the truth. They were already lost. Their destruction had been assured the moment he appeared on the field. Walking in a slow circle, he turned and angled the Fool's Tesseract to block incoming attacks while mentally directing his spinning weapons. The black discs flew unerringly to find first one, two, then more of his enemies. The dimensional fields passed through the armored behemoths as though they were made of air, leaving severed wreckage in their wake.

Unfortunately, there were still dozens of tortuses active, and he only had the two weapons with which to dispatch them. As their situation quickly became hopeless, those on the farthest edge of the battle accepted their fate and instead turned their railguns toward Castle Lancaster, hoping to inflict at least some damage before they were destroyed.

He had expected that, though, and the spinning discs went after those first, ignoring the ones still firing on him. *But I can't get all of them in time,* he thought regretfully. He knew, because he had been studying the possibilities for hours before the battle happened.

Studying the future was tricky business. The farther out one looked, the fuzzier things got, and it was only in the closest moments that near certainty could be found. This was the best possibility he had been able to find, and it was nearing completion. His dimensional blades tore through his enemies, destroying all but one.

He needed to redirect the blade closest to it, though. There were four tortuses firing on him from different directions, and if he didn't kill one of those first, he would be hit by an attack he couldn't block. That meant the final tortus aiming on Lancaster would get a single shot off with its railgun. Some things simply couldn't be helped.

An image flashed through his mind, Karen and Gram's bodies, torn and mangled into almost unrecognizable lumps of flesh. *She didn't go to the dungeon,* he realized. She had gone to help Gram instead, and the increased resistance in that area had lent weight to the machine's decision on which part of the walls to target.

Ignoring the warning of his danger sense, he sent the blade back toward the tortus that was about to fire on the castle. If he could hit one of its legs, he could spoil the shot—but it would be close. As he did, he created an impromptu shield to protect his back, pouring his strength into it and hoping it would be enough.

The spinning blade tore through the tortus's leg just as its railgun fired. Part of the castle wall exploded into rock and dust, and then Matthew felt the gatling gun of the one he had ignored open up on his shielded back.

He was thrown forward by the force of hundreds of impacts against his shield. When he hit the ground, the staff that controlled the Fool's Tesseract flew from his hand, and as the other three tortuses opened fire, he felt his concentration begin to falter. He was taking fire from four gatling guns now, and even his impressive strength could only take so much.

I need to go down, he thought. Creating a hole to shelter within was the only way to survive the withering onslaught, but he couldn't spare the strength and concentration to attempt it. Redirecting even a fraction of his power would result in near instant annihilation. Instead, he redoubled his efforts to maintain his shield while directing his dimensional blades toward his attackers.

One down, two, three... He was so close. *Just a few seconds longer.* The last tortus was still firing when he felt his power fail. His mind shattered into painful fragments as his shield collapsed, and the agony was so great that he almost didn't feel the impacts as the gatling gun's bullets tore into his body.

The world dissolved into streaks of red and black.

CHAPTER 3

I floated above a city of shining metal. Well, 'city' might not have been the best term for it. ANSIS didn't really create cities. If Karen were here she probably would have called it a factory. Whatever it was called, it was impressive. It stretched for ten miles in every direction, producing who knew what sorts of monstrosities.

How fast do they build these things? I wondered. This was the third one I had found since my moment of transcendence.

Transcendence was what I had decided to call my transformation. It sounded a lot better than 'descent into corruption.' I honestly had no idea what to think of my current state. I had become a living paradox, or perhaps an unliving paradox—either term was applicable. Possessed of unthinkable amounts of aythar, the stuff of life itself, I was nevertheless riddled with the dark power of the void. I was living fire, bound in chains of death.

Unlike my first transformation years ago, when I had been trapped as a shiggreth, this one was different. To begin with, I was truly myself, at least in the sense that my soul wasn't trapped within a prison, watching a simulacrum of my mind pretend to be me. My emotions were still present, but my perspective was skewed.

Very little seemed important to me. I still felt things—anger, love, hatred, even guilt—but they were more distant. The world—no the universe—was huge, and my place in it was much larger than before. The small problems of my previous existence seemed somewhat petty.

At some level, I tried to act according to my former priorities. ANSIS certainly seemed like an important problem. But then again, what was one world when there was an infinity of worlds? The cycle of life and death played out on all of them. In some, the void won; in others the living heart of aythar, the soul of awareness, the Illeniel, came out on top.

I was neither, and both, and it didn't matter. No matter which side I chose, nothing would change. The void was greater, an endless backdrop of night that made the brilliant stars of living worlds seem small, but even if I chose to snuff out the light, there would always be more. By the same token, eliminating the endless march of death and entropy was also impossible.

I could choose a victor here or there, but in the grand scheme of things, the battle would go on for eternity. There could be no ultimate victory for either side.

There was no point to it all.

The world exploded around me, again. ANSIS was well aware of my presence, and they were continuing their usual efforts to put a stop to my meddling. They had used something new this time, causing my body to disperse into a cloud of burning particles. I would have laughed, if I'd had lungs—or a throat.

Instead I descended, letting the diffuse plasma that currently constituted my body float downward. My first instinct was to reform myself, but I quickly changed my mind. Sometimes being big is more fun, so I spread myself even farther, making myself into a tenuous cloud so vast that it covered the entire ANSIS facility. Then I began to increase my temperature, slowly.

I could have done it faster, but I was bored and had no idea what I would do with myself once I was done playing here, so I dragged it out. Fifteen minutes later, and the heat had become so intense that things began to melt. Some of the buildings were putting out plumes of toxic smoke as their more flammable portions burst into flame. Eventually, the temperature got so hot that even the smoke began to burn as it was driven to still more energetic reactions with the atmosphere.

All of this cost me an enormous amount of aythar, enough to make me notice, at least, but aythar wasn't a real problem anymore. Once everything had been reduced to burning slag, I reversed the process; instead of pumping more energy into the system, I began removing it, letting the void drink its fill of the chaos and entropy I had created.

Everything cooled, until the temperature was so low that cracks and fissures formed in what few structures were left. I didn't stop, though. In the past I had thought the void only affected living creatures, and in a sense that was partly true. It affected living things more strongly, but all things have order and entropy within them, whether they are living or inanimate.

I removed all the energy I could, and then I continued, removing the order that naturally results from such a low entropy state. When I had finished, even the remains of the metal that had melted and cooled dissolved into a fine dust that settled to the ground.

Nothing remained of the factory, city—whatever you might want to call it. It was gone. A plain of unremarkable grey ash extended for fifteen miles in every direction, flat and featureless. My body had reformed, and the power within me was greater than ever. I gazed at the wasteland, studying what I had wrought, and it was *good.*

My reverie was interrupted by a flash, an image in my mind. *Matthew.* He was fighting somewhere, and his death was imminent.

Unfortunately, despite my premonition, I still had no idea in which direction Lancaster lay. I would have to search the world to find it, a task that would take me a considerable length of time. But then again, time, in a certain sense, is a product of entropy. Removing most of the entropy from the world was one possible solution, but it might be difficult given my current size. It would also have a host of undesirable effects for the world itself.

Far easier would be increasing my own entropy, increasing my own speed and causing the world to seem slower in comparison. Rising into the air, my body began to darken; the white flames that formed my body became grey, and then went from grey to black as I transformed into a creature of almost pure void. Then I began to move, and even light could no longer touch me.

***

By the time Tyrion reached the Wester Isle, he was feeling much worse. Everything ached, his joints, muscles, even his teeth hurt, and whenever he ran his hand over his head, it came away with a scattering of hair between his fingers. Death was only hours away.

I almost feel sorry for the krytek, he thought wryly. *Three months of perfect health only to fall apart in less than a day.*

He dismounted from the dormon and walked toward the new Illeniel Grove. It now consisted of nearly ten trees, his, Lyralliantha's, and eight saplings that were so new they stood barely ten feet in height. His tree was the largest of course, stretching several hundred feet into the air, but Lyralliantha's was slowly beginning to catch up. Her body stretched up nearly seventy feet in height, though her main trunk was still relatively slender, and her limbs and branches were still similarly lithe and small.

The other eight were technically adults by She'Har standards, though they had spent less than a day as 'children' before taking root. It would be at least a year before they could contribute anything to his efforts, but Tyrion had hope for them in the future.

In less than a hundred years, we could replace every human and cover the world with our forests—if I were so inclined, he thought smugly.

That wasn't his plan, of course. If anything, in the past he would have preferred to wipe out every one of the remaining She'Har, including himself if that was necessary. He had changed over the past four thousand years, however. He no longer desired the utter annihilation of the She'Har, or any other race for that matter.

Just let me settle the problems of the present so I can go back to sleep, he thought. After that, the world could do whatever the hell it pleased. *And if anything else goes wrong in the future, I'll decide then whether I care enough to sort it out for them.* It was entirely possible that after another several thousand years, he might not care enough to do anything, even if they came to burn his own tree.

He entered the grove, but didn't walk toward his own tree; he headed instead for that of Lyralliantha. *Wake,* he commanded, putting his hand against her trunk. *Wake.*

Nothing happened for several minutes, but eventually he felt a faint response. Her mind was aware of him, but it was still moving far too slowly to communicate with him. *Wake!* he commanded once more, sending a painful jolt of aythar into her.

Several more minutes passed before he received the beginning of a response from her, *My love…*

I have no time, he sent to her. *Rouse yourself, now!*

It's difficult, she replied slowly.

Do it, or I'll set fire to your branches to hasten the process, he insisted.

It was almost half an hour before she managed to bring her thought processes up to a speed close to that of humans. *What need is there for such haste?* she asked.

This body is almost done, he informed her. *A few more hours and I would be dead.*

You could have rejoined your tree, she thought back to him, somewhat sourly. *There was no need for threats.*

I need to return right away. Events move quickly in the human realm. I couldn't afford to spend weeks talking to you in the usual way, he returned. *Is the child ready?*

Yes, she replied. *But if you were in such a hurry you could have used another krytek body.*

They're inferior, he argued. *I'm sick of replacing them.*

You will need to eat calmuth regularly with this new body, she cautioned. *Otherwise it will take root and you will wind up in dire straits.*

Better than having to replace it every three months, he told her. *I'll store plenty of your fruit in stasis to take back with me.*

Take some for Lynaralla as well, suggested Lyralliantha. *She hasn't returned for some time. She must be running low by now.*

If I can even find her, said Tyrion. *She has gone into hiding with the majority of Mordecai's rebellious children.*

They talked for a short while longer, and then he went to the massive pod hanging from one of Lyralliantha's lowest hanging branches. It was so heavy that the bottom rested against the ground. He waited beside it for several minutes, until Lyralliantha's will caused its exterior to split and release her latest offspring.

Within was the lean, muscular figure of what appeared to be a human male with silver hair. It was covered in a viscous, sap-like fluid that coated Tyrion's hands as he pulled it free and stretched it out on the ground. Normally when a She'Har child was born, they woke up right after the pod split open, but this one remained comatose.

He stared at its features. *What a handsome devil I am,* he thought silently. Then he bent down and put his arms beneath its head and knees. He used his power to strengthen his back, legs, and arms, making the weight of the body easy for him to lift, but his joints still complained. Then he carried it back to his own tree. When he reached it, he opened his mind and listened, letting his self expand. After a few seconds, he walked forward and his body merged with that of his tree.

Silence fell over the grove then, broken only by the sound of the wind as it played in the branches. An hour passed before he stepped back out of the Father-tree that was his true body, and when he emerged, he was no longer carrying another body. Tyrion was alone.

He stood in the sunlight, stretching and getting used to his new flesh. "This is much better," he said aloud. Once he was done becoming accustomed to his new body, he went to a large root that had sprung up from the ground while he was within the tree. It possessed a large, rectangular knob of wood at the top. It was the size of a large footlocker, and when his hand came in contact, it broke away. Using his power, he lifted it and set it to one side, then opened it. *Now it just needs the appropriate enchantment,* he thought.

A stasis enchantment would take hours to craft, though. Tyrion smiled, then stretched out his hand. With a thought, magic grew from his fingers in a vine-like protrusion that stretched out to surround the wooden box before sinking into it. *Spellweaving certainly has its advantages,* he thought.

That done, he went to collect calmuth from Lyralliantha's branches.

Chapter 4

My search took what might have been days or even weeks of subjective time. It was hard to say; my sense of time was distorted to such a degree that was impossible to guess. The important reality, though, was that only a few seconds of time passed for the rest of the world.

Lancaster had definitely seen better days. The landscape around it was torn and littered with old corpses and more recently destroyed machines. The castle was missing a large section of one of its walls but was otherwise intact.

None of that mattered to me, though. On the western side, close to the trees, my son was stretched out face-down across a dark portion of torn earth, his blood just beginning to soak into the soil. There were pieces of what had once been deadly war machines strewn all about, testimony to what must have been an impressive battle.

One machine was still functional, a tortus with its gatling gun still trained on my son's body. Pieces of metal flew from it in slow motion, making their way toward Matthew's collapsed form. The easiest solution was simply to destroy the machine and the projectiles that were still in the air, but using that sort of concentrated aythar or its counterpart, entropy, might be lethal to Matthew, simply because of his proximity.

Instead I erected a simple shield around him, to protect him from further attacks—as well as my presence—then I moved closer. As I approached, I increased the power of the shield, for even the power that emanated passively from my body was such that a normal shield wasn't enough to keep him safe.

The tortus collapsed by the time I had gotten with fifty feet, though I hadn't taken any overt action against it.

My son was still alive. Only three bullets had struck him before I arrived, but the damage they had done would probably be fatal if something wasn't done quickly. *The question is what to do?* I couldn't risk trying to heal him directly, as I would have done before my transformation. Just being this close to him without a shield would kill him; attempting to do something directly would be much worse.

But I could feel a connection between us, a thin, silver thread of something familiar. It reminded me of Kion. I thought about it for some time, while a leaf drifted toward the ground in my peripheral vision, moving so slowly it felt as though it would take all day before it came to rest on the earth. *The Illeniel gift?* Maybe that was what I sensed, though I couldn't be sure.

Regardless, I had to do something, so I tried gently drawing some of the entropy from his body, enough to slow the progress of his death. Then another thought came to me. *I could make him like me.* Threads of black and white drifted in the air above my hand as I considered it.

Wrap him in chains of fire and void, I thought. *Then I wouldn't be alone. He could be a god. Even Penny would agree it's better than letting him die...*

No! The answer cut through my mind, a shout of denial so loud I couldn't ignore it, and it sounded like Penny's voice.

The hand I was staring at changed, becoming human flesh for a moment. I recognized it as Penny's hand, though it disappeared almost as soon as it appeared, burning away into ash, replaced by my living flame. Flesh was too fragile to persist in such close proximity, even if it was my own, or hers.

I felt her inside me, struggling to assume control, but her body burned to dust as soon as it started to appear, while her voice screamed in pain within my mind. *You can't do this!* she silently cried at me.

"Fine," I said aloud, in a voice that caused the nearest trees, already dead and dry from my nearness, to splinter and crack. *Relax,* I replied mentally. *You're killing yourself.* I couldn't be sure what Penny's struggle was costing her, but I suspected it wasn't something she could replace.

A feeling of sorrow washed over me. I didn't want to lose what was left of her, but at the same time I didn't want to lose my son, either. I studied him once more. It would take considerable time for his body to resume its normal course of dying. My other children were not far away; they could heal him. There was plenty of time for them to find him.

Backing away from my son, I decided to let them handle it. I spent the next second or two eliminating the remaining ANSIS machines in the area, a period of time that subjectively felt like hours for me, then I left.

***

Irene was on the wall when it happened. Tired beyond belief, she had put her back against one of the merlons to rest. The attack on her portion of the wall had ended, and she didn't have the strength left to help anyone else, though she had seen Karen appear across the yard and take Cyhan and Alyssa somewhere to help with what was probably a crisis elsewhere.

She didn't have the energy to even wonder what they were doing. It was hard enough just to breathe. Her fatigue went so deep that she worried that if she fell asleep she might not wake up.

A flash of aythar swept across the area, so wide and vast that to her magesight it felt as though the entire region had been blanketed by some massive presence. But it was a familiar presence. "Father?" she mumbled to herself.

The strength of it kept increasing, until it felt as though she was being pressed down into the stone she sat upon. The sensation continued to grow, as though the sun had somehow come down from the sky and was now so close that its brilliance was blotting out everything else. Eventually, she lost consciousness.

She woke after an unknown period, though whether it was seconds, minutes, or even hours, she wasn't sure at first. Her father's presence was gone, and after examining the sky, she saw that the sun hadn't moved much. *What happened?* she wondered.

Struggling to her feet, she looked over the wall and saw that the field beyond the castle was still and silent. Nothing moved. Then she looked west, and gasped. The trees on the west side of Lancaster were gone, and the broken machines that littered the field on that side were also gone. It had become a flat featureless plain, unremarkable except for the slight rise and fall of the ground. Even the grass was missing, and the ground seemed to be covered with a thick coating of grey dust.

Only one thing stood out, a shield of pure aythar that covered something. It was located somewhere close to where the tree line had once been, though it was hard to be sure now with so few landmarks.

Turning to examine the interior of the castle, Irene found no movement there either. The other defenders on the wall were all slumped to the ground. She feared they were dead, but after a few seconds her magesight confirmed that most of them were alive. Focusing her perception, she located her friends and family. *Lynaralla, Karen, Chad, Elaine, Gram...* Only Cyhan, Alyssa, and Matthew were missing.

She had witnessed Karen taking Cyhan and Alyssa away somewhere, but she wasn't sure what had happened to her brother. Irene felt something then, a feeling, or perhaps intuition, but she knew her brother must be under the shield to the west.

"Something's happened to him," she muttered dully, unable to muster the energy to express the panic she felt inwardly. Putting one foot in front of the other, Irene began to walk. None of the others were moving yet, so it was up to her.

Descending the stairs was a nightmare compared to walking along the wall. *Who knew it could be so difficult to go down?* she thought as she swayed, fighting for balance. There were no handrails on the stairs inside the wall, so falling was a real concern. She managed to get down, but her next major obstacle was the gate itself. None of the men were awake, so she had to figure out how to release the mechanism that lowered the drawbridge by herself. Thankfully it operated via a series of counterweights, so once she pulled the release and removed the rope holding it in place, it slowly descended.

She wouldn't be able to close it again on her own, though. It probably took several men to operate the crank that lifted it, and without her magic, it was beyond her means. She was grateful the portcullis was still up, or she would have had to find another way; as it was, just removing the massive bar that held the outer gate shut took all her strength.

If there are enemies left out there, we're in trouble, she thought. *Unless someone wakes up who can close the gate and raise the drawbridge.* She had her doubts, but it was more important to find her brother.

Crossing the drawbridge, she began the long walk across the eastern field. The ground felt strange under her feet, scrunching and compressing as she walked across the strange, grey dust. It wasn't long before her skirts were covered in it.

As she drew closer to the dome of aythar, she began to have doubts. The shield was so strong that to her magesight it was completely impermeable. She could discern nothing within it. It was definitely a product of her father's aythar, though. *How could he have made a shield like that, though?* she asked herself silently. It was too strong to have been created on a whim. It held more power than any mage could produce or control. *It might even be stronger than the shield around Castle Cameron,* she thought.

That was patently ridiculous. The shield that protected Castle Cameron and Washbrook was the product of an elaborate enchantment that was powered by the God-Stone.

She stared at it. If Matthew was inside, there was no way to get him out. Even if the shield was a product of raw magic and would fade with time, the amount of power in it meant it might last for years—or longer.

Then she felt another pressure wave of aythar—her father. Irene fell to her knees, struggling to remain conscious as a message pounded through her mind. *Heal him.* The shield vanished, and so too did the presence. Her father, wherever he was, had gone. Opening her eyes, she saw Matthew stretched out, prostrate on the ground, a pool of blood around him.

"No!" she cried involuntarily when she saw her brother. Stumbling to her feet, she went to him and crouched down beside him. She could feel Matthew's aythar, and his skin was warm, but he wasn't breathing, and his heart was still. *Please, don't be dead!*

Irene examined him carefully. Over the past couple of months, she had gained considerable experience with traumatic injuries, and what she found in Matthew confused her. The wounds were serious, but relatively simple—broken ribs, bruises, and several damaged veins. Matthew wouldn't die so long as he didn't bleed too much, and he didn't seem to be bleeding at all, even though the veins were still torn.

He should be conscious, and bleeding, she realized. When she put her hand on his skin, he still felt warm. Unsure what to do, she began correcting the most obvious problems. His veins felt hard and stiff when she began using her power to knit them back together, almost as though some power was resisting her efforts.

Sweat beaded on her brow, and her breathing became labored. Irene didn't have much power left, but she refused to give up. It took her far longer than normal, but she fixed the broken blood vessels and realigned Matthew's ribs, fusing them back together. Then she noticed his heart. She had been working for several minutes, and it appeared to have moved. It had been relaxed when she arrived, but it was now clenched, as though in mid-beat.

Irene waited, watching as his heart slowly relaxed again. It was beating, but at an impossibly slow rate. *He's alive! But how?* It was almost as though time had been slowed down, but just for Matthew's body, leaving everything else unaffected.

She didn't have enough strength to levitate him and take him back to the castle, so she sat beside her brother and made herself as comfortable as possible. Sooner or later the others would wake up, and then perhaps someone could help her get him back inside. Or, in the worst case, eventually her power would recover, and she would move him herself.

Irene gently rolled her brother onto his back and then propped his legs up across her lap to improve the blood return to his heart. Then she watched the afternoon sun slowly slide down to the horizon.

CHAPTER 5

Lady Rose Thornbear tried to open her eyes. Nothing seemed to happen, though. She remained in darkness, with very little sensation to inform her of her condition. *Am I asleep?* She didn't know. It was as though she was disembodied, a spirit set adrift in an endless, empty shadow world.

You are awake.

The voice seemed to echo through her, and Rose wasn't sure if it was a product of her imagination or an actual sound brought to her awareness via her ears. Either way, she didn't recognize it.

I am Kion, said the voice, answering her unspoken question. *You are awake, but your body is currently resting in my care.*

Rose pieced together the relevant facts quickly. *You're the She'Har elder I met with Mordecai,* she stated. *Where is he?*

Gone, responded Kion. *You were left in my safekeeping, though there is no longer any such thing as safe. The universe winds down to its completion. Soon even our memories will be lost.*

You seem pessimistic, said Rose. *You attacked us, yet Mordecai left you alive. What do you fear?*

She felt a sensation of amusement coming from her host. *Fear is meaningless to the Illeniels. Our time is at an end. Our worries and struggles are over. Fear, hope, conflict, peace, these are all things for the people of the new world. They have nothing to do with us any longer.*

Why? asked Rose.

Because I failed, replied Kion. *The corrupted fruit has taken hold in your lover. The end has begun. This world, this universe, will collapse as it grows in him, until nothing is left. All will be joined, all will be lost, and then a new world will begin.*

Mordecai won't let that happen, said Rose confidently.

He cannot stop it, Kion told her. *His every action from this moment on will hasten the end.*

Rose thought on his words for a while, then asked, *What was supposed to happen, if you hadn't failed?*

A limited use of the void, stated the She'Har elder. *The expulsion of ANSIS from this world, along with a warning serious enough to make them avoid it henceforth. That done, my own destruction would follow to ensure its safety. The future would have been left in the hands of humanity and the new grove.*

Perhaps Mordecai could accomplish those things in your stead, suggested Rose.

Unlikely, returned Kion. *The future we spent millennia studying is gone. I have spent eleven thousand years guarding this world, preparing myself for this burden. Your lover is a child, a momentary spark in the sea of time. He cannot do what is necessary.*

Kion, she returned, *if you were him, what would you do?*

It matters little what he does now, said the elder. *If he destroys himself soon, he might save the world from his own power, but ANSIS will inevitably become the victor. If he devotes himself to destroying ANSIS, he might succeed, but his power will accumulate until he reaches a state of singularity.*

Rose was unfamiliar with the word. *Singularity? What does that mean?*

Aythar and the void, order and chaos, they are drawn inevitably to one another. Once his power reaches a certain point, his will to preserve becomes irrelevant, and his power will collapse in on itself, destroying him and devouring the universe itself. This is the inevitable fate of all existence. Time goes on for unfathomable stretches, but every universe eventually fails in this way. From the ashes of each singularity, a new universe is born. Your lover's choice to defy me has brought about the conclusion much sooner than necessary, explained Kion.

Surely there must be something I can do? asked Rose.

Flee this reality, said Kion. *Find a child of Illeniel and escape to another world. This one is doomed.*

Release me then, Kion, said Rose, making her decision.

I will send you back into your half of the world, the one you know, said the elder. *You must make your own way from there.*

Thank you.

I wish you well, said Kion, *though you have little chance of survival.*

***

"What happened to him?" asked Karen.

"I don't know," Irene answered honestly. "Our father was here—I felt him, though he seemed to be everywhere at once. I think he's the reason everyone fainted. When I came to, I found Matthew protected by a powerful shield, wounded and—well, like this."

Chad Grayson reached out and touched Matthew's cheek, pressing one finger against it. "He feels stiff, like a two-day-old corpse. Are ya sure he's alive?"

"His heart is beating," said Elaine. "Just like Irene said. But it's very slow, maybe one beat a minute."

"I think it's getting faster," said Irene. "It was closer to a beat every three or four minutes when I found him."

Lynaralla frowned. "It can't be."

"Can't be what?" asked Irene.

"When we were studying the Erollith writings—I came across a theoretical description of this, but it's impossible, or at least the treatise said it was impossible. It requires manipulation of forces that are inimical to existence itself," answered the She'Har woman.

"You're going to have to explain it better," said Irene.

"It's like a stasis spellweave, or enchantment," began Lynaralla. "Those function by isolating a given volume of space from entropy, preventing all change. To do something like this means something similar happened to Matthew, but it wasn't isolated within a magical structure. Whoever did this directly manipulated the intrinsic level of entropy within his body. That isn't supposed to be possible. For one thing, no one has ever found a way to affect it using aythar, and besides that, if you, for example, were able to do such a thing, it would almost certainly kill you."

Elaine and Irene exchanged glances, and then sighed. Elaine spoke first, "That didn't help much. What does entropy mean?"

Karen broke in then, "It's complicated. Entropy is a measure of randomness, what you might think of as chaos. You could also think of it as heat, but that isn't quite right either. Imagine a giant stone. As a solid stone, it has a great deal of order, but if you grind it into sand, you've removed most of that order and created something with a lot of entropy. Entropy is a measure of energy that is unavailable for work."

Irene rolled her eyes. "Thanks, that helped," she said sarcastically. "How did you know all that, anyway? I thought you didn't have magic on your world."

"I was always a bookworm," explained Karen. "And entropy isn't magic. I learned about it in physics."

"It applies equally to our world and hers," said Lynaralla. "If we think of aythar as magic, or a power with the capacity to do work, then entropy is its opposite—energy without order, energy that is unable to do any work."

"Did that make any sense to you?" Elaine asked, looking at Irene.

The youngest Illeniel nodded. "Yeah, I think I'm starting to get it. It's like the shiggreth. My father spent a lot of time talking to us about them and the strange force within them. This sounds sort of like that."

Elaine sighed. "I want to pull my hair out just listening to this. How can energy do work?" She paused, looking over Irene's shoulder. "What are you doing?" she asked sharply, directing her question at the one person ignoring them.

Chad looked up and grinned mischievously. "If you poke yer finger into his skin it doesn't spring back." He was crouching down beside Matthew's body. "He's like a clay tablet."

"You're drawing on him?" exclaimed Irene, shocked.

The hunter shrugged.

Karen leaned over. "What is that?" She studied the faint lines that had been pressed into Matthew's forehead. They had a distinctly phallic shape. "Really? He could be dying and you're…"

Chad chuckled. "An opportunity like this doesn't come along very often. It'd be a shame to waste it."

"He's my brother," said Irene, disgusted. "That isn't funny."

Elaine took the archer by the arm. "Come on. Let's take you somewhere where your vulgar sense of humor isn't liable to get you killed." She led him away.

Karen laughed. "It *is* a little funny."

Lynaralla watched her seriously. "Why are male genitalia humorous?" When Karen only laughed louder, she turned to Irene. "Don't worry. The marks will fade. It's just happening more slowly because of the state his body is in."

Irene was gently rubbing Matthew's forehead, trying to get the marks to disappear more quickly. "Is there anything we can do?"

"Warm him up," said Lynaralla.

"But he isn't cold," observed Irene.

Lynaralla spread her arms wide and vine-like projections of aythar grew from her fingers. The spellweave spread and lifted Matthew from the ground, cradling him in a protective structure similar to a hammock.

The spellweave began to radiate a gentle warmth. "While heat isn't directly equivalent to entropy, the connection between the two is very strong. Warming him should increase the rate that he returns to normal. We will need to watch him carefully, though. Once he gets close to normal, the extra warmth could be too much."

"I'll stay with him," said Irene immediately.

"Me too," added Karen.

Lynaralla nodded. "Then I'll go help Gram and the others."

CHAPTER 6

Gareth Gaelyn coughed, drawing everyone's attention.

The Council of Lords was seated in a small chamber room within the palace in Albamarl. It was a meeting of the most important and powerful nobles of Lothion. Normally, the council only met once a year, but with all the tumult of the past few months, the Queen had requested they reconvene to discuss important matters.

"Since Lord Illeniel isn't present, I think there's a topic we should broach in his absence," began Lord Gaelyn, "that of the recent rumors among the populace."

Ariadne arched one brow. "Why would Tyrion's absence matter?"

"Because the rumors concern him directly, Your Majesty," answered Gareth.

She stared evenly at him. "This council is not normally concerned with rumors, Lord Gaelyn, but if you feel it is important, then do explain."

Gareth nodded. "The opinions of the populace are important, especially in this regard. Many people on the streets are discussing Duke Illeniel's past. Specifically, they are speculating that he was the first King of Lothion."

"That's ridiculous," protested Roland Lancaster. "Lothion wasn't established as a kingdom until after the War with Balinthor."

"I agree, Your Grace," said Gareth agreeably, "but unfortunately the mob doesn't concern itself much with logic. In their minds, the fact that Tyrion and his children founded the city of Albamarl is proof enough of some divine right to rule, and that coupled with the recent discontent over the actions of the Royal Guard could lead to riots."

Brendan Airedale, occupying the seat recently left vacant by his father's suicide, responded dismissively, "They can riot all they want. They don't make the decisions. Flog enough of them and put the loudest of them in prison and they'll settle down."

Duke Cantley grunted in agreement, but Count Malvern and Earl Balistair looked uncomfortable at the young lord's remarks. Ariadne spoke up first, "Lord Airedale, you are young and new to your title, so I will forgive your ignorance. We are not in the habit of oppressing our people in order to keep the peace. That is, and should always be, our last resort."

Cantley interjected, "Sometimes it does the people good to see their ruler isn't afraid to use a little violence when necessary."

Ariadne's eyes were cold as she turned them on the Duke. "I'm sure my late-husband, Prince Leomund, would have agreed with that sentiment. It is *my* opinion, however, that such is not a good foundation for ruling a nation. Surely you can see that."

Gregory Cantley blanched at her rebuke. "My apologies, Your Majesty. I meant no offense. I only meant to suggest that the people should be aware that Your Majesty is not afraid to use stern measures when necessary."

"It is the definition of *necessary* that is often a point of dispute in these cases," opined Count Malvern dryly.

Ariadne stared down the table, letting her eyes drift to take in each person, one by one. "So long as all of you recognize that *I* am the final arbiter on what is necessary and what is not, we won't have a problem."

There was a chorus of voices as everyone hastily agreed, then Gareth returned to the topic. "The point of my bringing this up was not to debate our reaction, but rather to consider the origin of these rumors. The common people don't usually manufacture such rumors from nothing. Lord Illeniel's history was known only to a few until very recently; mainly to those of us here now. I believe the seeds of these rumors were deliberately planted."

His pronouncement brought an uncomfortable silence to the table. Even the Queen was unsure how to continue. At last Malvern responded, "And do you have any suggestion as to who among us might have been motivated to do such a thing?"

Suggesting that one of the council members might be a traitor was not something to be done lightly. But there was one thing that could be said about Lord Gaelyn. He was not faint of heart. Outwardly, he still seemed relaxed as he continued his conjecture. "The Prince-Consort could have been behind it, at least in part, but I doubt he was alone. David Airedale is another who might have decided to shift the current power structure, but I have—"

Brendan Airedale shouted over him. "You dare accuse my late-father?"

Gareth stared coldly at the young man. "As I was saying, I have no proof of that. At the very least, your father's sudden suicide is suspicious."

"As I have repeatedly said!" said Lord Airedale vehemently.

"You misunderstand me," said Gareth, "and to your own detriment. If your father's death is something other than a suicide, then *you,* as his heir, would be the prime suspect. I was referring to his motivation for taking his own life. I suspect he felt guilty, perhaps over these rumors, or perhaps for his part in falsely accusing Mordecai Illeniel of the Prince's murder."

Lord Airedale paled at Gareth's words. "You have no evidence of any of those suppositions."

The Queen appeared pensive. "Take care with your words, Lord Gaelyn. The court has already rendered a verdict on that matter."

Conall, now occupying the seat as Lord Cameron, spoke for the first time. "I don't think my father was guilty either." He glanced up and down the table, then added, "Though I recognize the court's authority, and I remain a loyal servant to the Queen."

Duke Cantley gave Conall a look of disgust, then said, "Is there a point to your speculation, Lord Gaelyn, other than provoking dissension among us? Whether your conjecture is true or not, both David Airedale and Prince Leomund are now dead. Or are you accusing Lord Illeniel of working with them to put himself on the throne?"

"Not at all," responded Gareth. "From what I've seen of the man, he has no desire for the throne, but there are those who might see a change in power as an opportunity. Lord Cameron's trial has done serious damage to our Queen's position. She has lost not one, but two powerful supporters. This is aside from the fact that Lady Hightower was possibly the only one of us skillful enough to ferret out who the real traitor is."

Cantley snorted dismissively. "Lady Hightower marked herself as a traitor when she attempted to murder both you and Lord Illeniel, or have you conveniently forgotten that fact, Lord Gaelyn?"

Ariadne broke in, "We have no proof that she had a hand in the assassination attempt."

Lord Malvern responded, "We don't need proof. She incriminated herself by aiding Lord Cameron in his escape."

"I have lived a long time," began Gareth. "Long enough to gain a certain perspective. While the attack on my life angered me, I cannot help but note the end result of all this. Two powerful and well-connected supporters of the Queen are gone, while this council itself is increasingly populated by young and inexperienced lords." He dipped his head in Conall's direction. "No disrespect meant to you, Lord Cameron."

"None taken," said Conall. Brendan Airedale ground his teeth, though, for Gareth had pointedly not made the same mention for him.

The doors of the room opened and the Queen's chamberlain, Benchley, stepped inside. "Lord Illeniel has returned," he announced.

The man that entered had Tyrion's appearance, but his hair was drastically different. Where before it had been so dark as to be almost black, now it was a shimmering silvery white, as though each strand had been coated in metal; it fell in glittering waves to his shoulders. "Forgive me for being late, Your Majesty," said Tyrion. "I had urgent business at home and only just returned. I trust I haven't missed anything important."

All eyes were glued to the Duke of the Wester Isle, but it was the Queen who spoke first. "Your hair…"

Tyrion's teeth flashed white beneath eyes that seemed even bluer than before. "Pardon my appearance, Your Majesty. As you know, while I was born human, my time as a She'Har elder has changed me in certain ways. In the past I've made cosmetic changes to avoid unsettling my peers with my strange differences, but today I had little time. I hurried to the council chamber as soon as I heard a meeting was in progress."

Gareth Gaelyn's eyes narrowed at Tyrion's words, but he said nothing.

Count Malvern was more welcoming. "If I had hair like that, I'd never hide it, though my wife might die from jealousy." Several at the table joined him in laughter.

"Is all well with the She'Har?" asked Ariadne.

Tyrion nodded. "All is well with them. My problem was a matter of personal health. After Mordecai's escape, my injuries were more serious than I was willing to admit. I was forced to return and rejoin my tree for a time."

"And how are you now?" asked the Queen.

Tyrion bowed slightly. "Fully recovered, Your Majesty. Thank you for your concern." He took his seat then, and the meeting resumed. The next item on the agenda was the state of affairs in Cameron.

"I returned home yesterday," began Conall. "Washbrook is fine, but the castle is sealed off behind the protective shield my father created. No one can enter."

"What about the teleport circles?" asked Lord Gaelyn.

Sir Conall shook his head. “They aren’t working. Someone must have disabled them.”

Duke Cantley looked angry. “You mean your father.”

Conall shrugged. “Possibly. It hardly matters. The castle isn’t habitable.”

The Queen leaned forward. “What about the dragon eggs?”

“The circle to the dragon eyrie was disabled as well, but I went there the long way. The eggs are gone.” The young lord looked distinctly uncomfortable.

“How important are these eggs?” asked Tyrion.

Gareth Gaelyn answered first. “Each one contains approximately as much aythar as one of the Shining Gods. Their value is beyond calculation.”

“How many are there?” said Tyrion, probing further.

“I don’t know,” admitted Conall.

“I helped Mordecai create them,” offered Gareth. “At the time he had me make forty vessels for them.”

“Vessels?” asked Count Malvern.

“Small dragon bodies,” clarified Gareth.

“And how many do we have?” asked Duke Cantley.

The Queen answered, “Five. My dragon, Carwyn, plus the dragons that were given to Sir Harold, Sir Egan, Sir Thomas, and Sir William.”

“This is outrageous,” complained Cantley. “The Crown should control all of the dragons. This is just another example of Count Cameron’s brazen arrogance.” He paused. “I mean, the prior Count, of course. In any case, I recommend Your Majesty move to secure the rest of the dragon eggs. By all rights, they should be in your hands.”

Lord Gaelyn held up a finger. “While I agree the eggs represent significant power, I think you overreach your bounds, Duke Cantley. Mordecai created the eggs, with my help. They do in fact belong to him, though I think it might be wise for the Crown to lay claim to them. It is for the Queen to decide whether to attempt to claim them for the benefit of the people, not you, Your Grace. Her Majesty might wish to consider the implications of taking them by fiat. However we feel about the man, making an enemy of him might not be wise.”

“Moira claims ignorance regarding her father, and the circumstances surrounding Castle Cameron,” said Ariadne. “It might be good to question her once more.”

“I’ll go,” said Conall at once.

Cantley snorted. “Of course, you want to see her! You simply want to further your conspiracy with her and your father.”

The Queen glared at the Duke. “You have no basis to make such a claim, Lord Cantley. I have no cause to doubt Lord Cameron’s fidelity.” She paused for a moment. “That being said, it would be wise to send someone else with him.”

“I’ll do it,” volunteered Tyrion.

“Considering your overzealous behavior in the past, Lord Illeniel, I would prefer someone else,” said the Queen. “Lord Gaelyn, perhaps you would undertake the task?”

Gareth bowed his head. “As you wish, Your Majesty.”

Ariadne smiled. “Then it’s settled.”

CHAPTER 7

Moira was outside, enjoying the sunshine that flooded down on the mountainside in front of her family's home. Humphrey bounded from place to place, exploring the thick grass with his nose and searching amid rocky outcroppings for hidden treasures. The half-grown dog was a source of constant amusement for her, and the only remedy she had for her loneliness.

Through most of her life, home had been a place filled with people. Her brothers, sister, parents, and friends had made the place lively and sometimes chaotic. She hadn't really appreciated it at the time, but now her isolation gave her plenty of time to consider the past.

For once, she was alone, utterly and completely, except for Humphrey, of course. Technically she was still under guard, but the guards were hers; they no longer had their own minds. With Myra gone, she had no one to talk to but herself. Consequently, she spent a lot of her time thinking about the people she missed, most of all, her mother.

I never appreciated her, thought Moira for the tenth time that day. Penny had been her world as a child, her obstacle as a teen, and only recently, had become her most trusted confidante when she had no one else she could talk to. And now she was gone.

Humphrey finished his latest investigation and ran back to her, yipping to gain her attention. She stroked his head and ruffled his ears. "It's just you and me, Humphrey." Then she looked back at the house, where her spell-twin/guards were. "And me, and me, and me, and me—well, you get the idea, don't you, Humphrey?

"Everyone else is off somewhere else, doing who knows what, and here I am stuck on the mountainside." She thought it was somewhat ironic that she was also probably doing more than anyone else while simultaneously being completely bored. While she was doing next to nothing, her proxies were prosecuting a secret war on her behalf.

Gareth and Conall are here. The silent message came from one of her guards inside. Rising to her feet, Moira dusted off her skirts and walked up the slope to the front door, encouraging Humphrey to follow. She didn't want the young dog to get lost while she was inside.

She was waiting in the living room by the time Gareth and Conall got there. "Would you like some tea?" she asked them politely, keeping her expression aloof.

Gareth Gaelyn ignored her question, while Conall moved closer to her. "How have you been? Have any of the others come home?"

Are you asking for yourself or for the Queen? Moira responded mentally, making no attempt to hide her mistrust from her younger brother.

Before Conall could respond, Gareth spoke up. "Please don't do that again. If I sense your aythar moving again, I'll take it as a hostile action. Do you understand?"

"She was only greeting me," said Conall, turning to his companion with exasperation.

Moira smiled. "Lord Gaelyn is right, Conall. As a Centyr mage, anything I do should be viewed as a threat. I might scramble your brains or turn Lord Gaelyn into a puppet."

"She wouldn't do anything like that," protested Conall.

How little you know, brother of mine, thought Moira sourly. *You're too trusting, both of me, and those that currently surround the Queen.* She kept her thoughts to herself, though, to avoid rousing Gareth's ire.

The archmage moved forward and took a seat without waiting for an invitation, giving the impression he owned the place. "Have you seen any of your family?" he asked pointedly, repeating Conall's question.

Moira had never felt particularly close to Gareth, but now she found herself developing a newfound dislike for the man. She studied him for a second and briefly considered attacking him. It would give away her hand, but if she could take control of the archmage, it would greatly strengthen her position. There were four guards in the room, three of them krytek. If they acted in concert, they might be able to overwhelm Gareth's defenses before he could react.

She decided in favor of discretion. Giving the archmage a polite smile, she sat down across from him. "No. I'm afraid I haven't seen anyone. The rest of my siblings are too smart to put themselves within the Queen's grasp." She gave Conall an accusatory stare as she finished her remark.

"The Queen is only trying to do what's best for Lothion," argued her brother.

"She betrayed our family, Conall, *her family*, as do you, by continuing to support her," Moira replied, rebuking him. "You helped her arrest your own father. Do you still have any shame left?"

Conall's face grew pained. "I'm not a traitor, Moira."

"The Queen is," she responded sharply. "She'll pay for what she's done."

"One more threat and I'll act to remove you as a threat to the Crown," warned Gareth. "Here and now."

"I'll speak as I please in my own home, Lord Gaelyn," said Moira coldly. "You should consider where you are before threatening me. Either that, or you should bring more guards. I'm not sure ten would be enough to protect you if you make me angry."

Gareth's eyes narrowed. "If you'd like more guards, that can be arranged."

"Please do," said Moira sweetly. "I'm sure we'd all feel safer."

"Enough, Moira!" interjected Conall. "We didn't come here to argue. We came because Castle Cameron is locked behind the shield."

"Does that inconvenience you, Your Excellency?" said Moira in a voice that practically dripped acid. "I assure you I had nothing to do with it."

Her younger brother winced at her words, but he didn't give up. "What about Myra?" he asked.

"Who is Myra?" asked Gareth.

Moira closed her eyes, annoyance written on her features. "My spell-twin, or as I prefer to call her, my sister," she answered, then turned her eyes on Conall. "She's with me, as always."

"I'd like to talk to her," said Conall. "Just to verify that."

Moira nodded. "Certainly, so long as Lord Gaelyn promises to behave himself. I don't want him to think this is an unprovoked attack."

Gareth's shield, already strong, became even more intense. "Do as you wish."

A second later Moira's aythar began to move, sliding away from her body and splitting into a separate being, one composed entirely of aythar. Then her doppelganger said, "Hello Conall."

Gareth growled. "So your mother was right. You have been continuing your evil tricks."

"How have you been, Myra?" asked Conall.

"Well," said the spell-twin. "Though I don't like the direction of current events."

Moira spoke as well, directing her words to Gareth. "You can tell your wife I've been behaving myself. Myra was a product of the war in Dunbar. I haven't broken any more of the rules since then."

"This thing's very existence is an abomination," spat the archmage. "Why haven't you gotten rid of it?"

Furious, Moira glared at him. "You should consider *what* you married before you start hurling insults and suggesting people be eliminated."

Gareth's power flared. Raising one finger, he signaled to the guards. "Separate the two of them. I'll take care of this one right now."

The krytek stepped closer, hands going to the spellwoven weapons already on their belts. Moira's eyes flicked from one side to the other, as she debated whether to blow her cover and escalate the situation or let Gareth have his way to continue her façade.

Everyone froze in surprise as Conall stepped between Gareth and the spell-twin, his own shield increasing in strength and his hands held away from his body, as though he was preparing to fight. Coruscating sparks of actinic power flickered around his fists. "That's enough, Lord Gaelyn. I won't tolerate threats against my family. Not in my home or anywhere else for that matter. If you intend to do violence here, we have a problem."

Gareth's face hardened. "You'd throw away your position to protect that monstrosity?"

Conall lifted his chin. "I'd give my life to protect any of my sisters, and that includes the *two* who stand here now."

Moira was touched by her brother's gesture, while at the same time, in the back of her head, she was reconsidering the odds. If Conall threw in with her against the archmage, it would significantly improve her chances of breaking Gareth's defenses quickly enough to take his mind. Assuming Conall didn't realize what she was doing and change sides in mid-battle. Her younger brother was naïve, but his sense of honor virtually guaranteed he wouldn't approve of her plan.

Unless Gareth manages to kill my spell-twin in the opening exchange, thought Moira coldly. *Conall doesn't realize she isn't the real Myra. He might be so enraged he would switch sides completely, or at least long enough for me to take control of Gareth.*

It was such a cold-hearted plan that it even gave Moira pause for a moment, but she had no room in her heart for self-doubt. *If the spell-twin moves toward Gareth, and one of his supposed allies, the krytek, kills her, it might be enough,* she thought, preparing to send the commands.

Just before she did, Gareth relaxed his posture and stepped back, waving at the krytek to stand down. "This is a mistake, Conall," he said warningly.

Conall held firm. "If so, it's none of your concern. I answer only to the Queen, and if she were here I feel certain she would agree with me."

"Thank you," said Moira softly behind her brother's shoulder. The emotion in her words was genuine, and she felt slightly guilty for her plan to manipulate his protective nature to her advantage.

Her brother glanced back at her, offering a wan smile. "We're family," he said simply.

"I think we're done here," announced Lord Gaelyn.

"Feel free to leave, then," said Conall. "I'd like to talk to my sister. We haven't seen each other in a while."

"I'm afraid not, Count Cameron," returned the archmage. "You know very well that I'm here to prevent you being alone with her. She's too dangerous. Unless you're proposing to join her in house arrest. Is that your intention?"

Conall sighed, then looked at Moira. "Sorry, Mo'."

Looking into her younger brother's eyes, Moira was seized with a desire to hug him, but she knew better than to attempt it. Gareth would interpret it as a hostile action. "It's alright," she told him. "Do what you feel necessary."

He nodded. "We're both just trying to do what we think is right."

"I know," she answered. "But I still think you're a brat."

Conall smirked for an instant, and then he left. Gareth followed close behind him. Once again, Moira was alone.

Humphrey nudged her leg, reminding her of his presence, and she bent down to scratch behind his ears. "What's taking Myra so long?" she asked the young dog, but Humphrey didn't have an answer for her.

CHAPTER 8

Myra had been waiting at the boundary for just over three days when a small opening finally appeared. Lynaralla looked out at her from it.

"Moira?" asked the She'Har girl, then she corrected herself. "No, you must be Myra."

Myra smiled. "You spotted the difference pretty quick."

"Your aythar is almost identical, but the lack of physical substance within your spell-body is more apparent," explained Lynaralla. "Come in." She stepped away from the opening, and Myra accepted the invitation.

Studying her surroundings, Myra saw that the land had changed significantly. The trees on either side of the road were gone, replaced by a featureless, grey landscape that almost looked as though it was covered in snow, if snow were the color of slate. "What happened?" she asked.

"Our father," said Lynaralla.

The answer took Myra by surprise, and it was a second before she realized that Lynaralla was referring to Mordecai. *That's right, he told her he was adopting her.* Although she was a spell-twin, she didn't feel like one. In her mind she had been raised by Mordecai and Penny. She *remembered* it. Of course, in those same memories, they had called her Moira. Sometimes it was hard to accept that she was just a little over a year old, that she hadn't actually been the one sitting on her father's knee, looking up and wondering why his chin was covered in hair.

She should have been happy just to be accepted, but she felt a small pang of jealousy knowing that the She'Har girl in front of her was now counted as one of their daughters. It hardly seemed fair. *I shouldn't be so petty,* thought Myra. *I should be happy to have a new sister.*

After a few seconds, she shook herself from her reverie. "He was here?"

Lynaralla nodded. "None of us saw him, but Matthew swears it was him. I believe him."

"I need to talk to Matthew," said Myra.

"He's different now," said Lynaralla. "It's hard to explain. We'll have to walk. Karen left as soon as she dropped me off at the boundary."

Myra could have flown. One advantage of not having a true body was that she could freely change her form. She could even attempt flying the way Mordecai did, since crash landings weren't really a danger to her, but the walk would give her a chance to find out what had happened. "You can catch me up on what's been happening as we go."

Lynaralla did, beginning with the events before she had arrived herself. She described the unremitting attacks and their complete isolation from the world they knew. She explained her own arrival with Irene and the later appearance of Cyhan, Elaine, and Chad. Once she had all that out of the way, she told Myra about the past week. The increasing intensity of the attacks and their desperate defense while Matthew remained aloof, directing their strategy while refusing to commit himself.

"His plan was nearly flawless," said Lynaralla as she finished up. "He anticipated the enemy's final assault and wiped out nearly all their reserves just as they gathered, but he made a mistake at the very last. I'm not sure what went wrong, but Karen blames herself. Apparently, she didn't follow his last instructions completely."

Myra coughed. "I can't blame her for that. I'm sure he was pretty full of himself when he was giving orders."

"She knew better," said Lynaralla coolly. "We all did. Over the previous days we had lots of time to learn to trust his predictions."

"Predictions?"

"His gift has developed," Lynaralla explained.

"His danger sense?" asked Myra.

The She'Har woman shook her head. "The Illeniel gift takes several forms. The children, such as myself, sometimes display the more limited form, which you call a danger sense. That form is always present in our krytek as well. The elders, however, develop a much broader type of foresight based on probabilities observed in closely aligned planes of existence."

Myra nodded; she had heard as much before.

"Our brother, though, has developed something akin to the predictive powers of the Illeniel Elders. From what I was taught, that was thought to be impossible, as the human brain functions on such a brief and rapid temporal scale."

Myra made a face. "Trust Matthew to find a way to be different. He's always been weird."

Lynaralla didn't catch the humor in her remark. Instead she nodded in agreement. "What he's done is extremely impressive."

"So he can predict the future now?" asked Myra. When Lynaralla began shaking her head to correct her, she hastily added, "I know, I know, it isn't really precognition. Just let me simplify the terms a little. It's too much work to say 'probability forecasting' over and over."

Lynaralla pursed her lips, clearly not liking the simplification, but she gave a short nod after a few seconds. "As you wish. His ability seems to be more limited than that of the Elders, who could discern things thousands of years in the future, but that makes it all the more incredible. While long-term probabilities are less affected by the vast number of small variables present in everyday life, discerning probabilities in the range of an hour or two is entirely different, since almost every small bit of chaos in the system can radically change outcomes."

Myra followed the reasoning, but she found Lynaralla's overly precise language tiresome. *No use complaining, though,* she thought, *that would just cause her to give a long explanation for why she feels it necessary.* She smiled and shifted the topic. "Where is he now?"

"Resting in his room," said Lynaralla. "Karen and Irene have been taking turns watching over him. What news do you have?"

"Wait until we get to the castle," responded Myra. "Otherwise I'll have to tell it over and over again."

They were already in sight of Lancaster's walls, and a figure there was waving at them. Myra and Lynaralla answered by waving back. The figure vanished, and after a few minutes Karen appeared beside them. "Moira!" she exclaimed, but she frowned almost as soon as she said it. "Oh, not Moira—Myra. Sorry."

"It's to be expected," said Myra. "I'm starting to consider changing my appearance to make things easier for everyone."

"Not a bad idea," opined Karen. "I'm surprised you haven't done it already."

Myra winked at her and made a show of stroking her hair. "It's hard to mess with perfection."

Karen laughed, but Lynaralla stared blankly at her, missing the joke once again. Then she asked, "I understand you're considered pretty, but you're hardly perfect, at least in the physical sense."

"That's not what she meant," offered Karen.

But Lynaralla went on, "Symmetry is a critical component of beauty and your nose isn't perfectly aligned, not to mention the proportions of your breasts and hips being slightly unbalanced. Also, smoothness of complexion is…"

"Lynn!" warned Karen. "It was a joke."

"Oh," said the She'Har woman.

Meanwhile, Myra found herself inspecting her own form. Her body was a deliberate construct, and she had never really thought about altering it, even to fix the normal variances in shape or skin tone that humans typically lived with. There wasn't any reason not to do so, however. *I could be buxom, blonde, slender, short, tall, whatever I wish,* she realized. *Why do I remain as a duplicate of Moira?* She wasn't sure, but she guessed it was simply force of habit. On impulse she changed her hair to a honey blonde.

Karen grinned. "It looks good. Moira will be jealous." She held out her arms. "Take my hands. I'll save you a walk."

A second later, they appeared within the main hall of Castle Lancaster. Most of the others had already gathered there to welcome her, and after a long round of greetings, Myra took stock of who was present and who wasn't. Chad, Cyhan, Elaine, Alyssa, and Gram were there, but notably, Matthew was absent. "Where's Matt?" asked Myra. "He needs to hear this too."

They glanced at one another, though Myra noted that after a few seconds their eyes invariably rested on Karen, who sighed. "He can't really talk," admitted Karen. "He was injured in the battle."

Worried, Myra asked, "Is he alright?"

Karen nodded. "His injuries have been healed, but your father did something to him. We think it's starting to fade, but it may be a while before he can communicate normally."

Myra frowned. "Maybe you should explain exactly what happened. I'm confused."

Chad Grayson spoke first. "His dad turned him to stone, an' he's so naturally hard-headed it's takin' forever for him to return to normal."

Elaine glared at the woodsman. "If you don't have anything helpful to say, kindly refrain from speaking." As soon as she turned her eyes back to Myra, the archer began silently mouthing words at her back.

Myra listened as they tried to explain what happened, but their combined responses only made matters worse. In the end, it was Lynaralla and her overly precise language that saved the day. "Mordecai extracted most of the entropy from his body, effectively slowing time for him so he could be healed. We've been keeping him warm and he's gradually returning to normal, but it's difficult to speak with him since his perception of sound is still too far removed from ours."

"Lynn says we probably sound like birds chirping to him right now," added Karen helpfully.

"An' he sounds like he's croaking," said Chad. "It's borin' as hell."

"We've worked out a temporary solution, though," said Karen. "We write down what we want to say and then wait for him to pen a response."

Chad Grayson snickered. "It's about as much fun as watchin' grass grow."

"I'll have to write everything out then," said Myra. "I'll explain what's happened as I write."

Gram went and brought writing tools and paper from Duke Roland's study, and after they had Myra comfortably seated at the high table in the great hall, she began to write, stopping now and then to relay her news to the others.

> *Matthew,*
>
> *Moira sent me to bring news of events in the city and at home. Karen and the others have already informed me of what happened here.*
>
> *First and foremost, Lady Rose and our father did escape, though I suppose that given events here you already know that. We still have no word of Lady Rose's whereabouts, but I trust that if our father survived she must be with him still.*
>
> *The Queen has kept me under house arrest, though I'm sure you can guess how well that's working. Tyrion seems to have become her closest confidant and there are rumors that the two of them are also involved in a more physical sense. Conall continues to serve as her champion, though his loyalties are somewhat divided.*
>
> *Ariadne stated plainly in front of me that she does not wish to actually capture Father, but Tyrion is another matter. He has developed a serious grudge against both Dad and Rose. His stated intention is to kill them both if he has the opportunity.*
>
> *Gareth Gaelyn remains loyal to the Queen, but his motivations are complicated. Moira and I have had little time to study him, but his problem lies more with Moira's continued existence (as well as mine). If we were not in the picture, he might be more inclined to support Dad's innocence, or at least withhold his support from Ariadne.*
>
> *Tyrion has introduced krytek guards to supplement the Royal Guard in Albamarl as well as to bolster the defenses of all the other major cities. This seems to have*

been effective at rooting out the hidden ANSIS units within the populace, but it has created more problems for Ariadne. In Albamarl the citizens are disconcerted by the unexplained disappearances of their friends and loved ones. It wouldn't take much for them to start rioting in the streets.

At present, Moira is isolated at home, but she has already begun taking measures. I hesitate to put them down on paper, even here, among friends (who are reading along as I write). I'm sure you can infer what I mean. She has limited herself to the krytek guarding her thus far, but as they rotate back to duty in Albamarl, she is expanding her allies.

She is trying hard to prevent another situation like Dunbar, but it is difficult given that we have two enemies now, ANSIS and the Queen. To simplify that, Moira has devised a plan to unify the kingdom and reconcile our father with Ariadne. It isn't without risk, however, and certain casualties are to be expected. If you have any thoughts on the matter, please put them in your reply, especially regarding Tyrion and Gareth.

Other than such principal movers, Moira doesn't intend to endanger or harm any of the human retainers. For myself, I worry about whether she can succeed without causing significant damage to Lothion in general and to the nobility in particular. Again, your input might be helpful. Moira intends to move as soon as I return with your reply.

Love (from your youngest sister),
Myra

Gram chuckled as he read her closing over her shoulder. "Youngest sister, huh? Irene's going to love that. She's always been the baby."

Myra smiled. "In a sense, I'm also the oldest, or one of the three oldest, since I have Moira's memories. They're all middle children now."

Chad broke in. "Am I the only one that's a little worried about the fact that, according to this she's planning to overthrow the government?"

"No," said Elaine, looking at the ranger with obvious disgust. "For once, we're agreed."

"Mordecai should have done it years ago. We wouldn't be having these problems now if he had," said Sir Cyhan flatly. Gram seemed shocked at his mentor's words.

"He would disagree with you," declared Lynaralla. "Father believes in the rule of law."

"And I'm sure Lady Rose would say the same," responded the big warrior, "but the fact of the matter is that he's been the power behind the throne for too long. The reason everything has fallen apart isn't because of this murder trial, but the fact that he's stood on his principles rather than practicality. If he had taken power, Lothion wouldn't be fractured right now."

Alyssa looked at Cyhan, and then nodded in agreement. "Mordecai is a good man, but my father is right."

"I'm more worried about *how* she's plannin' on doin' it," explained Chad, then added with a shudder, "She's been in my head before. I still have nightmares about it."

Karen stood. "Let's take it up so Matt can start reading. It'll take hours for him to write a reply. The sooner we let him start reading, the better. We're not going to decide anything arguing amongst ourselves."

Myra looked around at them. "Matthew is your leader then?"

"I sure as hell don't want the job," swore Chad. "And big, tall, an' ugly there won't do it." He nodded at Sir Cyhan as he finished.

The big knight was unfazed. "My life has been devoted to war. Politics is a spectator sport for me."

"Personally, I prefer Irene," said Elaine candidly. "Matthew is arrogant and overconfident, but Irene is too young, and she defers to him anyway. That said, Matthew is still a good choice. As much as he irritates me some of the time, he's smart and he has that special insight."

"Let's take this to Matthew," said Myra. "The sooner the better."

CHAPTER 9

Rose Thornbear, formerly Lady Hightower and commander of the garrison in Albamarl as well as the head of logistics for the Royal Army of Lothion, rode quietly in the back of a farmer's cart, keeping company with a load of turnips.

Reflecting on the past week was less than pleasant, and only served to remind her of the drastic change in her station in life. After Kion had sent her back to her own half of the world, she had found herself in the countryside, not far from the city of Issip in Gododdin.

Penniless, friendless, and only half-clothed, the first day had been a trial, for country wives weren't partial to half-naked women showing up on their doorsteps, and the men—well, they presented an entirely different challenge, of equal parts danger and disdain. It was only after two humiliating attempts at gaining assistance that she had found someone sympathetic enough to offer her a used dress and information regarding her whereabouts.

She had gotten to Issip shank's mare, which is to say, she walked. Lady Rose had never considered herself to be in poor shape, but walking for eight hours in the remains of her court shoes had been agony. The blisters on her feet were enough to convince her to risk the World Road, which had an entrance in Issip, but King Nicholas had decided to capitalize on Mordecai's wonder by taxing its use. While the fee to enter had been small, any fee was too much when one was utterly broke.

Rose counted herself fortunate to have convinced a riverboat to allow her to ride down the Sterling River to Relliton. The two-day journey had allowed her feet a chance to heal, although the boatman was none too pleased with her cooking, for that had been her exchange for passage. It was a testimony to the man's charity that he hadn't refused to let her continue with them the second day after the first meal she had prepared.

Relliton had been exactly as she remembered it—unpleasant. The port city was built on marshland, and aside from trade, its main point of interest was a surfeit of mosquitos and vermin. Visiting as a noblewoman in her youth had been bad enough, but returning as a vagrant was ten times worse.

She had eaten twice while on the riverboat, but once in the city she did without, for the city residents weren't as charitable. Several men had offered her money, but only in exchange for services she wasn't prepared to render. Consequently, she had begun the trip to Iverly the next morning on an empty belly.

Rose's feet had begun developing calluses, so the first day's walk didn't do her as much harm as before, but hunger was a serious problem. Water she could get, since most farmsteads and small holders would allow her to drink from their wells, but food was another matter. Two days without food had left her light-headed and ravenous. *For the first time in my life, I find myself wishing I had gone to fat in my middle years,* she thought to herself.

The walk from Relliton to Iverly was generally considered to be four days on foot, but for a small woman with sore feet, it would likely take five. Four more days without food might have been the end of her. If it hadn't been for Farmer Tiggle's kindness, she wasn't sure she would have made it. The elderly man had offered her a ride on her second day out of Relliton and had been kind enough to share his meager food with her.

Rose wasn't a picky eater, and hunger was definitely a powerful spice, but after several days of boiled turnips she was ready for almost anything else, not that she would have dared say as much. She was very grateful for the farmer's aid.

"We're almost there," said the old man, looking over his shoulder at her. "Once we get over this rise, you'll see it."

"I can hardly wait," Rose replied honestly.

The old man squinted at her, his concern showing through the extensive wrinkles on his face. "You sure you'll be alright on your own there?"

Rose nodded. "Yes, I have family waiting to meet me."

Farmer Tiggle turned his face back to the road. "That's good. This world's no good for a girl on her own."

Girl? Rose almost laughed at that. It had been a long time since anyone had called her a girl, but she supposed from the old man's point of view she was just that. He may have underestimated her age as well. Women in the countryside showed their years sooner thanks to hard labor and overexposure to the sun.

"I appreciate your concern," said Rose. "I can't thank you enough for the past few days. If you'll tell me where your home is, I'll do my best to repay you later."

The farmer waved his hand in the air without looking back. "No need for that. I wouldn't have gotten as old as I have without a helping hand now an' then."

"Still, I'd feel better knowing how to reach you," said Rose. "One good turn deserves another."

"My daughter and her husband live in Iverly," said the old man. "I'll give you her address before you get off. And while we're at it, if anything goes wrong and your family isn't there, don't be too proud to look her up. Just tell her my name and she'll give you a place to sleep."

Rose was surprised by his generosity. Times had been good lately, thanks largely to the increased trade brought by the World Road, but it was still unusual for someone offer a bed to a stranger. In the past, such a gesture would have touched her heart, but after a week alone, without friends or support, it brought a tear to her eye.

When they finally stopped inside the city gate, Rose embraced the old man and kissed his cheek, causing his face to flush slightly. The old farmer chuckled and gave her a smile. "Damn. Been a while since a pretty girl did that. I'll be in trouble if the missus hears of it."

"It's been a while since I was called a girl by a young lad like yourself," returned Rose.

The wizened farmer laughed so hard he fell to coughing, and Rose worried about him for a moment, but eventually he collected himself and his breathing returned to normal.

After listening to his directions, she set off into the city of Iverly. It had been many years since her last visit, but she still remembered the streets. Iverly was probably her favorite place, and if she hadn't been born into the Lothion nobility she would have wished to live there. Unlike Albamarl, it was a coastal city and unlike Relliton it wasn't built on a marsh. The weather was mild year-round, and the ocean breeze swept the city clean of foul odors.

Walking through the city was a fascinating experience in her current circumstances. Always before she had visited as a wealthy young woman with station and power. For most of her life, and especially when away from home, she had been constantly escorted, by guards, ladies-in-waiting, and a multitude of servants. Today she was alone, with no one to curtail her curiosity. Not only was she unescorted, she was anonymous. Dressed as she was, she felt practically invisible, and the feeling was exhilarating.

Unfortunately, her anonymity also came with significant disadvantages. Finding Carissa would be difficult. That was by her own design, of course, but when she had imagined coming to search for her daughter, she hadn't anticipated being bereft of money or connections.

As far as she knew, she did still have connections; the Viscount was a friend, but she couldn't present herself at his home in her current state. It would be embarrassing at best and humiliating or even dangerous at worst. Lady Rose had no illusions regarding how a vagrant would be greeted if one appeared and requested to see a landed nobleman.

That was aside from the fact that revealing her identity would put Carissa at risk. Agents from Lothion were very likely present in the city, and if she was discovered they would put significant pressure on King Nicholas to arrest her and return her to face the Queen's justice.

She had other resources, but meeting with figures from the underworld would be even more dangerous in her current condition. They wouldn't hesitate to turn on her if she were found to be alone and without protectors.

As she walked, Rose's feet took her down River Street. It was one of the most scenic walks in Iverly, following the west side of the river. She took that route rather than Dock Street, because the east side was dominated by docks and numerous warehouses, as well as the people that worked in them, making it entirely unsafe for a woman alone.

Just one companion would make all the difference, thought Rose. It almost didn't matter who it was, though as much as she hated to admit it, Chad Grayson might have been the best choice. With him along, she could visit the taverns and get information directly. Gram would have been almost as useful, not in the search, but simply for protection and intimidation.

Walking into a tavern by myself would be the next closest thing to suicide, she noted silently, *although Elise could probably pull it off.* Of course, her mother-in-law was old enough to not have to worry about certain dangers, but Rose had little doubt the formidable woman would have been able to manage even in her younger days.

"What's a lovely woman such as yourself doing wandering River Street by herself?" said a masculine voice behind her.

Rose's heart jumped. She had been so lost in her musings that she hadn't paid close attention to her surroundings. Covering her surprise, she turned and answered without hesitation, "Enjoying the breeze from the ocean." Her eyes took in the appearance of the stranger, and within seconds she had his measure.

Well dressed, but the clothes are worn. He wears that coat every day. She could see scuff marks and wrinkles that no proper gentleman would permit. The stranger's hands were rough and calloused, and not with the callouses that might indicate a scribe or scholar, nor were they the sort of callouses to be found on a swordsman's hands. *He might be trying to portray a down-on-his-luck nobleman, but the hands ruin that story.*

"Care for some company as you stroll?" he asked. "The sun is beginning to set, and the streets aren't safe for a woman alone after dark."

Not with you around, observed Rose silently. She still didn't know his game, but she knew she wouldn't like the end result. Turning him down would make things immediately unpleasant, however. Accepting his invitation was equally dangerous, and she knew the conversation that followed would be designed to uncover whether she was truly alone, or whether she had family or a husband.

"I was just thinking the same," said Rose agreeably, her mind racing through dozens of possibilities.

"My name is Roger," said the stranger, giving a slight bow. "Perhaps I could walk you home?" He paused, then added, "Or elsewhere, if you prefer. I find myself lonely this evening. I know a good place to get a meal." His eyes twinkled with mischief.

Rose had faced similar proposals many times over the years, but they had all been in entirely different circumstances. This man had no reason to make such an offer. *No honest reason, anyway.* In fact, given her current state of disrepair she had trouble envisioning a honest reason for him to have taken an interest.

A realization hit her then, *He's a pimp.* Her mind went blank for a moment. Certainly, she understood that such men sought out young, vulnerable women, but she couldn't imagine herself fitting the profile he was seeking, as she was neither young, nor (in her current state) attractive, at least in her own opinion. *Ignore the absurdity and deal with the present,* she chided herself.

Pretending at hesitation, she chewed her lip while her mind worked through the possibilities. "There is a place I've been wanting to visit. I don't know if they have decent fare, but I hear there's plenty of excitement to be found."

Roger frowned; he obviously hadn't expected her to take the initiative. "Where would that be?" he asked.

"Red Tom's Parlor, have you heard of it?" Rose responded innocently.

His eyes widened with surprise. "That's a gambling den. They don't serve food there, nor is it a good place for an unescorted lady. Why don't we try the Painted Lady? I know the name is off-putting, but I assure you the food is excellent."

Unescorted waif, you mean, corrected Rose mentally. *That must be the establishment he works for.* "I'm afraid I'm not hungry at the moment," she lied, "but I'm just *dying* for some excitement. Why don't we play a few hands? After I've worked up an appetite, I'd love to accompany you wherever you'd like to eat."

Roger clucked at her in admonishment. "You seem to have some misconceptions, Miss…? I still haven't had the pleasure of your name."

"Angela," she answered, using her chief maid's name.

"Miss Angela," continued Roger, "places like Red Tom's don't allow people to come in and play for free. You have to have coin to lose."

"Oh, that won't be a problem!" Rose enthused breathlessly. "I won some yesterday. They have a marker for me."

Roger's jaw went slack. "A marker?"

"It wouldn't be safe to carry money around on the street, would it?" said Rose.

"Well, of course not—," began Roger.

She seized on his arm and began pulling him along. "I just adore playing cards. I think it's the best thing about the city, to be honest. That's why I came to Iverly. You won't find anything like Red Tom's Parlor in the country."

Roger stared at her in shock. "You came to the city to—gamble?"

Rose nodded happily. "I'm very good at it. Once I've won enough, I'll rent a place to stay. I've already had some luck. A little more and my dream will come true. After that I'll play just for fun, and for money to spend." She smiled vapidly.

"Where did you get the money to start with?" asked Roger suspiciously.

Without missing a beat, Rose answered, "I stole it." When Roger stared at her she added, "But it was mine to begin with. It was my dowry. My parents wanted me to marry a farmer." She rolled her eyes to illustrate what she thought of that idea. "Once I've made enough, I'll send back what I took and repay them."

"I'm sure you will," agreed Roger, humoring her.

He thinks I'm mad, or naïve, thought Rose, smiling inwardly. *Now I just need to make the most of this opportunity.* She had her escort, and that would open many doors and greatly increase her options.

She led him several blocks before he began to pull against her. "Why don't we just go to the Painted Lady?" he suggested. "They play cards there, you know."

"I don't have a marker there," said Rose flatly. "Though I suppose after I cash it in, we could go there to play."

"How much is it for?" asked Roger.

"Seven gold crowns," said Rose matter-of-factly.

The pimp's face froze for a moment, then he resumed his act. "Well, that's a respectable amount. I suppose we should claim it first."

Rose merely nodded. *I'm sure you think so, now,* she thought.

After walking another seven blocks, Rose saw the sign for Red Tom's, which was simply a painting of a pair of cards with red backs. She felt her heart speed up, for she wouldn't be able to keep up her lie much longer. Her eyes scanned the street, hoping… *there!*

Clutching Roger's arm tightly, Rose pulled herself close against him. The pimp glanced down at her in surprise, but then his eyes widened as he felt the cold point of her dagger against his side, concealed beneath their arms. "What?"

Rose smiled innocently up at him, but her eyes were as hard as steel. "There are a few things I've neglected to tell you," she began.

He tried to push her away, but Rose held on and pressed the point harder. The enchanted steel was razor sharp, and blood began to drip from his side where it had begun to cut into skin. "There's a watchman right there," hissed Roger, his eyes rolling to one side. "If you murder me in the street, you'll never get away."

"I have no intention of murdering you, dear Roger," said Rose calmly, "providing you behave yourself. Besides which, do you recognize the guardsman you just mentioned?"

"As a matter of fact, I do," said Roger, his expression malicious. "His name is Carl. I've dealt with him a few times in the past. Things won't go well for you."

Rose cursed silently, but her mind continued to work. *So, the patroller is on the take.* She would have to wager that the pimp didn't know much more about the man. "You know his name; do you also know his family?" she asked lightly.

"Why?" asked Roger suspiciously.

She only knew a few names in Iverly, aside from that of Viscount Ledair, but she did know the name of the guard-captain. "Did you know he's a nephew of Guard-Captain Neiman?" she lied. "After I tell him you assaulted me, and I was forced to defend myself, I only have to mention the good captain to see that *justice* is done."

Roger studied her. "Assuming I believe you, *why* are you doing this?"

"That's better. You're starting to think," said Rose condescendingly. "In fact, I haven't been in Iverly in some time, nor do I have a marker to cash in, which is why I'll need your cooperation."

"I don't have much coin on me, if you're planning to rob me," he informed her.

Rose couldn't help but laugh. "I've never robbed anyone in my life, but I suppose there's always a first time. No, I need your help to see someone."

"Who?" asked Roger apprehensively.

"The Roach," she answered, giving the name of her long-time informant.

The pimp's eyes widened. "I don't have any dealings with him. You chose the wrong man. I'm a pimp, working for Madame Lenore. She doesn't work with him. I don't even know if Old Tom has dealings with him."

"He does," Rose pronounced confidently, "but I can't walk in alone and expect to talk to Tom. That's why I need you. We'll go in and play a while, and after I've got their attention Tom will come and find us."

Roger had the appearance of a man who was seriously considering attempting to bolt, despite the risk to his life and limb. Rose kept the blade firmly against his skin. "How are you going to get their attention?" he asked after a moment.

"You'll see inside," said Rose. "Now, you mentioned coin. How much do you have?"

"So, you *are* robbing me," said her hostage, almost sounding relieved.

"If I'm mistaken, possibly," she admitted. "If things go as they should, I'll repay you. If not, you're out a little coin—it's better than the alternative."

The man glared at her. "You haven't given me any choices."

"Oh, you certainly have choices," she explained. "You can join me inside and loan me your purse, or you can spend the night in the city jail with a serious stab wound and charges of assault."

"Why do I have to come inside? I'll just give you my money," offered the pimp. "I don't want any part of this."

"I need an escort," she told him. "Dressed as I am, no one will take me seriously without someone to back me up. So, back to my question—how much do you have?"

"Twelve silvers," admitted Roger.

"I'll return double that to you," said Rose. "Now, let's go in."

"You can't keep a knife on me in there and still play cards," observed Roger defiantly.

Rose smiled at him, flashing a set of teeth far too perfect for the sort of woman he had thought she was. "Trust me, Roger. I'm a better liar than you. Try anything after we step through the door and I'll ruin you, knife or not."

Chapter 10

It was apparent to everyone that Rose was out of place at the table. In the smoke-filled interior of Red Tom's, she was the only woman playing cards and she was far more shabbily dressed than the women who lounged in shadowy corners of the room, drinking with their companions.

No, Rose looked like a fishwife, or perhaps a laundress, except for the man standing behind her chair, acting as her servant or bodyguard. The hard-faced men she was playing against had found her presence amusing at first, but they had begun to take her seriously now. Winning had that effect on people.

Things had been a little dicey at first, as she had suffered several bad hands in a row, but she had kept her losses small. After she had won her first big hand and replaced those losses the men around the table had begun to play more seriously, to their detriment. When they hadn't taken her seriously, they had played frivolously, making their actions hard to predict, but now that they had lost some skin, they had become easier to read.

As the hours passed, the pile of wooden chips in front of her had grown considerably. Of course, the wise thing to do would have been to cash in after she had won a reasonable amount, but that didn't fit into Rose's plan for the evening. Not only did she in fact need the money represented by the chips, but more importantly, Rose needed their attention, even if it was not of the positive variety.

Rose studied the men around the table. The bald one across from her, whose name was Liam, kept glancing at his cards, though his face remained expressionless. *His hand is bad,* observed Rose. She had already gotten a firm grasp of the man. He rarely looked at his cards when they were strong. Simon, the tawny and rough dockworker to her right, was a different story. Over the past hour she had observed him deliberately creating false tells, but behind his façade he still had signs he couldn't hide.

Simon rubbed at the rough callus on his right thumb, subtly indicating he was nervous, but Rose knew better; the man's eyes told a different story. *He's hoping I'll go in big on this hand,* she noted. She met his eyes and smiled.

The last man, a jolly fool who had probably once been brawny but had now gone to fat, was named Tony. He was the most difficult for Rose to figure out. The pudgy fellow played the harmless fool, joking even as he lost, but she could sense more behind his act. Rose strongly suspected that he had thrown several good hands. That meant he was playing a deeper game. Either he was hoping to make her overconfident or the money on the table meant little to him.

Or both. Rose made her decision. Rather than fold or increase the bet, she called Liam on the last round of betting. It was a costly move, since she knew she didn't have the cards, but she needed to lose a little to keep Liam in the game.

Once the cards were down, Liam did indeed have the best hand and he rubbed his hands together in excitement as he raked in the pot. Rose pouted faintly, pretending at disappointment. She lost smaller amounts over the next two hands, but on the third round she drew them in with a false bluff and took the largest pot yet.

The majority of the chips were in front of her now, and both Liam and Simon wore expressions of frustration and annoyance on their faces. Only Tony continued to smile.

"The bitch is cheating," grumbled Liam.

Before she could respond, Tony spoke up. "Don't be a sore loser, Liam. You never had a chance."

"But To—"

"Shut yer damn mouth, Liam," said Tony, breaking his character with his previously friendly persona. Then he turned to Rose. "So, how much do you think you've won?" he asked.

Rose gave him a sly look. "Never count your chips while they're on the table," she replied.

"I'll wager you know exactly how much is in that pile," said Tony, producing a small twig and picking at his teeth. "A girl as smart as you, Angela, or whatever your name is, I'm sure you've kept a careful count."

She knew exactly how much she had won, down to the last copper. The pile of wooden tokens represented thirty-one crowns and twelve silver. "A lady never tells her secrets," she replied, "and a gentleman never asks."

"I ain't no gentleman," said Tony abruptly. "Why don't you tell me why you're here?"

The moment had come. "I need to talk to Red Tom," said Rose.

"Tom doesn't talk to just anybody, 'specially not uppity bitches," answered Liam.

Rose had been watching their eyes during the entire exchange, and she had her answer already. Liam's remark only clenched the truth in her mind. Ignoring the bald man, she looked directly at Tony. "I really doubt that, since he's sitting right here. Isn't that right, Tom?" Simon and Liam's faces tensed, confirming her guess.

Red Tom broke the ensuing silence with a deep belly laugh, then pulled out a pipe and began to pack it. He glanced at Liam. "I told you she was out of your league." Then he leaned forward and studied Rose. "You guessed right, little lady. Now why don't you tell me what you want so I can make up my mind about whether you and your pimp bodyguard get to walk out of here or not?"

Roger leaned forward and spoke softly beside her ear, his voice anxious, "Just let them have the money so we can leave with all our parts intact."

Tom's eyes watched Roger, and Rose worried that his advice might have cost her. She knew that the money on the table wasn't Tom's concern. It probably was of major interest to Liam and Simon, but they weren't the ones she needed to convince. Ignoring her 'partner,' she spoke, "I need to talk to the Roach."

Tom lit his pipe and drew deeply on it. "I run a respectable business. What makes you think I'd know someone like that?"

Without hesitating, Rose prevaricated, "The word is that you know everyone in Iverly. I'm new here and I don't have many contacts yet. Talking to you seemed like a good place to start."

Red Tom exhaled, blowing a thick cloud of smoke in her direction. "That's as may be. What's in it for me?"

The smoke made Rose want to wrinkle her nose in disgust, but she carefully schooled her expression. "The goodwill of my employer."

"And who would that be?"

"I'm not at liberty to reveal that information. As you can guess, my purpose is to keep their identity safe. I can tell you that most would jump at the chance to earn his goodwill. If that isn't enough, we could discuss money, or an exchange of information," she replied.

Liam leaned toward Tom. "Boss, this bitch is bluffing. She's no one. We should just dump her in the river."

Rose arched one brow but kept her gaze steady on Tom's face.

Red Tom pulled on his pipe for a moment, his expression thoughtful, then, with a nonchalant sweep of his arm, he backhanded the bald man so hard he fell from his chair. The move was sudden and violent, and yet somehow also relaxed. "Shut your fuckin' mouth, Liam. I won't have you talking about a lady like that."

Liam looked up from the floor, his mouth bloody as he responded weakly, "Lady?"

"A lady," repeated Tom, staring at Rose. "If you knew how to use those useless balls of jelly you call eyes, you'd know yourself. Look at her hands, her skin—hell, look at her goddamn teeth. Angela here comes from gentility, as does her employer I'd wager."

Rose covered her disgust at the violent display with a disdainful smirk but said nothing.

Red Tom glanced at Simon. "Take the lady's chips and cash them in for her." Then he addressed Rose, "Come back tomorrow evening, after the seventh bell. I'll introduce you to someone."

She nodded. "Seventh bell." Then she glanced back at Roger, indicating he could get her chair as she stood.

A few minutes later as she and Roger stood outside she handed the pimp three crowns. "For your trouble," she told him.

The pimp's hand shook slightly as he accepted the coins. "Who are you?"

Rose flashed a quick smile. "Someone you want as a friend." Then she added, "Can you recommend a decent inn for the night?"

"The Green Goat is nice, though a little expensive," he answered. "But it would suit you better than one of the dockside inns." He followed that with directions.

Before he could leave, she caught his sleeve. "If you know someone who would like to make a few coins, have them meet me there tomorrow. Someone with some meat on their bones. I'll need a more impressive escort tomorrow."

Roger nodded. "I'll see." He made no effort to hide his desire to be quit of her as quickly as possible.

Rose watched him leave, smiling faintly at his back, then turned and began making her way to the inn he had suggested.

***

In the Queen's bedchamber, Tyrion brooded in the dark. Ariadne slept beside him, exhausted from their most recent passions. Her energy constantly surprised him, as well as the desperate need he felt in her lovemaking. *Though, perhaps it shouldn't surprise me. Her adult life has been devoid of physical intimacy,* he thought.

While there was no light to speak of, he watched her breathing with his magesight. When he had initially contrived to seduce her, he hadn't expected to care about her as much as he currently did. It had simply been a matter of lust and advantage. Then again, nothing about his return to humanity had been as he expected.

Was this really what it was like before? His memories of his original human existence were all second-hand, after all, granted to him by the true Tyrion Illeniel. While those memories carried a painfully intense amount of emotion, experiencing such things first-hand was still different. *Should I really be engaging in things like affection and investing myself in these people?*

He wanted to protect her, and while that was nominally his mission, he wasn't sure he was supposed to *want* to do it. What if the Grove changed his mission? How would he handle it?

Hate was infinitely simpler and easier to manage. He wanted to kill his descendant, Mordecai, and Rose Thornbear, but if he was ordered not to, he could deal with it. Hate was a matter of business, and his business was hate. Love, and the gentler emotions—those he had trouble with.

With a sigh he turned his mind back to more practical matters. His biggest concern was the fact that his progenitor, Tyrion the Elder, couldn't continue to produce enough krytek to protect the entire world. They were already stretched thin covering the major human cities, and they only lasted three months. If he couldn't find a solution to assure the complete elimination of the ANSIS presence within a few more months, his creator would begin to fall behind. As prodigious as the massive father-tree's ability to supply krytek was, it was still limited.

Which is why I hoped collaborating with the humans of this age would provide some new solutions, he reminded himself. *Starting a feud with the father of most of the world's living wizards was not an ideal outcome.*

But what choice had he had? He had offered his assistance to Lady Rose on several occasions, and still she had chosen to assassinate him instead. He had lost his temper when the arrows found him. Pain was one thing, but it was the betrayal that hurt him most, and he still nursed a deep-seated rage over the turn of events.

At such moments, he seriously considered just letting the world burn, but watching Ariadne sleeping beside him, he knew he couldn't. *Why did he have to create me?*

The answer was obvious. *Because he couldn't bear to face the world himself.*

CHAPTER 11

Matthew studied Myra's letter with great interest. As he did, the others came and went, flitting by like moths, moving too fast to observe clearly. Time had become a strange thing. He was fairly certain his personal perspective was slowly speeding up to match theirs, but he couldn't tell how long it would take.

Take the letter, for example. He had read through it carefully, over a span that seemed like a matter of minutes for him, but at his best estimate had actually been at least an hour. It was clear from the content that they expected some guidance from him, and for that he needed to study the probabilities of the future. He hesitated only because he wasn't sure how long it would take.

On prior occasions, he had found that his sense of time was distorted, or even absent while doing so. He feared that if he did so now, he might spend weeks or months in a trance without realizing it. Obviously, that wouldn't be helpful to his friends and family. But what else could he do?

Making a snap decision, he pushed his uncertainty aside. The sooner he began, the sooner he would know. Clearing his mind, he relaxed, stretching out his perception in the strange way he had discovered, letting go of his immediate surroundings and embracing the infinite. Reality dissolved into a complex pattern, one so vast it beggared the imagination.

It was beyond the ability of the human mind—or of any mind, for that matter—to grasp, but he was aided by a native intuition that existed outside of himself. The greater mind of the universe itself, composed of all the aythar in existence, guided him to the insights he needed. That was the deeper secret he had discovered in his previous explorations. The Illeniel Gift wasn't a matter of magic, or of the She'Har, or people like himself or Irene. It was a connection to a greater whole that could inform the user, if he or she were capable of listening and understanding.

The first thing that became apparent to him was that the pattern was unravelling. Not at the edges, as a tapestry might, but at a point in the center, a place of such intense power that it was threatening to tear a hole in reality itself. He recognized it immediately. *Father.*

It was a sobering realization. To stop the destruction, his father would have to be removed, and there were no easy ways to do that. Only a few remote parts of the pattern could still exercise any leverage over the thing his father had become—was becoming. *We need Rose.*

But the current state of Lothion made recovering her difficult. That needed to change. He studied the pattern for an unknown time, letting it inform the deeper parts of his consciousness, and then he brought his awareness back to the present. The room snapped back into place around him, and he saw a blank sheet of paper in front of him, a pen and inkwell close beside it.

Back in the real world, his emotions struck him as he considered what they must do. Blinking, he rubbed at his eyes, which were damp. Then he picked up the pen and began to write.

***

Karen watched Matthew hold the pen and begin to move it over the paper with agonizing slowness. She had always considered herself a patient woman but seeing him slowly scrawl letters on the page was an exercise in frustration.

A hand on her shoulder made her look up. "Come eat," said Irene. "You'll go mad if you watch him writing like this." The smile on her face was meant to be reassuring, but Karen could see that Irene was just as tense.

"You're right," she answered.

The meal was fairly standard, but the conversation revolved mainly around what they were all waiting for. "Anything yet?" asked Elaine.

Irene shook her head, but Karen replied, "He's begun writing."

"'Bout damn time," opined Chad Grayson. "It's been two days."

"Considering his current perspective on time, he's moving quickly," offered Lynaralla.

"Considerin' mine, I might die of old age before he finishes," said the ranger.

Myra looked at the ring Moira had given her. *In my case, that's a real concern.* "Hopefully he'll finish within a day or two. I can't stay long."

"An' they call me impatient," remarked Chad.

Elaine glared at the archer. "She's dependent on Moira for her life. It isn't a matter of whim."

Chad raised his brows in surprise. "Oh."

"Perhaps we should consider our options," suggested Irene. "At least we can lay out what our situation is, what we have and what we need."

Sir Cyhan spoke first, "We have Lancaster, though it's isolated in a foreign realm. No one can touch us here."

"'Cept ANSIS, if they come back," pointed out Chad.

"That's a fair point," agreed Irene. "We're relatively safe here, but we're also limited in our ability to affect what occurs in the rest of the world."

"Meanwhile we've been declared outlaws in our homeland," noted Elaine. "And our country is controlled by Tyrion and the She'Har."

Myra shook her head. "We don't know that. Ariadne is still Queen. As far as we know Tyrion is just acting as her vassal."

"Do you really believe that?" asked Alyssa, who had been silent until then.

"Moira does," said Myra. "She observed him closely during one of his visits. While she couldn't risk interfering with him directly, she didn't think he was trying to control the Queen."

"That doesn't help much," said Chad. "That just means the Queen's lost her damn mind all by herself."

"As much as I disagree with her actions," said Irene, "her hand was forced by political factors. The question in my mind is who set things up to force her, *and us*, into this situation."

Karen sat straighter in her seat, intrigued. "You think there's someone working behind the scenes to orchestrate this mess?"

Irene pursed her lips. "Maybe."

Cyhan broke in. "Then the question is who stands the most to gain from recent events?"

"Tyrion," said Chad firmly.

"ANSIS," countered Alyssa.

Lynaralla cleared her throat softly, drawing their attention. "It's entirely possible that matters arise from random factors. Especially given the difficulty arranging something as improbable as what has happened. Even ANSIS couldn't predict all the chaotic events that have occurred."

"The Illeniel She'Har could," observed the ranger, giving Lynaralla a flat stare.

"Not those present today," said Lynaralla without showing any sign of discomfort at his remark. "I don't believe Tyrion has the ability, and Lyralliantha is probably still too young. I can't discount my distant ancestors, but I don't think they could arrange such specific events from across such a vast gulf of time. My instinct tells me this is a result of natural chaos rather than a deliberate plan."

Chad chewed on the last bit of his bread. "I'd sooner believe things have been cocked up by plain stupidity and happenstance."

Lynaralla frowned. "I believe that is merely a paraphrasing of what I just said."

"Stupid never dies," stated Irene, echoing her father's old motto.

There was laughter at that, but as it died away Myra stood. "I'm going to go see what he's written."

"It won't be much," cautioned Irene. "It took him two days just to start."

"I don't care. I need to see," said Myra, and with that she left the room, heading for the stairs that led up to the room Matthew occupied. Karen and Elaine rose to follow her.

Chad glanced at Elaine's cup, then reached for it. "Well, if you aren't going to finish your wine…"

When Karen and Elaine caught up with Myra they found her leaning down to study the parchment Matthew was still writing on. Karen frowned as she saw it. "That doesn't look like his handwriting. It's too messy. What does it say?"

Elaine looked at her in surprise. "You can't read?"

Karen shrugged. "I've just gotten a good handle on your language. I still haven't mastered your writing."

"Then how do you know that's not his usual handwriting?" asked Elaine.

"Because he was teaching me," replied the curly-haired young woman. "I've seen plenty of his writing. It's small and tight, not like this."

"He's rushing," said Myra. "Read it."

Elaine moved to stand behind Matthew and began reading aloud for Karen's benefit. "Send Myra back. Tell Moira to unify Lothion. Don't wait to read the r—" She straightened up. "That's all there is so far."

"That's my answer," said Myra. "Karen, can you take me back?"

"It isn't finished, though," complained Elaine.

"It's clear enough. 'Don't wait to read the rest'," said Myra. "He thinks we're pressed for time. He knows it may take too long for him to write it all out. You can tell me the rest in a few days."

Karen nodded. "I can take you to the border, but we'll need Irene or Lynaralla to cross. After that I can teleport you back home."

Irene had just entered the room. "I'll do the crossing. I need the practice." She glanced at Lynaralla with a slightly sour expression. Her She'Har sister had mastered the technique much more quickly than she had.

Lynaralla nodded, and Karen held out her hands to the others.

"Shouldn't we inform the others first?" asked Elaine.

Myra shook her head. "You and Lynaralla can tell them. Karen and Irene can have me there in a matter of moments and then they'll be back." She paused, then corrected herself, "Actually, Moira may want their assistance, but I doubt it will take long." Reaching out, she wrapped her hand around Karen's; at her nod Irene did the same.

"Wait—," Elaine started to protest, but the three women were gone. She pursed her lips and looked at Lynaralla. "And they leave us to clean up the mess."

The She'Har woman frowned. "Mess?"

"We have to explain where they've gone, and everyone is going to have a different opinion. If any of them disagree, they'll blame us for not talking to them first," said Elaine.

Lynaralla shrugged, consciously employing the human gesture to communicate her lack of concern. Inwardly she felt a sense of pride at remembering to use the bit of body language. "It's simple enough. We merely report what happened. Their decision was rational enough."

Elaine sighed. "Sometimes I envy you, Lynn."

CHAPTER 12

Irene managed to open the barrier with less difficulty than she had anticipated, and once they were back in Lothion proper, Karen teleported the three of them to Mordecai's workshop. "You're sure the guards won't report our presence to Tyrion or the Queen?" asked Irene anxiously.

Myra nodded. "She has them firmly under her control. Well, except for the humans. She's avoided tampering with them much."

"*Much?*" said Karen, raising one brow.

Myra looked uncomfortable. "Just little things, like erasing a few memories, if they see something they shouldn't."

"That's a little thing?" observed Karen with obvious distaste.

"It's the lesser of two evils," said Myra defensively.

Irene spoke up to head off an argument, "How are we going to get into the house without them seeing us? We didn't bring Elaine with us."

"No need," answered Myra. "She already knows we're here. I'm talking to her now." She tapped her temple with one finger.

Irene frowned. "The workshop is warded. She shouldn't be able to sense us in here, much less communicate telepathically."

"She can't sense us directly, but our telepathic skills are a little more advanced than you may realize—," Myra informed them. Irene blanched, and Myra hurried to add, "You'd feel it if one of us tried to tamper—at least at first."

Irene remembered a warning her father had given her. "Then what Dad said…"

Myra nodded, already aware of what she was referring to. "He was right. If you ever do find yourself facing a Centyr mage, go for the kill. Given enough time, anyone can be manipulated."

Suddenly uncertain, Irene stared at Myra. "But the only living Centyr mage is my sister."

"Sisters," corrected Myra.

"But you couldn't," began Irene stumbling over her words. "You need her to survive, so you couldn't…"

The door to the workshop opened and Moira stepped in, closing it behind her. "She could," she said, answering for her twin. "The only reason she's tied to me is because she hasn't turned to evil. If she wanted, she could steal one of your bodies, and claim your aystrylin. That would be murder, though."

Irene paled, but Karen shrugged off the dark mood and spoke boldly. "Why would you tell her that? Even if true, you're only undermining your sister's trust."

Moira smiled. "Because our father isn't here, and while I think I'm safe now, I don't know for sure that I always will be. Every time I'm forced to—" she paused, searching for words, "*do things*, I become a little less sure of myself."

Myra frowned, then interrupted. "What she hasn't told you, though, is that she's implanted a geass in her own mind to prevent her from tampering with her family."

"And are you sure it will work?" Moira glared at her spell-twin. "What's been done can be undone. It's better they not have a false sense of security. I have no idea what I may or may not be capable of in the future."

Karen shivered, then muttered, "And I thought my world was scary."

Moira smirked. "Are you still sure you want to marry into the family?"

Straightening, Karen answered, "If I ever have any doubts, it won't be on your account."

"That's enough," said Irene. "We need to focus on matters at hand."

"Myra's already given me the details," replied Moira. "I was unsure before, but Matthew's message is clear enough. I already have a plan in place."

"What do you need?" asked Irene.

"Just to borrow Karen for a few minutes. The portal to the palace is heavily guarded. If she can take us into Albamarl, it will simplify matters," said Moira. As she spoke, Myra stepped closer and the two of them merged.

"That's all? What are you going to do?" said Irene wonderingly.

"What our father was always too high-minded to do," said Moira. "Take control of the Queen and thereby the country."

"I'm not sure that's what Matt intended," responded Irene.

Karen nodded in agreement. "That's going too far."

Moira laid her hand on Karen's shoulder, and Irene felt a faint movement of aythar as her sister replied, "Of course it's what he intended. He knows me better than anyone. He knew exactly what his message would set in motion."

Karen's eyes fluttered for a moment, then her gaze cleared. "You're right. I should have thought of that."

Irene's eyes went wide, and her mouth formed an 'o'. "Myra just said you couldn't…"

"Karen isn't family—yet," interrupted Moira. "And apparently time is short. I can't waste it by arguing."

Irene's power flared, and her shield began to glow intensely. "Undo what you did," she warned, her voice threatening.

"Relax, Rennie," said Moira calmly. "I didn't do much. I just took a shortcut around the argument. She'll be fine, though you should probably make her spend some more time working on her shields. That was far easier than it should have been."

"Undo it, Moira," repeated Irene.

Moira found herself reflexively beginning to squint. The vivid glow of Irene's shield was invisible to normal sight, but the power of her aythar was so strong that the air around her began to shimmer visibly, like heat waves on a sunny day. Moira could feel its resonance in her teeth. *She's so powerful, like Father,* she realized, then shrugged mentally to herself. *I could get around it, though, if I wanted to risk her searing the flesh from my bones before I could rein her in.*

She had no desire to test her theory, however. *No matter what else I become, family first,* Moira repeated to herself. "I will, Rennie," she reassured, then she sent a silent command to her latest pawn.

Karen's eyes focused on Irene. "I'll be right back." Then she glanced at Moira and the two of them vanished, leaving Irene alone in the dark workshop.

In the silence that followed, it was all Irene could do to control her impulse to shatter the stone walls of her father's shop. With an effort of will, she relaxed her power, but it was several seconds before she realized the growling noise in the air was coming from her own throat. Being alone, she finally vented her irritation in a stream of invective she had previously heard from Chad Grayson, "Toad-sucking dandy trollop!"

***

Karen and Moira appeared in a shadowed alley just a few blocks from the palace in the central district of Albamarl. "Is this what you had in mind?" asked Karen.

"Exactly," chuckled Moira, knowingly.

"I'm going to have a hell of a time calming Irene down when I get back," observed Karen ruefully.

Moira nodded. "Not to mention yourself."

Karen blinked, her eyes framed by her curly, almost black hair. "Huh?"

"I tampered with your mind," Moira informed her. "But it was only temporary. I didn't do anything permanent. When you return, my influence will fade and you'll likely find yourself extremely angry."

Karen seemed confused. "That can't be," she muttered, then she felt an image enter her mind, one she knew came from her companion.

"Remember that," advised Moira. "A shield that can block normal attacks isn't necessarily the best thing for stopping my sort of intrusion. No matter how strong, once I find a pattern or resonance, I can get in. You have to keep it shifting, almost random, if you hope to thwart me for very long."

"Why would you show me this?"

Because you might need it someday, thought Moira to herself. "Teach the others, and make sure you practice. Now, go."

Without hesitation, Karen teleported back to the workshop where they had left Irene. Moira was alone.

You're never entirely alone, communicated Myra from within. *I live here too.*

Stay out of this, said Moira silently.

You don't want my help?

No, this is my task, answered Moira. *I don't want you getting your hands dirty.*

Why? asked Myra.

Who knows how much this will affect me? If you can keep from becoming tainted like I am, you can serve as my conscience.

Myra wasn't particularly happy about that statement, but she knew it was pointless to argue. *How do you plan to proceed?* she asked.

Moira reached down and smoothed her long black skirts with pale hands. She had dressed for the occasion. With her magesight she could already sense the approach of several krytek, moving to investigate the appearance of a new mage in the area. "I won't touch the people, if I can help it, but I'm going to need soldiers. Thankfully, Tyrion has provided the perfect solution."

You won't touch any of the people?

"Except the Queen, of course," explained Moira, "and possibly a few of the nobles, if they seem likely to rebel against their monarch's new directives."

You realize everyone disagrees with your plan, including me, Myra informed her.

"Except Matthew," corrected Moira. "He knew exactly what I was considering, I'm sure of it."

This is wrong.

"Ariadne gave up whatever right she had to free will when she decided to cross my family," Moira stated firmly. "Don't worry, though. She won't even realize it's gone when I'm done." She began walking toward one end of the alley, moving to meet one of the krytek advancing toward her. It would be easier if she could take one first, rather than fighting both at once.

From within, Myra watched Moira's transformation with fascinated horror. It wasn't external, of course, but she could see the change in her twin's spirit as she approached the human-like krytek guard. In the blink of an eye Moira's inner self became dark and hard, almost reptilian. Lifting one hand, she reached toward the krytek with invisible claws.

The contest was swift and brutal, yet bloodless, as Moira ripped at a weak spot in the krytek's simple shield and seized its mind. Seconds later she had control, and with its assistance she subdued the second krytek easily. Then she coldly crushed their souls, devouring their free will and replacing it with newly constructed spell-minds of her own design.

Unlike Myra, these new spell-twins were more independent. Moira had effectively murdered the krytek and given their bodies and aystrylins to her new servants. Where one Centyr mage had entered Albamarl, now three stood in the darkened alleyway. Summoning a mental image, Moira shaped her aythar and covered herself in an illusion, making herself appear as one of the krytek guards.

"That won't fool anyone with magesight for very long," cautioned one of her new servants.

Smiling, Moira replied, "Anyone with magesight is an ally, or will become so."

You're referring to the krytek, clarified Myra within Moira's head. *What about Conall, Gareth, or Tyrion?*

Moira responded aloud, for the benefit of her two servants, "If we encounter my brother, he must not be tampered with. Disable him, even if it costs us. We have lives to spare, but I only have two brothers. Gareth is a different story. Incapacitate him if possible. If that turns out to be too difficult, destroy his mind and bring me his body. It would make a powerful vessel."

Moira! cried Myra silently.

Shut up.

She went on. "Tyrion is to be taken. If possible, I'll bring the She'Har under control, but I won't shed any tears if he dies today." With that said, Moira strode from the shadowy alley into the light, but she carried her darkness with her.

Chapter 13

Lady Rose sat in a darkened corner of Red Tom's Parlor, at a table he had directed her to when she arrived. In front of her was a glass of cheap wine, doubtless the best they had to offer. She sipped at it slowly, doing her best to hide a wince at the sour taste.

Rose felt considerably better today, having bathed and dressed in new clothes. She smirked at herself as she looked down at the green fabric of her dress. It was well made, but the quality of the material was inferior and there was a notable lack of embroidery, trim, or lace. *A few weeks ago I wouldn't have been caught dead in something like this,* she thought. *Now I'm just glad to not look like a laundress.*

She glanced at her escort, a young man named Glen. He was the youngest son of a local butcher and had no experience at being a bodyguard, or any other type of servant for that matter. His most important quality was that he was unknown to the men frequenting the establishment. If she had hired one of the usual mercenaries, the man she was about to meet would have known it. Glen helped provide the illusion that she had some power and influence of her own, beyond what the people of Iverly knew.

It also helped that he was tall, muscular, and somewhat ugly. Whether or not he'd be of any use in a fight she had no idea, but if things turned to violence she would have already lost. Glen's entire purpose was as a stage prop for the role she played.

The butcher's son saw her looking at him and he met her eyes, then glanced longingly at the glass of wine in her hand. Given his part, she hadn't bought him a drink or allowed him to sit at the same table. Instead he sat at the next table, looking thirsty and uncomfortable.

Rose didn't feel bad, though. She would pay him enough to enable him to drink as much as he wished for several days.

She watched the room while she waited, wondering about the other patrons. Almost any of them could be the Roach; she had no idea what the man looked like. He might well be studying her before coming over to speak.

Lady Rose passed slightly more than half an hour that way before a small, slender man approached. She had taken note of him earlier, as he sat at the bar, but he was easy to dismiss. He was short, with lanky hair that looked as though he oiled it. There was nothing special about his clothes, his face, and certainly not his stature.

When he pulled the back the chair across from her and twirled it around, Glen stood up as a warning, but the man didn't even glance at the looming butcher's boy. "Tell your dog to sit down or this meeting is over before it begins."

Rose nodded at Glen, and he resumed his seat. "You're much as I expected," she observed.

The stranger's brows went up. "I don't hear that often. Usually people say the opposite."

"Which is exactly what you strive for, I'd wager," said Rose.

"I'll have to disappoint you, milady," said the rogue. "You expected the Roach, but I am merely his messenger."

Rose sipped her wine, then replied, "I doubt that very much."

"Oh?" said her visitor with some surprise. "What makes you say that?"

"The Roach is known for his skill and efficiency. Unlike some in his position, he's created a reputation for being quicker, smarter, and more effective than his competitors, and more importantly, his underlings. Having someone like you in his employ would counter that reputation. I have trouble imagining two men such as you in one small city such as this," posited Rose.

"You have an active imagination," said her guest, before reaching across the table and taking her wine bottle. He turned it up and took a healthy swallow of wine.

Glen had been watching, and he stood once more at this affront. "Watch your tone with the lady," he warned.

Perfectly played, thought Rose, but she gave Glen a harsh glance. "Sit down," she ordered.

The stranger smiled, then swept his arms out wide as he performed a mock bow while sitting. "Thank you, milady. Few such as yourself would show such concern for an insignificant cutpurse."

Rose stared at him without blinking. "I simply don't like having to replace good help."

The butcher's son took his role too seriously, however. Stepping closer, he leaned over the small rogue. "I'd make short work of a jackanape like—erp!"

His words were cut off short as a blade appeared at his throat, held in the stranger's slender hand. Glancing down, he saw another, larger piece of steel threatening his manhood. Glen tried to step back, but the rogue used his leg to slide his chair behind the large man, causing him to stumble and fall, crashing heavily to the floor.

The small man recovered the chair and resumed sitting almost before Glen hit the floor. He took another swig from her bottle and then lifted it in her direction as though making a toast. "I salute your powers of observation. You were right to be more worried about the boy than me." The large knife had vanished, but the smaller dagger twirled around his fingers before coming to a stop. He then began to trim his nails.

Rose's bodyguard got up, red-faced and angry, but she pointed at his chair and he found enough reason to obey her this time. Then she lifted a hand and waved at the serving girl. "Another bottle, please." While the server went to fetch it, she turned to her guest. "You've only confirmed your identity."

"Think what you will," said the rogue, but then he paused. "Did you plan that?"

She smiled. "You're terribly paranoid, even for someone in your line of work."

The thief stared at his dagger thoughtfully, then glanced up at her. "You're taking a big risk coming here. That shows desperation."

Rose felt a chill run down her spine. She had underestimated the man, a potentially fatal mistake considering that her only real leverage was a bluff. She kept her features smooth, but her hand inched toward the long, enchanted blade hidden in her skirt. *Another stupid idea,* she reminded herself. From what she had just seen, the man sitting across from her could kill her and Glen both in the blink of an eye. It wouldn't even cause him to work up a sweat.

As if to underscore his point, the rogue twirled the small dagger in his hand before making it vanish with a move so quick her eyes couldn't quite follow. "Why don't we cut the shit and speak honestly," said the thief. "After all, you've already guessed my identity. Why don't you tell me who it is that you represent?"

Maintaining her composure, Rose answered, "My employer is in Lothion, more than that I'm not allowed to say."

"Unlikely," responded the Roach. "No one would send a woman such a distance to attempt to negotiate with me. There are far more reliable channels."

"Manfred is dead," she stated flatly, gratified by the look of faint surprise on the stranger's face. "The usual channels are no longer satisfactory."

The Roach leaned forward, his face thoughtful, then he sighed. "I'm starting to understand why you came in person."

Rose frowned. "In person?"

"Don't be coy," said the thief, then he tilted his head back and opened his mouth in an expression of mock surprise. "Did you think you were the only one who could act? I've known about Manfred's death for more than a week now, but your knowledge of the same tells me everything I need to know about you, Lady Rose."

"You're mistaken."

The Roach grinned. "I don't think so. There aren't many noblewomen from Lothion who would dare the road to come here. Not only that, but you're desperate and bereft of allies and assistance. Your Queen has declared you an outlaw and there's a significant bounty on your head. Why else would you come here and try to lie to me?"

The man's face darkened as he added, "I dislike liars, milady, even when the lies come from the lips of someone as beautiful and intelligent as yourself."

"I'm not the only one with a bounty on my head," reminded Rose.

"Threats do not become you," said the Roach. "You're a cat with no claws. You could scream my name to the rafters and it wouldn't matter, not here, not now. Look around the room. Who do you think these people are? Customers of Red Tom?" He laughed. "I could cut your farmhand into little pieces and one of them would clean up the mess for me. After that, I could do whatever I wished with you and no one would object. You're alone here. The only real question left is whether you have anything more valuable to offer me than the price on your head."

Rose's mind raced as the man spoke, searching for something, anything, that might salvage the situation. She needed more information to work with, and she knew little about the man across from her other than what she had been able to glean from her recent observations. Smiling confidently, she spoke even as her thoughts solidified, "You sound a lot like Manfred did. Are you really so sure of yourself? It didn't do him much good."

The Roach said nothing for a moment, staring intently at her, but his eyes betrayed him for a second as they darted to one side to scan the room. "You've got a lot of nerve, trying to double down when you've already been caught in your bluff. You sure you want to try that tactic with me?"

She refilled her glass, grateful that her hand was steady as she poured, then took a sip before replying, "You've already guessed who I am, and you know my reputation. You should know better. You know who my friends are and, more importantly, you know what they're capable of. If you really think I came here unprotected, you're welcome to test the theory, but I won't be held responsible for the consequences. It would also be unfortunate if I had to find someone else to do business with."

The Roach studied her as she spoke, silently impressed with her performance. Herw words gave him pause, for over the course of their conversation he had come to realize he was dealing with someone whose wits were just as sharp as his own. That in itself was something of a novelty, and combined with his own native caution, he was tempted to accept her words, but he hadn't climbed out of the gutters by playing it safe. Rose Thornbear was worth a great deal of money.

He decided to call her bluff, and he felt the familiar joy of adrenaline surging in his blood. The muscles in his body tensed almost imperceptibly as he prepared to move. In the blink of an eye he went from sitting to standing, and then he was flying through the air in a leaping somersault that would put him behind her bodyguard.

It happened so quickly Rose had no chance to react; even her eyes were barely quick enough to follow his movements, and her heart shot into her throat as she saw the Roach sail into the air, steel glittering in his hands.

***

"She's going to die."

I ignored the voice. It was simply another sign of my impending madness. At first, I had thought it might be Penny, whispering to me from whatever crevice she occupied in my heart, but over time I had come to the conclusion that it wasn't her.

"Don't you want to do something?" it suggested.

No, I cautioned myself. The voice was always tempting me to do more. In some way it was connected to the gift I had inherited, but it was anything but benign. At first it had been subliminal, almost subconscious, but now it was ever present and easy to hear, like a friend whispering in my ear. And it was always urging me to act.

But with every action, the power within me grew. Soon I would no longer be able to contain it. That was why I had come here. Or rather, that was why I had created this place, an empty pocket hidden away between dimensions.

After saving my children, I had continued onward in my quest to eradicate ANSIS from my world. Whether I had succeeded was an open question, but gradually I had come to realize that with every exercise of the powers I held, they grew stronger, as did the voice. It had fed me hints and knowledge, giving me the locations of hidden places where ANSIS thought itself safe.

And for a while, I had listened, gladly accepting its help and destroying them at every turn. Eventually I had come to realize its intention, however. It was egging me on, urging me to greater uses of power to hasten the end.

An image flashed in my head, and I saw a man leaping up from a table, twin daggers in his hands, but his target wasn't Rose, it was the large man that sat nearby. *He isn't going to kill her,* I thought silently.

"What do you think will happen to her after he kills her bodyguard?" asked the voice. "Shall I show you?"

No! I screamed within my mind.

"Don't you want to save her? You're in love with her."

"If I do she'll die anyway," I finally answered, speaking to the brilliant void that surrounded me. "Everyone will. They're only safe if I remain here."

"That isn't remotely true," argued my invisible antagonist. "The process you're undergoing is irreversible and unstoppable. Even if you do nothing, your struggle to contain it will only slow it down a little. You might as well do as you wish while you still can."

"If it happens here, it won't affect them," I responded.

A chuckle sounded in my ears. "In that you're mistaken."

"I don't take advice from mysterious spirits," I replied. "It's a long-standing policy."

"That can be remedied."

My tiny little private universe vanished, replaced by a wood-paneled office. The agony of straining to contain my power also disappeared, causing me to gasp with relief. Looking down at myself, I saw my body was much as I remembered it, before my transformation.

Two large, padded chairs with small side tables beside them occupied the center of the space, and the walls were covered in shelves loaded with books. A man sat in one of the chairs, sipping a cup of tea and looking up at me over the rim of his glasses. "Is this better?" he asked. His face was familiar, though I had no idea who it was. It felt as though I should know his name, but my mind was blank on the subject.

"None of this is real," I said flatly.

He nodded. "Neither are you, or your world, or even me for that matter. What's your point?"

I grimaced. That was a philosophical rabbit hole I wasn't in the mood to jump down. "I don't feel like sophistry at the moment. Who are you?" I demanded.

"You already know the answer to that," said the familiar stranger.

"Piss off," I replied. "I didn't put up with mysterious doublespeak from my now deceased spell-twin, Brexus, I'm damn sure not putting up with it from you. Answer plainly or leave me the hell alone."

The man put his cup down with a frown. "Since you insist on being unpleasant, I don't have a name. Are you happy? I may have had one once, but its long lost to me."

"Then what are you?" I asked.

"I could say 'God,' but that isn't really satisfactory. I could also say that I'm you, but that wouldn't convey the meaning you need to understand. 'The Dreamer' might suffice, but I prefer to think of myself as an author, or maybe a storyteller," he answered.

I chuffed in annoyance. "For an author you're terrible at names. I'll just call you Tim."

"As you please."

"So, from what you've said, you'd have me believe the world is just a dream you're having. Is that correct?"

Tim nodded. "That's the easiest way to describe it."

"And what does that make me?" I asked.

"Part of the dream."

"You're a twisted son of a bitch," I accused, not bothering to hide my anger.

He smirked faintly. "I can't really deny that."

"If you're God, then you're responsible for all of this, all the suffering, all the evil, all the deaths. Why would you put us through such things?"

"That's true," he admitted. "I'm also responsible for your family, your loves, every sunrise—every bit of joy you've ever felt."

Staring at him, I felt a sense of sorrow, or perhaps wistfulness, and my curiosity began to get the better of me. "The real question is why. Why would you do these things? If you're that powerful, why don't you put things right? Why should people suffer?"

"I wish I could tell you the answer," he replied. "I have spent eternity watching you and those like you, and still I do not know. I think I once held hope that by observing, I could finally discover that secret, but at some point I gave up. I no longer believe the answer exists. All we can do is make the best of what we're given."

Faced with someone who claimed to be an all-powerful being, I found a sour taste in my mouth from his answer. "Then leave that aside. You could still do something about it. You could do away with the suffering."

"Can I?" he asked, his mouth quirking up on one side. "You'll see, when your time comes."

"My time?"

Tim nodded. "What's happening to you is not the end, at least not for you. The destruction will bring an end to me, and all my willful stubborn dreams, except for you. It will also be a new beginning. The new world will be a product of your dreams, and hopefully, I will finally be at peace."

With those words, I finally understood his motivation. "You want me to kill you. That's what this is all about, isn't it? You want out, so you've been pushing me to bring about this apocalypse of yours."

He sighed, then picked up his cup and took another sip. "I wouldn't put it that strongly. Let's just say that I don't object. Since you've put things in motion, however, I see no reason not to move on to the conclusion."

Something else occurred to me then. "Is this how you got here? Were you like me once?"

Tim shrugged. "Probably, though to be honest my memories of before are vague at best."

As I chewed on my lip another thought came to me. "Let's say this does happen."

"It will," he said immediately.

Impatient, I waved my hands at him. "Suppose I believe that, for the moment. What if I recreate this world? Could I fix the things I think you've screwed up?"

He looked intently at me, his gaze piercing me and driving a spike of sudden sadness through my heart. "What you really mean to ask is could you bring your friends back, your wife, your father, all those you've lost."

Defensively, I replied, "Well, among other things, but yes."

"No, not really," he said frankly.

"Why not?" I challenged.

"When you lie down to sleep at night, do you choose your dreams? Can you control them?" he responded. When I didn't respond, he continued, "Neither can I."

Agitated, he stood and approached me, his form blurring before me, his face changing, until Penny was in front of me, looking down. "Do you think I would choose to leave you, or our children?" A second later, Dorian had taken her place. "Do you think I would choose to suffer, if I could avoid it? Or that I would leave Rose for another man to love?" Next came a face I had seen only in a painting, Elena di' Cameron, my long-dead mother. There were tears in her eyes. "Would I choose to leave my only child behind?"

They appeared and vanished, one after another, leaving their questions hanging in the air like accusations. "Stop, please. This is too much," I begged. The pain in my chest was unbearable.

His form changed once more, and Marcus was before me. Returning to his chair, he sat down and lifted the cup. He sniffed it once and his lip curled in disgust. Then he waved his hand, causing it to vanish. A moment later it was replaced by a glass of wine. "That's better." He took a long drink from the glass. "If I have to do this, I might as well have something good to drink."

Blinking away tears, I couldn't help but ask, "Is that really you?"

My best friend's wry expression was exactly as I remembered it. "Yeah, unfortunately it is, thanks to your stubbornness. Apparently, I'm the only one you'll listen to, which doesn't say much about your judgement, I might add."

"But it can't be you. This is some sort of dream, or illusion." I spoke to him, but I was reminding myself.

"That's the point, dunderhead," said Marc. "For a genius, you're really having trouble with this one."

I knew it was still the stranger, but his words, his voice, his manner, they were all Marc. "What's the point of putting on false faces?" I argued.

"They aren't false," said Marc. "Unfortunately, they're very real. It's actually me, plus an uncountable number of others. I just happen to be the one who has been put in charge for the moment."

Narrowing my eyes, I thought for a moment. "If it's really you, help me. Stop what's happening to me."

Marc downed the rest of the glass before staring down at his feet. "I can't. That's the piece you're missing. For all that talk about gods and whatnot, I'm effectively powerless. I can do almost anything, here and now, in this tiny moment, but in what you think of as the *real* world, I have very little control. Dreamer really is the best term for it. The world is me, and I am the world, including *you,* but things just happen. That's why I don't mind dying. Every moment, every life, every joy, sorrow—everything, good and bad—I'm living them."

"You must have some power to change things," I insisted.

He looked up at me from beneath hair that was just a little bit too shaggy. "It's like writing a story, or dreaming it. I can push things one way or another, but I can't do much more. And the one thing I most certainly can't change—is *you*. You've gone too far. That power inside you, that's a big part of me, and as it grows, I become weaker. Eventually, it will destroy me, and a new dream will emerge from you, like a butterfly from a chrysalis."

"Fine," I said at last. "What do you think I should do? And by that, I mean *you*. I don't give a damn what the rest of the world thinks."

My old friend picked up the bottle and, forgoing the glass, took a long slug directly from it, then handed it to me. I did the same. "Well, the answer is the same whichever one of us you're talking to."

"You know me best," I replied. "You know what I want."

"You can't have that," he said solemnly, before looking directly into my eyes. "You should enjoy the time you have left as best you can. Do what you want, save Rose, but *eventually* the end will come. It's unavoidable. *Trust* Matthew."

Having known him for most of life, I caught his emphasis on certain words. *Eventually.* A faint hope bloomed in my heart, but then his face dissolved, and Tim was back.

"That's enough of that," said Tim. "Don't read too much into what he said."

I gave him a disdainful look. "Next time you should be more careful who you let do the talking."

Tim appeared worried. "You're only going to make things worse for everyone."

"He wouldn't lie to me," I responded, "and I already know there's not a thing you can do to stop me."

"What if I kept you here?" he suggested.

Free now of the despair that had clouded my thoughts, I took note of his phrasing. "You can't, just like you can't lie. Otherwise you'd have made that a statement rather than a question."

"I know what you're thinking. It's a bad idea," warned Tim.

Smiling, I answered, "Good, bad, it's all a matter of perspective in a dream, isn't it? You made that perfectly clear." Searching inside myself, I found the pain that had been hidden from me and touched it, letting my power fill me. It ripped through my awareness, searing my soul as though I was burning from the inside out. Exerting my will, I dissolved the illusion around me and then did the same for the private sanctuary I had created to hide within.

Standing in Lothion once more, I stretched time until the world stood still, and then I took to the air, heading for Iverly.

Chapter 14

Rose reached for the longknife strapped to her leg, but she felt as though she was moving in slow motion. It was too late, and the Roach was far too fast. Glen would be dead before she could even get to her feet.

Then the world vanished, obliterated by a searing flash of light accompanied by a sound too loud to be heard. A wave of pressure ripped through the room, flinging the Roach back in mid-leap. The rogue flew across the room and over the bar, slamming into the wall. The shockwave knocked down most of the other patrons as well, though it didn't seem to touch Rose.

Glancing behind her, Rose saw that the doors of Red Tom's Parlor were gone, as well as some of the wall that had held them. Smoke rose from the street outside. *Lightning?* she thought. *No, it's too big a coincidence.* Looking back, she saw the patrons rising from the floor. They were shaken and fearful, but otherwise no worse for wear. The Roach was rising from behind the bar, a trickle of blood running from his scalp to his jaw.

Ever quick, she knew what to do.

Rose remained in her seat, keeping her features cool and composed. As the Roach stalked toward her, new blades in his hands—for he had lost the old ones—she took a sip of her wine. Her eyes were cold when she glanced up at him. "Care to test me again?" she said calmly.

The wiry thief stared at her and his face began to pale. Putting away his weapons, he scavenged a chair from nearby and sat down across from her once more. "How can I help you?"

"Since you forced me to such a distasteful act, I'm afraid the nature of our relationship will have to be made very clear," Rose told him. "You work for me now."

The Roach nodded. "What do you need?"

"First, I need to find some people. Two women who came to Iverly to hide—," she began.

Her new accomplice's face took on an expression of confusion. "You came to me to find missing persons? Am I hearing this right?"

Rose didn't bother responding, the look in her eyes was enough.

"They must be very important," said the Roach at last, "and you're seeking to avoid involving the Viscount in this."

Her brows went up. "You already mentioned the bounty on my head."

"In Lothion," countered the thief. "I happen to know you're well connected with the King of Gododdin."

"The Iron Queen is even more important. If I put Nicholas in an awkward position, who do you think he will choose to support?" asked Rose. "It's better not to strain my relations. I'll solve my problems with the Queen myself."

"Fair enough. What do they look like? I'll need a good description if my men are to find them."

"One is young, with light hair and a fair face, the other is older, closer to my age, with darker hair. They aren't using their own names, but they entered the city with a modest sum. They should have found lodgings and be living quietly somewhere out of sight," explained Rose.

The Roach frowned. "That isn't much to work with."

"I have faith in you," said Rose, somewhat sarcastically.

"And what's your plan for them? Are you planning a more permanent disappearance?"

She grimaced. "I want to help them. Make sure your men don't expose them when they're found. I need to see them privately."

Red Tom burst into the room then, his face stunned as he saw the destruction. When he found his voice, he bellowed, "What the hell happened here?!" Everyone else had long since abandoned the space, so he marched toward them.

Furious, he glared at the Roach. "I loaned you the use of the room, I didn't expect *this*! Who's going to pay for the damage?"

The Roach shrugged. "It was an act of god. I can't help it if lightning struck your establishment."

Rose answered as well, turning a slender finger in the Roach's direction, "He'll pay for it."

The thief's jaw dropped, and he pointed at himself, silently mouthing the word, 'me?' Artfully, Rose arched one brow, and the rogue hurried to respond. "It was my fault. I'll take care of it, Tom."

***

Conall feigned interest in the roses, wishing he could be somewhere else. Being knighted and named the Queen's Champion wasn't nearly as exciting as he had originally thought it would be. Ariadne, the Iron Queen and sovereign of Lothion stood a few feet away, studying the flowers and occasionally remarking on their colors. Conall fought to avoid yawning.

Despite the impressive title, he felt as though he wasn't much more than a courtier these days and considering the state of his family, he couldn't help but wonder if he wasn't wasting his time. *Dad's an outlaw, Mom is gone, Moira's under house arrest, and who knows where Matthew and Irene are,* he thought, mentally reciting the litany to himself for the thousandth time. *Meanwhile, I'm touring the gardens.* He felt useless, and it didn't help that his siblings probably thought he was a traitor to the family. *Maybe I am.*

He had always admired his father. From a young age, everyone had repeatedly told him his father was a living legend and the stories of his battles and struggles against the Dark Gods and the shiggreth had been too incredible not to leave a lasting impression on him, but in the end, his dad was just a man. Conall knew that all too well. Growing up under the same roof, he had emerged from adolescence and come to the realization that his father was fairly ordinary in many ways, and he had plenty of flaws.

Conall had never known Dorian Thornbear, though, and consequently he had been far more impressed by his tales. Early on he had wished he could become a knight, and being born a mage had seemed rather lackluster to him. It wasn't until he had come into his power that he had realized how much better it was, but he had still romanticized the nobility of the knights in stories.

Now he was both, a dream come true, and it was boring as hell. Consequently, rather than enjoying the flowers, he found himself continually reviewing the steps that had led him to where he was now, reconsidering his decisions and wondering if he could have done anything differently. His choice at each turn seemed good and right, but he still felt guilty.

"Are you bored?"

Conall's eyes snapped into focus and he found Ariadne staring at him. "No, of course not, Your Majesty."

The Queen growled faintly.

He hastily amended his statement. "No, of course not, Ari." She had repeatedly told him to relax around her when there was no one else present. He glanced back at the people following them; two guards, a messenger, and two ladies in waiting—all of them well out of earshot.

"Even if they were close, servants don't count," she reminded him. "And you are definitely bored. What are you thinking about?"

Conall shrugged. "Nothing of consequence."

Ariadne's lips firmed up. "You're worried about your family."

He said nothing. Conall was fairly proficient with courtly phrases, but he was still terrible at dissembling.

"I don't blame you," she pronounced. "I'm worried about them too. Do you blame yourself?"

Conall looked at her in surprise. "Not really—maybe, I don't know. I can't see that I've done anything wrong, but even so…"

"Multiply that feeling by a thousand, and you'd know how it feels to be a king," she replied. "You aren't to blame for any of it. You've only acted according to your conscience."

Her statement was enlightening, and he felt suddenly selfish for his self-absorbed mindset. Trying to make her feel better, he responded, "The same is true for you."

Ariadne shook her head. "A conscience is the one thing too expensive for a monarch to afford, yet still I have one, and it torments me. I have *not* acted according to it, though; otherwise your father would never have been jailed and convicted."

"But…"

She held up her hand. "I'm not making excuses. If I had acted according to my conscience, I very well might not be Queen anymore, and who knows what state the kingdom would be in now."

"I'm sorry," he apologized. "I didn't mean…"

"I just want you to know I understand how you're feeling," she continued. "I've done what I thought was necessary, even though it required me to act against my conscience. More importantly, it means that you have been caught between your allegiance and your own conscience. It's put you at odds with your family." Ariadne moved closer and fixed him with her eyes. "You don't have to do this. You can go home. I won't take your lands from you. You don't have to be here. You don't have to actively support me. If I had the option, I'd go with you."

His breath caught in his throat for a moment. The look in her eyes was heartbreaking. She couldn't say it, couldn't even show it on her face, but deep behind those eyes he could feel the pain her inner conflict had created. It was the same as his own, but she had no choice. The Queen was a prisoner here, wrapped in gilded chains and royal trappings.

And if he did leave, how long would she survive? As much as he respected Tyrion's strength, Conall didn't trust the man any more than his father did. Without Conall's support, and the support of Gareth Gaelyn perhaps, what would keep Tyrion from putting her under his thumb? Having driven out most of the Cameron family, she only had Tyrion and Gareth to prevent the nobles from dethroning her.

Overcome by emotion, Conall could feel his eyes beginning to water. Dropping to one knee, he took her hand and bowed his head. "Never," he said, his voice almost hoarse. "When I swore my oath, I meant it. I am your man, through and through, Your Majesty. As long as I live, you will never be alone. You have my strength, my sword, and my power, to support you through whatever may come. Body and soul, I am yours, through fire and storm, I will never desert you."

Ariadne was silent for a while after his declaration, and when he finally looked up to see her expression, she had a scowl on her face. "Enough of that," she told him. "I need a friend, not another vassal. Stop reminding me of the crown I'm forced to bear."

Conall regained his feet, feeling somewhat sheepish. "I am your friend, but it's all true. Don't forget."

She smiled. "I won't. Thank you. I do feel better."

He noticed something strange then. "Did you call for more guards?"

The Queen shook her head. "No, why?"

"Several of Tyrion's special guards just entered the garden," said Conall. "Just beyond those trees. They're heading in this direction." He pointed toward the far side of the garden.

She frowned. "The krytek?"

Conall nodded.

"Is Tyrion with them?"

"No."

Ariadne looked thoughtful. "That's odd, but he may have sent them with a private message."

"That seems likely," agreed Conall. "But why would he send five? No, wait—seven. Two more just entered from the southern end of the garden."

"We will discover that when they get here," said Ariadne, straightening her back and smoothing her skirts.

Conall didn't like it and he didn't bother asking for permission before creating two shields, one around himself and another around the Queen. They were invisible to normal eyesight and she wouldn't notice anyway, unless she moved.

When the krytek arrived a minute later, they appeared calm. They weren't shielded or showing any signs of overt use of power, but Conall still didn't trust them. They remained spread out, as though covering any possible routes of escape. "Tyrion needs to see you," announced the one in the middle. Another glanced at Conall. "No need to take a defensive position. We all serve the same Queen."

Ariadne answered, "Give me your message and I will decide whether he needs to attend me. One does not summon a queen. Your master needs to improve your education on human matters."

The original speaker replied, "My apologies, Your Majesty. We are indeed ignorant of your customs. Unfortunately, I do not know what he wishes to speak to you about, only that he is waiting in the council chamber."

The Queen sighed. "Perhaps I will indulge him this once." She glanced at Conall then, and he could see uncertainty in her eyes.

"We will escort you to him," answered the krytek.

Conall's stomach fluttered. He knew something wasn't right, but seven of the krytek would be too many for him to handle alone. They were created for battle, without fear or reluctance, while he—deep down he knew he was merely a boy pretending at being a champion. He had saved the Queen once, but it had been a rushed chaos at the time; he hadn't had time to think. Self-defense in the heat of the moment was entirely different from coldly confronting an overwhelming number of enemies.

If he let them escort her away, he would be safe. They probably wouldn't start a fight if they could avoid it. *And they are Tyrion's servants. They couldn't possibly mean to harm the Queen—could they?* That was the coward talking, of course. He knew better. He could feel it in his bones. Sweat began to bead at his temples, his heart was racing, and despite his previous combats he felt paralyzed by sheer terror. *I don't want to die.*

Ariadne tried to take a step and was brought up short by the shield he had placed around her. "Conall, remember what I said. You can go home. Remove the shield so I can go see the Duke." Her voice was calm, but her eyes were intense, as though she was pleading with him.

She wants me to save myself, he realized. *What do I do?* His father had always lectured him on keeping his head clear if it came to battle, but his mind wasn't just clear, it was utterly blank. He couldn't think.

"The shield, Conall," repeated Ariadne.

He snapped, his fear and terror fueling action born of pure instinct. Instead of lowering the shield around his cousin, he lowered his own. As he did, he felt the krytek begin to gather their aythar, but he was already lashing out with his own power, transforming the aythar that had once been his defense into arrow-like shards of destruction. They lanced outward, and a few of them found their targets, tearing through the bodies of three of the krytek.

The four remaining krytek reacted almost instantly, working in unison. One spoke a word, putting the Queen's nearby guardsmen and servants quickly to sleep. Two clamped their power around Conall in a rushed attempt to smother his power with their own, while the last one began forming a spellweave to contain him more permanently.

Three might have been enough, but trying to lock him down with just two, that was a mistake on their part. Conall's fear was gone now, transformed into a blind rage as his power surged, shattering the shield they had placed around him. The two krytek holding him fell back, stunned by the feedback as their magic broke. Conall leapt forward, sweeping his sword from its sheath and using it to cut away the half-formed spellweave before plunging it into the krytek's chest.

Something struck him then, and he staggered. He had lost track of the krytek that had put the servants to sleep. Turning, he sent a blast of gold fire in its direction, but his fiery assault was deflected by a hastily erected shield. Beneath that protection, his final foe began to construct a spellwoven shield, something his magic would be unable to break.

A roaring filled his ears, though whether it was from himself or some external source Conall didn't know, nor did he care. Focusing his power this time, he broke the krytek's shield while simultaneously propelling his sword through the air like a spear. As the shield broke, his enchanted blade tore through the spellweave and lodged itself in the krytek's heart.

He couldn't rest yet, though. The two stunned by feedback could recover at any time. A shadow fell over him as he turned back. Looking up, Conall saw Carwyn's massive bulk pass over to land nearby. *She summoned him,* he realized, feeling a sense of relief. After the dragon landed, he took two steps toward them, deliberately stepping on the two still living krytek, crushing them beneath his clawed feet.

"Conall!" yelled Ariadne. She was still trapped inside the shield he had put around her, and she was staring at him worriedly.

Feeling numb and strangely calm, he smiled. "It's alright. I'm fine." He expanded the shield around her and moved it, so she could walk over to him. He wasn't about to release it. When she was close by, he opened it and stepped inside with her.

"No. No, you're not. You're bleeding," insisted the Queen, her hand moving to indicate his stomach.

Looking down, he saw blood on his shirt, and after a moment's exploration realized he had a hole in both his belly and his back. Something had passed completely through him. *I didn't feel a thing.* His thought was interrupted as he realized they were not alone; another mage was present. *Moira?* He recognized her aythar immediately. *How did she get here? Was she riding Carwyn?*

CHAPTER 15

Tyrion stalked the halls of the palace, his feet moving quickly across the tile floors. Only a short time before, he had received a disturbing report from one of his krytek. An unknown mage had appeared in the city, but those he had sent to investigate hadn't returned.

Could it be Mordecai? he thought. *Surely not.* He had sent another of his servants to the Queen's chambers to use the portal there to check on Moira Illeniel, but he hadn't heard back from that one either.

All of it served to give him a bad feeling, and now the hairs on the nape of his neck were tingling. Something was wrong. "Where the hell is everyone?" he shouted in frustration. The halls were empty. He had yet to find even one of the servants in what was normally a very busy section of the palace.

His magesight couldn't locate anyone either, possibly because of the abundance of privacy wards set up in the various rooms of the palace, but even with that, he should have been able to find *someone.*

He increased his pace. He needed to find Ariadne. Whatever was happening didn't bode well, and her safety was his first concern.

Tyrion went to the council chamber first, and when he reached it he threw open the doors using his power. Then he knew something was badly wrong. The room was occupied, but those within were all slumped on the floor, as though asleep. Searching with both eyes and his magesight, he quickly identified most of the occupants: Benchley, Harold, several courtiers, and a variety of mundane servants and guards. They were all alive but unconscious.

"Useless, all of them," muttered Tyrion. Striding quickly across the room, he found Harold and began shaking the large man. "Wake up, fool! The Queen is in danger!"

It took a long and precious minute to wake the knight up, which was another obvious sign of a magically induced slumber. When Sir Harold's eyes finally opened, he stared at Tyrion in confusion. "Why did you do it?"

"Do what? I'm trying to wake you up. What happened?" asked Tyrion.

"It was one of your men, those krytek things," said Harold. "Don't they take orders from you?" Harold's gaze was suspicious as he slowly sat up and rubbed at the back of his head. He had bruised it when he collapsed.

"They do," answered Tyrion. "What did it do?"

"It came in and just sort of looked around," began Harold. "Then everyone started collapsing to the ground, like puppets with their strings cut."

"If you'd been wearing your armor you might have been protected," declared Tyrion. "Where is it?"

"In my room," replied Harold. "I was wearing this, though." With one hand, he drew out the enchanted pendant Mordecai had given him years before.

Tyrion knew then, and he felt as though a cold stone had settled in his stomach. *Moira.* She was the only one capable of such a thing. *And she's suborned the krytek.* "Get your armor, and make sure you keep the helm on at all times," ordered Tyrion. "If you meet any more of the krytek, kill them quickly." Rising to his feet, Tyrion activated the enchanted runes that covered his body, and he was comforted by the familiar feeling as a shield of force encased him in armor stronger than any steel.

"Where are you going?" asked Sir Harold.

"To find the Queen," stated Tyrion. "Warn anyone you find, especially Conall. Don't waste your time trying to wake the guards. They won't be of any help in this fight." With that said, he left.

He headed for the Queen's chambers first, but as he neared the outer door, two of the krytek stepped out.

In the moment before most conflicts, men hesitate, even if only for a second. Humans are social creatures by nature, and violence is instinctively preceded by a pause to consider consequences, but the krytek were not men. They were bred for battle, without human instincts or compassion, and their orders were clear.

Tyrion was faster. He had given up his humanity ages ago, long before he had become one of the She'Har. The endless battles of the arena were permanently etched in his heart. It was the main reason he was so ill-suited to civil society. Violence was always his first reaction. The self-restraint of living among peaceful people was exhausting for him.

But today, for the first time in a long while, Tyrion was relaxed. He was at home.

His first blast struck as their shields were just coming to life, and the two krytek were slammed back through the stone wall that flanked the door. He leapt through the stone dust even as they struck the other side of the antechamber he had blown them back into.

Tyrion's right armblade cut through one of the krytek before it could recover, then he spun and cut away the spellweave snaking toward him from the other. Reaching out with raw aythar, he seized on a chair behind the second krytek and pulled it toward his remaining foe.

The krytek spent a precious second reinforcing its new spellwoven shield against an attack that could not possibly injure it, but that wasn't the point. The chair sent it flying toward Tyrion, and he was waiting with open arms and a feral smile. A second later it was over, and Tyrion marched across the bloody remains of his former servants.

Ariadne's bedchamber was empty. He stared at the room for a moment before he heard the unmistakable roar of Carwyn, the Queen's dragon. The massive creature's voice reverberated through the halls, coming from the other end of the palace, and then fell silent.

Turning back, Tyrion began to run.

He had no time for turns or detours. Using his memory of the palace layout, he took a direct path, destroying the walls that presented themselves on the way. As he went, he hoped to hear the dragon's call once more, for that would mean that the fight was not yet over, but nothing reached his ears. *She has to be safe.*

The last wall he destroyed was also one containing a privacy ward, so he was surprised when he passed through it. It opened onto a terraced walkway that surrounded the royal garden, and it was there that his enemies finally converged upon him. Several beams of power and two long, vine-like spellweaves struck him as he came through the new-made hole in the wall.

He was unable to avoid them all, but his enchanted shield withstood the assault. Unfortunately he couldn't escape the stone ceiling that the attacks brought down on his head. As the covered walkway collapsed, the heavy weight drove him down against the paving stones, but his defenses kept his body from being crushed.

Though he was now entombed, Tyrion wasted no time. *The next attacks will be focused to tear through both the stone, my shield, and finally, me.* Exerting his will, he summoned a dense fog laced with aythar, an old tactic to block magesight. That would prevent precision attacks, but it wouldn't be enough on its own.

In the past he had escaped similar predicaments by burrowing through the earth, but the heavy paving stones beneath him would slow that sort of tactic, and he instinctively knew they expected it from him. It was time to show his cards. Imagining what he wanted, he diverted some of his aythar to his new body's seed mind. Threads of aythar shot forth, flowing through the rubble around him and creating a complex web, a spellweave with several distinct functions as power struck the pile from multiple directions.

His spellweave absorbed the attacks, repurposing the energy to negate the inertia of the stone around him. When it finished, he gathered his will and *pushed.* He released the spellweave a split second later.

Tiles, building blocks, and broken rubble exploded outward in all directions, regaining their true masses as they took flight. They ripped through everything close by—krytek, trees, support pillars—only the grass and smaller plants of the garden near him were spared. Rising from the center of destruction, Tyrion gazed upon the results and felt a swell of pride at seeing his handiwork. The smile that he wore was entirely genuine.

He wasn't one to stand and gloat, though; such activities were for fools waiting to die. Most of the krytek had survived, their defenses too strong for simple stone to destroy, but the blast had thrown them into chaos. Calling up another magesight—blocking fog, Tyrion simultaneously sent runners of aythar along the surface of the ground, creating a faint grid to allow him to locate his foes. Then he began to dance, weaving through the mist, hunting and slaying his one-time servants.

When he thought most of them were dead, he dismissed the fog and scanned his surroundings. On the far side of the garden he saw Carwyn, Ariadne's dragon. In front of it stood Conall, sheltering the Queen behind him. There were dead krytek scattered around them, the apparent product of the young mage's enthusiastic defense of his liege. *Good job, boy,* thought Tyrion.

Two of the krytek that had attacked Tyrion were still alive, hovering several feet off the ground to avoid the grid he had used to locate their companions. Seizing the air currents, Tyrion used his greater strength to hurl them into the sky, flinging them up and out of the palace entirely. It wasn't likely to kill them, but it would get them out of the way until he could secure the Queen.

Running again, he headed for Ariadne and the others, and as he did, he noticed several strange things about the situation. Carwyn stood perfectly still, seeming more like a statue than a living, breathing dragon. Conall held a vivid golden shield of power between himself and the dragon, and his face appeared strained, as though he was struggling against a powerful force, though Tyrion didn't see any other foes present. *No—there!* A woman stood on the other side of Carwyn, a mage, her body sheathed in power. He recognized her immediately.

Conall saw her too, and his expression changed to one of confusion. "Moira? Why are you here? Is this your doing?"

"No," answered the woman. "I'm trying to help you."

Ariadne straightened, ordering, "Then release my dragon, immediately!"

Tyrion was still twenty yards away, but he knew he had almost no time. *If she reaches them, all is lost.* Channeling his anger, he sent a meteoric blast of pure hate and aythar at the woman, who had stepped out from behind the dragon and was now in his line of sight.

Conall sensed his intent and shifted his shield, moving it to include his sister and block the thundering blast that Tyrion had sent at her. The air shuddered as their powers met, but the young knight's shield survived the assault.

"Try that again and I'll answer in kind," challenged Conall, turning his body to face Tyrion's approach.

Frustrated beyond endurance, Tyrion screamed back, "You fool!" but it was too late. Moira stepped close to her brother and laid one hand on his shoulder. A second later the young mage slumped to the ground, unconscious.

He was almost to them by then, but Moira reached toward Ariadne with one hand and barked a command at Tyrion. "Stop or she dies." A black claw of aythar extended from her arm across several feet. It had long, slender digits tipped with deadly talons and it wrapped entirely around the Queen without quite touching her. The central talon was poised above Ariadne's heart like a dagger, ready to plunge itself into her chest.

Tyrion didn't pause, he leapt forward, his arms outstretched and sheathed in deadly power. Moira's eyes widened in surprise and the dragon's head dipped down, whipping toward him like a striking snake, but he was faster than both of them.

His arm blades plunged through Moira's chest as Carwyn's jaws closed around his torso. Blood erupted from her torso, and Tyrion's hands were buried up to their wrists in her body as Carwyn's teeth pierced his shield and bit into his flesh. Ordinary teeth wouldn't have managed it, but Mordecai's dragons were armed with enchanted teeth and claws, backed by more power than any mortal mage could resist.

Moira died near instantly, while at the same instant, Carwyn's jaws stopped just short of crushing him completely. The dragon released him, and Tyrion fell to the ground, bleeding from the equivalent of a dozen serious stab wounds, but he lived.

Ariadne stood nearby, staring down at him in shock, too numb to move or react while Tyrion quickly set about fixing the more serious wounds. Some of them were deadly, and without fast action might have killed him. He muttered to himself as he worked, glancing at Moira's dead body. "You misunderstood me. I'd rather kill an enemy, even at the risk of a friend. Better to be a live bastard than to die a hero."

The magic covering Moira's body sloughed away, and as the illusion faded he saw it was yet another of his krytek. Tyrion stared at it in confusion. *It was definitely her aythar. There was no mistake.*

Then Moira's face rose from the body, ghost-like, and it stared at him with disdain. "She's in love with you. Did you know that?"

Tyrion seized the strange spellbeast with his aythar, ripping it to shreds, but she wasn't done speaking. "You've already lost," it said with Moira's voice. It sounded as though she was whispering in his ear. *How long did you think it would take me to get inside after your shield was destroyed?*

He could feel the tendrils of her will winding through his mind, trapping him inside his own body, but they were weakening rapidly. Her power had been cut.

Tyrion fought, tearing at the shadows that surrounded him, filling his vision, and the darkness began to fade, but he still heard her laughter in his ears. He shouted at the ghost within him, "You were a fake all along!"

More laughter answered him, *Just as you are.* Her voice was growing faint.

"I'm alive, you've lost," he replied. She was dying, and he was still strong, his core untouched, but as she faded away he heard her final words.

You don't deserve love.

She was gone then, and Tyrion lay on the ground, weak and exhausted. He could no longer keep his eyes open, but he thought he had done enough for his wounds to keep from dying. After a time, he heard voices calling out, searching for the Queen and he recognized Sir Harold's baritone.

Ariadne must have recovered from her shock by then, for she answered, "Over here."

He listened to the big man's footsteps as he hurried to them. Tyrion was too weak to speak, and his consciousness was beginning to fade, but he heard the next exchange.

"What happened?" asked Harold anxiously.

"Tyrion has betrayed us," said the Queen in a clear voice. "Take him."

CHAPTER 16

Hours later, Ariadne sat beside a bed in one of the palace guestrooms. More specifically it was Sir Conall's bedroom and the young knight himself was stretched out upon the mattress, still sleeping soundly.

Soundly, but not peacefully; Conall's face was pale and his skin was hot to the touch. A man stood on the other side of the bed, his hand stretched out over the young man's belly. Gareth Gaelyn had been there for some time, but his face was resigned as he withdrew and spoke to the Queen. "It isn't good."

"You're an archmage, Lord Gaelyn. Surely you can fix whatever is wrong," she responded.

The taciturn mage grimaced. "Not without risking my own life."

"Then do it," she insisted.

Gareth's answer was calm, without a hint of the stress or conflict most would feel at refusing the Queen. "No."

Ariadne stood, her eyes catching fire at his defiance. "I command you."

"I have done all I can reasonably do," said the archmage. "The wound itself wasn't too bad; none of the major blood vessels were damaged and the injury to his liver wasn't serious. I've sealed the skin and repaired most of what was wrong, but his stomach was pierced. Sickness and fever will almost certainly take him in the days to come."

"Then do whatever is required to prevent it," said Ariadne.

"No," said Gareth again, unfazed. "Doing so would require more than ordinary magic and could potentially kill me. I will not do so for one of Mordecai's heirs."

"You would defy my command?" asked the Queen.

"How you choose to interpret my choice is up to you," said Gareth smoothly. "I would caution you, however, with Tyrion in chains and young Conall dying, I am the last pillar supporting your rule."

She glared at him, unbowed by the implied threat. "You would let him die, just to increase your power?"

"If I were to try and fail, you would have no mages left to aid you," explained Gareth calmly. "The manacles I have placed on Tyrion will not last indefinitely. Without a constant guard, he will escape eventually. I would counsel you to execute Tyrion soon. Wasting your resources on Mordecai's child will not profit you at all."

Disgusted, Ariadne pointed at the door. "Get out."

"As you wish." As Gareth stepped out, an old serving woman entered, carrying an empty basket, presumably to collect the dirty linens.

Ariadne paid little heed to the other woman's presence. Instead she resumed her seat, taking Conall's feverish hand in her own. "You deserve better than this," she muttered.

"Most would say it is an honor to have a queen attending him as he dies," said the laundress in a clear voice.

Surprised and mildly affronted by the servant's boldness, Ariadne looked at the woman. The washer woman was removing her head covering and had already placed her basket on the ground. Ariadne was shocked to realize she recognized the old woman's face. "Lady Thornbear?"

Elise Thornbear nodded diffidently, almost ignoring the Queen as she leaned over to examine Conall. She placed one hand on his forehead before lifting his shirt and studying the new scar on the young man's belly.

"How did you get in here?" asked Ariadne in a subdued tone.

"No one pays attention to servants," replied Elise distractedly, "especially old women."

"Where have you been?"

Elise snorted, then glanced up at the Queen. "With Mordecai and my daughter-in-law both declared outlaws, I thought it better not to be seen. Albamarl hasn't been the friendliest place for my family over the past month."

Insulted, Ariadne drew herself up. "That may be, but I would not have touched you, whatever their crimes were. None of it was your fault. I am wounded that you think so little of me."

The old noblewoman's eyes fixed her in their clear gaze. "*You* are not the only power in Albamarl, Your Majesty. Now let me focus on my patient."

Ariadne's anger dissipated as quickly as it had appeared, and she deflated, letting her eyes drift down toward the floor. "Lord Gaelyn says he will not live."

"I'll judge that for myself," growled Elise, then she pointed at the scar on Conall's abdomen. "Since he closed the wound, I'm assuming he repaired whatever was damaged within. It's a shame, though. I can't tell if the stomach was punctured without opening him back up."

"It was," said Ariadne. "He fixed that as well." Then after a thoughtful pause, she asked, "How would you tell if his wound was open?"

Elise lifted a cloth sachet filled with pungent herbs. "I'd brew a tea with this and feed it to him. If you can smell it in the wound, then you know the stomach or intestines have been compromised. He's saved me that trouble at least."

Ariadne shuddered. "Is there anything you can do?"

Elise pursed her lips. "Perhaps, but not here. I'll need him moved to the kitchens."

"The kitchens?"

"I can't boil enough water here. I'm going to need assistance. We'll have to boil a lot of water, as well as towels. Send your herbalist to see me. I don't have everything I need," commanded Elise.

"What about the royal physician?" suggested the Queen. "He was here earlier, though he said there was little to be done."

Elise shook her head. "He'd just be in my way and probably complain that I was killing him."

Alarmed, Ariadne asked, "What are you going to do?"

"Save his life, if possible," declared Elise. "My methods may be a little shocking, but he has almost no chance if we do nothing. Do you trust me?"

Ariadne wasn't entirely certain that she did, but she nodded anyway.

"Then I'll need you to stay with me. Bring Harold as well. The servants will probably balk at some of what I want to do. It will take your authority to keep them in line," said Elise.

The hours that followed were strange, as Elise organized and directed the boiling of water and towels in a variety of pots which she insisted be cleaned and recleaned first. After the towels were boiled, some were used to cover additional pots of boiled water, though the old woman refused to say why that was necessary.

Ariadne couldn't help but feel the arcane procedures were more like some strange magic ritual than most of the actual magic she had seen in her life. She also had serious doubts about their effectiveness, but she held her tongue—for the most part.

"Where did you learn all this?" she asked at one point.

"This is part of the hidden teachings of the Church of Millicenth," replied Elise as she watched over the boiling pots.

The Queen frowned. "The Church…?" The Church of Millicenth was still active in Lothion, but its numbers and power had diminished greatly during recent years. One of the consequences of having had their deity extinguished. Of course, those that still worshipped believed that their goddess was alive and well, despite all evidence to the contrary.

"I was a Lady of the Evening Star in my younger days," added Lady Thornbear, as if that simple remark explained everything.

Ariadne was stunned. *She was a prostitute?* She had no idea what to say.

Elise laughed, watching the younger woman's discomfort with evident humor, then she nodded. "Yes, I know what you're thinking, and yes, you're correct. What you might not know, however, is that some of the Ladies of the Evening were trained in additional arts."

That made some sense to Ariadne, at least, since Millicenth had been the goddess of healing, but the goddess was gone now. How could their rituals work without the deity that had empowered them? Unsure what to say, she finally stated her concern flatly, "But Millicenth is dead."

"This isn't magic, Your Majesty," returned Elise. "I was trained in poisons and healing medicines." She stopped briefly to reprimand one of her helpers. "What are you doing? I said I needed salt, not that you should add it. It has to be measured first."

As Ariadne watched, Elise added a large batch of herbs, wrapped in cheesecloth, to one of the pots. Then she began measuring salt using a set of scales the royal herbalist had brought. *What sort of tea has salt in it?* Eventually, she asked, "How is he going to drink all that?" The pot in question held at least a couple of gallons of water.

The old woman began laughing. "This isn't for drinking, Your Majesty. There will be medicinal teas, of course, but that comes after. This is an irrigating solution, a bath of sorts, for his innards."

"A bath?"

Elise nodded, adding, "For his insides."

"But how?"

The older woman pointed at a freshly boiled cloth that held several small knives that had been similarly cleaned. "I'm going to open him up, so we can wash out the filth his stomach released when it was ruptured."

Ariadne's cheeks lost their color and she felt as though a cold breeze had swept through the room. Everything swayed as her vision narrowed down to a long tunnel stretching out before her. Faintly she heard Elise barking orders to one of the guards, "Get her out, quickly! If she vomits in here, I'll have to start all over."

Harold and one of the other guards hastened to usher her outside, and while the Queen didn't actually throw up, it was several minutes before she felt completely herself again. She went back in. Later, when Elise's 'irrigating solution' had cooled sufficiently for use, she stepped out again. She didn't trust herself to watch what was about to happen.

Sir Harold and the guards were forced to escort several more of the kitchen staff out, most because they were near to passing out, but the cook's chief assistant because he seemed to think what was happening was some sort of evil witchcraft. After things had calmed down, and only Elise and the more strong-stomached servants remained, Harold joined Ariadne in the hall, his face visibly pale.

"Is it that bad?" Ariadne asked him.

Sir Harold shook his head. "I've seen worse on the battlefield, and afterward, but there's something wrong about opening a man up and pumping his belly full of water. It's unnatural."

She shivered. "I've never doubted her before, but I'm struggling to believe this will help."

Harold said nothing, but his expression was clear. It had been her choice to allow Elise to do what she was doing.

The Queen sighed. "Both Lord Gaelyn and the palace physician agreed he would almost certainly die. There weren't any other options." Another thought occurred to her then. *Unless this causes him to die in a more painful way.* She pushed it aside, such thinking wouldn't help.

***

In the shadows of a dark alley several miles from the palace, Moira Illeniel's body sat, huddled against one wall. A casual observer might have thought she was alone, though a mage would have quickly noted the powerful spellbeasts hidden at both ends of the alley, protecting her privacy.

Wrapped in cold solitude, Myra wept, for she was, for the first time in her life, utterly alone, the sole inhabitant of Moira's body. "I told you not to do it," she muttered miserably. "You should have sent me, or let one of the new ones do it."

Isn't this what you really wanted? came a dark thought, unbidden. *You have a true body now. You're alive. You're Moira.*

She cried harder, tears and snot mingling on her chin. "Not like this," she sobbed. "Never like this."

As she hid, a multitude of messages flooded in, reports from the various krytek that Moira had taken control of, but she couldn't bear to face them. Her entire being was focused on her creator's last moments, for they had been connected, right up until the last seconds. Myra had even felt echoes of Moira's pain as Tyrion's armblades had torn through her chest.

This was for the best, Moira had told her. *You were the version of myself I truly wanted to be.*

"I don't want this," mumbled Myra, closing her eyes. Deep within she could see her aystrylin, Moira's aystrylin, the source of life and aythar that maintained the body she resided within. It was hers now, hers alone, but she didn't want it. Not anymore.

She hadn't claimed it yet, not truly. She had been holding it in trust for Moira's return, keeping her body alive while she was away. *All I have to do is let it slip away. It won't even hurt...* She could fade away and leave the pain of the real world behind. A soothing grey calm passed over her as she relaxed her hold on it.

NO!

The mental command came as a silent shout that stunned her with its sheer force. A being had appeared in the street at the far end of the alley, a being composed of seething black fire, and even at that distance its presence made her skin burn and tingle with pain. Myra struggled to create a shield powerful enough to preserve her flesh, and only barely succeeded.

I will not lose two daughters, thundered the voice, shattering her thoughts and despair. *You must live.*

It vanished as quickly as it had appeared, leaving a gaping silence in its wake. Myra stared in the direction of where it had been, her eyes idly noting the way the buildings had begun to crumble where its power had touched. "Father?" The experience had been so intense it had been difficult to recognize at first, but as her mind processed what had happened, she became sure. *That was him.*

Her tears had dried without her noticing. Drawing herself to her feet, Myra shrugged off her self-pity and embraced the living flame in her heart. Moira might be gone, but her life was still there, waiting to be lived. She began paying attention to the messages coming in. There were over five hundred krytek under her command, and while the original mission had been fulfilled, they needed new instructions.

Myra felt embarrassed by her stupidity. A moment ago, she had nearly forgotten their reason for coming to Albamarl. *But I won't forget again.* Using her sleeve to wipe her face, Myra began to give new orders. *We're going to save you, Father.* Then she remembered she was alone, so she rephrased her thought, addressing it to the emptiness inside where her sister had lived, *Don't worry Moira. I'll save him for you.*

CHAPTER 17

Karen kissed him again, enjoying the slow reaction that played across Matthew's face. He still hadn't reached what she would consider a normal speed, but there were certain advantages to having him react slowly. She could watch the subtle movements of his eyes and lips to judge his true feelings better.

Matthew's face was always difficult to read, but the slowness of his response made it easier. She could see the faint signs of surprise and pleasure that normally happened so quickly they were disguised by his taciturn expression.

He blinked. "Please…"

"I can tell you're enjoying it," she said mercilessly.

"… stop," he finished.

"Make me," she replied, kissing him again and laughing at his pitifully slow attempt to dodge her tender assault. When he tried to roll from the bed, she tossed the sheets over him and twisted them to keep him from escaping.

"I have work," he began.

"*I'm* the first item on your schedule," she told him firmly, pinning him down and throwing one leg over his midsection.

"…to do."

The night before had been memorable, not the least because Matthew's altered sense of time had drawn certain things out to excruciatingly lengthy periods. Karen wasn't about to waste the opportunity to enjoy the more interesting aspects of his malady before he completely returned to normal. Pressing down on his shoulders, she let her eyes explain her intentions as she slowly stretched out her torso above him.

Matthew's face changed, showing resignation and anticipation simultaneously. "Fine…"

Unfortunately, it was at that moment that the door to the room opened and Alyssa stepped in. "Lyralliantha says there's a messenger here for you," she announced, her gaze taking in the situation without any sign of judgement, or embarrassment.

In contrast, Karen's light blue cheeks turned purple as she blushed, and she hurried to reclaim the bedsheets to cover herself with, inadvertently exposing Matthew's body in the process. He sat up slowly, not bothering to protest. Alyssa smirked and left.

They dressed quickly, the mood having been broken. Well, Karen dressed quickly, anyway. Matt did his best and she did what she could to speed things up for him, gathering up his clothes and putting them in easy reach for him after she had finished.

In the main hall, they found everyone gathered around a small bird. It wasn't a true bird, of course, but rather a spellbeast. As Matthew approached, it flew to him and settled on his hand before dissolving into his skin, its message delivered. His face grew pensive as he considered the mental images and words it had brought. Almost five minutes passed before he spoke, "Moira has accomplished our goal."

"*Your* goal," countered Irene, her tone sour. "None of us agreed to it." Her eyes met Karen's and they both nodded. Everyone else in the room looked vaguely uncomfortable, and none of them looked directly at Matt.

"You chose to make me your leader," said Matthew slowly. "You read my message to Moira and you delivered it. Whatever misgivings all of you may have, you've accepted my directions. I'll say it again, Moira has accomplished our goal."

Chad Grayson had been examining one of his knives and began stropping it on the leather of his jerkin, though the enchanted weapon needed no such attention. "I never thought you'd take to treason so easily, lad."

Matt smiled. "I doubt the Queen would define it as treason."

"You mean your sister," argued Chad, "since she's the one that rules."

Matthew blinked, his slightly slower speed making the action seem almost languid. Then he replied, "Control is an illusion, but a handy one, and it rests in my hands now."

"You think you can control her?" asked Irene incredulously. "Moira holds the reins now, and she's shown no compunction about using her power as she sees fit. Don't forget what she did to Karen."

Matthew's power flicked out, seizing Chad's hand as it started to slip, stopping the blade it held from slicing his finger. The hunter glanced up, a faint shiver running through him. "That's just creepy," said the archer.

"Would you rather cut yourself?" asked Matthew before continuing. "Let that serve as a reminder. The world is ending. The best we can do is guide it to a conclusion that suits us."

"It would be best if we decided together what conclusion suits us best," Irene declared.

Matt looked at his youngest sister carefully and Karen saw almost imperceptible flickers of silver aythar shimmering in his eyes. "That won't be necessary," he replied before turning his attention back to Chad. "You'll be heading to Iverly. You'll find Lady Rose there. Karen, you'll take him."

Karen glared at him. "How can you be so rude?"

"Because I already know the choices you'll make," Matt answered, letting his gaze roam the room. "I choose my words according to which ones will produce the actions necessary for success." When Karen started to argue he held up his hand to silence her. "Let me finish. Starting tomorrow, we are no longer outlaws. The Queen's next proclamation will exonerate us. We'll be returning to Castle Cameron. I need to see your father."

Irene looked back and forth between the two of them. "You mean Gary?"

Matt nodded.

Chad growled, "What are these *necessary* actions?"

"The ones that don't end in our deaths," said Matthew, before adding, "hopefully."

Elaine had been silent until then. "You don't sound very certain. You expect us to follow some hidden plan of yours, but you're not even sure of the outcome? I thought you could see the future."

Matthew sighed. "I see possibilities. Most of them I know to be failures, but a few lead to a singular event, one that I can't see beyond. The threads of reality converge there, creating a knot of uncertain fate. All I can do is steer us toward it."

Chad glanced at Cyhan, wondering if the big knight would put forth an opinion, but he seemed to have no interest in the conversation. Irritated, he started to speak, but Matthew interrupted him. "The argument you have in mind won't do anything for your mood. Get your gear together. Karen can take you to Iverly as soon as you're ready." The young mage addressed the rest of the room, "The rest of us will proceed to Castle Cameron this evening."

"What about Roland's family?" asked Irene. "We can't abandon them, or the other people here."

"There won't be any further attacks here," Matthew stated confidently. "We can bring Roland back to oversee his estate after we settle in at Cameron."

Irene nodded. "He's probably been mad with worry since he left."

Matthew was already walking away, heading back in the direction of the stairs that would take him to his room.

"Where are you going?" asked Karen. "Shouldn't we talk about this more? You haven't explained anything."

Matt stopped and looked back, his expression faintly apologetic. "I'm not that good with words. My explanation would only confuse things more. I have something important to prepare for." Then he left.

"What an arrogant prick!" spat Chad.

Karen frowned. "He has his reasons. We'll just have to trust he knows what he's doing."

Gram walked in a moment later, just as Chad was leaving to collect his gear. "What did I miss?" he asked the archer as they passed by one another.

"Your friend is a jackass," said Chad without stopping.

Gram paused, then looked at the others. "I already knew that. What did he do this time?"

***

Karen and Chad stood beside the road that led from Relliton to Iverly. Iverly was less than two miles to the west. "Are you familiar with the city?" she asked the older man.

The ranger shook his head. "No, but I'm sure it's much like other towns. There'll be pubs and such. That's all I need."

"You aren't here to drink," she replied disapprovingly.

"I am *always* here to drink," shot back Chad, "but that's not the point. Taverns are where I'll find out what I need to know. Besides, can't your boyfriend tell the future?"

Karen was still angry with Matthew herself, and having been forced to defend him had made her even more irritable. "What's that got to do with anything?"

"If the best way to find Lady Rose was to ask the city guard, or visit the local lord, he'd have sent someone else. He sent me. That means the answer will be found while sitting on a barstool. Ye ken me?" When she didn't reply immediately, he went on. "I am destined to get drunk. Who am I to defy fate?"

Karen shook her head, sending her dark curls flying in every direction. "The world is doomed if it's relying on you to save it." Then she gave him a serious stare. "I'll check this spot every morning, so meet me here when you find her."

"Sunset," said Chad firmly. "I only do mornings when I'm hunting in the wild."

She sighed. "Morning, if you expect me to take you home. Hopefully, I'll see you here in a few days." Then she vanished.

Setting his feet to the road, Chad began walking in the direction of Iverly. As he went, he opened his pack and drew out a wide-brimmed hat that he set firmly on his head, pulling it down and slightly at an angle to obscure his features from casual onlookers. He hadn't been to Iverly, but he was fairly sure that some of those who knew him lived there now. *It wouldn't do to be recognized by the wrong sorts,* he thought to himself. *Best to be cautious.*

While he walked, he kept his eyes on the roadside, scanning the trees and brush for a good place to hide his treasure. When he found a spot he liked, he took a moment to memorize the landmarks before tossing a rope into a tree hidden from direct view of the road and using it to hoist a long oilcloth wrapped package into its limbs. *It'll be safe here,* he thought, staring up at his longbow. He hated to be parted from it, but such a weapon always drew eyes and unwanted attention.

Back on the road he felt confident he wouldn't be easily remembered now. The only visible weapon he carried was a long knife, which wasn't that unusual. His clothing was worn but durable, neither too shabby nor too notable. He could pass for a crafter or dockworker, perhaps even a farmer if the observer wasn't too perceptive.

Less than an hour later he passed through the city gate, not that it deserved such an appellation; to the ranger's appraising eye it didn't look as though the structure was functional. They probably hadn't tried to close it in years. The two guards who stood at their posts looked bored and disinterested. That suited Chad just fine.

He didn't bother asking directions to the nearest tavern. Some things were the same almost anywhere you went. There'd be a place within shouting distance of the gates, a few others near the docks, and very likely some more expensive establishments in the heart of the city. Chad let his feet guide him, and minutes later he had found what he sought.

It was called 'Gate Inn,' but it was more of a pub than a place to seek accommodations. If it did actually have rooms for rent, he doubted he would have wanted to stay in them. The customers were mainly farmers and tradesmen, and the floors were heavily coated with dirt from the road. Even so, he withheld judgment until he had tasted his first pint of ale.

Rat piss. His lip curled in disgust. The ale was poor and had been watered, enhancing its lack of flavor. Ordinarily he would have left immediately, but he was there for more than just a drink so, with a sigh, he leaned back in his chair and pretended to be nursing his mug slowly.

He watched the crowd, not with any hope of finding Rose there, but simply to get a feel for the area. His eyes sorted through the customers as they came and went, passing over farmers and tradesmen quickly and spending more time on those whose professions were more questionable. He took note of several cutpurses and petty thieves, recognizing them from experience and intuition more than any particular defining mark.

Unfortunately, they noticed him as well, for newcomers were their bread and butter. After only half an hour a large friendly man came over to his table. “Mind if I sit here?” asked the stranger. “I’ll buy a few rounds if you have news.”

Chad glanced up, making a conscious effort to keep the menace from his features. Despite the stranger’s friendly demeanor, the ranger knew his purpose. It was an old tactic. The stranger would buy him a few drinks, get him drunk if possible, then his friends would rob him when he left.

His usual response would be a subtle warning, but that would get him noticed. Accepting the offer and then facing several assailants later in an alley would also do him no good. Win or lose, they’d remember him. *As if I’d lose to this trash,* he thought disdainfully. “No thanks,” he answered, standing. “My friends are waiting on me.”

“Why the hurry?” asked the big man, putting a hand on his shoulder. “Let me buy you a drink.”

Chad resisted his first, second, and third impulses, each of which was worse than the last. The first two would end with the stranger unconscious or badly injured, the third would have him howling with rage when he found his purse missing later. Instead, Chad gave the man a friendly pat on the shoulder and then slipped around him. “Maybe tomorrow. I can’t stay any longer today.”

The stranger frowned but let him go, likely in part because he thought he’d have a better chance the next day. Chad grinned to himself as he left. “Who says I can’t be diplomatic?” Then he set off in a direction that his nose indicated would probably lead him to the docks. The dives there would be rowdier, but the ale was almost certain to be better. Dockworkers didn’t put up with watered ale.

Chapter 18

Tyrion stared into the darkness until his eyes began to water from not blinking. He knew where he was; his magesight had already confirmed the dimensions of the room, which was very familiar to him. It was the same room that Mordecai had previously been imprisoned in.

It had been several days since he had awakened there. He thought. It was hard to be sure, since time lost all meaning without the normal cycle of light and dark, events and conversation. In the black silence time meant nothing at all, other than a slow decline into madness. *My how the tables have turned.* The irony of his current situation wasn't lost on him.

Moira Illeniel had turned the tables and now the world was against him. *Nothing new there.* He had won the battle, defeated his enemies, and yet had lost everything anyway. At least Mordecai had had Rose to visit him. Tyrion rather doubted the Queen would be making an appearance. Based on Moira's last words, he suspected her heart had been turned against him.

A dim square of light appeared as one wall vanished, nearly blinding Tyrion's darkness-accustomed eyes. He sat up and squinted against the glare as he studied his visitor, Gareth Gaelyn.

"Are you enjoying your stay?" asked the red-bearded archmage, his face betraying little humor.

Tyrion ignored him.

Gareth walked into the room and stood still for a moment, then continued, "Your food is better than his was."

Tyrion grunted. "That's true, unless you count the food Lady Rose brought him."

"Should I arrange a bath for you as well?" said Gareth dryly, raising one brow.

"If you think you can keep me in here long enough for it to be necessary," Tyrion challenged. "You're alone. You can't keep watch over this cell indefinitely."

"A good point," agreed Gareth, "but in your case an invalid one. You might manage the manacles, but this cell can hold a mage indefinitely." He stared intently at Tyrion, his gaze conveying an unnamed accusation.

He knows, thought Tyrion, feeling uneasy. "When did you figure it out?"

"I started having doubts when the first Tyrion was here, but I had nothing to base my suspicion on," said Gareth. "When you appeared I at first thought I was wrong, since there were no scars or other signs of the grievous injuries that Mordecai inflicted. It wasn't until later that I realized it wasn't because you had healed them, but rather because your entire body was newly made."

"You're very observant."

"I'm a Gaelyn," stated Gareth. "Matters of the flesh do not escape my notice. This body isn't decaying the way your previous one did. Was it was created by Lyralliantha?"

Tyrion gave a faint nod. "Does it matter?"

Gareth smirked. "You could live a long life."

"Not likely," said Tyrion. "You'll either kill me or leave me to rot. You don't have any other options."

"Unless you escape."

Tyrion let out a short bitter laugh. "Only an archmage could escape this cell, and you already know my secret."

"The key there," began Gareth, "is that *only* I know you aren't the original, that you aren't an archmage."

A strange feeling crept over Tyrion as he realized Gareth had some hidden agenda. "Your point?"

"Why don't we talk about what's happened since you were put down here?" suggested the archmage. "I might be interested in your opinion on current matters. Would you like some wine?"

Tyrion stared at him with open suspicion. "What game is this?" When Gareth failed to answer he finally gave in. "Fine. I could kill for a cup of wine about now."

The red-bearded mage barked, emitting a dark chuckle. "Is that a euphemism?"

Tyrion held up his wrists. "Take these manacles off of me and you'll find out."

Gareth stepped out and returned a moment later with two wooden cups and a bottle of Dalensan Red. Filling the cups, he handed one to Tyrion, who sniffed it before taking a small sip. His nose wrinkled a bit. "You think I would poison you?" asked Gareth.

"It's sweeter than I prefer," said Tyrion sourly. "Next time bring one of those whites they make in Turlington."

"There won't be a next time," said Gareth flatly, his eyes cold and dead.

"So, you *do* have the balls to do what's necessary," complimented Tyrion. "I always liked that about you."

"Don't be so eager to die just yet," responded the other mage. "We haven't talked yet."

Finishing his cup with a long gulp, Tyrion held it out for a refill, but said nothing. Gareth obliged and then began to speak. "As you might imagine, Moira has taken control of Lothion."

"Are you sure?" asked Tyrion. He was fairly sure he had killed her surrogate before she could do much to the Queen.

"On the surface, things are much the same as they have been," continued Gareth, "with the exception of you being here and the Queen having issued a full pardon for Mordecai and his family."

"She wanted to do that before," remarked Tyrion. "Though I warned her it was too risky."

"She's gone ahead and done it," said Gareth, "and the nobles have been remarkably complacent. Most notably the Duke of Cantley hasn't raised any objections."

"If he's planning to organize a revolt, he might play the obedient lamb for a while, at least in public," observed Tyrion.

Gareth shook his head. "I've observed him when he thought he was alone. In fact, a few minor nobles approached him with their concerns and he told them in no uncertain tones that he supported the Queen, no matter what she decided."

"You think she's manipulated his mind," stated Tyrion.

"I can't prove it, but it's the only thing that makes sense. Everyone who previously might have caused trouble has mysteriously decided that the Queen's word is law."

"Has she done anything else, aside from the pardons?" asked Tyrion.

"No," answered Gareth. "Although she has made very clear that she hates you."

That stung more than it should have, but Tyrion hid his dismay. "If she believes I betrayed her that's understandable. I know better than most how betrayal feels."

"Perhaps," said Gareth. "But I think it's more than that."

Tyrion held his cup out for another refill. "What do you expect a condemned man to do about any of this?"

"I'm hoping you'll escape and eliminate the last Centyr mage," said Gareth coldly.

Even Tyrion was surprised by that and his eyes grew wide. "She's your step-daughter."

"The Centyr are a plague on mankind," countered Gareth. "The only thing that kept them in check in my time was the fact that they policed themselves, and even that wasn't perfect. This incident, as well as what happened in Dunbar, makes it very clear to me that she has passed beyond redemption. If she isn't stopped, eventually she'll rule the minds of every man, woman, and child."

Tyrion mulled it over in his mind for a long minute. He had developed a strong grudge of his own against Mordecai's daughter, and killing her wouldn't bother him in the slightest, but he hadn't expected such hatred from Lord Gaelyn. Unlike most, while hatred often motivated him, Tyrion never let it cloud his judgment. "I don't think the girl is that ruthless," he said in a neutral tone. "Are you sure this isn't about her father?"

Gareth laughed. "I actually *like* her father, except when it comes to this matter. I counseled him to put her to death after what happened in Dunbar. *That* was the source of the trouble between us. Hell, I wouldn't even object if he set himself up as king. It matters little to me."

"But not her?" prodded Tyrion.

"If a Centyr goes bad and is left unchecked, it will result in unparalleled tyranny. Imagine a world in which one person controls everything, including the thoughts of her subjects. Free will would become nothing more than an illusion."

Tyrion sighed. "You sound almost noble. Aren't you worried what I might do if you release me?"

Gareth finally finished his first cup of wine. "Frankly, I don't care what else you do. Any evil you commit will be limited to your lifespan. Humanity will recover from your petty acts of violence and revenge. If that girl isn't stopped, she could become effectively immortal, and her evil would never end."

"The She'Har never had this problem. Do you know why?" prompted Tyrion.

"You mean with the Centyr She'Har?"

Tyrion nodded. "The Illeniel Grove kept them in check."

"Mordecai may have the name, but he doesn't have their gift," observed Gareth. "I fail to see your point."

"His children have it," corrected Tyrion. "I've heard quite a bit about his son Matthew, and I've seen hints of it while training with Conall."

"Are you trying to talk me out of helping you?" remarked Gareth dryly.

"Not at all," replied Tyrion, standing up and holding out his manacled wrists. "Just sharing my observations. I have plenty of reasons to kill her already."

With a touch and a brief effort of will, the other man released him from his bonds. "Leave quietly."

"Shouldn't we fight a little? Aren't you supposed to be guarding me?" asked Tyrion.

"I'm not here," said Gareth. "Since I'm the only mage in the palace currently there haven't been continuous watches on your cell. I'm in bed as far as anyone knows."

Looking disappointed, Tyrion responded, "That's too bad." Stepping out of his cell, he began to walk down the hall. He glanced back for a moment and saw the archmage walk into the stone wall, passing through it as though it were made of air. *I guess that explains how he got down here unseen.*

Alone at last, he stopped for a moment, propping himself up against the wall to brace himself against a sudden wave of dizziness. His injuries still hadn't healed completely and his time wearing the aythar-sapping manacles had left him weak. The wine probably hadn't been a good idea, either. Breathing slowly, he waited until his balance returned, then continued on.

As tired as he was, he kept his escape simple. Once he had reached the upper levels of the dungeon, where there were actual guards, he restricted himself to merely putting them to sleep. He had to conserve his strength, for he worried that some of the krytek that Moira had suborned might still be within the palace. If he encountered one of them in his current condition, it might well be his last fight.

He didn't sense any of them within his range, however. Moira had probably removed those that survived to further her pretense that they were part of some sort of rebellion on Tyrion's part. *But did she kill them or hide them away somewhere?* he wondered. Most of them had less than a month left to live, but it would still have been a waste of a valuable resource to eliminate them. *She probably hid them outside the city,* he decided.

Once he emerged onto the ground level of the palace, he detected Conall's unmistakable presence. The boy was in one of the rooms across the palace, one that hadn't been given a privacy ward. The young mage's aythar seemed weak, as though he were recovering from a wound, and after a moment Tyrion decided he was probably unconscious. *Good,* he thought, *otherwise I might have to kill him to get out of here.*

Using a simple illusion, he disguised himself as one of the palace servants and began making his way to the main gate. No one questioned him as he went, but his fatigue and injuries worked against him as he struggled to walk without staggering.

Then he felt the arrival of a powerful source of aythar, one he recognized. It was Carwyn, the Queen's dragon, flying in from the east. He had been fortunate the dragon hadn't been there when he emerged, but his luck had run out. Just as he sensed the dragon, it recognized him as it landed in the courtyard near the gate and its head immediately swiveled to stare in his direction.

Shit.

At his best, the dragon would have been an opponent worth careful consideration before confronting, but in his current state, it would be a disaster. The beast was a creation of flesh and magic, and although it couldn't use magic, it contained as much aythar as one of the Shining Gods. It was resistant to magic, had magesight, could fly, and its teeth and claws were enchanted.

Carwyn was also fully grown, and consequently possessed a body the size of a small farmhouse. The dragon's roar as it spotted Tyrion was loud enough that it seemed to shake the palace all the way down to its stone foundations.

The blue sky above beckoned him, whispering that freedom was close at hand, but he discarded the idea of trying to fly immediately. He didn't have Mordecai's skill at flight, and any construct he created to allow him to take to the air would be too slow to escape the dragon. *If I even had the strength to do so...*

Running was likewise foolish but facing the monster in the courtyard was utter suicide. The palace gate might as well be miles away. He would never make it.

Tyrion turned and ran back toward the door leading into the palace. For a second, he attempted to create an aythar-laced fog to block the dragon's magesight, but the effort nearly caused him to collapse. He abandoned the idea and hoped he could reach the door in time. If he could get back inside, the dragon's size would work to his advantage. It couldn't follow him without destroying the building.

He heard the beast's loud inhalation and dove behind a low stone wall that divided a covered walkway from the rest of the open courtyard. Servants, groomsmen, guards—everyone ran to get away from the area the dragon's mouth was facing and Tyrion could hear their cries of fear and terror for a brief second before the blast came. Using what little power he had, Tyrion activated his shield tattoos and hoped they would be enough as a wall of flame rushed over the courtyard and covered the stone wall he hid behind.

It seemed to go on forever, and he felt his skin begin to burn as the blistering heat bled through his inadequate shield. The stone beside him cracked, crumbled, and began to melt along its edges.

"Betrayer!" roared Carwyn when the flames finally subsided, his voice too deep for any human throat to reproduce. "Tyrion is loose! Guard the Queen!"

As soon as the dragon's breath stopped, Tyrion was up and running once more. The great beast leapt after him, and he passed through the stone archway that led into the front hall of the palace with barely a second to spare. Behind him Carwyn smashed into the stonework, sending stone chips and fragments flying in every direction. A second later the arch collapsed as the dragon forced himself in, his great jaws snapping at the air behind Tyrion.

Carwyn continued to bellow warnings to the palace staff as Tyrion pelted down the corridor and ducked into the first crossway he found. He wasn't sure if Carwyn would risk using his fire inside the palace, but he wasn't going to tempt fate.

Where to run? It was an open question. His intent was to get out of the palace, not back in, but with the dragon outside that was no longer possible. Mordecai had taught him the method for creating teleportation circles, but he hadn't made one yet, and without a circle to teleport to it was pointless. *The Queen's chambers.* It was his only hope, he realized.

If Moira was at home, he would be unable to handle her, but he doubted she was there. *No, she'll be hiding here, in the city somewhere to oversee the activities in the palace.*

His illusion melted away as he ran, for he didn't have the strength left to squander maintaining it. Most of the staff were too surprised to do anything when they saw him anyway, other than gape and stare. He didn't meet organized resistance until he was just outside the royal chambers. Four armsmen waited for him with bared steel.

"Shibal," he put them to sleep with a word, though he could feel the strain it put on him. Without pausing, he threw the door behind them open and charged in.

He nearly lost his head as Sir Harold's enchanted blade whistled through the air. The knight had been waiting for him, using the Queen's privacy ward to his advantage, since he knew Tyrion would be blind as to what waited within.

Tyrion had been expecting something like that, however, and he had gone in low. If his opponent had been a normal man, it would have been enough, but Harold was inhumanly fast. The knight changed the angle and sweep of his blade at the last moment, cutting a long, bloody slash down Tyrion's back. The pain shot through him like fire as he dove forward and rolled, leaving bloodstains on the floor as he went.

He came back to his feet and dodged to the right, narrowly avoiding Harold's follow up. There was no time to think; the big knight's attacks came at him without pause, delivered with a speed and strength no normal human being could hope to match. Tyrion evaded the next few strikes only because he *didn't* think; years of life and death struggle were burned into his body and mind.

Tyrion didn't need to fight, he only needed to escape, but the door that led to the portal was also the door to Ariadne's bedchamber, and it was locked and barred. Retreating before Harold's relentless assault, he made full use of the furniture in the room to buy precious time and within seconds most of the furnishings were ruined beyond repair as the knight's sword cut through wood and marble alike with ease.

He marveled at Sir Harold's combat prowess. He had watched him in the practice yard and sparred with him a time or two in the past, but that was nothing compared to facing the man in a real fight. In a fair fight, without armor and using his own power to increase his strength to something comparable to Harold's, he would probably lose. *Of course, if I had my usual power, I wouldn't fight him on those terms.*

"Can't we talk about this?" said Tyrion, scrambling back behind the pieces of a recently bisected divan.

Harold's voice sounded strange as it echoed from within his metal helm. "You lost the right to speak to me when you betrayed the Queen. Coming here to complete your treachery only reaffirms my decision to end your miserable existence."

As the knight answered, Tyrion's eyes searched the room, looking for something he could use. He found his answer sheathed on Harold's right side, an enchanted misericord. The weapon was similar to a dagger, but with a triangular cross-section and a needle-like point. It was designed for dispatching an armored opponent, as it had no edge to speak of, only a strong, slender point for driving through the joins and weak spots in a foe's armor.

His plan formed in an instant, and Tyrion leapt forward as though ready to attack. Harold responded perfectly, whipping his sword across into a guard position, but Tyrion stumbled before getting within reach and fell to the floor. Seeing his chance, Harold stomped the ground as he moved forward, setting his stance for the deathblow as he brought his blade over and down at Tyrion's vulnerable head and neck.

Tyrion was waiting. As Harold stomped, his foot came down on an invisible object of pure force that sent his foot sliding awkwardly to one side, causing him to lose his balance. With a thought, Tyrion used his power to draw the misericord from the knight's belt and pulled it to his open hand. Harold's left arm went out reflexively to catch a side table and prevent himself from falling.

At that moment, Tyrion attacked. Directing all his remaining power into strengthening his own body, he struck like a snake, driving the point up and over, straight into the knight's armpit.

The armor Mordecai had crafted for Harold so many years ago was strong and well made, and even the vulnerable spaces, like those beneath the arms, were protected by mail. A normal point would have failed, and even the enchanted blade Tyrion held wouldn't have succeeded, if he hadn't driven it in with the force of a charging bull. It tore through steel links, linen padding, skin, ribs, and finally, Harold's heart.

Harold's sword swept inward, but Tyrion stayed close, pulling himself up against the knight's chest. Even so, the force of Harold's armored arm landed on his back like a hammer, nearly driving the wind from his lungs. Then the big man began to collapse. Tyrion held onto him and eased him to the ground, ignoring the pain in his back.

He stared at his defeated opponent, watching him die, and all he could feel was regret. "Damn it."

The only reply Sir Harold could manage was a thick gurgling noise, and then he was gone.

Though it went against his every instinct, Tyrion paused for a moment. "I really liked you, Harold."

CHAPTER 19

A blazing beam of brilliant light seared into Chad's private agony, forcing him to consciousness and dragging him into the waking world. His head was pounding, and his tongue felt fuzzy and dry. Closing his mouth, he tried to moisten it, but that only made him keenly aware of the fact that he had apparently been eating shit the day before, judging by the taste.

"Fuck me if I ever drink in that dive again," he rasped out. He'd had his doubts the night before. The ale had seemed passable, but he'd already had too many to taste properly when he got there. Now he knew for sure it had been bad. Good ale never hurt this much the next day.

Two days of heavy drinking while he explored the various pubs and taverns of Iverly, and he still had found nothing. "Investigative work is hard," he muttered to himself as he stumbled across the room to see if there was any water left in the pitcher on the nightstand. There was, but as he lifted it to his lips he paused, then took a sniff. A vague memory of the previous night came to him, and his keen sense of smell confirmed it. *I had trouble finding the chamber pot last night,* he remembered.

Going to the window that had offended him, he tipped the pitcher out of it before thinking to look and see if anyone was below. That wasn't such a big deal in some cities, but Iverly had strict laws about waste disposal, so the citizens weren't as wary about walking beneath them, since people generally didn't empty chamber pots out of them. He waited a moment, listening rather than revealing himself by looking out. He didn't hear any swearing, so he assumed no one had gotten a foul bath.

He was near to dying of thirst, so he found his jacket and went downstairs quickly, admiring his own agility as he nimbly made his way down. The stairs had been a formidable opponent the night before. The common room was empty when he got there, it being too early for customers, and the innkeeper was nowhere in sight. Then the main door flew open as a woman stepped in.

Chad could tell at a glance that the woman was as angry as a wet hen, his impression being strengthened by the fact that she was indeed wet. Her hair was heavy and dripping, as though she had just poured water over herself. *Oh damn,* he thought, as a terrible realization sank into his still foggy brain.

She glared at him, then barked, "You! Where is the proprietor of this place?"

He stared blankly at her for a moment while his brain ran through possible answers, none of which did any good for his headache. "That would be me," he answered finally.

Her eyes narrowed with obvious suspicion. "I am here to lodge a complaint, and *you* are not the proprietor. Where's Ham?"

Ham was the name of the man who had rented him the room two days prior, and clearly the woman knew him. "He's upstairs dealing with a problem. I'm his cousin," corrected Chad hastily. Then, to add a dramatic touch, he studied the woman's wet hair with concern. "You weren't outside under the window just now, were you?"

She turned for the stairs, ignoring him, as what he knew to be urine dripped from her hair to the dusty floorboards.

"You can't go up there right now!" Chad barked.

The woman glanced back, fixing him with dark brown eyes. "Why not?" she asked angrily.

"There's been some violence. It's not a scene fit for a sensible woman's eyes," he improvised. "He caught one of the boarders flinging something unmentionable out the window, and a fight broke out." Moving around the main bar, he found a towel and held it out to her. "You'll want to wipe your face."

She didn't respond at first, but after a second she took the proffered towel and used it to wipe her face and dry her hair and shoulders. "I hope he gave him a good beating," she added.

"He knocked the fool unconscious," offered Chad with a grin. "Might have broken his jaw. Mind if I ask yer name?"

"Priscilla," she replied dourly.

His brows went up in surprise. "I have a friend by the same name," he answered, thinking of his dragon. He hadn't seen Prissy since his abrupt flight and escape from Albamarl after Mordecai's rescue. Presumably, the dragon was still somewhere in the vicinity of Lothion's capital, but it had been so long he couldn't be sure anymore.

She grunted with obvious disinterest.

Chad needed to get her out of the inn. It was only a matter of time before Ham returned, and then his house of lies would collapse. "I'm sure Ham would want me to compensate you for your misfortune." He reached into his purse and pulled out two silver coins. "This should be enough to pay for a bath, laundering your dress, and some extra besides." Gently he took her elbow and began steering her toward the door. "I was just heading to the bathhouse myself."

Priscilla's eyes searched him, up and down, but she let him guide her. "You do reek of alcohol and sweat."

He bit back his near automatic response; it wouldn't be helpful. *An' you smell like piss and vinegar.* He couldn't help smirking, though, and Priscilla scowled at him when she saw his expression. She pulled her arm from his grasp and quickened her stride, exiting the inn ahead of him.

"You don't need to follow me. I know the way," she said as they stepped outside.

"I already told you I'm going to the same place," he responded.

She kept up her brisk walk. "Don't walk beside me. I'd rather not have people thinking I know you."

Stuck up bitch, he thought silently. "Have it yer way." As they walked, he studied her figure. He'd always had a weakness for watching women walk. Or breathe. *Or pretty much anything,* he added mentally. Priscilla looked to be a townswoman of average means, going by her modest clothing, but her stride was firm and purposeful, with just enough femininity to distract him from his normal watchfulness.

If he had to guess, he thought she might be a merchant's wife. She was of a similar age as himself, though she showed less gray in her hair. *Probably has four brats and a mangy dog waiting at home,* he decided. He caught himself staring at her hips as she walked and made a conscious effort to bring his gaze back up to the back of her head, where he found himself admiring the curve of her neck. Blinking, he looked around and studied the street. *It's been too damn long.*

He found himself thinking about Danae, the barmaid back at the Muddy Pig in Washbrook. He hadn't seen her in well over a month, and he wondered how she was doing. The two of them had had a few intimate encounters in the past, but he still thought their relationship was purely casual. They were merely friends who happened to be of different genders. Friends who had let themselves get carried away by too much drink a few times.

Why did he keep thinking about her, though? *I'm just worried about her,* he decided. The turmoil of the events surrounding Castle

Cameron could have caused all sorts of trouble in Washbrook. *I hope she's alright.*

It was just normal concern, however. The huntsman was wise enough to know the difference between lust and love. She was just a friend that happened to be a little more fun than his male drinking buddies. *I should have left Priscilla to keep a watch on her, instead of taking her to Albamarl,* he thought. The damn dragon was certainly doing no one any good wandering around the countryside near the city.

While he had been lost in thought, they reached the city bathhouse. The building was divided into two separate sections, and Priscilla looked back at him briefly before heading for the women's entrance. "Thanks for your concern. I have to get back to work, so I won't linger. If I do see you again in future, I pray it will be under better circumstances."

Chad's jaw fell as he tried to decipher the subtext of her words. "Linger?"

She gave him a look of barely disguised pity. "I mean I'll wash quickly and be on my way, so this is goodbye."

Her meaning finally sank in. *She thinks I'm interested in her,* he realized. "Oh, that's fine. I was coming here anyway. I'll be having a long soak." He waved his hands in dismissal, but as she turned away a sudden question came to him. "What do you do?" he asked to her back.

She paused, then answered. "I'm a dressmaker."

Something clicked in his head then, but he didn't have time to understand his hunch. On instinct, he continued, "So you're a seamstress?"

Her lips formed a line, and he knew he had offended her somehow. "I have several seamstresses who assist me and handle everyday items. I create dresses for women of quality," she corrected with a reproving tone.

"Oh." Chad watched her enter the bathhouse while scratching his head. When she was gone he muttered to himself, "Why do I care?" It felt as though his brain had an itch, but he wasn't sure how to scratch it. With a shrug he went in to the men's side and paid for a private tub, fully intending to have that long soak. It had been a week since his last bath in Lancaster, and that had been little more than a cold splash of water.

His muscles were looking forward to the heat.

He had only been in the water for a minute before his gears clicked into place. *If Rose came here after that hurried escape, she probably didn't have any clothes,* he reasoned, *at least nothing she would consider acceptable. If she had the means, she'd find a dressmaker.* He couldn't recall the last time he had seen her wearing anything less than what most would consider regal. "In fact, I've *never* seen her in anything but dresses of high quality," he told himself.

With a sigh, he knew his bath wasn't fated to be of the long, relaxing sort. Dunking his head beneath the water, he scrubbed his hair quickly and stood. "What a waste of five pennies." He rushed to dry and reclaim his clothes from the boys who were beating them to get the dust out. Still damp, he put them on and went back outside to wait. He needed to talk to Priscilla again.

Half an hour passed, and she still hadn't emerged. "I could have had that soak after all, damn it," he swore quietly. He was beginning to wonder if she hadn't been even quicker and already left when he saw her emerge. Her eyes spotted him immediately and a look of surprise showed on her face. "Is that what you call a quick bath?" he asked sarcastically.

Priscilla watched him warily. "Why are you still here? I'm a married woman, you realize?"

He nodded impatiently. "Yeah, I understand. I'm not after yer virtue. You said you were a dressmaker, right?"

Her answer was hesitant. "Y—yes?"

"I'm looking for a lady, and I think she probably has need of your services, or those of someone like you," he went on. "How many dressmakers are there in Iverly?"

"Several, if you'd call them that," said Priscilla, her eyes questioning. "But I'm the only one who specializes in gowns and dresses for ladies of breeding."

He clapped his hands together briskly, causing her to step back. "Then you're the one I need!"

"Pardon?"

Warming to his subject, he found his words tumbling out quickly. "You probably know most of your clients, right? Given that you make dresses for the rich?"

Priscilla glanced around, probably wondering if any of the city watchmen were nearby, but she looked at him from the side of one eye as she answered, "Yes."

Realizing he was scaring her, Chad softened his tone. "Look, I'm not a bad fellow. I'm sorry for startling you. The woman I'm looking for is a friend, but I think she might be in trouble. I can pay you for your time." Pulling at his belt, he reached for his coin purse.

A look of anger crossed her features. "Don't be so vulgar. I'm not a street urchin looking to do favors for coin. What is it you want?"

"I'm grateful for whatever ye can tell me," he responded, his accent thickening briefly. "My friend came here not long ago, but I don't know how to find her. I think she would probably come to you for dresses. She's a noble lady and she was traveling light, so she wasn't able to pack much to wear."

With a sigh of long-suffering, Priscilla faced him squarely. "What's this lady's name then? If I've seen her I'll have heard it."

Chad's eyes went to the side for a moment. "Well, that's the trouble. I can't really say. She wouldn't have given her right name. She's in trouble. I can describe her for you."

"Are you some sort of bounty hunter?" asked Priscilla, her eyes narrowing in suspicion.

He shook his head. "No, not at all, but there are some who are hunting her. I need to find her first."

It was clear from her expression that she didn't believe him. "I don't know who you are, but I'm not telling you anything more."

"Listen," he said desperately. "I'm tellin' the truth here. I'll swear to it. I mean her no harm, exactly the opposite, in fact."

"You expect me to believe a stranger's oath?"

Chad thought for a moment, trying to come up with something to convince her, but his mind was blank. At last, in desperation, he pulled out the metal flask he kept inside his jacket. Grabbing her hands, he pressed it into them and then wrapped his own hands around hers. "Fair enough," he responded. "You don't know me, but this is the truth. I don't care for much in this world, other'n my friends and my drink. I'll swear it to you now, on this flask, which is as dear to me as me own life. I mean that lady no harm. I need to find her before those that mean to hurt her do."

Priscilla stared into his eyes for a long moment, before asking, "Are you serious?" She half laughed as she said it.

"What?"

"You're swearing on a flask?"

He nodded. "Yeah."

She did laugh then. "This is the most ridiculous thing I've ever heard."

"But you believe me, don't you?" he prodded.

She pulled it out of his hands and lifted the flask to examine it. "What's in here?"

Chad answered proudly, "Nothing less than Joe McDaniel's finest."

Priscilla unscrewed the cap, sniffed, then took a long swallow, grimacing slightly. “That’s not bad.” Then she pushed the container back into his palm. “Fine, I believe you.”

Chad shook the flask lightly, judging how much remained with some regret. “It’ll be sometime before I can replace that,” he announced sadly.

Her look was one of mirthful sympathy. “I’ll tell you what I know—for a price.”

He gave her his best haughty gaze. “I thought you were too good for coin.”

“I don’t want coin,” said the dressmaker. “I want two bottles of—what did you call it—McDaniel’s finest?”

Chad rubbed his chin. “That could take a while. It comes from Lothion…”

Priscilla waved her hand. “Not now, later. I’ll trust you to owe it to me.”

“Deal.”

“As you said, I know all my customers, but I did have a new one several weeks ago, a woman near my own age,” began the dressmaker. “She bought four gowns, two for herself and two for a younger girl. I didn’t see the girl, though; she came alone.”

Two women? “What did she look like?” asked Chad.

“She had brown hair, turning to gray.” She held out her hand to indicate the woman’s height. “About so tall, with grayish-blue eyes.”

“What name did she give?”

“She didn’t,” responded Priscilla. “But the dresses are to be delivered to her home. I have the address at my shop if you want it.”

“I do,” he answered immediately. “But I’m surprised. Why are you trustin’ me?”

She stared at his shoulder for a moment, as though she was giving it thought, then she answered, “I’m a good judge of people. You lied earlier, when you said you were Ham’s cousin, but you were serious when you swore on the whiskey.”

The hunter felt his cheeks begin to color. “Now hold up, just because you—”

“It was you who dumped the chamber pot out the window,” she accused, her eyes flickering with subdued anger.

“I already told ye it weren’t me!” he declared.

The dressmaker poked his jacket, prodding the place he kept his flask. “Swear it on McDaniel’s finest then,” she challenged.

That stopped him cold. He wasn't about to dishonor Joe McDaniel's memory by swearing false on his treasure. Chad deflated and let out a long sigh. "Fine, ye got me."

Priscilla nodded. "Good. You admitted it. Lying is a bad habit. You should avoid it in the future." Then she started walking. When the hunter didn't follow immediately, she looked back. "Are you coming?"

He hurried to catch up, and together they walked up the slight incline that led to High Street, where the shops frequented by the noble and wealthy were located. Chad suppressed the urge to whistle as they went, keeping his attention instead on his surroundings. Even the watchmen in this section of town stood straighter, and it made him feel somewhat self-conscious.

"That's my shop ahead," said Priscilla, pointing to a store with a neat front and a well-made sign that included not only a picture of a red dress but actual lettering beneath it, 'Bell's Finery.'

He glanced at her curiously. "Bell?"

"My mother," she informed him. "I inherited the shop from her."

"Ah," he said noncommittally. His eyes scanned the street up and down as they entered, and he fought the urge to pull the brim of his hat down. Once they were inside, he waited until the door was closed before turning to Priscilla. "There are spotters outside."

She seemed confused. "Spotters?"

"Two boys and a man," he explained. "They were positioned to keep an eye on your shop. Have you made any enemies lately?"

Priscilla gave him a funny look as she rummaged through a box behind the front counter. "You're paranoid. I make clothing. If I upset someone, they'd just demand a refund or have me redo my work."

"I *am* paranoid," he admitted. "It's why I'm still alive. I also know my work. They're watching this place. Has anyone else been askin' questions of you?"

Taking out a short piece of ribbon, Priscilla tied her hair back in a business-like fashion. "One person did, but he's a regular customer. I've known him for years. I don't think he was that interested."

"If he wasn't interested, why'd he ask?" replied Chad with some exasperation showing in his tone.

"It was casual conversation," she answered. "Tarol was here to order a new gown for his daughter. There was nothing strange about it. It was small talk. He asked if I'd had any new customers, and I told him about her. He didn't seem particularly interested in it."

Chad chewed his lip. "He was interested enough to put men outside."

"Tarol is a liveryman, a gentleman's gentleman," she said reassuringly. "He keeps an honest living. He wouldn't be mixed up in anything like a search for refugees. It's silly to even think such things."

"Ye think they'd send someone rough in here to ask questions?" asked Chad. "The people I'm talkin' about have money. They'd send someone nice and well mannered. He was just a face to keep you from gettin' suspicious."

She gave him a dry look. "Yet *you* asked me. You're pretty rough around the edges. You're overthinking it."

It was useless arguing with her, and yet he wanted to pull his hair out in frustration. The woman she had described was obviously not Rose, but he couldn't shake the feeling she was connected somehow. *And if she isn't Rose, why are they lookin' for her?* he wondered. None of it made sense.

CHAPTER 20

Priscilla tugged on Chad's sleeve as he prepared to leave. "If you really think they're watching the place, shouldn't you sneak out the back or something?"

The archer snorted. "I thought you didn't believe me."

Easing to the left of the door, she peeked through a crack in the shutters. "Well, I'm not saying I *do* believe you, but now that I look at them it's occurred to me that I've seen them several times over the past few days. Maybe you should go out the back. What if they waylay you and steal the dresses?"

He gaped at her. "You're worried about the dresses?"

Priscilla gave him a sour look. "Do you have any idea how much those dresses are worth? Besides, I hardly know you."

Chad sighed. "I promise you, they aren't watching this place to steal dresses. It's more likely they're hoping to find out where your new customer lives. Watch when I leave and see if one of them follows me." Then he paused. "How much are these dresses worth?"

"More than you make in a span of months, I'd wager," she replied seriously. "If anything happens to them I'll have to return the payment, *and* I'll be out the cost of the fabrics."

You'd be surprised what I make in a month, he thought to himself, although it was obvious the dresses were costly. Her words still rankled, though. "I don't work for money."

She looked him up and down, judging him once again by his appearance. "What do you work for then?"

Danae's face flashed through his mind, but he ignored it. Then he smiled and patted his jacket, his hand over the spot where his flask was safely nestled. "Good booze, fine songs, and warm company. The world provides everything else I need." When Priscilla laughed, he felt compelled to go on. "Listen up, good woman, you may have mistaken me for a bounty hunter or hired man, but in truth I follow the highest of callings. I'm huntsman by trade, and though I have a lord who provides for me, I have no need of one. The forest provides everything I need; food, shelter, and wood for a fire. What I do for my friends, I do because they give me things I cannot find in the wilderness: a table, beer, smiles, and songs."

The shopkeeper shook her head. "It seems I was mistaken. I thought you were a bounty hunter, but it turns out you were a fool all along. You're not married, are you?"

"What of it?" He bristled.

"Strong drink leaves only a hangover, and songs fade as soon as the singing is done. A woman wants love and shelter. You'll die a bachelor if you don't learn that lesson."

Chad squinted at her. "You forgot the friends I mentioned."

"You're getting up in years," she responded, undaunted. "Your friends will be too busy with their own wives and children to waste time drinking with you, if they aren't already."

That hit a little too close to home, and Chad felt a familiar pain in his chest. Over the past few years he had spent entirely too much time drinking alone. "Heh, shows how little you know," he bit back and then he opened the door to step out. "I'll take my leave," he said, tipping the brow of his hat. *I plan on dying of a pickled liver anyway,* he thought to himself. *If someone doesn't stick a knife in me a'fore then.*

On the street again, he started down the gentle decline that would take him toward the riverside docks and away from the glowing affluence of High Street. After traveling only a single block, he made a right turn down a side street and used the opportunity to check on the spotters. As expected, one of them was missing from his perch, the older man. That meant he was being followed, though he hadn't laid eyes on the man stalking him yet.

I figured they'd just stick one of the brats on me. They must think I'm a serious lead, he realized. Chad smiled to himself. He preferred it this way. Threatening a child would have left him with a bad taste in his mouth.

Continuing on down the street he had taken, he stopped the first person he met, an old man. "Beggin' yer pardon, mister, but does this road lead to the docks?" He made sure to position himself so he could watch the corner, and while the old man replied he caught sight of the one following him as he turned on the same street.

"You'll never get there going this way," the old man answered. "Take a left at the next street there and you'll find it."

He tipped his hat and thanked the man, then resumed his walk. He hadn't needed directions, of course. He had spent the first day in Iverly walking the streets and learning its ways as he roamed from pub to pub. It always paid to be prepared. Chad took the left that the old man had advised, but afterward he plotted his own course, making turns here and there to take him to a good spot he had noticed two days earlier.

A quiet alley, one where two men could have a conversation without being seen or overheard.

Ten minutes later he had arrived, after having set a pace that probably was of some concern to his tail. It was hard to follow someone moving at a fast walk while also seeming inconspicuous. *But then again, makin' his job easy ain't my concern,* he observed silently.

A brick chimney jutted out from the building on his left, a feature he had made note of previously when scouting the town, and after he had entered the alley he stepped past it and into the shadow on the side opposite the street. Then he put his bundle down and waited. He considered drawing one of his long knives but decided against it. His weapons were enchanted and consequently far too sharp for what he had in mind. If his target struggled or moved suddenly, he could wind up with a large mess to clean up.

After a minute or so he heard footsteps as his tail stopped at the entrance to the alley. Chad figured one of two things would happen at that point, either his pursuer would be foolish enough to enter, or he'd decide it was a trap and walk away. If it was the latter their roles would reverse and he would begin stalking the fellow, which might yield more information anyway.

The stranger swore quietly to himself, though Chad could still make out the words. "Damn it, he's on to me." Then the man advanced ten feet into the alley, cautious and wary of a possible ambush. As he passed the chimney, he spotted the hunter and reached for his belt knife.

That wasn't the ideal setup Chad had hoped for, but it was better than having to follow the man for the next few hours. He stepped out of the shadows and gave his visitor what he thought was a deadly smile. "Afternoon, friend."

The man was slightly shorter but heavily muscled, with dark hair and eyes that seemed almost black in the dimly lit alley. He faced the hunter, knife in hand, and asked, "Who are you?"

"Someone with questions," responded the archer casually, showing none of the customary fear that being faced with a knife normally caused. "Want a drink?" He patted his jacket and started to reach for his flask.

The man with the knife stepped forward, threatening. "I'll be asking the questions."

Holding out his other hand as a sign of peaceful intent, Chad drew the flask while stepping away. "No need to be testy." Showing the flask to the stranger, he unscrewed the cap and took a sip before offering it to the man. "I was serious about the drink offer."

"I asked who you were," said the rogue. "I also want to know who the dresses are for."

"You have strange interests," Chad replied with a grin. When the stranger raised the knife, he added, "Careful, friend. If you manage to scratch me with that thing I'll give back fourfold what I've gotten."

It was obvious from his features that the man who had been following him was unnerved by his relaxed manner, but he came forward anyway in a sudden lunge. The hunter kicked his attacker's leading foot out from under him before it could land on solid ground, sending the rogue into a twisting fall. Unfortunately, his wildly flailing blade still managed to graze Chad's jacket, leaving a light score line across the leather.

"You pus-ridden cock dribble," cussed the hunter. "This was my favorite coat. It's gonna look ridiculous after I stitch up the front." He stepped on his fallen foe's hand as he swore, forcing the man to release the knife. Then he leaned down to leer at the man. "You shouldn't have refused the drink. That was rude, and cutting my jacket really pisses me off."

The fallen stranger scrabbled back and, his bravado gone, jumped up and began to run.

"Godsdamn it all," spat the hunter. Reaching down, he picked up a loose brick he had noticed earlier and tossed it in the air, getting a feel for its heft. Taking aim, he threw it with moderate force at the man's back, aiming for the middle of his shoulderblades. Regrettably, he underestimated his strength and the heavy brick caught the man in the back of the head, dropping him to the ground like a fallen sack of potatoes. "Shit!" swore Chad. *Don't tell me I killed him. That's why I didn't take out my knives.*

Rushing over, he pulled the fallen man away from the alley entrance before checking the man's head. Blood covered his fingers as he felt the back of the fellow's head, but the skull seemed whole; there was none of the mushiness he had feared. *So much for my cunning plan to interrogate him.* Staring at the unconscious man, he felt some relief the fellow was alive, but only some. Mostly he felt irritated. "Dumbass," he spat.

His only option now was delivering the dresses for the shop owner. "Cuz I'm damn sure not going to spend hours nursing your stupid ass awake," he told the senseless rogue.

Chad dragged the man to one side and propped him against a wall, trying to make it appear as though he had passed out, but he was doubtful of the efficacy of his attempt. "Bastard looks dead," he muttered as he wiped his hands on the man's shirt, leaving red stains there. Seeing what he had done, he swore again, "Shit. That didn't help."

Standing up, he decided to leave well enough alone. The man would wake up some time later—or not, but he figured the fellow's chances were pretty good. The best thing he could do now was to keep moving and put some distance between himself and the unfortunate consequences of his failed interrogation. Hefting his bundle, he took his leave.

He hadn't quite gotten out of the alley when he spotted the girl staring down at him from a rotting wooden balcony three floors up. She looked to be around eight at most, and her eyes were round with surprise, or possibly fear. Chad grimaced. *Fuck my luck.* Then he called to the girl, "He was an asshole. Here." Reaching into his purse, he pulled out a silver coin and tossed it up to her.

She missed the catch, but the coin landed on the balcony close beside her. The girl quickly pocketed it.

"I'd appreciate it if you forgot about seein' me," he told her, and she nodded in response. "Thanks," he said, tipping his hat and walking away.

"He was an asshole," she murmured, repeating his previous words.

Chad grinned to himself and kept his pace casual, but he had barely gone a block before he heard the distinctive whistle of the city watch. Glancing back, he saw a man talking to a guardsman. The little girl was standing beside them, and as he watched she lifted her hand and pointed in his direction.

"Really?" he said with disgust, then he turned and ran. *Can't even trust people in the slums anymore, especially kids,* he observed as he put on speed.

With Chad's dragon-bond, the watchman would never be able to match his pace, but that wasn't the problem. It was the damned whistle. Every guard within blocks would hear it, and they'd all be looking to stop the fool trying to run past them, but he couldn't very well stop running with the first watchman chasing him.

Of course, he could evade or disable them as well, but his problems would only grow larger the longer it went on, and he didn't particularly want to injure or potentially kill watchmen who were only trying to do their jobs.

But the hunter had been running from guards since long before he'd had the dragon-bond. It wasn't something he practiced, naturally, but the lessons of youth are hard-won and even harder to forget. Being fast was helpful, but the key was to break line-of-sight and hide; if the runner tried to stay in the open and keep running, eventually they would be caught. He sped down streets and narrow lanes, dodging the occasional new guard who appeared in front of him all while keeping his eyes open for what he needed.

He was zigzagging through rows of two-story houses, stone at the street level and wooden above, when he turned a corner and saw a promising spot. A closed and locked cellar door stood to his left, close against the side of the building, while a sturdy balcony leaned out from the second floor above. He was at least thirty seconds ahead of his latest pursuer and there were no people in sight.

Grasping the cellar door's handle, he braced himself and pulled, exerting his strength until the wooden bar that held the cellar closed snapped and the door banged open. Then he tossed his bundle onto the roof and jumped, clearing the ten feet to the balcony rail with ease. In years prior, it would have been a scramble to climb up and he'd probably have been forced to trust his luck by lying flat against the floor of the balcony, but not today. Setting his feet on the rail, he jumped again and easily caught the eave of the roof above before pulling himself over to flatten himself against the rooftop. Then he waited.

The principle was simple—gain distance, get out of sight, and then hide somewhere close to a more obvious hiding place. The guards would check the cellar, and after not finding him assume that he had kept running while they had wasted time searching. So long as no one had heard him landing on the roof he was probably safe. *And I was fairly quiet getting up here,* he told himself, *if there's even anyone inside in the middle of the day.*

He knew better than to risk peeking over the roof's edge. Instead he scooted closer to the center of the roof and made a pillow of the bundle of dresses and settled in for a long wait. Lying on his back, he found the sun beating mercilessly into his eyes. *This is when a nice hat comes in handy,* he observed, pulling the brim of his own down and covering his eyes.

Chad smirked quietly while listening to the frustrated watchmen searching for him below. The sun was just strong enough to offset the cold wind, and the warm roof beneath him seemed almost comfortable. After a short time, he napped.

CHAPTER 21

"Come to finish what you started?"

Ariadne's voice was laced with venom when it greeted him. She stood across the room beside her massive four-poster bed, a slender sword in hand. Tyrion had several good memories involving that bed, but they were spoiled by the cold and hostile expression on his former lover's features. "Do you think you can stop me with that?" he asked disdainfully, letting his eyes rest on the weapon she held.

He could see the fear hidden in her eyes as she answered, "No, but I won't die without defending myself. James Lancaster's daughter is no coward."

The fear hurt him more than her words. He knew her mind had been twisted, but it still bothered him to hear the anger in her voice. *One more thing the mind-witch will pay for,* he noted silently. "I don't want your death," he declared, advancing on her.

Tyrion almost died then, for he had miscalculated the Queen's incredible speed. While she wasn't a trained warrior, she did possess the dragon-bond, and the point of the sword she held came up and straight for his chest in a blur that he could barely follow.

Using a minimum of motion, he sidestepped and used his forearm to push the blade out of line before punching the enraged Queen solidly in the jaw. With his power almost gone, anything else would have likely meant his death, for she was far stronger than he could hope to match at the moment.

Ariadne fell sideways, crashing into the bed post and slumping to the stone floor, stunned but not quite unconscious. Tyrion took possession of the sword, absently noting the blood dripping down his hand from a shallow cut along the forearm. Then he dragged the dazed monarch to her feet before turning her away from him and holding the sharp steel against her throat. "I'm not here to kill you, but my back is against a wall at present. Push me any further and I'll do something we'll both regret," he warned.

"You killed Harold," she hissed as her gaze fell on her fallen defender in the adjoining room. "Have you no shame?"

"He didn't give me much choice," returned Tyrion. "Don't make the same mistake."

"My only mistake was in ever trusting you, you treacherous bastard," she declared angrily. "Finish me and be done with it. I'm sick of being in your presence."

Strangely, Tyrion felt only sadness at her words, that and an overwhelming sense of loneliness. It wasn't something he expected, not of himself at least. Anger he could deal with, like an old friend, but this was a reminder of a part of himself he had thought long dead. *I'm just tired,* he told himself. His exhaustion was extreme, that much was definitely true. He knew his body, and it was telling him that he was close to collapse. It would be best to finish his escape quickly. "Just get me through the portal and I'll be out of your hair," he replied. "I've no wish to hurt you."

The portal Mordecai had created between his personal dwelling and the Queen's chambers was protected by several clever safeguards, something Tyrion knew from his previous use of it with Gareth Gaelyn. The Queen and the Illeniel family were the only ones who could use it, and they could only bring others through by using a secret password, otherwise the portal would fail to operate.

"I won't help you," said the Queen. "You want to hurt Moira, don't you?"

Actually, he did, very much so, but admitting as much wouldn't help him. Besides, he was in no shape to face another mage, much less her. "She isn't there. I just need a way out and currently this is the only path available to me."

"How do you know she isn't there?" asked Ariadne, a faint curiosity evident in her voice.

"Because the spider is in the city, where she can pluck the strings of her web," he answered, pushing her forward toward the portal door. When they were only a foot from it, he pressed the sword's edge against her throat. "Now, open it, or Lothion will have to choose a new monarch."

He could feel her back stiffen along with her resolve. "No."

Violence wouldn't help; he knew her better than that. He had to appeal to her sense of responsibility. "Think about the people that will die trying to rescue you if you trap me here," he said softly, whispering in her ear. "I won't die easily, you know that, and I'm perfectly capable of taking a lot of your followers with me."

Ariadne lifted her chin proudly. "I'm not new to this throne. I've had to make many hard choices over the years. Letting you go free could lead to many more deaths in the future. Nor will I be tricked into accepting responsibility for your actions, now or in the future. The blood is on your hands, not mine."

"I wonder how many would die if I brought the palace down on their heads right now," he speculated. "I might even be able to escape in the confusion afterward." It was a bluff, of course. Even if he weren't exhausted, doing such a thing purely with his own aythar would be foolish, if not suicidal, and he didn't have access to his creator's special abilities.

But Ariadne wasn't aware of that.

The Queen's trembling fingers reached for the door handle while she muttered something softly under her breath. When the door swung open, he could see the portal had activated, for Mordecai's home lay on the other side. Carefully, Tyrion turned the two of them around and then shoved the woman away from him. She stumbled and almost fell, but catching herself in time, Ariadne turned her eyes back on him accusingly. "You never cared about me in the slightest, did you? I was just a means to an end, wasn't I?"

Tyrion paused, his hand gripping the edge of the door. He desperately wanted to slam it shut, to block out the image of her face. "Anything I say is pointless. That mind-bitch will just change your memory of my words to match her wishes."

"As I thought," said Ariadne bitterly. "Nothing but excuses."

His anger flared then. "Yes, you were a means to an end, but you were also more than that. I loved you, in my own way."

"Liar," she hissed.

The way she said it caught him for a moment, reminding him of a time long ago, when another woman whom he had loved more than anything had said the same. Slamming the door shut, he crossed the small room and opened the second door, letting himself into Mordecai's home before shutting that door behind him as well. His magesight quickly confirmed that he was there alone, although he couldn't be sure of the warded rooms yet. Regardless, he was tired to the bone. Relaxing his resolve, he slid to the floor, breathing heavily.

In his mind's eye, he could still see Kate's green eyes filled with tears. *"Liar."*

He laid his forearm across his face, as though he could block out the vision. "She's a lot like you were, Kate," he muttered. There was an obvious difference, though. Kate had believed in him no matter what, whether he was right or wrong, despite his lies. Ariadne's mind had been twisted, and she believed he was lying even though he had spoken only truth.

Tyrion did his best to push those thoughts aside. He had no idea how much time he might have, for his enemies knew where he was. He needed rest. Time to recover, time to think, and once those things were accomplished, time to decide. Getting back onto his feet was hard, and his back screamed at him with every movement.

I should destroy the portal, he realized. Otherwise pursuit would be far too quick for him to escape. That was easier decided than done, however. The enchantment that operated the portal was a work of art and it stored a significant amount of magical power within it. In his current state it would be difficult to damage, and even if he could, the resulting release of power might kill him.

Then a thought came to him, and he smiled. From what he had seen, the portal activated when one of the two doors leading into the closet was opened, but not both. When one door was open, the other had to be closed, or the enchantment wouldn't activate. It was a fundamental part of the protections that his descendant had built into the magical device. All he had to do was prop the door on this end open. Someone would have to travel to Mordecai's home by other means and close the door here before it would function again.

That done, he made a quick search of the house and nearby workshop, ruining every teleportation circle he found. He couldn't be certain there weren't others nearby, but it was the best he could do. At the very least, the World Road had an opening in Arundel, so his pursuers would only be an hour or two behind him.

He rummaged through the kitchen and came up with dried peas, hard cheese, and a surprisingly fresh loaf of bread. It hadn't been *that* long since Moira had been here. He ignored most of the rest of what he found, since it wouldn't be practical to try and cook while he traveled.

Tyrion set out then, following the gentle grade of the mountain downward, but he had gone only a mile before the pain in his back forced him to stop. Every step pulled at the damaged skin and muscle, causing it to bleed again. Ordinarily he would have healed it at the first opportunity, but he had been shepherding his remaining power, thinking it to be more precious than a little blood. That was no longer the case.

Being as careful as he could, he sealed the wound and knitted the damaged tissue back together. Even so, the effort left him faint and in danger of losing consciousness. He also sealed the shallow gash on his forearm. Walking after that was an exercise in stubbornness. The world kept going dark, narrowing into a tunnel in front of him as his brain struggled to hold onto awareness. On several occasions he awoke to find himself laing facedown on the ground, with new bruises to add to his collection.

At some point, after the sun had disappeared behind the mountains, he reached the bottom, where the base of Mordecai's mountain met its neighbor and a small stream trickled by. Tyrion sat beside its edge, though his movement might be better described as 'collapsed.' Rousing himself momentarily, he drank, and then he allowed his eyes to close. Just before he drifted into oblivion, he closed his mind. If they were looking for him, he wouldn't make it easy for them.

When he awoke, sometime later, he was shivering in the darkness. There was no moon, and being in a mountain valley, few stars were visible. With his mind closed he felt completely blind, at least until he opened it again and his magesight began to function. His body ached, not just from its wounds, but also the shivering, which presumably had been going on for a while. It was one occasion when he felt he might have preferred his previous krytek body.

The krytek body he'd had before had been human in form, but krytek, whatever their form, were produced with the guiding principle of function before survival. They didn't get cold, they experienced little pain, and they could continue to operate normally right up until the point that they fell over dead. The body he had now was an exact replica of his creator's former human form, which meant, like most natural living bodies, that it prioritized survival over function. He got cold, he shivered, he felt pain and experienced fatigue. All the natural mechanisms that human bodies had to prevent death and warn them of impending injury or death were in place, and consequently, he was absolutely miserable.

And based on what he was feeling now, there was a decent chance he might not survive long enough to find proper shelter.

Dying wasn't a particular fear for him, and at present he was too tired to even feel his usual anger or drive for revenge. Lying down and going back to sleep was tempting. *I probably wouldn't feel the cold much longer and then I could rest peacefully,* he thought to himself.

He didn't do that, however. Instead, he sat up and forced himself to eat the cheese and drink some water, though he felt no real hunger.

Then he got up and began walking, hopefully away from Mordecai's home. There was no way to tell for sure. He followed the flow of the stream, on the general principle that it would eventually lead him out of the mountains.

Eventually, the sun rose behind him, confirming his guess. He was headed west. The sun warmed his back, a welcome change, and he plodded along steadily. As the day wore on, he ate the dried peas, chewing them in small handfuls. Tyrion still wasn't hungry, but he knew he needed something to keep him going, whether he felt it or not.

In the early afternoon, a companion joined him, a woman perhaps. She trod along beside him, though he couldn't see her when he turned his head to look directly. She was known to him more as a feeling, a presence, and occasionally he caught flashes of light glinting from what he presumed were her weapons.

This didn't seem strange to him, though he suspected it should. As the day wore on, he began to hear her footsteps more clearly, and when he began to stagger he finally caught a glimpse of her from the corner of his eye. Brigid.

She was naked, as usual, and the glints of light were coming from her snake-like metal weapon, hovering around her as it often did when she fought. She met his eyes for a moment and smiled, the expression half-feral and half twisted as it always was when she attempted it.

His daughter turned away a second later, her raven hair hiding her face as she continued to march onward, leaving him behind.

Straightening up, he followed, unwilling to show his weakness in front of her, or behind her as the case might be. Brigid's figure blurred in and out of focus as he walked, but he could see she walked with strength and confidence, as she always had, her long, dark hair swaying behind her.

She's a perfect reflection of my best and worst, he thought idly. Then his eyes misted. *But she's dead.*

Brigid turned back just then. "Hurry up, Father. We can't have you dying here."

"You aren't real," he muttered, too low for her to hear.

"And you are?" she returned, hearing him anyway.

That made him grimace. He was, after all, only a copy of her true father. "More than you."

Brigid stopped, then turned to face him, appearing as a naked goddess with the sun creating shining highlights in her hair, but none of that was what caught his attention. It was the deadly, enchanted steel blade at the tip of her chain that was racing toward his face.

Activating his arm blade, he batted it away, albeit more awkwardly than he normally would have, then he stumbled and fell sideways to avoid the slicing chain that whipped toward him from the other side. The third attack would have killed him, for he had no way to avoid it, but Brigid stopped. She stood over him, looking down with blue eyes hidden in shadow.

Seizing his chance, he surged upward and caught her throat in one hand, but his daughter's body felt as hard as stone beneath his fingers. Her face devoid of expression, Brigid lifted one hand and pulled his hand away, her strength greatly exceeding his own in his weakened state.

His strength gave out then, and his legs collapsed beneath him. Tyrion wound up on his back, staring up at her, while his body trembled from the sudden exertion.

Kneeling beside him, Brigid brought her face close to his and then kissed him before sitting back to stare at him with serious eyes. "You have a fever, Father. I think you may die soon."

"What's it like?" he asked with genuine curiosity.

"I don't know," she answered immediately. "The living have no knowledge of such things, and for now…" She gestured at herself, as if indicating her all too real body. "… I feel alive."

"This is a fever dream," he declared quietly. *Unless my original self created her from his memories, but if so, she isn't the real Brigid.* His mind was too foggy to decide what was real and what wasn't.

A malicious look crossed her features and Brigid lifted her right hand before pressing it against his heart. Focusing her aythar at the tip of her thumbnail, she cut a small red line into the skin of his chest. She sealed the cut a second later, knitting the skin in a lazy fashion that would leave a noticeable scar afterward. "There," she said, satisfaction in her voice.

"What was the point of that?" he asked weakly.

"None," said Brigid. "Unless you live." Then she eased one arm behind his shoulders and the other beneath his thighs. He could feel her aythar moving as she strengthened her body, and with a smooth motion, Brigid stood, lifting him with her, like a babe in her arms.

Tyrion was vaguely aware of her walking after that, as he passed in and out of consciousness. It was dark again when he woke fully at the feeling of cold grass beneath him. Brigid was staring down at him again, her eyes serious and sad. "Try not to die, Father. The god hates you, but he isn't done with you yet."

He chuckled hoarsely. “God? There is no god. This is a fever dream.”

Thunder cracked, seeming so powerful that it shook the sky itself, and Brigid began to fade. “Watch me burn,” she whispered, and then she was gone. Rain began to fall, and the fat, cold, drops of water felt good on Tyrion’s skin.

He closed his eyes and waited to die.

“Are you alive? Can you hear me?” asked an anxious woman’s voice.

Tyrion opened his eyes again, but the face in front of him wasn’t Brigid’s, it belonged to a stranger. The woman stared at him worriedly before putting her palm against his forehead. Then she stood and began to run. “James! There’s someone here!” she called.

CHAPTER 22

Matthew stared back in the direction of Lancaster as the opening his sister Irene had made closed. Slowly, almost languidly, he turned back to the others, his eyes meeting first Karen's and then Irene's and Lynaralla's. "I need your help," he announced, the cadence of his voice sounding almost normal now.

Karen nodded immediately, but Irene asked, "What is it?"

"I want to return Lancaster to its previous place," said Matthew simply.

"You can do that?" exclaimed Irene. "Is that possible?"

Lynaralla also responded at the same moment, "No."

Irene glanced at her. "It isn't possible?"

"Possible and probable are two different things," said the She'Har woman. As she stood in the early dawn light, the wind plucked at her hair, strengthening her already ethereal appearance. "It may be possible, but the probability is low and the chance of death or worse is very high."

Elaine spoke for the first time from her position behind them, "I thought you didn't have any working knowledge of how the Illeniel She'Har constructed these magics." Her statement was addressed to Lynaralla rather than Matthew.

Lynaralla nodded in agreement. "I do not."

Irene, whose expression had been wavering between hope and uncertainty, asked, "Then how can you say that, Lynn? What do you understand about this that we don't?"

Without any hesitation, Irene's newest sister replied, "The basics of magic."

Elaine coughed. "Ouch."

But Lynaralla wasn't done. She continued, "From what I do know, the magical construct that was created to divide our world was the work of thousands upon thousands of my people, possibly both children such as myself and the elders. For an individual, or even a small group, to attempt to shift any part of it is akin to a single worker trying to remove or replace the keystone of an arch in a stone wall. The task is too great. Without proper support the wall will collapse, probably killing the individual as well as destroying the wall."

Matthew smiled. "She's right."

"Then we shouldn't attempt it," asserted Irene.

"Why would you even suggest it?" asked Karen, her eyes narrowing as she stared at him.

Matt sighed. "I mean her reasoning is correct, based on the information she has. However, I am certain, based on mine, that it is not only possible, but almost certain that we will succeed." He received only sour looks from them at those words.

Gram took Alyssa's hand. "Let's take a walk. I have a feeling this is going to take a while."

For her part, Alyssa seemed torn. "But, what if…?"

"They won't need us," said Gram.

"I'll join you," put in Cyhan, and Grace chimed in a second later, "Me too."

Moments later, only the mages and their dragons remained at the dimensional boundary line. "What is this information you possess?" asked Lynaralla, nothing but pure curiosity in her voice.

"I can't put it into words," said Matthew. "You aren't truly an Illeniel yet. For that matter, maybe I'm not one either."

"You're human," said Irene. "Illeniel is just our last name. Lynaralla actually *is* an Illeniel She'Har."

"That's not what I'm talking about," said Matthew. "Rennie, do you know what the word 'Illeniel' actually means in Erollith?"

Elaine began muttering loudly under her breath, "Here we go again. I'm so sick of this mystic prophet routine."

Irene shot the older woman a warning glance before answering her brother, "No. You know I don't speak Erollith. I wasn't born with the Loshti like you were."

"The closest word in Barion would be 'potential,'" said Lynaralla helpfully.

Matthew nodded. "I always thought it was an odd name for a She'Har grove, or for our family. It never really occurred to me that there might be a deeper meaning until I crossed the void to go to Karen's world. I really didn't connect the name to our gift until a few weeks ago, while I was considering the changes my gift has undergone. I don't know what to call it, to be honest."

"Just get to the point," snipped Elaine.

"Illeniel is a reference to what lies between worlds," explained Matthew, "or maybe it's a reference to those who can communicate with it, those with the Illeniel gift. The terminology doesn't really matter I suppose. The important point is that the place between worlds, between universes, isn't empty, it's alive—and aware. Aythar is a manifestation of that. That's why everything is conscious to some degree, however slight. But when you travel between worlds, everything else falls away and you lose your sense of self, you get a glimpse of the unlimited potential that underlies the fabric of reality."

Karen was nodding, a distant expression on her face. "I felt something like that, when you brought me here."

"That's where my 'mystic prophet' routine comes from," said Matthew, giving Elaine a wry look. "The potential guides me, showing me possibilities I haven't considered."

"You have become an elder," said Lynaralla.

Irene frowned. "He isn't *that* much older than me."

"I think she's referring to the She'Har elders, those who have become trees," suggested Elaine.

Karen laughed. "He's pretty rough around the edges but he's a long way from having bark."

"Elaine is correct," said Lynaralla. "Since he is human, he cannot become a tree, but his mind has undergone a transformation similar to that of an Illeniel elder."

"What does that mean?" asked Irene with some exasperation.

Matthew answered first, "It means I can probably reverse the dimensional boundary around Lancaster."

"This is crazy," said Elaine.

"Will you help me try?" asked Matthew.

Lynaralla responded immediately, "Yes."

After staring at the She'Har woman for a moment, both Irene and Karen nodded affirmatively, but Elaine's response was more pessimistic. "This is stupid, but I guess I have no choice but to go along."

"What do we do?" asked Karen.

"Each of you will connect your minds with mine and allow me to control your gift. Zephyr will supply the aythar needed," began Matthew.

Elaine was quick to point out the obvious flaw in his plan. "Only Irene and Lynn have the same gift. Karen and I can't work with this 'potential' you mentioned."

"You do," countered Matthew. "It's the secret behind all the She'Har gifts, no matter which one you consider. Teleportation, invisibility, mind control, shapeshifting, they all require control and calculations that no human mind is capable of alone. A mage without one of those gifts can often replicate the results, but only with extensive preparation—a teleportation circle for example. The other gifts are more specialized, but they all rely on the same connection to the 'potential.'"

"Is this something you learned from that Loshti thing you were born with?" asked Irene.

He shook his head. "No. It's just my guess. Dad used to speculate about it, but as time goes on it seems like the only explanation that really fits, at least to my way of thinking."

A few minutes later they stood together at the boundary with their hands linked. A voluntary mind-link was something any mage could manage, even without the physical contact, but the degree of control Matthew required was difficult. It took a while for each of them to still their thoughts and relax their self-control, subordinating their power to his will. Compounding the problem, he had to draw aythar from Zephyr at the same time, which made it feel a bit like juggling, a physical skill he had never mastered. *This would be a lot easier with Moira's help,* he thought, forgetting their close link for a moment.

As if any of us would trust her in our minds, came Elaine's mental response.

The link wavered for a moment as each of them began to verbalize mentally, forcing them to spend time silencing their thoughts once more. Thoughts weren't the only distraction, however. Emotions flowed between them as well, and with five people things got confusing. Matthew felt a jumble of unexpected feelings—love, irritation, affection, and even jealousy. It wasn't always clear from which person each emotion originated, but he quickly realized that beneath the veneer of ordinary daily existence, the four women around him had far more complex relationships both with him and one another, than he had really appreciated.

Elaine's eyes met his for a moment before she looked away, her face coloring, while at the same time he felt a surge of anger, presumably from Karen.

"This isn't working," remarked Irene, staring at the other women while through the link she radiated both disgust and some sort of sisterly protectiveness.

Perhaps if we dealt with the affectionate and reproductive urges first, things would be easier, sent Lynaralla. *It might eliminate the competitive tension between some of us.*

How? asked Matthew, before immediately regretting the question, as the She'Har woman projected her idea to them visually.

The vision she presented was as vivid in its clarity as it was shockingly lewd. Matthew shuttered his mind instantly, breaking the link. He fervently hoped none of the others had caught a glimpse of his first, less-than-civilized response.

Meanwhile, Karen was blushing so furiously her cheeks were purple, and Elaine turned completely around to hide her face. Irene was making gagging noises. "I think I'm going to be sick," she announced.

Only Lynaralla seemed unaffected. "Was it a bad idea?"

"Yes!" The response was uttered instantly by the other women, while Matthew merely grimaced.

Karen punched him. "The answer was *yes.*"

"Of course," he told her. "I was just embarrassed." Looking up, his eyes went to Lynaralla for a moment.

Karen punched him again, harder this time. "Don't even *think* it. In fact, just erase that memory completely."

Unfortunately, Matthew had perfect recall, thanks to the Loshti, and he suspected Lynaralla's vision would haunt him for some time to come, but he knew better than to say as much. "I already have," he answered instead.

Irene had been taking deep breaths, but she paused to give Lynaralla a serious stare. "Later, you and I need to have a serious talk about jealousy and interpersonal relationships. I think you have some very bad misconceptions regarding men and women."

"Especially regarding brothers and sisters," added Karen sharply.

"Karen, please!" barked Irene. "I really am going to be sick."

"Let's just stop talking about it," suggested Elaine, still facing away from all of them.

"I already know the things you are going to tell me, Irene," said Lynaralla, attempting to defend herself. "The image I produced was not meant to be taken seriously."

"What?!" yelled Elaine.

"That was your idea of humor?" asked Karen incredulously. "Please never tell me a joke again," she added earnestly.

Caught by the nervous tension and ridiculousness of it all, Matthew let out a half-snort, half-giggle. It quickly turned to strangled laughter as Karen and Irene both began hitting him. He fought to contain his laughing. "I can't help it. It's funny!" he cried as they pounded on him. "Why are you hitting *me?* She was the one that did it!"

Eventually they all calmed down and silence reigned for several minutes. "Are we ready to try again?" asked Matthew. "I have a better idea this time." The response he got was a collection of suspicious glares, but after a time they consented to try once more. As they joined hands he explained, "This time focus on me. Ignore your inner feelings and just listen to my thoughts." *That will help avoid distractions,* he added mentally as the link between them solidified.

Matt kept his own thoughts on the task at hand, letting the dimensional boundary fill his attention as the link with the other mages strengthened. He made a point of ignoring the variety of emotions that filtered through to him, letting it all pass him by unnoticed, like the wind on a mild afternoon. As the seconds dragged on the others began to resonate with him, as their own mental states matched his own.

Once everything felt right, he began to draw power from Zephyr, directing it toward the others and using their minds to tune it to the dimensional boundary. It was easiest with Irene and Lynaralla, whose gift matched his own. They had become almost transparent within the bond, extensions of his own power, while Karen and Elaine both exhibited different degrees of resistance.

He took his time, and as they relaxed the resistance seemed to wane until it was almost unnoticeable. When he was ready, the five of them, acting in unison, pushed their power outward and attached themselves to the vast boundary.

A note of satisfaction vibrated between them, a single thought with no definitive originator, *step one complete.* Then things got weird.

With a single thought, he shifted his—no, their—perspective, passing beyond the world and into the potential that lay between realities. Everything vanished, except the boundary, which was formed within that potential, both underlying and overlying the familiar world. Now they could see it in its entirety, not just the small section they had been standing beside. It was a giant lattice work of lines and planes, stretching out in every direction, dividing and organizing the physical reality they had been born within.

It was a vast matrix of power, and yet, built into its very structure, within each vertex, were the tools needed to control it.

Crouched inside, a sentience existed, an ancient mind, old, powerful, and slowly dying. The last of the gatekeepers. Its roots extended into the matrix, and its mind was connected to the potential that lay between worlds, an Illeniel elder. *I am Kion,* it announced suddenly. *Why have you come?*

They responded as one, for only Matthew remained. *Because you have grown weak. Mistakes have begun to propagate through the structure.*

It no longer matters, answered Kion. *The seed has stolen my power. All is lost. That is why the errors appear.*

No, Matthew declared. *They began before your loss. Age has taken its toll on you.*

That may be, but causes are no longer relevant. The end of beginnings is near. Your sire will destroy it all, the elder replied.

It is not gone yet. Help us repair it.

No.

Matt was genuinely surprised. *Why?*

Nothing but spite remains to me. Your progenitor ruined the only purpose I have lived for.

Then we will replace you, Matt warned.

Laughter echoed through the place that was no place at all. *Even if your sire didn't destroy us all, you would be dust before my death is finished.*

Something stirred within him, and Lynaralla's thoughts emerged. *The She'Har have returned. A new elder will be found to take your place.*

Do what you will then, child, said Kion. *I will neither assist nor resist your effort.*

That was enough. Refocusing their mind, Matthew returned to the specific portion of the dimensional matrix that needed shifting, and then he relaxed his boundaries, letting the potential blend itself with them. It absorbed his sense of self, destroying his ego, even as it accepted his purpose.

The power being drawn from Zephyr increased until it burned them, searing through their souls until even the infinity they had joined seemed to consist of nothing but fiery pain. Their aythar enveloped the boundary enclosing Lancaster and began to press.

For the briefest of instants, Matthew knew doubt, and with it came fear. Their power was barely sufficient and even the tiniest of mistakes, the slightest moment of hesitation would cause everything to unravel. The result of such a blunder would be annihilation.

That was why Kion didn't interfere, he realized. *He wants to die.*

THEN HE WILL BE DISAPPOINTED.

The voice that thundered through him was not that of the potential, nor was it any of the others that composed him now. He recognized it without being aware of where his recognition came from. *Father!*

DO IT, WHILE YOUR COURAGE HOLDS FIRM.

The power that resonated within those words was so great that it threatened to destroy them, but Matthew found comfort in his father's presence nonetheless. Seizing the moment, he pushed his doubt aside and with one last surge of will, he inverted the boundary that Lancaster lay within.

He knew he had succeeded, and wasting no time, he released the power coming from Zephyr and shifted them back to the world they were familiar with. But things were still not back to normal. In the distance he could see the road stretching on toward Lancaster—the world had been repaired, but he perceived it now through five sets of eyes.

The bond that connected them was still in full force. He had five bodies, but his mind was still his own. Looking back and forth, he studied his bodies from all the perspectives available to him. Four of them were undeniably female, but he was still male. It was disconcerting and fascinating all at once.

Their minds were present, he could feel them, but their wills were gone. A sense of power washed over him. *Is this how Moira feels?* he wondered. *How does she manage to control herself?* The power was intoxicating. He could do anything.

Once again, he studied his subordinate bodies before fixing his attention on Lynaralla. She was perfect, her body without flaws, immortal and unchanging. Her physical form was also incredibly beautiful.

And it was his, to do with as he pleased.

In response to his unspoken will, Lynaralla's face turned to him and smiled before licking her lips. The expression was unlike her, for it was entirely human, and it mirrored his subconscious desire.

He forced his attention away from her, and his many eyes came to rest upon Elaine. She was not perfect, but she was also desirable. Even her minor flaws held their own charm. Her eyes sparkled as she looked at him, and he saw himself through them.

The expression on his face was predatory. In his face he saw hunger—and evil.

For a moment—or to his shame, perhaps longer—he thought maybe he could live with that. Until he let his attention shift to Karen. She gazed back at him like the others, though with her blue skin and curly hair she was the most visibly different of them all. His heart moved when he saw her, and more importantly, he saw genuine emotion within her, true affection that wasn't a product of his own will.

Angry at himself, he broke the bond and all four of the women around him collapsed, like puppets whose strings had been cut. Taking deep breaths, Matthew sat down in the grass, studying his unconscious friends.

"Damn. I hope they don't remember any of that," he muttered, feeling incredibly tired.

Chapter 23

Karen woke after a short nap, feeling worn and exhausted. The others roused themselves not long after, and Gram, Cyhan, and Alyssa rejoined them a short while later, but Karen was in no shape to teleport them back to Matthew's home just yet.

Matthew had been sitting nearby when she woke, but he had yet to speak. While he was usually quiet, his silence on this occasion was almost unnerving. His wan face looked tired, but there was something more there, as though he was haunted by something. Karen pulled him aside not long after they were all together again. "What's wrong? It looks like it worked."

His eyes met hers, but only for an instant before they shifted to something to one side. "It did work. I'm just tired."

"You aren't the only one," she agreed, though she sensed something hidden in his words. "But something else is bothering you."

"A little," he admitted.

"What's wrong?" she asked. "Was it something you saw on the other side?"

No, something on my inside, he thought sourly. "How much do you remember?"

"Not much," she answered honestly. "After we joined, things were confusing at first, but once you started everything sort of faded away. I remember a lot of pain at one point, like I was holding a piece of red-hot iron. When we came back, I remember everyone staring at each other, but I think I passed out right after that. Did something happen?"

"No," he said, perhaps a bit too sharply. Seeing the look on her face he softened his tone. "Do you think I'm a good person?"

He's doubting himself, she realized. "What's that?" she returned, her voice joking. When his face didn't change, she went on, "Listen, I'm not a kid. I don't believe in heroes and villains like they have in comic books."

"Comic books?"

"Stories," she supplied. "People aren't that simple. We're all a mixed bag. Even the definitions of good and evil are relative to the observer."

Matthew nodded but didn't respond. If anything, he looked worse than before. Karen kissed his cheek. "I didn't fall in love with you because I thought you were a hero," she added. "Although, if anyone fit that description, you certainly come damn close. You've ticked me off something fierce a few times, usually when you try to exclude me out of some misguided desire to protect me, but overall I think you're a pretty decent human being."

"I might be more mixed than you think," he told her, understating his feeling.

She fixed her eyes on him. "Why do you say that?" When he didn't answer, she pushed harder. "Come on, tell me. Don't let it fester."

He still didn't reply right away, but after a long pause, followed by a tired sigh, he said, "I think I understand what Moira's been going through a little better."

Karen studied him for a minute. "From controlling us?"

Matt nodded. "After it was over, I waited a bit before releasing you and the others. I didn't want to let go."

"Not because of how close you felt to us," she clarified.

He shook his head. "It was the power, absolute power."

"It couldn't have lasted forever," she said, trying to divert his guilt.

"I'm not so sure. I think it could have been permanent."

Karen frowned, causing her freckles to wrinkle. "So we'd have been what, your slaves?"

Matthew refused to look at her, studying his sleeve instead. "Something like that."

The suggestion made her angry. The thought was repugnant, but the man in front of her was not. They had been through too much together. After gathering her thoughts, she responded, "But you chose to let it go."

"What if I hadn't?"

Karen wound her hand through his hair and then gripped it painfully, tugging until his face was in front of hers. "But you did. It's what you do that counts. Should we start judging people by every ugly thought they have? If so, I'm probably a murderess at least three times over every day before I go to bed."

"It's not just what I did," he insisted. "I didn't *want* to let go."

Lynaralla's perfect face popped into her mind then, and Karen gritted her teeth. He hadn't said it, but she had a fair idea what sort of depravity might have run through his head. She wanted to punch him, or worse.

Later, she told herself. She suppressed the urge to bite and kissed him instead. “Let’s look at this from a different angle,” she began. “Think about your father.”

For the first time, Matt laughed. “Bad example. I know exactly how messed up he is.”

“Stop using your brain for a minute and think with your heart,” Karen explained. “Sure, you know he’s made a lot of mistakes. You know he’s done some bad things. That’s not what I’m talking about. I’m talking about how you feel about him.”

Matt pushed her hand away, freeing his head. “What do you mean?”

“In your heart, you’re a little boy,” she explained. “A little boy who idolizes him. He’s your hero, and he probably feels the same way about his father. You don’t think he’s evil, no matter what he’s done.”

“He’s saved the world several times over,” said Matt defensively. “I don’t think he’s perfect but he’s definitely not evil.”

“And he probably feels the same way about his dad,” added Karen. “And there are a lot of people who feel that way about you, myself included. Stop judging yourself by a higher standard.”

Matthew sat down but stayed quiet for a while after that. Karen found a seat beside him and let the silence soak in before she asked, “Feeling any better?”

“A little.”

“Good,” she pronounced, pulling him back to his feet. “Let’s go back before the others start making up stories about us.” They walked hand in hand on the way back, but just before they reached the group, she said something else, sending a cold chill up his spine. “Don’t think I don’t know what you were thinking. I’ll forgive you, but I’m still going to punish you later.”

***

They didn’t bother traveling home. There weren’t enough dragons to carry everyone, so even having to wait a few hours for Karen’s strength to recover was still faster than walking. When she felt ready, she took them in three groups.

Matthew was among the first, and something felt off as soon as he arrived. He glanced at Irene and stated his feeling, “Something’s not right, Rennie.”

Lynaralla, Irene, and Zephyr stood with him in the yard, and they looked back and forth at one another for several seconds. Karen reappeared with Gram, Alyssa, and Grace a moment later. Gram took one look at their faces before asking, "What's wrong?"

"Moira's not here," said Matthew. "She was supposed to be here."

Irene frowned. "You sent her to Albamarl, remember?"

Matt nodded. "This doesn't match my vision. It was almost certain that she would be here when we returned."

Alyssa and Gram looked at each another. As always, she was already armored, and with a word, his armor appeared and encased his body. The two of them strode in unison toward the door, while at the same time Karen returned with Elaine and Cyhan. After a few words, Elaine volunteered to scout the other side of the house where the workshop was.

"I'll come with you," suggested Sir Cyhan.

Elaine waved him away. "That would defeat the purpose of having a Prathion do it." She vanished even as she said it, and the rest of them resigned themselves to waiting.

"I don't like this," said Karen.

"Me either," responded Matthew. "It feels weird whenever Gram acts like he's my bodyguard. I should have gone in with him."

"You're more important than the rest of us," said Lynaralla matter-of-factly.

"Although clearly your omniscience isn't everything you thought it was," added Irene.

Gram stuck his head back out from inside the house. "It seems empty. Come use your magic sniffers to see if we missed anything."

They all started forward immediately, though Matthew made sure he was the first to enter. "Magic sniffer?" he asked, giving Gram a curious look.

The young knight shrugged. "Whatever you want to call it."

The house was empty, and after a thorough search they found nothing, though Karen was the first to note that the door leading to the portal to Albamarl had been propped open. Matt joined her and after rubbing his chin went to check on the portal room next to it. "They've all been damaged," he announced.

Gram and Alyssa joined them, and a second later Elaine appeared behind them without warning. "The teleportation circle in the workshop was damaged too."

Matthew and Karen jumped, but neither of the two warriors even flinched. Alyssa winked at Gram and then said, looking at the two mages, "You get too wrapped up in your thoughts. We heard her walk in."

Karen scowled, but Matthew merely composed himself with a deep breath. "I'm sure everyone's hungry. Why don't you see if there's anything to be had in the kitchen?"

Alyssa smiled wryly, then stood to attention. "Certainly, my lord. Your warrior-maid stands ready to serve."

It turned out there wasn't much in the pantry, but the garden still held vegetables. Karen and Cyhan helped gather and clean them while Alyssa got the kitchen stove burning. An hour and a half later they had a simple but filling soup.

The room was silent, but for the sounds of slurping. Everyone ate quickly, while Matthew sat staring into his bowl, hardly touching his spoon. "It was him," he muttered. "It had to be."

"Who?" asked Elaine.

"Tyrion," said Lynaralla immediately.

"You think so too?" asked Matthew.

She nodded. "Who else would have cause to try and keep anyone from following him here? Moira must have succeeded, and he was forced to escape here."

Sir Cyhan looked alarmed. "That means he escaped through the Queen's chambers."

Gram and Matthew both stood, but Karen caught Matt's sleeve. "Eat your soup. Going hungry won't help. Whatever happened was likely days ago."

Cyhan agreed, "Besides, if you step through that portal in a rush, you're likely to lose your head. They'll probably have it heavily guarded, and Sir Harold is sometimes a little too quick with his sword."

"What if it was Moira?" offered Irene. "Suppose she lost and had to escape. Maybe Tyrion had the Queen issue an order for her arrest."

"That might explain propping the door to the portal open, but not damaging the teleportation circles," Matthew pointed out. "Tyrion doesn't know the keys to the circles here. I'm not even sure he knows how to create a teleportation circle at all. The enchantment was devised long after his time."

"He knows," said Lynaralla. "Mordecai taught him."

Angry, Elaine stood up, nearly knocking her chair over. "Why would he do that? He hated the man! Lynn, are you sure that's true?" When the She'Har woman nodded, Elaine sat back down. "How stupid could he be?" she muttered, before adding more loudly, "Do you think Tyrion could have learned the keys here?"

"Possibly," answered Lynaralla. "He checked on Moira while she was staying here at least once. It's possible he could have looked at them during that time."

"So we can't be sure who came here," said Irene, summing things up. "Or who they were running from."

"Don't forget about Gareth Gaelyn," reminded Sir Cyhan. "He's made no secret of his stance on Moira's right to keep breathing."

Matthew shook his head. "That's true, but he's respected Father's decision this long. I don't think he'd try to do something to her on his own."

"Your father is gone," said Cyhan. "Gareth is capable of worse than that if he believes in his cause."

As though he had suddenly remembered his hunger, Matthew began eating. "Fine," he mumbled around a mouthful of soup.

"What does that mean?" asked Karen, her exasperation showing on her face.

Swallowing, he answered quickly before shoveling another spoonful in. "We'll have to go to Albamarl. Speculating will prove nothing."

Everyone else had already finished their bowls, but they were forced to wait while Matthew ate, for he refused to say more. To make matters worse, his idea of eating quickly was infuriatingly slow. So much so that Cyhan began to laugh quietly to himself, while the others argued among themselves.

Ten minutes later, Matt carefully placed his spoon on the table and raised his head to stare at them. The conversation stilled as they saw his eyes fade from silver back to blue again. "I was using my time productively," said Matthew. "We'll rest tonight. Tomorrow morning Karen will take Cyhan, Zephyr, and me with her to the capital. The portal would probably be safe, but there's a slightly higher risk taking that path."

"And me," announced Irene.

Matthew blinked to keep his eyes from going damp. *She looks so much like Mom when she's being stubborn,* he thought silently. Then he nodded. "And you, Rennie."

His sister seemed surprised by his quick acceptance, then her eyes narrowed in suspicion. "You already knew I was going to argue about it."

Matt fought to conceal a smirk. "I lost the argument. It's easier to skip the fight."

Irene stood, her mouth making a wide 'o' that combined both shock and irritation. "Oh, oh, oh! No, we're having the fight! I have as much right to go as you do. She's my sister, and Conall's there too."

Her brother bowed his head in acknowledgment. "You're right."

"But you'd prefer to keep me here, since it might be dangerous," Irene insisted. "How is that fair?"

"It isn't," he agreed.

Irene glared at him. "You should at least be honest! Why can't you say what you're feeling?"

Matthew sighed. "Obviously, you already know exactly what I'm feeling, and I already know you won't be dissuaded. Can't we leave it at that?"

Cyhan, Gram, and Alyssa were already laughing at the argument that wasn't, but Irene was incensed. She started toward her brother, until Elaine grabbed her by the shoulders. "Let me go," said Irene half-heartedly. "I want to wipe that smug look off of his face."

Sir Cyhan leaned over to Gram and told him, "Be ready to leave with them tomorrow."

Confused, Gram replied, "I thought he said you were going."

The veteran warrior only chuckled. "I was thinking of telling him you'd be a better choice, younger, faster, better armor." He glanced at Matt and winked. "But he already knows that."

They separated after that, with each attending to their own needs. Irene headed for the workshop, and when asked, her only response was, "I have something to finish. Something I started before everything went crazy."

CHAPTER 24

In a place that wasn't a place, I sat and pondered. How long I had been there, I had no idea. Time was too vague. Sometimes it passed in a blur, and at others the world would slow to a creep so sluggish that I could only stare in wonder at raindrops hanging in the air. It obeyed my will when I focused on it, but my mind was occupied by many things, too many to keep a close watch on time.

Brigid. That was the thought that plagued me now. *Was she real?* I had watched my ancestor's escape from Albamarl, and while I had been tempted to destroy the man after Harold's death, at some point I had been moved by pity.

Seeing Tyrion so close to death as he pitifully made his way down the mountain had reminded me too much of my own past. *How often was I like that, alone, friendless, and dying?*

It had only been an impulse, a thought that came to me from my ancestor's memories, Brigid, the raven-haired warrior daughter. And yet, she had appeared. *This must be a dream,* I decided.

"It is," said the stranger who appeared suddenly beside me. This time she wore a different face, but I recognized her anyway, or him. It was the self-named god of reality.

The god frowned as if sensing my thoughts. "I told you, I prefer 'author' or 'dreamer.' 'God' implies too much control."

I ignored the woman's mild rebuke, focusing instead on her previous statement. "Is this your dream or mine?"

There was a twinkle in the dreamer's eye. "They're the same."

"What does that mean?"

"I am waning, dwindling—while you are growing, but until it's over we're connected. You began as part of my dream, now I am becoming a part of yours," explained the god.

Frustrated, I asked her directly, "Was that you? Did you bring her back from the dead?"

The woman smiled, her face was aging even as she stared back at me. "Brigid is still dead, but for a while she was alive. That was your doing, not mine."

"But I didn't want that," I protested.

The dreamer laughed, growing young again, her grey hair shifting to a soft brown. "It isn't a matter of *wanting.* It's a matter of whim, not conscious decision. Right now, you may still be able to do things of your own volition, but as your power grows it will change. Your conscious desires will only last as long as you keep them in mind, but your subconscious thoughts will begin to gain permanent substance."

I thought about that for a while before responding. "So my thoughts can affect reality? I can change the dream?"

"This is still my dream," said the woman, her skin darkening until it was a deep brown. "Your conscious thoughts and whims can have some effect, but only to a certain degree. Eventually, when your power surpasses my own, you'll fall asleep and your newborn dream will rip mine to shreds."

"Sleep? I'm going to sleep?" I asked. "That's not quite how I pictured it."

"I'm slumbering," said the dreamer, "as I have for all of eternity. All of this is a dream, but dreams aren't so bad."

I wasn't buying it. "If that's true, why do you want to die? You could halt this. I've figured that out already. You could take the power from me, if you wanted it."

The author's eyes showed a hint of hidden pain, but it disappeared as quickly as I spotted it, replaced by a smiling face. "I've seen too much," answered the god. "I'm tired and I want to forget. Only you can give me that."

***

The sun dipped low in the west, making the haze from the ocean seem to catch fire. Sunsets were one of Rose's favorite things about Iverly, and she sighed as she sipped from a porcelain cup. "The tea could be better, though," she intoned dryly. "Still, it's improved since last I was here."

She had visited frequently on summer trips when she was much younger. Back then the only thing she had found to complain about was the poor quality of Iverly's tea, but Mordecai's World Road had drastically improved trade. She made a mental note to thank him if she ever saw him again. Her jaw clenched at the thought. "When," she said firmly. "I will see him again."

Pushing her dark thoughts aside, she stretched languorously, extending her legs the full length of the cushioned divan. It was positioned outside on the veranda, which made her feel absolutely decadent, and slightly guilty.

The past week had given her a chance to recover from her ordeals while traveling alone. Her aches and pains were gone, though she could still feel her ribs a little too clearly through the fabric of her gown. Not that she wanted to become plump, but near starvation had caused her wrinkles to deepen. *I'm at an age where a little extra is better than not enough,* she thought ruefully.

A bell rang inside the small house, loud enough to be heard even where Rose reclined. After a moment, a young woman with a rather sharp, almost pinched nose appeared, wearing a stiff cotton dress. It was Mary, the house maid she had hired.

"Who is it?" asked Rose.

Mary's face showed her distaste clearly. "It's him again, mistress."

Rose fought to conceal a smile. She knew who the young woman was referring to, but she asked anyway, "Him?"

"The vermin," answered Mary as though she might spit before saying the man's name.

"Let him in," ordered Rose, "and bring him out here. Be polite." *He's paying the bills after all,* she thought to herself.

A minute or so later a slender man appeared, dressed in dark leather and wearing a black velvet cap. He gave a perfunctory bow that was just barely passable. "I see you're enjoying yourself," observed the Roach.

Rose gave him a sharp look. "And I see your fashion sense is just as stunted as your height. Didn't I tell you to dress better before visiting? You look like a cross between an assassin and a dandy."

Irritation flashed across the Roach's features before disappearing. "I am what I am," he replied. "None of your new neighbors saw me approach your door in any case."

The rogue sighed. "Ahh, I never get tired of your sharp words. I suppose the old adage about roses and their thorns is true, Lady Angela."

Her eyes narrowed at the indirect threat to her identity. "Careful with your words. I may decide to rethink the nature of our arrangement." She waited until his face blanched slightly before asking, "Do you have news, or is Tom wanting me for another of his parlor games?"

The Roach recovered his composure quickly, smiling as he replied, "I believe you've poisoned that well. You won too much at the last game. I have news."

Rose waved her hand at him, encouraging him to speak.

"One of your suggestions may be bearing fruit," said the rogue, "though it's too early to say for sure."

"Which one?" asked Rose, arching one brow.

"The dressmaker. My men spoke to several over the past week and one seemed to have a possible lead, although she refused to divulge her information. We've been watching her over the last few days."

"And?"

"We had planned to follow her clients, but today a rather interesting fellow showed up at her shop. One of my men followed him but wound up being ambushed instead," explained the master thief.

Rose frowned. "I thought your men were skilled," she noted disparagingly.

"This one wasn't one of my best, but he was good," said the Roach. "He was caught, and the stranger tried to interrogate him. He tried to escape and nearly died. I don't think he gave away any information. The city guard caught wind of their scuffle before the man could finish him off. They're still hunting the fellow, but I suspect they won't find him."

Intrigued, Rose sat up straight. "How does this help us?"

The Roach held up two fingers. "Two ways. First, while the city watch probably won't find him, my people will spot him sooner or later. I have eyes on every street and corner. When he emerges from his hole, we'll know it. Second, we found this." With his other hand, he held up a small scrap of paper, then offered it to her.

Rose scanned it quickly, her eyes lighting up. "An address? You think this might be it?"

The thief nodded. "The man was carrying a bundle. We think he somehow convinced the dressmaker to give him her information and allow him to deliver her products to the customer. He likely lost it while he was fighting."

"It's not far from here," observed Rose. "We need to confirm this quickly. The man you met was almost certainly a bounty hunter or mercenary of some sort." Overtaken by nervous energy, she rose from her seat. "Let me change. We can go now."

The Roach held up one hand. "No need to rush. You'll only give yourself away if you move with too much haste. I've set men to watch the house, my *best* men. They'll take care of the bounty hunter if he's foolish enough to show himself. Once they've confirmed that two women are living there, we can make contact with them."

Frustrated, Rose found herself pacing. *That's my daughter!* she wanted to yell, but she wasn't foolish enough to give away her precise relation to Carissa in front of the Roach. He might just decide the target was valuable enough to use as a hostage against her. Only fear kept him under control. If the assassin thought he had leverage strong enough to protect him against even a presumed mage, his allegiance would become uncertain. "Very well," she said at last.

"You seem impatient," observed the rogue slyly, his eyes watching her carefully.

She forced herself to relax. "A little," she admitted. "It's almost time to eat and I'm feeling peckish."

"Shall I stay and dine with you?" asked the Roach.

The look in Rose's eyes perfectly communicated her opinion on that subject. *I'd sooner dine with a snake.* "I'd rather eat alone," she responded coolly. "Send me a report in the morning. I want regular updates until you know who is living there."

"As you wish," said the rogue, bowing once more.

"And send Roger next time," she added. "He blends in with the neighborhood better. I'd rather have you watching that address."

The Roach looked surprised. "Personally? I told you my best men were there," he replied, sounding as though the task was beneath him.

Rose showed her teeth in an expression that was nothing like a true smile. "Obviously they weren't good enough to deal with the mercenary the first time."

Chapter 25

Chad lay on top of yet another roof, looking down on the house that he thought might hold Rose and Carissa. It was in the merchants' district, a place where those with money but no title made their homes.

The house in question was a modest affair for the area, being only two stories tall, the lower floor of stone while the upper floor was wattle and daub, with a fresh coat of plaster and paint over it. The houses nearest it crowded close by, such that the alleys were narrow while the upper floors nearly touched. That had been important for his purposes, since he had done most of his traveling via rooftop. The streets were full of watchful eyes.

He had left his bundle tied to a chimney not far from his most recent violent encounter. It simply hadn't been practical hauling it around while trying to avoid being seen. Thankfully he remembered the address, since the written address had been pinned to it and he had forgotten to bring it with him.

Peeking over the edge of the roof once more, he made a new count of the men loitering in the area. Most of them had perfectly respectable reasons for being there. One was cleaning the windows of a nearby house, another was sweeping the street, and one enterprising fellow was pretending to be sleeping off his drink in an alley.

The street sweeper might have been believable, *if* he hadn't already finished the job and started over twice in the hour that Chad had been watching. The window cleaner was also polishing a perfectly clean piece of glass, while the drunk was completely out of place. The people of the merchants' district didn't put up with such conduct.

And those were the ones in plain sight. The others hid in alleys and were only visible when they occasionally moved. Chad had to thank his dragon-bond for the ease with which he spotted them, for his vision worked much better these days at showing him details hidden within shadows.

Not that he needed it. He knew his work; that was part of the reason he had waited so long. Waiting an hour gave him plenty of time to spot those who were too well hidden, since they'd had to move eventually. *Eleven,* he noted mentally.

It was the same number he had come up with fifteen minutes ago, which gave him some confidence that he hadn't missed any. He found his hand once again unconsciously reaching for his bow stave. That would've been the easiest solution. In a minute or less he could have eliminated all of them. He was still debating with himself whether he should go back and recover his bow.

Then again, killing eleven men in broad daylight would draw an awful lot of attention, he told himself. Even if he went for non-lethal shots, some of them would wind up maimed or crippled for life. *An' I don't have any particular grudge against these fellows—yet.*

Still, he couldn't think of any reasonable explanation for so many obvious rogues and thugs to be congregating near Rose's possible hideout. The only reasons he could come up with were dark indeed, and he was growing anxious at the thought that she might leave the house unaware and be ambushed.

His best hope would be to get inside without alerting the watchers, but that was nigh impossible in the current situation. Even if he could get to the building's roof, there was no window he could enter without being seen. There were men scattered around the building on every side, not to mention the one perched on the roof. He had nearly been noticed by that one when he first approached.

"This stinks," he whispered.

As things stood currently, if he tried to reach the house, he'd either have to accept being apprehended or instigate a bloodbath. For some reason Cyhan came to his mind. What would he do in this situation? "He'd probably walk up the street, casual-as-can-be, and as soon as they approached him he'd start knockin' 'em flat," Chad murmured, chuckling to himself.

He could try the same himself, but the knight seemed to have eyes in the back of his head. The ranger worried about catching a knife in his back. The dragon-bond made him stronger and faster, but it didn't make him invulnerable.

Once again, he wanted his bow, but this time the thought gave him an idea. Using the chimney to remain hidden from the spotter on the roof across the street, he slowly eased himself to a standing position. Then he worked his fingertips into the dry and crumbling mortar that held the chimney bricks in place. One particular brick was slightly loose, and he used his exceptional strength to pull it free before taking a moment to feel its heft in his hand.

He was an exceptional marksman, but that was a far different thing from being a good thrower. He couldn't be sure of hitting the man on the other roof. But he had other options. Taking aim at the next house down, he threw the brick with everything he had, hoping it would make enough noise to suit his purpose.

Luck was with him. It not only hit the other building, but also struck a shuttered window with such force that it tore through the thin wood and crashed into something within the dwelling. A few seconds later, a man's voice rose in a cry of alarm and outrage. Chad had planned to use the moment to try a running jump across the street, but this was too good to waste. Instead he crouched down and listened as the angry homeowner came out and began yelling at the people in the street.

The streetsweeper and window cleaner both claimed ignorance, and even more foolishly, were too surprised to even lie properly, saying they had seen no one throw the brick. An argument began, and as the yelling continued a whistle in the distance announced the arrival of the city watch. Chad began to grin as the chaos below grew louder. Another man had emerged from the house beneath him and was loudly taking his neighbor's side against the strangers claiming innocence.

The watchman arrived and as some of the rogues in hiding began to quietly slink away, he spotted them. More cries of alarm went up, and the guard's whistle was piercing as he called for help. More whistles sounded in the distance as other watchmen answered. Several more residents came out of their homes, and all hell broke loose when the streetsweeper lost his nerve and took off at a run.

The hidden rogues ran in one direction, the streetsweeper and window cleaner in another, and the residents and watchmen split up to chase them. A minute later and the street was empty.

There was still the other man hidden on the roof, though. Chad tensed for a moment and then began to run before launching himself across the street. He judged the distance well, but the landing was rough, and he crashed onto slate tiles and began to slide. He was only saved from a fall by grabbing onto a stovepipe as he slid past.

Dignity gone, he found the rooftop watcher staring at him in dumbfounded amazement as he got back to his feet and found his balance. The man's hand reached for the dagger at his waist.

“I wouldn’t do that if I were you, sonny,” the ranger warned. “There are several ways for this to end, but if you pull that blade the only one you’ll see ends in your death.” Leaning forward in a crouch, he slowly advanced up the sloping roof toward the stranger.

The spotter shifted, as though he might run, but Chad held up a hand. “Try to run and you’ll fall, I’ll make sure of it. Just stay still a moment. I’ll see that you get down safely.”

The rogue looked down, and one foot slipped uncertainly on the slate. “What are you going to do?” he asked nervously.

“Let’s get down first,” cautioned Chad, then he pointed to the left. “See that?” As soon as the man’s eyes turned to look, he brought his right hand up in a palm strike that rocked the rogue’s head back. He caught the fellow’s shirt as he fell and landed on top of him, adding a few more well-aimed punches to make sure the man was thoroughly unconscious. Then he rolled him over and draped him carefully over the arch of the roof so he wouldn’t slide down. “Sorry about that,” he muttered. “But it was the only way I could think to keep you quiet without killin’ you.”

After a moment’s thought, he checked the man’s pulse to make sure he hadn’t inadvertently killed him accidentally. His heart was still beating. Wasting no time, Chad eased his way down the roof on the side of the house that faced the river. Once there, he slid over the edge and held on for a second before letting go, dropping to the veranda with a minimum of noise.

A lightweight double door was there to allow entrance to the second floor, but it was locked, as he had assumed it would be at such a late hour. Reaching down into the top of his boot, the ranger pulled out a small, thin-bladed knife, then slipped it between the two door panels, easing it upward to push the latch out of the way. That accomplished, he pulled one door out an inch before pausing to listen.

It was quiet, but not quiet enough to fool his dragon-enhanced hearing. He could hear the short, quick breathing of a woman within the room. He had been spotted, and the woman was terrified. *Can’t say that I blame her,* he thought. *Best not to draw it out and frighten her even more.* With that determination, he pulled the door wide and stepped inside. “Don’t worry, I’m not a robber. I’m here to help.”

His world spun out of control as something hard and heavy slammed into the side of his head. Shadows danced and swirled in his vision as he fell to the floor, unable to catch himself with arms that had gone limp. Staring up, he saw a familiar woman holding a large brass vase. He knew her from somewhere, though he couldn't recall exactly where or when he had seen her.

The woman kept her eyes on him as she spoke to someone he couldn't see, "Carissa, go to the front door and call for help. Yell as loudly as you can. There should be a watchman somewhere in the vicinity."

"Wai..." Chad's words came out half-formed as his eyes struggled to keep the number of women standing over him to a respectable two or three. "I'm helpsher. Na bad. Promish." He desperately wished he could recall the woman's name, that would have been tremendously helpful just then. Where had he known her from?

Carissa, that's Rose's daughter, so this would be... His thoughts were somehow much clearer than his speech.

The woman standing over him wore a light gown, and though it was dark and her hair was bound up, he got the impression it would be a soft brown color if the lighting were better. "Don't move!" she warned. "If you even twitch, I'll make sure you stop moving for good."

She had called Carissa by name, so it had to be someone who knew Rose personally, probably a close servant or—*her lady-in-waiting.* "Itsh mee. Chad Grayshun. One of Roshe's frenshds," he managed to gasp in an almost intelligible voice.

The woman frowned as she stared down at him, then she yelled, "Carissa, wait! Light a lamp and bring it here!" She raised the vase threateningly when he tried to sit up. "Don't! Stay still until I can see your face."

That was when he realized it was much darker than he had thought. With his dragon-bond Chad could see the room clearly in hues of black and grey, but it must have seemed nearly pitch-black to the woman who had tried to dash his brains out. "Chad Grayson," he repeated, getting his name out clearly this time. "Rose knows me."

"Quiet," she commanded.

"Fine," he mumbled. "I'll just lay here and bleed." He relaxed and lay still, wondering if he was indeed bleeding or not. If he was, it would be messy. Scalp wounds always were. As his eyes wandered the room, things came into focus and he spotted a shadowy figure in the far corner—a man.

The figure wasn't moving, but as he stared at it, he felt as though the man was staring back, meeting his eyes, though he couldn't be certain. *Who is that?* he wondered. *Does she know he's there?* His intuition told him she didn't, but the last thing he wanted to do was alarm his captor. He might not survive another blow to the head like the last one.

Carissa appeared a moment later, carrying a lantern that seemed like the sun to his night-adjusted vision. He caught a blur of movement, but when he looked, the man in the corner was gone. He heard the shadowy figure's footsteps, though, despite how quietly the fellow had moved. A second later his eyes had adjusted, and he saw that the room was empty, except for Carissa and the other woman.

That took skill, he noted mentally. He knew the technique, though he doubted he could have pulled it off so perfectly. It required cool nerves and a perfect understanding of people's line of sight and where their eyes would be drawn. *The bastard just walked out, easy as you please.*

But he hadn't walked far, or Chad would have heard it. His steps had stopped after he left the room.

"Master Grayson!" exclaimed Carissa as she examined him in the light. "What are you doing here? Oh, Angela, what have you done to him?"

Angela sniffed. "What any self-respecting woman does when a man creeps in like a burglar." The expression on her face said she recognized him as well. She leaned down to help him up to a sitting position, and Chad felt the world spin around him once more.

"I'll damn well knock next time," spat the hunter. "I thought you might be in danger."

"There was a terrible ruckus in the street not long ago," said Angela, then after a pause, she added, "Was that you?"

Chad nodded and immediately regretted it as a wave of nausea swept over him. "There were men watching the house. I wanted to get in unseen." As he spoke, he tried to think of a way to quietly warn the two women that they were being overheard.

"Did Lady Rose send you?" asked Angela anxiously. "Is she here to get her daughter?"

"Is Mother here?" asked Carissa, her voice becoming excited.

They're saying too much. Chad held a finger up to his lips, then pointed at the door. In a whisper he replied, "Actually, I was looking for her when I came here." Then he raised his voice to a normal volume. "Her daughter has already returned to Albamarl. I'm here to let you know you don't have to act as decoys anymore." He had no idea if the listener would believe it, but it was the best he could come up with.

"That makes no sense," exclaimed Carissa, but then her eyes went wide with understanding as Chad continued to make shushing gestures while pointing at the door. In a tight voice she continued, "We didn't expect to hear that news for months."

Angela was quicker on the uptake. Hefting her vase, she started toward the door while announcing, "That's good news. I can't wait to go home."

Chad caught the hem of her dress and shook his head. With one hand he mimed someone holding a knife. He knew the man at the door was far too skilled. The most likely outcome would be fatal for Rose's maid. *He won't be caught off-guard like I was,* he mused ruefully.

Angela made more gestures, indicating she would stand to one side with the vase ready while he opened the door. Chad shook his head 'no' once more. He was in no shape to fight, especially not if the man was as competent with his steel as he suspected. It would be better for them all if the stranger was allowed to sneak of and make his report.

Slowly, he got to his feet, testing his legs. As expected, they were wobbly. His body felt as though it was made of jelly. Angela's blow had nearly cracked his skull. Even so, he slowly drew his long knives, though he hoped he wouldn't need them. With any luck the man was already quietly padding away toward…

The bedroom door swung inward, revealing a short, slim man. Chad's eyes widened as the lantern light revealed the stranger's face, then they narrowed in disgust.

"I should have known it was you," intoned the Roach, his voice cold. "I'd heard you became the Blood Count's lapdog, but I never thought you would someday follow me here."

"I'd rather eat pig shit than follow your bony ass anywhere," swore the ranger.

The light flashed on steel as a small blade appeared in the rogue's hand, but he made no move to threaten them. Instead he polished the metal on his jacket. "You sound like you missed me," responded the Roach. His eyes flicked to Chad's face. "From all the blood on your cheek I'd almost think we had already met." Then he grinned. "Then again, you're still breathing, so it's obviously our first meeting today. You've fallen far. Now even women and children can whip your sorry ass."

"At least women are interested in my ass," Chad shot back. "Only a dog would sniff yours."

"Who is this?" interrupted Angela.

Something flew across the room, too quick to see, and Chad whipped the quilt from the bed, throwing it in front of Angela. A narrow blade fell to the floor, having gotten tangled in the fabric. "Speak again and

I'll kill you first," warned the Roach with a crooked smirk. "I only need the girl. You're just baggage."

Meanwhile, Chad was regretting his sudden movement as his stomach threatened to empty its contents onto the floor. "Get out," he hissed from the side of his mouth.

"This is too much cousin." The rogue chuckled. "There's no place for her to run. I still have a few men outside. Your little game didn't uproot all of them. I think you and I will have fun here. You're already hurt, but you intend to protect the woman too? You're a fool. You were never a match for me in tight spaces, but now you've just handicapped yourself."

Angela glanced at Carissa on the other side of the room. "When I give the word, run. He can't catch us both." *And he wants you alive,* she added to herself.

Chad knew better. "Don't."

"He can't be that good," remarked Angela. "No one is."

Another flash of steel, and this time Chad was unable to react quickly enough. Angela gasped and fell back, a knife handle standing out from her right thigh. She gasped in pain but clenched her teeth rather than scream.

The Roach lifted his hand and mimed tipping his cap to her. "*He* is that good, and now you understand that you won't be running any time soon. Why don't you lie down on the bed and have a good bleed, hmm?"

From the corner of his eye, Chad saw Carissa's hand reaching slowly into her skirt and he knew Rose well enough to know why. "Let me talk to him, Carissa. I'm the one he's angry with."

"You give yourself too much credit, cousin," said the Roach.

"Let's negotiate, then," suggested the ranger.

The rogue laughed. "Why? I have all the cards. Once I kill you and the wench, I can use the girl to control that bitch sorceress. All you need to do is die."

Bitch sorceress? Chad was confused, but he didn't let it show. *Does he think Rose is a wizard? Or is he talking about someone else?* He held his hands out in a gesture of peace. "Fine. Let's say you kill me. There are other profits you could gain from what I know. There's no rush for time here. Take a few minutes, and perhaps I can offer you something in exchange for letting Angela go."

The Roach grinned. "But not the girl? Who is the woman? Is she someone special to you?"

"No," said the ranger honestly. "But it's obvious you won't bargain for Carissa. The maid means nothing to you. There's no need for her to die."

The rogue scratched his chin while Angela glared daggers at Chad's back. After a second the Roach responded, "That is uncharacteristically pragmatic of you. What do you have to offer?"

Chapter 26

Reaching down slowly, Chad patted his vest. "You know what's in here, right? Mind if I have a sip?"

The Roach sneered. "Ever the drunken sot. You never change. Still trying to drink yourself to death over that slut?"

The hunter's face twisted with sudden anger, but he held it in. "There's enough for both of us if you want."

The erstwhile assassin shook his head. "No thanks." Then he glanced at Carissa and pointed at the bed. "Go join your nanny, girl. It'll be easier to keep an eye on you there."

Chad carefully drew out his flask and unstopped it before taking a long swallow. He wondered what Cyhan would have done in his situation. It certainly wouldn't have been drinking. *He'd probably kill the bastard like it was child's play and then say some bullshit about meditation or something,* thought Chad. *Some of us have to work at it.* The liquor began to burn in his stomach, sending a warm glow through his body and causing the nausea to fade. Chad took a second pull from the flask, longer than the first. *Damn that's good.*

"What are they calling you these days?" asked the ranger. He was feeling more relaxed, and his brain was beginning to sort through the possibilities.

"The Roach."

Chad snorted. "Vermin. It suits you perfectly."

The rogue's lips tightened. "Because I'm impossible to kill."

"Is that what Mal'goroth promised you?" asked the hunter. "You know he's dead now, right?"

The Roach glared hatefully, but spoke with pride, "I was never fool enough to ask for such a thing. Mal'goroth gave me other things. Gifts I still possess, whether he's gone or not. I was god-touched, something you'd never understand."

"You were pond scum before you joined the Shaddoth Krys, Oswald, but Mal'goroth really knew what he was doing. He took a glop of slime like you and somehow polished it into a shining turd." Chad took another lazy swig from his flask, enjoying the rage on his cousin's face.

"Say that again and our talk ends," warned the former shadow-blade.

Chad nodded amiably, then spoke to Angela in a not-so-subtle aside, "In case you're wonderin', this man was once the top turd among Mal'goroth's so-called Shaddoth Krys, but that's not what pissed him off." He looked back at the assassin. "I never understood why you hated your name so much. It's perfectly fine. A lot of honorable men have had that name." Then he snickered.

"I'm done waiting. Quit stalling and tell me what you have or I'll end it now," threatened Oswald.

The hunter sighed. "Alright, have it your way. I just wanted enough time to enjoy this last drink before you kill me. I don't have anything for ya, not that I'd share if I did," admitted Chad.

The Roach laughed. "You were stalling just so you could drink more? You really are nothing but a pathetic drunk." Twin blades appeared in his hands, promising death.

Chad lifted the flask, holding up one finger, then put it to his lips, taking a final pull. He closed his eyes. *Forgive me, Joe, for I'm about to sin against your finest gift to mankind,* he prayed silently. When his eyes opened once more they revealed smoldering brown pools brimming with malice, then he puckered his lips in a mocking kiss to his adversary.

Oswald leapt forward, then jerked back with a cry of pain as Chad sprayed him in the face with McDaniel's finest. Taking the initiative, Chad followed up with a solid punch to the rogue's stomach, for Oswald had raised his blades to guard his now-blinded eyes. The Roach flew back to crash hard against the wall. Then Chad swung the flask, splashing more alcohol on the assassin.

The Roach didn't stay put for long. Still blind, the rogue jumped to his feet, seeming to charge at Chad before leaping into the air and diving completely over the hunter's head.

The hunter had expected something similar, and his long knife came up to gut the thief, only to be blocked by the assassin's own blade. Even blind, the Roach was uncannily skilled. The thief struck the floor behind Chad and rolled several feet farther before springing up again, wiping at his eyes with one sleeve. His eyes were red, but he could see again.

Chad knocked a thrown blade aside, barely, and then the two of them met, not in a clash of steel, but in a lightning dance of sweeping slashes and hasty dodges. He held his own for an eternity of seconds, but as fast as he was, he could tell that Oswald was still—somehow—

faster. Eventually, he was going to get a bellyful of steel. "What are you waiting for, girl?" yelled the hunter. "The lamp!"

The ranger launched an aggressive series of attacks to force Oswald back toward the corner while Carissa puzzled out the meaning of his words, and he took several nasty cuts on his forearms in the process.

Carissa finally understood his plan, and the lantern flew through the air. Quick as a flash, the Roach dodged to one side, but Chad had anticipated him and forced him to change direction. Even so, the rogue managed to slip away on the other side—almost. As the lantern smashed to the floor its oil spilled out, and the flaming pool set fire to the assassin's leg before spreading upward to his shirt.

The assassin shifted his stance in the blink of an eye, and ignoring the flames, he drove his right-hand blade forward and up. Chad had no chance to dodge, but Oswald's leg slid sideways as he moved, a victim of the burning oil on the floor. The rogue fell, rolling away and screaming as his hair caught fire.

Somehow, the Roach still managed to rise, beating at his face and neck, desperately trying to smother the flames. Careful to sidestep the oil, Chad moved forward, leaned away from his adversary, and then lashed out with a vicious front kick. He felt ribs snapping as his boot landed, launching Oswald through the balcony doors, across the veranda, and into the night. "Drop and roll, asshole," he muttered to himself as his cousin fell to the street below.

Stunned, Carissa stood mute for a moment, then asked, "Is that man really your cousin?"

"Not anymore," answered the hunter, then he reclaimed the bedspread from the floor and threw it over the burning oil, hoping to put out the fire. Unfortunately, his effort met with limited success. Moving over to the bed, he helped Angela up, putting her arm over his shoulder. "I hope you didn't buy this place."

"We're renting," said the maid as they hobbled toward the door. The flames were already spreading.

Carissa started to turn back. "Let me grab some clothes…"

"Forget them," said Chad. "There's not enough time, and I need you to help Angela. I need my hands free when we get to the door."

Carissa took his place, and the two women began moving together. The stairs turned out to be the worst challenge, as they forced Angela to bend her leg several times, causing her considerable pain, though she didn't complain. Chad waited for them at the bottom, shaking his flask with disappointment as he tried to get a few final drops from it.

"Is that all you're worried about?" asked Carissa. "You're bleeding." She looked at his arms, which were covered in long, shallow cuts.

The hunter smirked as he answered, "Priorities, girl." Then he held up the flask and kissed it before slipping it back into his jacket. "Rest well, my friend. You made the ultimate sacrifice to save us."

Carissa shook her head in disbelief as she and Angela continued, making their way toward the front door. "Unbelievable."

Chad moved past them to open the door, drawing his long knives once more before he stepped out. Seeing no one, he looked back at them. "That's what they all tell me, lass, but the legends are true."

"You're an unrepentant drunk," accused Angela.

He turned to the maid and gave her a wink. "I see you've heard the Saga of Chad before."

Pulling out a small knife, the maid cut two long strips of cloth from her skirt and began wrapping his forearms. "You'll be of no use to us if you pass out from loss of too much blood."

In Chad's opinion, the cuts were too shallow to be dangerous, but he appreciated the concern. His headwound was what truly handicapped him, although the alcohol had helped with that somewhat. He still felt unsteady. As Angela worked on the second arm, he was forced to drape the other over her shoulder to prevent a fall. He almost felt bad about the bloodstains he left on her dress. "Before we step out the door, find a weapon and hide it under your cloak. I doubt he was lying about there being another man or two outside."

Angela gave him a doubtful look. "You think we're in any shape to fight? I can barely walk and you're having trouble keeping your balance."

The hunter nodded. "That's as may be, but I still have my strength. If it comes to it, I'll try to grab hold of them. Once I've tangled one up, try to repeat what you did to my head."

Carissa returned from the kitchen holding a large meat-carving knife. "I'll do it. I'm in better shape than either of you."

"Your only job is to run if there's trouble," admonished Angela. "You're more important than either of us."

"Too bad," said the younger woman as she pulled a cloak from the hall tree and draped it over her shoulders.

Chad left Angela and made his way to the front door before Carissa could reach it, swaying slightly as he walked. Fortunately, he'd had a lot of experience walking across unsteady terrain. In the past that was mainly due to excessive inebriation, but the skill seemed to transfer pretty well to his current situation. He gave Carissa a lopsided smile. "I'll open the door. If there's a problem, you can try your murder-kitten act then. Just be sure not to stick me in the process."

Angela hobbled over to them, and he opened the door.

Two men waited just outside the door, and neither hesitated. Adrenaline and McDaniel's finest helped the hunter as he gutted the first man with a speed neither Angela nor Carissa expected. The stranger grabbed hold of Chad's shoulders, dying but still dangerous, while his accomplice moved around to confront Carissa.

The maid pushed forward on her one good leg, pulling her ward back as the man advanced. Both women were surprised, however, when a crossbow quarrel erupted from the man's chest, having passed almost completely through his body.

Two shadowed figures stood in the street, one a man; the other was shorter, a woman carrying the crossbow that had just fired. Carissa recognized her first, her eyes registering relief. "Mother!"

Rose handed the empty weapon to her companion, Roger, and advanced up the steps to embrace her daughter. "I've been worried sick about you."

Angela stumbled forward, attempting to bow on her one good leg. "Milady."

Rose nodded quickly, then turned to Roger, her eyes having noticed the leg wound immediately. "Help her, quickly," she commanded.

"Don't mind me," said Chad from the ground as he shoved the now-dead thief off. He was thoroughly covered in blood.

Rose stared at him in disbelief. "What are you doing here?" Her expression turned to disgust as she watched the ranger rifling through the dead man's jacket. He found a purse, which he tucked into his own coat before smiling as he found a half-full wineskin.

"That's more like it," crooned the hunter. His smile turned to disappointment as he took a sip, then threw the wineskin to the ground. "Fucking water." He stood and wiped his blade on the fallen man's coat before putting it away. "I'm here to find you, but I found these two instead."

"You're the mercenary," said Rose, "or so we thought." She glanced at the two dead men. "These two were here to guard the house—from you."

Chad sniffed. "You need better help, besides…"

"They were going to kill me and kidnap Carissa!" interrupted Angela. Then she pointed at Chad. "His cousin broke in and tried to kill us."

Rose frowned. "Who?"

"Ex-cousin," corrected Chad. "His name was Oswald, though he was going by 'The Roach.' I think he decided Carissa would be good leverage once he found out she was your daughter." He looked up and down the street. "It would probably be a good idea to put some distance between ourselves and the burning building. We're drawing a lot of attention."

A crowd was gathering, and two enterprising citizens had already begun yelling for others to assist in forming a bucket brigade. Rose and the others agreed with him and they began moving away. One brave neighbor tried to stop them, but he backed away quickly when Chad snarled and started to draw his knife.

Once they had gotten a few blocks away, Rose began sharing an abbreviated version of her story, which soon prompted a question from the hunter. "How did you get here so quickly?"

Rose's companion, Roger, lifted a hand, then Rose answered, "I didn't trust the Roach entirely, so I paid this dear man to keep an independent eye on things here for me."

Chad was surprised. "You found an independent contractor? How'd you know he wouldn't report back to the Roach?"

"I'm not a thief," said Roger quickly.

"He's a pimp," Rose announced, grimacing as she said it aloud.

Carissa moved a little farther away from the newcomer, putting her mother and Angela between them, while Chad snickered. "It sounds like there's a lot more to your story than you've shared so far, Lady Rose. Or should I call you 'Madame' Rose?"

Rose sighed. "It will make more sense after I've explained things."

The ranger shook his head. "I think I'd rather guess." He nodded at Roger. "You thought she was new talent, didn't you?" The pimp didn't reply, but Chad saw a smirk on the man's face before he looked away. The hunter began to laugh.

Scowling, Rose interrupted his mirth, "If you're quite done—where are we heading? I don't think my place is safe any longer."

"I have a rendezvous point outside of the city," Chad informed them. "Karen should be there in the morning. She'll take us back to Matthew and the others." Then he pointed at a building to the left on the street they were walking down. "But first I need to retrieve something."

After a painful climb, Chad returned a few minutes later with the bundle of dresses that Angela had commissioned for Carissa. He handed it to Rose's daughter. "This might help make up for what you lost in the fire."

Chapter 27

They spent over an hour walking through the streets, following a route that Chad thought would garner the least attention on their way to the eastern city gate. Given the hour and the unusual composition of their group, they couldn't avoid all scrutiny, however. Twice they were stopped by a night watchman, and the second time Chad thought he might have to resort to violence, until Roger stepped in and bribed the man with a few silver coins.

That probably wouldn't be good enough once the news of the fire and the disturbance Chad had created reached all the watchmen, but they only had one last obstacle to overcome, the gate itself.

He looked over his companions again and sighed. There wasn't a single good excuse he could think of for three women and a man covered in dried blood to be exiting the city at this hour. His left forearm throbbed, and he rubbed at it through the makeshift bandage.

The best choice would have been to find a place to lay low for a few days. He wasn't in any shape for a fight, and his appearance was highly suspect. Every beggar, cutpurse, slam-thief, and street urchin in the city, not to mention the city guard, would be on the lookout for their group within a matter of hours. The Roach was almost certain to have contacts within the constabulary, and even if he was dead, some of his men would likely be able to use those contacts.

If he was dead. Chad was far less certain on that count than he had acted earlier. *If that bastard didn't break his neck in the fall, I can only hope the burns keep him in bed until we get out of here,* he thought to himself.

"I only see a couple of men guarding the gate," observed Carissa quietly. "It's open. Can't we just walk through?" She paused, then added, "Actually, why isn't it closed? Isn't that the whole point of having a gate?"

"Most cities only close their gates during time of war, dear," explained Rose. "It's far too much trouble the rest of the time. There's always someone wanting through for something urgent after you close them. Besides, Iverly is far from the border and they haven't faced a serious threat in generations. Even during the war with Lothion there was never an incursion into Gododdin itself."

The ranger grunted. "Yeah, they only had to worry about their own priests cutting their throats."

Carissa looked at him with sudden interest. "You mentioned the Shaddoth Krys earlier. Was that the priesthood of Mal'goroth?"

Chad shook his head. "No, they were religious assassins, sort of like the secret police of the priesthood. Most of them were just common cutthroats, dressed up and given a special place as enforcers, but some, like my cousin, were given special gifts by Mal'goroth himself."

"Was he some sort of channeler?" asked Angela.

"Doubtful," said Chad. "Oswald never had any special abilities as far as I know. He was just quick with his hands. Besides, the channelers lost their power once Mal'goroth died. Whatever Mal'goroth did to him was some sort of physical enhancement."

"Like the Anath'Meridum, or the dragon-bond?" suggested Carissa.

The hunter shrugged. "I ain't a wizard. All I know is that the asshole is faster than I am, though I doubt he's stronger. Also, I have one major advantage he doesn't have."

"What's that?" asked Carissa.

Chad patted his belly. "I can drink that bastard under the table any day of the week."

Roger laughed suddenly, then spoke for the first time since they had met, "All you need to do now is lure him into a tavern and drink him to death."

That earned the pimp a harsh glare from Rose. "Don't encourage him," she warned. "Do you have anything constructive to add, Roger?"

Roger smiled brightly. "As you've already guessed, trying to leave by the gate is going to draw attention to you at this hour. You could spend the night at the Painted Lady and try the gate in the morning when the farmers and traders start coming and going."

"The Painted Lady," mused Carissa. "Is that an inn of some kind?"

Chad began to chuckle while Angela's cheeks colored with embarrassment, but Rose answered without hesitation, "No, dear, it's a brothel, and I'd rather not expose you to that environment."

"Mama Bear doesn't want you to see how…," began Chad before the flash of anger in Rose's eyes stopped him from ending his sentence. *…how she's been earning a living,* he finished mentally. *No, that joke* *wouldn't have gone over well at all.* Recovering, he amended his words, "…how the other half live."

Carissa was perceptive, and her eyes moved back and forth between her mother and the hunter, noting the tension in the air. Finally, she broke the silence, "What about a distraction? You said you threw a brick earlier to draw the men away from our house. Would something like that work here?"

Chad sighed. "There's nothing on the other side of that gate but open road and flat land for half a mile. We might draw them away and slip through, but they'll spot us when they return to their posts. That would only make things worse. I doubt we could outrun a detachment of guards." He nodded in the direction of Angela, whose limp had become noticeably worse over the past hour. "Then again, we can't hide in an alley, either. I suspect there are a lot of people looking for us by now. People we really don't want to meet.

"And no disrespect to you, Roger," he added, "but they know about you and Rose working together. The Painted Lady is one place they're bound to look."

Lady Rose had closed her eyes, deep in thought. When she opened them again she met the hunter's gaze and addressed him, "You're sure that Karen will be at this rendezvous point at sunrise?"

He nodded slowly, seeing something dark and serious moving in her thoughts.

"Let's speak alone for a moment," Rose suggested, walking back down the alley they were hidden in. Chad followed. When they had gained enough distance to avoid being overheard, she said in a low voice, "Are you well enough to take the guards alone?"

The ranger's eyes widened slightly in shock. He knew Lady Rose to be a pragmatic woman, but he had never expected her to consider such a dirty solution.

She saw his surprise and responded before he could say anything, "She's my daughter, Master Grayson. I would do far worse to see her safely out of here. Can you do it?"

"Those men are innocent, as much as any of us are," he replied. "Are you sure about what you're asking me to do?"

Rose arched one brow. "You've never killed innocent men before?" Her tone implied that she knew otherwise.

He grimaced, and his hand unconsciously went to find the empty flask in his jacket. He put it back down when he realized what he was doing, then he fixed Rose with a hard look. "I can do it, but remember this the next time you wonder why I drink so much. There's a reason I have trouble sleeping at night."

Lady Rose never blinked. "Make sure Carissa doesn't see the bodies." Then she walked back to the others. "We're going to hide farther away. Master Grayson has a plan to draw the guards away from their posts long enough for us to escape cleanly. We'll wait there until he tells us it's clear."

A few minutes later, Chad approached the gate, alone. He made no attempt at secrecy, pretending to be only what he was, a man seeking to leave in the dead of night. When he came abreast of the guards, one started to speak, probably to ask where he was heading, but the guard never finished his question. The second guard died almost as quickly, just as he registered that his partner was falling.

Chad swallowed, fighting back the bile that threatened to choke him as it rose up from his belly. Then he dragged the two men into the small guard post they had occupied. After a brief search, he found a blanket and used it to cover the bodies, doing his best to make it look more like a shapeless pile than what it really was, two lifeless corpses.

He went back for the others, and they said their good-byes to Roger. As they passed through the gate, Carissa noticed the blanket-covered pile. A dark stain was beginning to show through the wool. "What's that?" she asked.

Rose tugged on her daughter's hand. "Come along, dear. It's probably just some contraband the guards confiscated. We don't have much time." Chad said nothing and avoided looking at his companions.

The night wind was cold on Chad's face as they walked down the road that led away from Iverly. The sharp bite against his skin made him painfully aware of his wounds, within and without. His forearms throbbed and his heart ached. He wanted a drink, or ten, to wash away the sharp edges of sobriety.

The three women stayed close together, with Rose and Carissa walking on either side of Angela to support her. It made for slow going, but the sun was still far enough off that they should make the rendezvous with some time to spare. The hunter lagged behind, his eyes and ears open for any sign of pursuit. He dearly hoped there would be none, for he was heartsick and tired of blood.

They had covered a solid mile and left the empty fields behind. Trees now crowded the road on both sides, when the ranger's ears caught the sound of horses behind them—many horses. "Fuck me," he muttered to himself, hurrying forward to catch up to Rose and the others. "They're after us," he announced.

Rose looked at him worriedly. "How far are we from the meeting place?"

His stride increased, and he passed them. "Doesn't matter," he replied. "Sunrise is still two hours away."

"Slow down," said Rose. "We can't keep up. Should we get off the road?"

"Do whatever you like," said Chad over his shoulder. "I'm going on ahead."

"You're leaving us?" asked Carissa, shock in her voice. "Aren't you here to help?"

Anger welled up in Chad's heart. After everything, they always assumed the worst. He was struck by the urge to swear at the girl, but instead he merely answered harshly, "I've done more than enough. When they catch up to you, tell them it was all me. They'll still arrest you, but you won't be harmed." He broke into a ground-eating jog.

"At least take Carissa with you!" Rose yelled, but the hunter paid her no heed. Moments later his form was lost in the darkness. "Bastard," she swore. Then she turned to Angela and her daughter. "We'll get off the road. We might have a chance if we hide in the trees."

They nodded and made their way to verge of the road, but the sound of loud hoofbeats came to their ears before they reached the trees. A shout went up behind them, "I see them!"

Seconds later they were surrounded by horses and men. Rose counted ten city guards and another man dressed in dark leathers who seemed to be some sort of scout. "That's them," announced the guide. "There was a man with them as well. He's probably somewhere close by."

"Please, sirs," pleaded Rose, adopting a submissive tone, "we've done nothing wrong. My friend is injured."

The guardsman in charge dismounted and directed them back toward the road with his sword. "Killing honest men at their duty isn't a crime? Is that what you're saying?" He sounded furious.

Carissa was bewildered. "What?"

But Rose lowered her head. "We are all women. Do you truly think we could have fought the guards and won?"

The man threatened her at sword point, herding them away from the trees. "Whether it was you or whether you're accomplices, I'll do my best to see that you all hang for it."

"Hurry up!" one of the men shouted, kicking at Angela's back with a booted foot, causing her to stumble and fall.

Carissa lost her temper and turned on the trooper. "Stop it! She's wounded, weren't you listening?" Her features were lit with righteous fury, though they changed as she saw the man lift his sword to strike her down.

"No!" screamed Rose, though in her heart she knew it was too late.

The sword seemed to rise in slow motion, but it never came down. It stopped in midair, and a strange gurgling noise rose from the soldier as he dropped his weapon and clutched at his throat. The fletchings of an arrow stood out in the lantern light.

The guard captain was the first to react. "Assas—!" He failed to finish the warning as a second arrow pierced his padded gambeson, directly over his heart. Chaos ensued as the horsemen turned their mounts, trying to spot the archer, but their efforts were too slow; two more were down before they had even determined the direction the arrows were coming from.

Horses screamed in equine terror as their riders fell, and several of the troopers spurred their mounts, some toward the source of the arrows and others back toward the city. Carissa watched the surreal slaughter with wide eyes, until Rose slammed into her, knocking her down and moving to cover her daughter with her own body.

One of the riders, a young man who had frozen in fear at the sudden attack, flew from his saddle as a heavy, yard-long war arrow slammed into his chest with such force that it emerged from his back. He fell less than five feet from where Carissa lay, and she watched him gasp unsuccessfully for air while he died.

Less than a minute after it had begun, it was over, and not a single rider had escaped. In the silence that followed, Carissa pushed her mother away and sat up, quiet tears upon her cheeks. Neither Rose nor Angela said a word as they regained their feet. There were no words that were adequate.

Eventually the quiet was broken as Chad Grayson returned, walking into the light of a fallen lantern, leading one of the soldiers' horses behind him. A massive warbow was in his right hand. The expression on his face was harsh and unforgiving, and Carissa's breath caught at the sight of him. Rather than relief, she felt fear in the presence of a man she had known for most of her childhood.

"It would have been nice if one of you fools had thought to catch some of their horses," intoned the ranger, his voice cold and angry.

Lady Rose started to apologize, "Master Grayson, forgive me. I misunderstood you when you…"

"Did exactly what you wanted," he said cruelly, cutting her off. "But that's what I am, isn't it? A tool for murder. Are you satisfied with my work? This is what happens when you kill people for convenience. It's just like lyin'. You kill one, then you have to kill ten more. If we stay here long enough, I'll wind up killin' the whole godsdamned city for you."

Rose was not one to be silent. She had lived her life exercising her authority, and her intellect was such that she rarely had cause to yield ground to anyone, but she closed her mouth then. While Chad and Carissa helped Angela onto the horse's back, she began searching the nearest bodies. By the time the time the maid was ready to ride, she had found what she was looking for, and she handed a heavy wineskin to the hunter.

He stared at her with narrow eyes. "Is this an apology?"

Rose shook her head, not quite meeting his gaze. "Would it matter?"

"No," he answered, sparing no time to open the skin and take a long swallow. Then he gestured to one of the dead men. "Maybe ask him. He might give you a different answer."

The rest of their journey to the rendezvous was uneventful, and they made better time now that Angela no longer had to walk on her injured leg. The hunter said nothing for the rest of the night, and though it took them less than half an hour to cover the last mile, he had drained the wineskin before they arrived.

Karen appeared as the sun crested the horizon, and she immediately felt the tension in the air. "You found them!" she said excitedly before changing her tone and adding worriedly, "What happened?"

"We'll explain later," said Rose as she, Carissa, and Angela gathered around the mage, more than ready to leave. Chad remained apart.

"Aren't you coming with us?" Karen asked the hunter, curious at his strange behavior.

"I'm done with this shit," said the hunter. Turning his back, he began walking down the road to the east.

"I'll come back after I take them!" Karen told him. "I can take you wherever it is you need to go."

Chad stopped in his tracks, considering. "Washbrook."

CHAPTER 28

Matthew, Gram, Karen, and Irene stood beside Zephyr, dwarfed by the black-scaled dragon's bulk. Karen ran her hand down the dragon's leg, marveling again at the cool, hard feel of his scales. Her eyes focused on Matthew's when he tapped her shoulder, breaking her train of thought.

"You're sure you can get us all in one trip?" he asked.

Karen nodded, she had returned with Lady Rose and Carissa that morning, but Matthew had insisted on making the trip to the capital. None of them had protested since Rose, Carissa, and Angela had obviously needed a good rest before facing the onslaught of questions they had for them.

"Why are we bringing Zephyr and not Grace?" asked Gram.

"This should be a peaceful trip," answered Matthew. "I didn't want to tax Karen by forcing her to bring a large entourage. If anything does go wrong, I can draw power from Zephyr, and he's large enough to carry the three of us if we need to travel for any reason."

"Grace is large enough as well," remarked Gram.

"But I can't draw aythar from her," returned Matt, "while you fight just as well with or without your dragon."

Karen frowned at him. "You *just* said this would be a peaceful trip. Are you keeping things to yourself again?"

"*Should be*," corrected Matthew. "Nothing is certain, even for me."

Karen twisted a finger in her dark curls, appearing uncertain. "Perhaps I should stay with you…"

"I want to keep our group small to simplify things," countered Matthew. "If the others need to travel quickly, you'll be there for them. We can return via a temporary circle since I put a new one down at the house." He gave her one of his rare smiles. "Don't worry, nothing will happen, and if it does Gram will be there."

"And me," put in Irene, taking Karen's hand in her own. "I'll be sure to keep him safe for you."

Karen grinned. "I feel better now. I don't trust these two on their own. Boys will be boys."

Gram and Matthew glanced at each other, rolling their eyes. A moment later they all joined hands, and Karen teleported the entire group, depositing them at the main gate that led into Albamarl from the direction of the World Road. After a few quick good-byes, she left, and they prepared to enter the city.

A voice entered their minds before they could start moving. *Matthew? Irene? Is that you?* It was Cassandra, Moira's dragon, her mental voice laced with worry.

Yes, it's us, replied Irene, broadcasting her thoughts so the others could hear her response. *Where are you? Is Moira with you?*

No, came the dragon's answer. *I'm in the woods, near the river. She asked me to wait here, but I haven't heard from her in days.*

After a short back and forth conversation, Matthew sent Zephyr to join Cassandra while he and the others entered the city. The gates were open, and a healthy amount of traffic flowed in and out as merchants and farmers carried goods between the capital and the World Road. By all appearances everything was normal, with no sign of war or unrest. The guards watching the city gate barely spared them a glance as they walked through.

Irene put a hand on Matthew's arm when they came to the first cross street. "Are you sure this is a good idea? We have no idea what's happened here."

"From what I've seen, the chance of physical danger is low," began Matthew. "But I know things didn't go as I had planned, or we'd have met Moira at home." He paused, a pensive look on his features.

Irene could tell he was holding something back. "You're worried about something. I can see that. Be honest with me."

Matt looked at Gram, who shrugged, then back at his sister. "There's bad news waiting for us. I haven't gone deep enough to know what it might be, and the near future has grown more chaotic, so I'm not sure if it would help anyway."

Gram growled faintly. "That's pretty vague, Matt."

He nodded. "I know. That's why I wanted the two of you here with me, rather than any of the others."

"You didn't want me here at all," reminded Irene.

"That's not entirely true," replied Matthew. "You're my sister, and I'd rather you never have to face the things we've seen over the past few months, but deep down, I need your strength, Rennie. I have a feeling that whatever we learn is going to test my resolve. I think I'm going to need your support."

Irene frowned. "Now you're really starting to worry me."

"Whatever happened is my fault, Rennie," said Matthew at last.

"Now it makes sense," observed Gram. "You're afraid of what we'll find, and you'd rather it be Irene than Karen who finds out what happened first."

Matthew didn't respond, but after a moment Irene took both their hands in hers. "Let's get this over then. We won't learn anything standing in the street."

Gram pulled his hand away after only a second. "I need my hands free—just in case."

They had gone only two blocks before a pair of uniformed figures met them, Royal Guards, one of whom was human while the other was one of Tyrion's special krytek. Matt and Irene had both sensed their approach, but the look of sadness and recognition in the krytek's face seemed out of place. "Matthew and Irene Illeniel, Sir Gram." It nodded at each of them. "The Queen has given orders for you to be escorted to her."

"Were they expecting us?" whispered Irene.

Gram nodded. "It seems like it."

Matthew said nothing, but a deepening sense of dread filled his stomach. The guards escorted them to the palace, and they couldn't help but notice the looks of fear and hatred directed toward their escort when they passed people on the street. Things improved once they entered the palace, though. A number of the soldiers and palace guards there recognized Sir Gram, and there was no shortage of them calling out greetings to him as they passed.

Inside the halls of the palace itself, a few of the higher-ranking servants recognized Matthew and Irene, offering quick bows of respect, but no one addressed them. The two siblings did recognize a familiar presence as they walked, however. "She's here," said Irene quietly, elbowing her brother.

Matthew nodded solemnly. "I noticed." Moira's distinctive aythar was present a few hundred feet away, in a separate but unwarded portion of the palace.

"Why isn't she coming to meet us then?" wondered Irene.

The two guards leading them stopped, and there was a sudden movement of aythar as the krytek raised a hand toward the human guard beside him. The man's eyes went blank and he stared off into space.

Then the krytek turned to them. "She'll find you later. She hasn't revealed her presence, so don't mention her when you see the Queen." The krytek turned back and the human guard's eyes cleared, and they resumed their former pace.

"That was…" began Irene, but Matthew shook his head before raising a finger to his lips. Gram nodded his understanding, and the three of them followed their escort without saying anything else.

A few minutes later they were brought into a small sitting room furnished with cushioned chairs, and their escort left. A serving girl appeared soon after, bringing a tray laden with wine and bread, which she left for them. Irene looked at the others. "I wonder if Conall is here. Hopefully we'll get to see him before we leave."

Matthew blinked, then reached for his wine. There was a hint of nervousness in the motion that Gram didn't miss. "I hope so too, Rennie," said the young knight.

A quarter of an hour later, the door opened once more and Ariadne passed through it. Two knights in full armor stood behind her, wearing the enchanted plate that marked them as two of the four surviving Knights of Stone, though they were members of the Order of the Thorn now, Sir Egan and Sir Thomas. They started to follow her in, but the Queen stopped them with a gesture. "Wait outside, please."

Sir Thomas stepped back immediately, but Sir Egan was more stubborn. "Your Majesty, we agreed that your safety—"

"Is not a matter of concern at this time, Sir Egan. I have pardoned Mordecai and his heirs. These are our allies now," interrupted Ariadne.

"You haven't even spoken with them yet. How do you know they intend to return meekly to the fold?" argued Egan, his face growing stern.

They had already taken to their feet at the Queen's arrival, and Gram moved forward, bowing first to Ariadne and then following up with a respectful nod to the senior knight. "Sir Egan, my allegiance to the Queen never left my heart, but as much as I respect your skill at arms, if I desired to do her harm you could not stop me, much less my companions. You need not worry on our account." Though his words were bold, there was no trace of boasting in his voice; it was a plain statement of fact.

Egan's face turned red at the affront. "Arrogant pup! You dare—"

The Queen's voice rang out, loud and sharp, "Outside, Egan! I'll not order you again." The angry knight trembled with rage for a moment before gaining control of himself and retreating from the doorway.

Once the door closed, Ariadne turned back to them. "There's a lot to be said and no good order for it, so let me clear my chest first." After observing their nods of acceptance, she went on, "I owe an apology to you, Matthew, and to your family as well. I doubted your father, but even when I did, I didn't believe his actions to be wrong. At the end of the trial I knew he was innocent, but I was too cowardly to overturn the judge's ruling. I feared more for the kingdom than for doing what was right. Now that I've pardoned him, I've seen that my fear was pointless, none of the turmoil I feared has come to pass. I hurt your family for naught."

"You couldn't have known that," offered Matt graciously. "The good of the kingdom should come before the needs of an individual or a single family." Irene gave him a sidelong glance of surprise before turning her gaze back to the Queen and giving a single nod of agreement.

"As Queen, I cannot apologize for my past decision in public, or show weakness by explaining my pardon, but I felt I should at least tell you this in private," finished Ariadne.

Gram edged forward on his seat. "What about his title?"

Matthew responded first, "Leave it as is. Father is in no state to hold it any longer, and I don't want it. Conall will serve better as Count di'Cameron."

Ariadne pursed her lips and took a seat across from them, folding her hands in her lap. "That's the other matter I need to tell you." She looked from Irene to Matthew and back again. "Your brother has been gravely injured."

Irene stared at her in shock for a second before glancing at Matthew. "This is what you were worried about, wasn't it?" she asked, her tone bearing suppressed anger. Matthew could only clench his eyes shut and lower his head.

Ariadne hurried to ease their fears. "He's still alive, and I have every hope he will recover. The wound was small, but his stomach was pierced. Lord Gaelyn gave him up for dead, but Elise Thornbear pressed me to allow her to treat him, and his fever has begun to subside. She thinks he may soon be out of danger."

Matthew expelled the breath he had been unconsciously holding with a loud sigh, and some of the weight bearing down on him lifted. "Tell us what happened, please," he entreated. A soft whisper sounded in his mind, surprising him, *Come find me after you see the Queen—alone.* He recognized the feel of the foreign thoughts immediately. It was Moira.

Ariadne explained Tyrion's betrayal to them, beginning with the krytek putting most of the palace guard and staff to sleep before his attack on her and Conall in the palace garden, and Matthew was interested to note that she made no mention of Moira's presence at any point. As he listened, he organized his thoughts into a message for his sister. *How are you reaching me? We're inside a privacy ward.* He was careful not to broadcast his message, though, assuming Moira would pick it from the surface of his mind.

Static wards are easier to peer through than even the sloppiest of personal shields, came Moira's thought in answer. She followed that message with a mental image of the palace layout, highlighting the place she would be waiting for him.

I'll be there soon, he thought silently to himself.

As his attention returned to the conversation at hand, Ariadne was winding down, finishing with a description of Tyrion's desperate escape through the portal that led from her bedchamber to their family home. He noticed that Irene's eyes were red and welling with tears, and she was watching him with a combination of sorrow and curiosity. Taking that as a sign he had missed something important, he went through his memory to replay the conversation, listening to the latter part of Ariadne's story that had reached his ears while he was distracted.

Harold was dead. The realization struck him like a hammer blow to the heart. The knowledge hurt, and he had to force himself to take a deep breath as his chest tightened. Glancing to his left, he saw that Gram's face was stern, almost statue-like in its stillness. His friend was in shock.

That made perfect sense, of course. Harold had been a recurring figure during their shared childhood, and Gram had been even closer to the man. Irene was showing her emotions more visibly, which was also understandable. She and Gram's sister, Carissa, had harbored crushes on the handsome young knight when they were children.

And he's dead because of me, thought Matthew. *Because of what I told Moira to do.* His heart hurt, but he felt no urge to cry, just a dull pain that somehow combined guilt and numbness. An even bigger question haunted him. Was that the news his premonition had warned him of? Conall wounded, Harold dead—his intuition told him it was something worse than just those two things.

"Don't you have any questions, Matt?" asked Irene, her voice bringing him back to the present while her eyes studied him with suspicion.

"No," he blurted out, unable to formulate a better reply. "It's a bit much to process. I'm sorry. It's just—Harold—I don't know what to think." After a moment he followed his words with a mental broadcast for Irene, *Moira wants me to meet her. She's hiding close by.*

Irene's gaze softened with understanding. Looking at Ariadne she said, "I'd like to visit Conall now, if it's alright."

The Queen stood. "Of course. I'll go with you. Elise will be happy to see all of you as well, especially you, Gram."

"I need some time alone," said Matthew. "I need to think, to come to terms with what we've just learned."

Gram gave him an odd look, but Irene stepped in to save him. "I understand." She nodded at Gram. "We'll go ahead. Come join us when you're ready."

Gram was looking back and forth between Irene and her brother, feeling certain he had missed something, but he made no objection. The two of them and Ariadne left, leaving Matthew to ponder the news.

Matt didn't get up immediately. He waited a few minutes to be certain they had gone beyond sight of the door before opening it to see if there was anyone in the hall. Sir Thomas and Sir Egan were gone, presumably to escort the Queen and the others, but another guard was posted there. He said nothing to the man as he left.

CHAPTER 29

The room Matthew found Moira in was small and modest, but well appointed. It was close to some of the other servants' quarters, but it was obvious that this was the dwelling of but a single person, while the rooms that most of the servants stayed in held at least several people.

Moira waited for him within, wearing a nondescript brown dress that matched that of the laundresses and scullery maids, probably part of a deliberate habit to avoid undue notice. At first glance she looked well, but her face was pale and somber. Matthew's first look communicated his concern for her, but his words avoided the topic, "Whose room is this?"

"Benchley's," she replied, knowing he would recognize the name. Benchley was a long-time retainer of the Lancaster family and currently served as the royal chamberlain. A man of dry wit and unshakeable loyalty, Benchley couldn't have been convinced to keep her secret, Matthew was certain. "No one remembers me," offered Moira, "unless I allow it. Plus, he's too busy to be here often, so I leave before he returns."

Matt understood immediately. His sister was minimizing her contact to avoid having to alter too many people's memories. That explained both her choice of clothing as well as the room she borrowed. "Why didn't you return home?" he asked. "I expected you would do that and then return after the announcement of the pardon, instead of going into hiding."

Actually, it hadn't been his expectation, it had been the most probable outcome. Tyrion's escape and Moira's failure to return home meant one of the less favorable possibilities had occurred, though he didn't know which.

She looked away, as though shy, or perhaps ashamed. "That was the original plan, but after everything that happened, I couldn't bring myself to go back. I needed time to myself."

Matthew wasn't the best at reading people, but even he could tell something was wrong, and he knew his sister better than anyone else. She seemed less confident, less dark, and more uncertain than he remembered, almost like a younger version of herself. A grim chill began to seep into his heart, a creeping fear he was afraid to look at directly.

His sister felt the shift within him immediately, reading his emotions as easily as some might read a book. When she lifted her eyes to meet his again, they were brimming with unshed tears. "I don't know what to do. How can I face them?"

"Myra," he said simply, using her name as a declaration of fact. The spell-twin that occupied Moira's body nodded in confirmation, her cheeks now stained by watery tracks.

Matthew felt himself standing on the edge of a limitless black abyss, one that threatened to swallow his reason and devour his heart. Unable to prevent it, he heard his mouth say the words, "Moira's dead." The words were followed by a silent sentence pronounced by his conscience, *and I'm the one that sent her to die.*

Myra shook her head in denial. "No! It wasn't your fault. It was mine. I shouldn't have let her do it. It was my job."

"Get out of my head!" screamed Matthew, losing control of himself for the first time he could ever remember. Cracks formed in the stone walls as his power unconsciously reinforced the power of his voice. He lost all sense of himself for a few seconds as he squeezed his eyes shut and his emotions ran riot, but in the silence after his shout he heard—as well as felt—Myra softly crying. She sat on the end of Benchley's bed, her legs drawn up and her arms around her knees, a pitiful sight as her shoulders shuddered.

A wave of guilt washed over him, piling onto the considerable weight he felt already. He didn't know what to do, and while he felt bad about lashing out, he didn't feel capable of comforting another person either. Reestablishing control over his emotions, he pushed them away and spoke in a neutral tone, hiding his pain. "What else do you have to tell me?"

Myra looked up at him, her face dreadful. "I saw Father. He appeared after it happened."

Matt wasn't surprised. It fit into a pattern, which appealed to his need for order. His father had last appeared when he himself had nearly died, so it made sense he would show up at the time of Moira's passing. *He should have been there sooner,* wished Matthew. "Describe it to me. Did he tell you anything?"

"He was frightening," began Myra. "A figure of black fire, radiating power so intense it almost overwhelmed me even though he never came close to me." She stopped then, reluctant to repeat the message he had given her.

Matthew's inner turmoil edged closer to anger as he ground out his question again, "Did he tell you anything?"

Myra's hair covered her face. "I was thinking about following her, letting myself die. He didn't say much, only a 'no' followed by stating that he didn't want to lose another daughter. That's why I waited for you."

His anger faded, replaced by an empty despair. "You were wise to listen to him."

She shook her head. "I didn't. I couldn't decide, not on my own. I haven't taken her aystrylin. I'm still fading; my strength dwindles even faster from maintaining her body. Now that I've seen you, I think it's probably best for me to let go."

Matthew was torn between the desire to strike her and the urge to hug her, but he knew his emotions weren't rational, and they didn't necessarily even reflect how he felt about Myra. They were born in large part from his own inner guilt. So he did neither. Instead he commanded her, "Get up. Look me in the eye."

She did, and he continued, "None of this was your fault, and your dying serves no purpose. I need allies far more than I need another dead body. Take her aystrylin, assume her life. That's what she would have wanted, and it's obviously what Dad wants as well."

"I—"

"Now, Myra. I don't have the strength to waste arguing with you. I'm hurting as much as you are," he added.

She closed her eyes, and he felt *something* happen within her, though it was too subtle for him to pinpoint what exactly she had done. When she opened them again, she merely nodded, and he knew it had been accomplished. Staring at her, he had a dark thought, *If we didn't tell anyone they'd never know Moira was gone.* It would be simple, and he'd never have to face Irene or Conall's judgment for what had happened to their sister.

"I could do that, if you want," said Myra, once again reading his thoughts.

He didn't shout this time. Instead he met her gaze, seeing the doubt in her eyes, the need for acceptance. Myra felt a guilt as great as his own, misplaced though it was. She was desperate for anything that might validate her right to continue existing. Rising above the anger, the guilt, and his need to hurt someone, anyone, made his next words some of the most difficult he had ever said. "No. I need a sister, not a slave to guilt. Go home and rest. I'll tell the others. If I don't, they'll blame me even more later, and possibly you as well for hiding it."

She looked at him for a few long seconds, and he knew she wanted to hug him, but she could also tell he wouldn't react well to such an overture. Pursing her lips, she stood and went to the door. Before she left she said only one thing, "Don't blame yourself too much. You're not the only one who made these choices. We've both made mistakes." Then she was gone.

Grateful to be alone, Matthew sat on the bed and cradled his head in his hands. His grief was a tangible thing, so thick he felt he could almost cut it with a knife, and at last he could face it without someone watching his every thought. He and Moira hadn't gotten along much of the time, for they had been polar opposites in most regards, but she had been his twin, even though they weren't truly related by blood. He had grown up with her as a constant presence, a huge part of the world that he defined himself within. Now that she was gone, he felt lost.

He allowed himself ten minutes, and then he went to find Irene and Gram.

***

Conall was in a lavishly appointed guestroom rather than the one he had been occupying while in the capital. It was a room ordinarily reserved for visiting heads of state, and its present use showed clearly how much the Queen valued her wounded vassal. The young count was awake and sitting up, his face drawn and pale as he glanced up at Matthew's entry.

Matt took note of the others in the room, the Queen and Irene, who stood by the bed, and Elise Thornbear, who sat on a large couch, having evidently just awoken from a well-deserved nap. Gram sat beside his grandmother, talking quietly with her, but all eyes turned to Matthew as he came into the room.

"Feel any better?" asked Irene, a hidden question in her eyes.

"Not really," admitted Matthew as he studied his brother. "Though I'm glad to see our brother recovering." He went to stand beside his sister. "Conall, what happened to your face?"

Conall gave him a confused look. "Huh?"

Matthew went on, "Rennie, you haven't shown him a mirror, have you?"

Irene scowled back. "What are you talking about?"

"Nothing happened to my face," insisted Conall, lifting a hand to touch his cheek. "Did it?"

Matt's brows went up as though with a sudden revelation. "You haven't told him?" he asked Irene, surprised. "I shouldn't have said anything. I'm sure it will be fine as long as we don't let him near any mirrors."

Gram chuckled, but Irene looked reassuringly at her brother. "Don't listen to him, Conall. Nothing happened to your face."

Matthew frowned, staring intently at Conall. "Are you sure? I don't remember him being quite this ugly before." Then he glanced around. "Maybe it's just the lighting."

Gram winked at him. "Perhaps I should open the curtains?"

"No, that would only make it worse," said Matthew in a deadpan reply.

"That's enough, boys," cautioned Elise. "I won't have you bullying my patient."

Conall growled for a second, then let out a weak laugh. "I must not be dying, or you wouldn't be picking on me again."

Ariadne leaned forward, kissing Conall's forehead. "He's just jealous since you're obviously the handsomer between the two of you." Then she straightened. "I should go and let you catch up. I have some matters to attend to."

"But we haven't talked about what happened yet," put in Conall. "I've been out for so long. What happened after Tyrion and M—" He was interrupted as Matthew tripped and fell against the nightstand, spilling a pitcher of water onto him. "Ack! What! Why are you so clumsy?" cried Conall, shocked by the cold.

Irene glared at Matthew, certain it had been no accident, while Elise hurried to Conall's side with a towel to dry him off. Ariadne didn't wait, and she was gone a moment later.

"Gram, go and fetch me some more towels," ordered Elise.

As everyone moved around, attempting to undo the chaos he had created, Matthew leaned close to his brother's ear. "Say nothing about Moira. She was never here. Understand?"

Conall was full of questions, but he met Matt's eyes and gave a tiny nod of agreement. Once things settled down again the conversation turned to matters of the past few months and Irene took up the bulk of the task of relaying what had happened to Conall.

Their brother seemed confused about the matter of the Queen's pardon for their father, but after glancing at Matthew once more he held his tongue.

"We can talk more after you come home," suggested Matthew. "Will that be possible soon?" he asked, addressing his question to Elise.

"My place is here," said Conall somewhat stubbornly.

"You *are* the Count di' Cameron now," pointed out Irene. "You can't ignore that forever. You should come home while you get your strength back. None of us will stop you from returning after that."

Elise broke in, "Now that his fever seems to have broken, I think he could return in a day or two."

Agitated, Conall struggled to sit up. "But the Queen—"

"I'll stay with her," volunteered Irene. "Her Majesty will be as safe as houses."

Conall surrendered, and with that settled Matthew stood and motioned to Gram. "We should head back. We can return in a couple of days and collect him as well as your grandmother."

Irene followed them into the hall, catching Matthew's sleeve. "What did she say?"

Matt stopped. "It wasn't good."

She motioned for him to continue.

"Rennie, I promise I'll tell you everything, but not here, not now," said Matthew, his countenance turning somber.

"Why not?"

He took a deep breath, framing his thoughts. "It's too important to say here. You'll be in the palace for a few days, and this is something we need to talk about, as a family. Once you bring Conall back, I'll tell everyone then. You won't be able to focus on our brother if I blurt it out now."

A figure approached them from the far end of the hall, Sir Egan. He stopped a few feet from them, but his attention was firmly on Gram. "I haven't forgotten your insult, Sir Gram," he announced, steel in his words.

Gram merely raised a brow, but Matthew spoke first, "Dueling has been outlawed, Sir Egan. I hope you remember that."

Gram put a hand on his shoulder. "It's alright, Matt. Sir Egan isn't as bloodthirsty as that. What did you have in mind, Egan?"

The senior knight answered immediately, "An apology would suffice, if it were sincere."

Straightening, Gram replied seriously, "I won't apologize for the truth. I may have sounded like a braggart to your ears, but my words were simple honesty."

"Then we should test that honesty," suggested Egan, a fierce light in his eyes.

"What did you have in mind?" asked Gram.

"Training swords and arming jackets," said Egan.

Matt groaned, but the two men were already in agreement. He glanced toward Irene for support but she merely shrugged.

Chapter 30

The training yard within the palace was just off the front courtyard. It was a smaller yard, enclosed by stone walls, and unlike other areas grass was not even encouraged to grow there. It would have been pointless, since the constant movement of men made any plant's dream of growing a hopeless endeavor.

There were pells set along the length of one wall, where new soldiers practiced their swings, but no one stood at them now. All eyes were on Sir Egan and Sir Gram. The news of their impending match had raced ahead of them, and by the time they arrived the barracks had emptied out and every guard, trainee, or soldier that wasn't stuck at a post had come to watch their fight.

Sir Thomas stood to one side, surrounded by a knot of men hastily placing bets. When they entered, he looked up at Gram and offered him a cheerful wink. Sir Egan marched straight over to him and began exchanging angry words with his fellow knight.

"You're the one who decided to create a spectacle of yourself," said Sir Thomas, an easy smile on his face. "I'm just making use of the opportunity to raise morale. The men could use a little entertainment."

"And enrich yourself," growled Egan. "Gambling is not among the knightly virtues. These men are supposed to look up to us."

Sir Thomas shrugged. "Last time I checked, having a stick up your ass wasn't a virtue either."

Sir Egan glared at him for a second, biting back another angry comment. Then his curiosity got the better of him. "What are the odds you're taking?"

"Four to one that you'll win," said Thomas.

Egan smirked. "You won't make much with odds like that."

"Oh, I'll make a killing. I bet on Gram," replied Thomas dryly. "Most of the men here don't know how good he is."

"You always were a fool," Egan retorted. "The boy has potential, but he's no Dorian Thornbear."

"And you obviously weren't paying attention when we went to Cantley. Would you care to place a bet on yourself?"

"Twenty gold marks," said Egan immediately. "And don't come crying to me when you can't meet your taxes next year."

Gram waited patiently through the exchange, and after it was over he and Sir Egan each selected one of the training swords from a long rack. There was a wide variety of sizes to choose from, and while some were made of wood, many of the practice swords used by the experienced guardsmen were normal swords that simply hadn't been given an edge. By mutual agreement both men picked steel weapons.

Gram's choice was a short falchion, a slicing weapon preferred against unarmored opponents, though since there was no edge it hardly mattered. Egan returned with a long one-handed arming sword, and he looked askance at Gram's choice.

"Trying to handicap yourself? Pick something else. I don't want you saying it wasn't a fair match," said Sir Egan gruffly.

Gram made a few practice swings, checking the heft and balance. The falchion was one of the best choices for real combat that didn't involve metal armor, since in times of war they were sharpened to a fine edge that could cut through even tough linen padding, but he had picked it today because its shorter length and lighter weight would make it easier to avoid breaking bones. Being struck edge-on by a blunted sword was enough to sometimes crack a bone, even through a heavy, padded gambeson, but when the weapon was wielded by someone with a dragon-bond—it was hard *not* to cause a serious injury. He eyed the longer blade in Egan's hand before answering, "This will do."

He considered refusing the arming jacket, but that would only further insult Egan, and that was the last thing he wanted. After he shrugged on the thick padded garment one of the pages helped lace up the sides, and then Gram walked onto the field where Sir Egan waited for him.

Sir Egan limbered his arm with a few practice swings. "Any rules you'd like before we start?"

"Makes no difference to me," responded Gram, "but I intend to avoid doing anything to you that might put you out of the Queen's service for more than a day or two."

Sir Egan nodded. "No rules then, other than we don't try to kill each other. Since you aren't in the Queen's service, I'll make no promises about not putting you in a bed for a month or two."

Sir Thomas strode out to stand between them, a green handkerchief in one hand and large mug of beer in the other. "I've witnessed your pledges and will require you to stand by them. When the cloth hits the ground, you are to begin." He took a long swallow from his mug, and then tossed the cloth in the air as he walked away. "The loser buys me another."

Gram relaxed as the linen fluttered to the ground, letting his mind go blank after one final mental caution to himself, *Make it last a while.* Then he began to walk forward, his stride seeming almost casual.

Sir Egan was one of the best swordsmen in Lothion, possibly *the* best, now that Harold was gone. Sir Cyhan was the exception to that rule of course, though he wasn't truly a swordsman, being more of a lethal jack of all trades. As Gram came into range, Egan's body uncoiled like a spring, and the sword in his hand whipped across in a low swing toward Gram's left thigh.

The strike was blindingly fast, to a degree that most opponents would have failed to react to it, much less block or dodge aside, but the swing was also a trick. Egan expected Gram to be fast enough to block, and at the last possible moment the blade shifted direction, angling upward.

Gram's falchion met the blade, batting it away before returning to threaten Egan on the backswing, a move that felt almost half-hearted to Gram.

What followed was a baffling display of rapid-fire strokes and counterstrokes that left the spectators goggling in amazement. Many of them were unable to follow the fight at all, and only the accomplished swordsmen were able to read the fight well enough to understand what was happening. To Gram, it felt like an absurd play, but he restrained himself for the sake of Egan's pride.

He let Sir Egan carry the offensive for a full two minutes before he began to press his own attack. Even so, he kept himself contained within the flow and meter of the dance, following Egan's patterns and attacking in ways that allowed the older man to defend himself with dignity. He knew if he shamed the senior knight, he might make an enemy for life, and that was the last thing he wanted.

After a minute or so of that, the two men broke apart, and Egan was breathing a little more heavily than his younger opponent. "You're a fine swordsman. I'll give you that," admitted the older knight. "But experience will teach you that the battlefield is a place with no respect for pretty swordplay."

Gram's only reply was a flat stare that showed nothing. He knew what was coming next, and when Sir Egan came to him again, he wasn't disappointed. The veteran fought aggressively, moving in ways meant to throw him off balance or distract him from the true line of attack.

And yet Gram never missed a parry, and his face remained blank and impassive, a fact that was slowly beginning to unnerve his opponent. Desperate, Egan lunged forward, feinting toward Gram's head before leaping back and ducking low. It appeared as though he had momentarily lost his balance, and he caught himself with one hand against the ground before springing back to his feet and flinging the handful of dirt he had gathered directly at Gram's eyes.

But Gram's eyes were already closed, and they remained so as the younger man flawlessly parried Egan's follow-up strikes. He opened them a few seconds later when Egan backed away, and he saw the older man staring at him in bewilderment. "Ready to surrender?" asked Gram, his features momentarily returning to life.

Egan ground his teeth. "You haven't convinced me yet. Neither of us have even landed a blow."

Gram sighed, his disappointment clearly evident. "If that's what it takes." Then his face went dead again, and he moved forward.

His movement was unusual, though, in that he didn't stop once he had come into range. Instead he moved forward implacably, parrying Egan's warning attacks and forcing the man to retreat to maintain his distance.

Egan found himself struggling to fend off an ever-increasing number of high-speed attacks, and he was surprised when the world shuddered for a moment and Gram retreated to give him room. His adrenaline was singing in his veins, and it took him a moment to register the stinging pain coming from his right cheek. He lifted his left hand and rubbed at his face, finally realizing he had been struck by the flat of Gram's falchion. "That wouldn't mean much in armo—"

The veteran knight never managed to finish his sentence as Gram stepped in again, knocking his sword out of line and moving close. Egan felt Gram's foot behind his own, and then he was falling, driven toward the ground at blinding speed by the younger man's left hand against his chest. The wind exploded from his chest and when his vision stabilized, he found himself staring at the point of the falchion just an inch from his right eye.

Unable to breathe, Sir Egan was utterly unable to say the word, 'surrender,' but Gram merely stared down at him. After a few long seconds the young knight rose to his feet and offered his hand to help Egan up.

Egan took it, and when he could finally draw breath again, he gave his answer. "I surrender."

Gram touched his blade to his forehead, saluting Sir Egan. "Well fought, Sir." Cheers went up around them, though they were slightly muted by the fact that so many had lost money on the outcome of the fight.

Sir Egan returned the gesture and then moved closer to speak softly in Gram's ear. "You drew the fight out, didn't you?"

He didn't want to admit that fact, but neither could he bear to lie, so Gram circled the truth. "Your skills are nothing to take lightly, Sir Egan. I started cautiously to avoid making a mistake due to overconfidence."

Egan studied him seriously. "You avoid lying directly, and you weren't boasting earlier in the Queen's chambers. I appreciate your kindness to this old man."

Gram clapped Egan on the shoulder. "You're hardly old."

Sir Thomas walked toward them, a broad smile on his face. "Pay up, Egan. I'm a rich man today!"

"If you're done, we need to go," reminded Matthew.

Still basking in the warm glow of his victory, Gram responded lightly, "The day is still young. What's so important that we need to get back right this minute?"

Matthew blinked, and for a moment Gram saw flecks of silver mixed in with the blue. Then his oldest friend replied in a somber tone, "I have sins to pay for and larger ones to commit if we're going to save the world."

Gram sighed and went to put away his weapon and the gambeson he had borrowed. As he walked, he muttered unhappily to himself, "You just couldn't let me have five minutes of joy, could you?"

Matt watched him, his sharp ears picking up the remark, but he kept his response silent, *You'll have years to be happy if all goes well, unlike some of us.*

***

Rose, Angela, and Carissa were still sleeping when they returned, but Karen had another surprise for them. She had used her ability to teleport into the central courtyard of Castle Cameron and returned with Gary, her machine-father. Karen's face split into a wide grin when she saw Matthew and the others.

"You'll never guess the news!" she told Matthew excitedly, and when he failed to ask, she continued, "The war with ANSIS is over!"

Everyone's faces lit up, but Matthew's countenance remained guarded. Gary had been left behind, still connected to the antenna array they had created while Castle Cameron was sealed away. Matt had been hoping he might learn something valuable during that time, but this information surprised him, even though it wasn't enough to lighten his burden. He looked at Gary. "What did you learn?"

The android responded with a smile, which was only mildly disconcerting on his not-quite-human features. "The past months have been almost boring, but I caught an unencrypted message a few weeks ago and was able to gather the keys they use. Since then I've learned a lot, which is now mostly useless."

Matt frowned. "Useless, why?"

"Because they're gone," answered the machine. "While you were away, I've been listening to an unending litany of distress calls from various elements of ANSIS. Something was systematically destroying them, both on this side of the dimensional borders and on the other side. I can only surmise it was either you or your father, but the end result is the same. A final message was sent out to deactivate the few remaining assets ANSIS had here, and the last large conglomeration traveled back to their home world."

"Would a machine give up?" asked Matthew.

"They decided it was a matter of survival. Either the threat you sent them or the actions of your father convinced them that if they continued their campaign here, they might all be exterminated."

Matt stared at his metal hand. That had certainly been his intention, but he had never expected the machines to take his threat seriously. He had assumed they would push until he was forced to make the ultimate choice.

Karen was practically bouncing with joy, and her enthusiasm was infecting the others. She hugged her father first, and then Matt. "Isn't this good news?"

Myra walked in, though the others still thought of her as Moira, and Matthew met her eyes. *You're not convinced,* came her thought, a statement of fact.

He didn't look forward to the conversation he would have to have with Conall and Irene about her, but that was still a few days off. He gave Karen a half-hearted smile as he answered her, "Maybe. I'm not sure yet. I need to meditate." Then he turned away from them and headed for his room. He locked the door behind him.

Gram took the opportunity to ask Karen a question. "I didn't see Chad with you when you returned this morning. Where is he?"

Her expression darkened.

CHAPTER 31

Tyrion kept his eyes closed. The first thing he noticed was the smell of woodsmoke, and his magesight quickly discovered the source, a brick oven across the room from where he lay. He was in a small dwelling of some sort, and a woman was tending a large pot that sat atop the stove.

Since the woman had her back to him, he slowly cracked the lids of his eyes and peered around, though he was still careful not to move his head. Any sound might alert the woman. First, he needed to determine whether she was his savior, or his captor.

Thus far the signs pointed to the more benevolent of the two options. A careful examination of his body revealed that he wasn't bound or chained. What disturbed him most was the fact that the wounds on his arms had mostly healed. Since he hadn't done so himself with magic, that indicated he had been there for a week at least. Had he been unconscious that long? Hunger and fatigue didn't seem sufficient to explain such a span of time.

Expanding the scope of his magesight, he explored the area around the house. It was surrounded by a bare earth yard enclosed by a short fieldstone wall that was barely three feet tall. Beyond that were scattered trees and open expanses of grass. Looking farther out, he found a river half a mile distant. *I must be in the valley near Cameron,* he surmised.

There was a young girl playing a game with sticks not far from the house, something that involved drawing lines on the ground, but he found no sign of a man or any other adults besides the woman in the room with him.

All of this served to put him at ease. His first instinct had been to leap up and seize the woman. The threat of violence would make her answer his questions, and if others had been near, he could have used her as a hostage, but since she was alone none of that seemed necessary. The fact that the only other person in the vicinity was a child made that abundantly clear. Slowly, he sat up, mildly surprised at the effort it took. His body felt like a wet rag.

The woman turned at the sound of him rising. "You're awake!" she exclaimed, stating the obvious.

Tyrion fixed her with predatory eyes, causing her to flinch back slightly, then rose unsteadily to his feet. He had something urgent to attend to.

It was when the woman's eyes drifted downward that he realized he was stark naked. The heat of the oven had made it easy to overlook that fact. What was not easy to overlook was the state of his manhood, given how full his bladder was.

He wasn't embarrassed, though; his past made such an emotion unlikely. "I need to relieve myself," he said flatly, then turned to the only door that led outside.

The woman overcame her shock and ran over to the bed. "Wait! My daughter is outside." Snatching up a blanket, she offered it to him.

He accepted it and draped it over one shoulder before tying the corners at his waist on the opposite side. He observed woman's gaze traveling across his skin as he did; most likely she was fascinated by the bizarre lines and symbols that covered his body. Pushing aside the flimsy wooden door, he went outside. The little girl took notice of him immediately and ran over to him.

"What's your name?" she asked. By her size, he guessed she was probably around six years old.

Tyrion ignored her question and walked around the house. The girl started to follow him, but a voice from the house called out to her, "Anna! Leave him alone."

With the house blocking her view, he emptied his bladder. His urine was a dark and unhealthy brown color, an indicator that he had either been badly injured or that he had been unconscious for quite some time. He returned to the house a few minutes later. "I'm thirsty."

The woman brought a pitcher and a wooden cup. She filled the cup and handed it to him.

Sniffing at it he looked at her with a question on his lips. "Water?"

"It's safe," she replied. "We have a well close by. You've been drinking the water for the past week, what little I could get into you safely. You had a terrible fever."

Tyrion watched her aura carefully, and while he was no Centyr, he was well versed in observing people's emotions and reactions. He didn't sense a lie. With a shrug, he drained the cup and held it out to her for more. Once he had had his fill, he glanced at her again. "You have food?"

She fed him, watching with curiosity as he put away everything she gave him. He could tell she had a lot of questions, but his appearance must have intimidated her, for she didn't ask them, which suited him just fine. With his belly full, he felt the need to rest again, so he lay back down on the bed. The room was almost stiflingly warm, so he didn't bother covering himself.

He almost chuckled when a light touch woke him a short time later. The woman had draped a blanket over his midsection. He said nothing, however, pretending to be asleep. Soon enough his pretense became truth once more, and he dreamed. As was almost always the case, his dreams were filled with fire, fear, and blood. The only peaceful moments were when the green eyes stared down on him, and even those moments merely filled him with guilt.

He awoke once during the night, needing to relieve himself. The woman and her child were asleep on the floor, wrapped in another blanket close to the stove. As he glanced back at the bed, it occurred to him then that it was the only bed in the house, and if her words were to be believed he had been occupying it for a week. He stared at them for a short time, deep in thought, then he went outside and took care of his personal needs before returning to bed.

When his eyes opened again, it was morning and the smell of something simmering over the stove filled his nose. Rather than rise, he remained in the bed, studying his hostess from behind while she labored over breakfast. She appeared to be a healthy woman, sturdy more than beautiful, at least according to the tastes one might find in higher circles. She wasn't fat by any means—hard work and the lack of abundant food made sure of that. Instead she was wide-hipped and somewhat muscled from her daily labors.

It was a combination he found attractive, more so than the wispy figures so popular among the ladies of Albamarl who often starved themselves. Even the long braid of brown hair she kept rolled up at the back of her head was appealing. He wondered where her husband was. He clearly remembered her calling a man's name before he had passed out.

Rising from the small bed, he walked across the room and leaned over her shoulder. "Smells good." Her reaction was gratifying. She startled, then turned, her face close to his. From her eyes and the shift in her aura, he could see she found him attractive. With a grin, he left the room.

The little girl was in the yard, hanging wet clothing over a line with the help of a wooden stool that still left her almost too short for the task.

After he had taken a quick trip behind the house, he returned and helped the child hang the clothes. She didn't protest, but took to watching him with interest.

"Are you a king?" asked the little girl.

Tyrion looked down at her. "It depends who you ask."

She pouted. "That's not an answer. Why don't grownups ever answer straight?"

He finished putting up the last pair of trousers. His own clothes were already hanging on the line, a sight that put him at ease. He had begun to wonder if the woman's husband had left to sell them somewhere. Putting his hands on his hips, he tightened the blanket tied around his waist. "Sometimes the answers are too complicated to give an easy answer," he replied at last. Then he stared into the girl's eyes somberly. "I have never been called a king, but I have been *like* a king. Not too long ago I was a duke, but I think that's probably over now."

The girl eyed him suspiciously. "But you were never a count?"

He shook his head. "No. Why do you ask that?"

"You look dangerous," she responded honestly. "The Blood Count is very dangerous. He used to be our Lord, but the Queen banished him."

"And you thought I might be him?"

She nodded.

"Your name is Anna, right?" he asked. The girl nodded again. "Well, Anna, I can promise you that I am not the Blood Count, but you were right about one thing."

"What's that?" she asked curiously.

"I am dangerous," he stated.

Anna looked him up and down, then moved closer and pointed at one of the lines on his lower leg. "What's this?"

"It's part of my magic," he told her.

"What does it do?"

"It protects me from monsters, and from people like your Blood Count," he replied.

She looked at him with interest. "Is he your enemy?"

Tyrion sighed. "One of many."

"Then you're dead," said Anna. "He'll kill you."

"People have been telling me that all my life," said Tyrion. "But I'm still alive, and all of them are dead."

"The Blood Count killed an entire army," Anna informed him, stretching her arms wide and swinging them around. "Right here. He flooded the valley and drowned them all, along with Papa's sheep. Mama said she and Papa had to hide in the hills until the water was gone." She stopped for a second, then added, "That was before I was born."

Tyrion eyed the little girl. The challenge written on her face was humorous, and he couldn't help but play her game. "I once killed an army's worth of wizards, but I didn't use a flood, just my hands." To illustrate his point, he activated his right arm blade, giving it a visible blue glow and holding it up for her to see.

He had half expected the girl to be frightened at his use of magic, but to her credit she barely flinched. "They say the Blood Count killed the Dark Gods," she boasted.

He struggled to keep from laughing at her serious demeanor. Instead he nodded, then drew himself up and stood straight, towering over her. "I killed the race that created the Dark Gods, as well as most of the people living in the world back then."

Anna glared at him. "Liar. There's lots of people in the world. Mama took me to Washbrook once. There's hundreds of people there."

"It's true, whether you believe me or not," said Tyrion, then he bent down and touched a weed growing in the yard. Using a spellweave, he sent a thread of magic through it, causing it to grow visibly as she watched. Buds appeared and yellow flowers bloomed, and when there were enough, he used his magic to sever the plant from its base and wove them into a wreath, which he placed on her head.

Anna was staring at him in wonder, more fascinated by his ability to create flowers than she had been by his armblade. Her fascination was interrupted by a shout from the house. "Anna! What are you doing? You should be done hanging the wash by now."

The girl ran into the house to answer her mother's call, and Tyrion was left alone, his mind wandering back across the exchange he had just had with the girl. He couldn't help but chuckle, not just at the girl, but at his own childish responses. Since his strength had recovered, he wandered around the house to a woodpile he had noted previously and made himself useful splitting wood.

He knew he owed the woman a debt for taking care of him, and he wanted to repay her somehow since he figured he would leave in a day or so. Oddly, he felt closer to these people than any others he had met since leaving the She'Har grove. The citizens in the capital were far removed from the people he, or rather his creator, had known thousands of years before. The woman and her daughter, by contrast, weren't very different from the people of his time. In short, they felt real to him in a way that the citizens and nobility of Albamarl never would.

That evening, after finishing a simple dinner that consisted of a pottage made from primarily peas and onions, he sat staring into the fire when a small hand tugged on his sleeve. It was Anna, staring up at him with large brown eyes. "Do you know any stories?" she asked.

Tyrion gave the woman a reassuring look. "It's alright." Then he paused. "I haven't asked your name. Pardon me for being rude."

Anna's mother looked down. "It's Brigitte."

He hid his surprise at the coincidence. *I hallucinated seeing my daughter, and now I'm saved by a woman with nearly the same name.* "Mine's Daniel," he replied, falling back on a name he hadn't used in millennia. For some reason it felt more comfortable here in this place, as though it matched the country farm. "I do have a story to tell, but I'm not sure you'll want to hear it."

"Anything would be welcome," said the mother.

So, he launched into a retelling of his life, or his creator's life. As far as he was concerned it was his own, since the original Tyrion had given up on being human. Who else could argue against it being his? Out of necessity, he shortened the tale considerably, as well as simplifying many parts of it to make it more understandable for Anna. Even so, his story took hours and though it kept the girl up long past her bedtime, neither she nor her mother showed any signs of sleepiness.

He ended the story at what seemed to be its natural conclusion, when he had been betrayed by his daughter and had become a She'Har elder, but once he had finished and the silence grew, Anna stared at him in exasperation. "That's it?" she asked angrily.

His brow furrowed as he looked down on the child. "Pretty much."

"He turned into one of the tree people? They were the bad guys!" stated Anna, outrage evident in her voice. "That's stupid."

"He needed to rest—" began Tyrion, but the girl interrupted him again.

"He was supposed to kill the tree people!" declared the little girl. "And he almost did, but then he turns into one?"

Brigitte broke in, "Anna, it's time to go to bed. We've stayed up far too late. Thank Daniel for his story and let's get some sleep."

"But Mom, it's a dumb story! He needs to fix it!" protested the girl.

Her mother's gaze was unforgiving. "Anna!"

The little girl glared back at her mother, then relented. She turned to Tyrion, her voice sullen, "Thank you for the story." Under her breath she added, "Even if it was dumb." Then she trundled away to roll up in the collection of blankets she and her mother had been using as a bed for the past week.

Her mother looked at Tyrion and shrugged, an apology written on her face, but once it was apparent that he hadn't taken offense, a question came into her eyes. "The boy in the story's name was Daniel," she said in a neutral tone.

Tyrion nodded. "It was."

She stared once more at the tattoos that covered his arms. "But it was just a story, wasn't it?"

He went to the bed and stretched out. "I'm tired. Thank you for the food." She didn't press him for more, and he pretended to fall asleep quickly, but he lay awake for an unknown time after that, lost in thought.

The next morning, he rose early and after eating what Brigitte prepared, he made his goodbyes. The look on the mother's face was a mixture of sadness and relief. "Are you sure? You've only just recovered."

"I couldn't impose any longer," he told her.

"Well, you cut some wood yesterday—"

"I finished all of it," he corrected. "I don't think it's enough to repay your kindness."

Her features froze. "All of it?"

It had been a considerable pile, but he hadn't relied on an axe to do the work. "All of it," he affirmed.

"There were almost two cords of wood out there," she muttered in disbelief. "James said it would take days."

He headed for the door, but Anna called out to him from her seat at the table, "Fix your story."

Turning, he fixed her with a genuine smile, but underneath it something sinister lurked. "I intend to." Then he addressed her mother, "Which way is Washbrook from here?"

She answered immediately, "North, across the river. You'll meet a road there; just follow it west a few miles."

He was gone before she could ask him any more questions.

CHAPTER 32

Breakfast had been finished for more than an hour, but Matthew and Rose, along with all the others except Conall, Irene, and Chad, still sat at the table. The conversation had ranged wide and far as they shared their stories, primarily covering the ground since Rose and Mordecai had escaped from Albamarl.

Naturally, some parts were shortened for the sake of brevity, on both sides, but Matthew knew Rose had left out something critical. Something he needed to know. He had spent the prior evening deep in meditation, meditation that had proven somewhat fruitless. Their future was as bleak as ever, with almost every choice ending in darkness. Not the foreboding sort of darkness that indicated bad things ahead—no, this was the sort that showed nothing, simply a blank void.

He had a strong feeling that what he had seen wasn't something metaphorical, but rather an abrupt end of everything, a stark line that marked the end of history. It varied slightly how far away it appeared, but along every branch of the future it came within two months. The only glimmers of a more normal progression came after his conversation with Rose, and only along a few of the lines that led on from there.

Nothing she had said so far hinted at anything that might give him an idea as to a course of action. Glancing at the others, he raised his voice, "Do any of you mind if I speak to Rose alone for a while?"

The question earned him some sour glances, particularly from Karen and Elaine, but after a short space punctuated by random comments and the clattering of dishes, they left the two alone, retreating to the kitchen with their plates and utensils.

Lady Rose didn't wait for him to begin. "You seem very different than the last time I saw you," she opined. "You've matured."

Rose had been a second mother to him for much of his life, or perhaps a close aunt. Hearing such a thing from her felt strange. "I don't think it's maturity," he replied. "It's more like a burden has landed on my shoulders. Without Dad here, it feels like I'm the only one who can carry it."

She smirked. "A burden, that's a perfect description of maturity." Lifting her tea-cup, she sniffed at it, realizing she had already finished the contents. Placing it back down on the table with visible disappointment, she added, "So what did you want to ask me?"

"I need your help," said Matthew frankly. "As they told you a little while ago, I can see branches of the future now, but what I didn't mention was that currently there isn't one."

She raised a brow. "No future, at all?"

"Almost," he nodded. "There are some murky paths that lead out from this moment. I think they'll become clear after we talk, if you tell me the right things."

Rose leaned back in her chair. "That would imply that I've not told you the truth thus far."

"Or omitted something important," suggested Matt. "Or that you haven't told me the right lie." When she looked askance at him, he continued, "I can't assume it's the truth I need to hear. All I know is that you know something I don't, and either that truth, or perhaps some version of it you've edited, will open a path forward."

Her lips were pursed in a sour expression. "That's not much help. You don't even know whether you need the truth or a fiction."

"But you did leave something out, didn't you?" he pressed. "Something important."

"I did," admitted Rose, "but I do not know whether it is the truth or not." Matthew leaned forward with interest, so she continued, "Your father and I met an Illeniel Elder, a gatekeeper of some sort, named Kion. Mordecai fought with him and took his power but left him alive. After that, something happened to him and he left me there. It was Kion that sent me back to this side, but not before filling my ears with dire portents."

"What did he say?"

"That no matter what he did, Mordecai would grow stronger. His every action causes his power to increase, until eventually it will overwhelm him, and he will destroy the world. Kion seemed to think it was a foregone conclusion, that all we could do was sit back and wait for it to all end," she explained.

His eyes lit with comprehension. "That's why he's been hiding. He's been trying to do nothing."

Rose smiled sadly. "Probably. He seems to know what's happening to him."

"Did the Elder know of a solution?" asked Matthew.

She chewed her lip, an uncharacteristic action for Rose Thornbear. "Kion said that if he had taken your father's power, he would have destroyed himself after accomplishing his task. I don't think that's possible for Mort."

Matthew thought about it for a minute, then responded, "When I met him, near Lancaster, his power was so great he couldn't get near me. When he met Moira, she said it burned her just being half a block from him. It's probably gone too far for anything to destroy him now."

Rose blinked, and an unbidden tear fell from one of her eyes. "He's your father. Could you kill him? Even if it were possible, could you do such a thing?"

His heart clenched in his chest, but then he asked Rose a question in response, "You have a daughter. If it would save her life, could you do it?"

Her face twisted with pain. "This is just a hypothetical. There's no way to do such a thing."

Matthew pressed on, "If I find a way, could you do it?"

Agitated and perhaps angry, Rose stood up from the table, turning away, but not before he saw more tears welling in her eyes. "Yes," she answered. "If you doubt me, just ask Chad Grayson." Then she left the room.

Matt stared at her empty cup, lost in dark thoughts. She had given him his answer. *If Rose can do it, then I can too,* he thought to himself. It might destroy him inside, but then again, he was already torn with guilt for what had happened to Moira. This would just be one more log to throw on his bonfire of regrets.

***

The next morning Matthew rose late. His sleep had been troubled by dark thoughts and even darker dreams. After rising he meditated, and despite his sleepless night, he found the sliver of light that represented a possible way forward into the future had grown brighter. *She told me what I needed to hear, but it gives me no comfort,* he thought. To guide his family and friends past the grim gate, he would be forced to destroy his father.

No, not destroy, he realized. *Destroying him would be like releasing the Fool's Tesseract after it has absorbed too much. I have to somehow eradicate him completely, as though he never existed.* But that was impossible. He knew that already, at a level so deep it went beyond knowledge or even intuition. Gary had even said something to that effect once, even though he came from a world without magic. *"Energy cannot be created or destroyed,"* the android had told him.

Just thinking about it made his head hurt and his heart ache. Still, there had to be some way, otherwise the small hope for the future he had seen wouldn't exist at all. Despite his normal reticence, he wanted to tell the others about his dilemma. It was a problem too large for him, if only because it tore at the very core of his emotions. But he had looked at that possibility directly during his meditation. If he shared what he knew, completely and honestly, Irene and Conall wouldn't cooperate and they seemed to be crucial to whatever it was he had to do.

That meant his most likely course would require a half-truth, something that grated on his nerves. He had never liked lying, whether doing it himself or receiving them from others.

Voices from beyond his room brought him back from his reverie. Irene and Conall had returned, creating a vibrant chaos of greetings and hellos as everyone reunited around the breakfast table. That brought him another sense of dread. He had promised Irene to tell her the truth when she came home.

Matthew drew himself up and took a deep breath before stepping into the hall and approaching the dining room. Everyone glanced up at his arrival, and as he had expected, Irene and Conall were seated among them, along with Elise Thornbear. Something else drew his eyes, though. In his younger brother's hand was an unusual staff he had never seen before. It was enchanted, much like the one their father used, but that wasn't what made it so strange.

It was composed entirely of magic, much like one of Moira's spellbeasts. From the way Conall held it, it had a physical presence, but there was no normal matter within it. In many ways it resembled one of the spell constructs the She'Har created with their spellweaves, but it was clearly made using human runes.

Ignoring everything else, Matthew asked, "What is that?"

Karen's face was a picture of stern disapproval. "Is that any way to greet your brother?"

Most of the others were looking at him strangely, but Irene seemed pleased by the question. "What do you think it is?" she returned.

"It's good to see you too, Matt," said Conall, before handing the staff to Irene. "It's just something Rennie loaned me to help me walk."

Myra, still pretending to be Moira, sat at the far end of the table, and as usual she had already begun skimming thoughts from the surface of his mind. *Is that staff really more important than what you're planning to say? You should have at least said hello to him first,* she told him, sending the thoughts to him privately.

Don't remind me, he thought, then added, *and yes, it might be. I'm not sure.* Looking at Conall, he inquired, "How are you feeling?"

Conall grinned, "Much better, thanks to Lady Thornbear. I'm still a little weak and the stitches in my side itch, but otherwise I'm right as—"

"Glad to hear it," interrupted Matthew impatiently. "Did you make that staff, Rennie?" he asked immediately after. Karen threw up her hands in despair at his rudeness, then covered her face with her palms.

The others were more used to his strange behavior, having long ago given up on him following social norms, and Irene's eyes actually twinkled at his sudden interest. "It was something that occurred to me when Father was teaching me about enchanting."

Matthew frowned. "He couldn't have taught you that. No one's done that before. How did you manage it?"

Irene's expression was supremely smug. She had finally stumped her brother and shown him something that amazed him. "I was learning to make rune channels, and Dad was telling me about the different uses for them depending on size. He suggested I might prefer a wand, but it got me to thinking I should make one that could be altered to whatever size was desired." Lifting the staff, she said a word and the weapon shrank in her hand until it was the size of writing stylus. "See? Now I can use it for fine detail work without having to have a separate…"

He nodded, still impatient. "That's not the point. It isn't anchored to anything." Creating an enchantment that could change size on command wasn't anything new—his Fool's Tesseract did that, as did their father's flying construct, stasis cubes, and shield stones, but those were all anchored to small objects that could move to accommodate the change in the structure.

Lynaralla seemed confused. "I do that with spellweaves all the time. Enchanting is fundamentally the same. Why are you surprised?"

"Enchanting is done slowly," explained Matthew. "That's why we use objects, because we don't have a seed-mind to create it all at once. There's no other way for us to stabilize the structure before it collapses."

Irene smirked. "Clearly, you are wrong. There is a way. You just never thought of it."

Irritated, Matthew replied, "Not just me. Dad never thought of a way, and not just him. I remember the Age of Magic. None of the enchanters of the past ever came up with a method either. How did you do it?"

"Wax," said Irene. "I watched Dad making a mold, and when he was melting the wax out, I got the idea. I made the staff out of wax, then inscribed the enchantment. I had to include an additional portion to control the size, of course, but it wasn't too complicated. After I was done, I melted the wax away and I was left with this. Neat, huh?"

Matthew stared at his younger sister as though she had grown a second head. Irene winked at him, then asked smugly, "Impressed, aren't you?"

He blinked slowly, twice, then replied honestly, "I think I am."

Elaine was standing in the corner of the room, and she snorted when she heard his response. "I never thought I'd hear you admit that."

Karen moved closer and put her arm around Matthew's waist. "I'm proud of you." Then, in a faintly malicious tone she added, "It'll do you good to have someone take the wind out of your sails now and then."

Enjoying the moment, Irene took the initiative to ask, "What were you waiting to tell me the other day, Matt?" Everyone paused to look at her, then at Matthew, who seemed to withdraw into himself.

Are you sure about this? Myra sent to him mentally.

He met Myra's eyes and nodded, then drew himself up to address the others. "I'm not sure if I should bring this up in front of everyone, Rennie. It might be better if it was just you and Conall. It's a family matter."

Irene hesitated, but Conall answered immediately, "Everyone here is family, Matt. Lady Rose, Lady Thornbear, Gram, Elaine, they're as close as blood."

Matthew looked to Irene for confirmation, and she nodded. Still nervous, he found himself looking down as he began, "There's been a tragedy, another death…" His words trailed off as he struggled to express himself. The room had gone deathly silent and all eyes were on him. "It was my fault," he added. "Just like Conall being wounded."

"What are you trying to say?" asked Irene, consternation filling her eyes.

When Matthew failed to speak for several seconds, everyone began to pepper him with questions. Conall stood, wincing in the process, and went to stand beside him. "Give him a second!" Then he looked at his older brother. "It wasn't your fault what happened to me. You weren't even there. I was just trying to do the right thing and bit off more than I could chew."

Matthew's eyes were haunted as he listened to Conall. "No, it was my fault. I was the one that sent Moira there."

Confused and irritated, Gram spoke up, “Just say it.”

Unable to stand by silently any longer, Myra answered, “Moira is dead.”

“You’re standing right in front of us,” put in Elaine. “Are you confused? That’s a real body I’m looking at, not like Myra’s…” Her words trailed off. Glancing around, she saw looks of confusion on everyone’s faces, confusion that was slowly being replaced by dawning dread, mirroring her own reaction.

Myra dropped her gaze, staring at the floor. “This is her body, but I’m not Moira.”

CHAPTER 33

Karen recovered from her shock first. "Myra? Is that you?" she asked. Lost for words, Myra could only nod in affirmation.

"Hold up," exclaimed Conall, glancing toward his older brother. "I know you told me not to mention this, but just the other day I saw Moira. How can she be dead?"

"Matthew sent her to the capital to overturn the Queen's decision regarding Dad and the rest of us as well," said Irene, her voice growing dark. Her eyes were focused solely on Matthew, and in them he could see a growing condemnation.

Rose watched them all with interest, keeping silent since she didn't have first-hand information of the events they were discussing, but her son, Gram, broke in, "Matthew's letter just said to 'unify Lothion.' There's no way he knew she would go to such lengths, or get herself killed."

Irene's gaze never left Matthew's face. "No, he knew exactly what she would do. She even said so herself, when I tried to stop her. Her words to me were, '*He knew exactly what his message would set in motion.*'" The tension in her body was growing visibly as she spoke. "Not only that, but he *knew* what would happen. He knew she would die, and he sent her anyway!" When Matthew didn't respond, she yelled at him, voice filled with rage, "Didn't you?!"

"I knew it was possible," admitted Matt, "but it wasn't probable…"

"So you decided to just roll the dice with your sister's life? Is that supposed to make this better? Do you think that would make me forgive you?" growled Irene between clenched teeth.

Conall was staring at his older brother with a look of growing shock and disbelief, but Irene's rage snapped him out of it. Stepping between them, he held his hands out toward her. "You need to calm down, Rennie. We don't even know how it happened yet. You aren't the only one suffering here either. I know Matt's feeling the same pain we are."

"Don't tell me to calm down," snapped Irene. "He's been playing with all of us. Using us like pawns in some grand game of chess!"

"It wasn't his fault," interjected Myra. "I was there. Moira changed her own plan at the last minute, putting herself in danger rather than using me, or one of the spell-minds she had created. I argued against it, but she ignored me."

Irene's cheeks were red and her eyes welling with tears as she turned angrily on Myra. "Would that have made it better? Should I be relieved to know that he thought it might be *you* who died instead? You're my sister too, even if you weren't born in a flesh and blood body."

"She's right," muttered Matthew, barely loud enough to be heard.

Karen gave him a look of concern, reaching out to put a reassuring hand on his shoulder. "It isn't as simple as that. We've all made hard choices. We can't lay the blame for any of our misfortunes at the feet of any one person."

Matthew flinched away, then took a step to remove himself from her reach. Then he raised his voice, "No, she *is* right. I have been playing a game. It's a hard, cruel game, and the cost of losing could be all of our lives, but I'm the only one who can play it. I'm the only one who can see the probabilities, and I've been taking chances with everyone's lives.

"But I'm not going to stop now," he declared, lifting his head to stare at them with cold determination. "Someone has to do this, or there won't be a future."

Irene seemed close to throwing herself at him as he made his declaration, but Alyssa and Lynaralla were holding her now. "As if we would listen to anything you told us to do!" yelled Irene. "Do you think we're fools to be played twice?"

"I do," said Matthew simply. "You have no choice. You'll do it because it's the only way to save this world. You'll do it because the only way to save the future is to save Dad." With that, he turned and left the room, leaving them all in shock.

His younger sister's voice started to climb in the back of her throat, promising a scream that would shake the rooftop, but Rose's cool command cut across the room, "Irene, enough."

The younger woman stared at Rose silently, a dazed expression on her face.

"We need to make some tea," announced Rose. "Come with me, Irene." Then she addressed the room, "We'll be back in a few minutes. We can discuss what happened then. I'm sure Myra has a lot to tell us." Taking Irene by the hand, she led the young wizard toward the kitchen.

***

Irene filled a large kettle with water and brought it back into the kitchen, where Rose placed it carefully on the stove-top to heat. The younger woman didn't say anything, for she was still trying to sort out her emotions and Rose was one person she didn't feel comfortable speaking rashly in front of. For one, the woman was like an aunt to her, an aunt who, unlike her mother, had never been one to tolerate ill-considered words.

As a result, Irene found herself reflecting on her emotions silently. She was angry. No, she was beyond angry. The shock of losing her mother, and then everything that had happened to her father, it was all still too recent. Now to discover Moira had died, quietly and without anyone being aware, as a direct result of one of Matthew's schemes—it was too much.

It doesn't matter what he was trying to achieve, it's still his fault, she resolved. *The end doesn't justify the means, and those means cost Moira her life.*

Rose's voice cut through the silence like a splash of cold water. "I don't know if I've ever said this to you before, Irene, but of all your siblings, your personality is the most like your mother's."

She had no idea how to respond to that, so she remained quiet, studying the table in front of her.

"Conall is a bit like her as well," continued Rose, "but he doesn't have the same sensitivity more commonly found in our sex. Nor is he as intelligent as you are, when you give yourself time to think."

"Thank you," said Irene after some hesitation.

"In fact, you're probably brighter than your mother. She could be remarkably dense at times, thanks in part to her incredible stubbornness," added Rose, her gaze focused on the window to the garden.

Irene felt her anger bubbling up toward the surface again. "Mom wouldn't have been any happier about what he's done than I am."

"The interesting thing about families is that every person has a role to play. People tend to gravitate toward the part that best suits them. Do you know what role best suited your mother?" asked Rose.

Hackles rising, Irene responded, "I'm not my mother."

Rose's eyes flicked toward the younger woman for an instant, and Irene could feel them weighing her worth, then they returned to the window scene. "No. You are not her. Nor did your mother fill the role you assumed I meant. When you were young, she held your family together. She was the glue, the unifier, but as you and her other children grew up, that changed. She became the family protector, the guardian. *You* took on the part of family peacemaker."

Irene's cheeks flushed with anger. "If you're suggesting that…"

"I am not telling you to do anything, young lady," said Rose calmly, her cool tone cutting Irene off. "You're old enough to make your own decisions. I'm simply sharing my observations about you and your siblings, so you can make intelligent decisions.

"When your mother died, your brother, Conall, took on the role of protector. Your departed sister, Moira, took on the role of nurturer, as odd as that seems. Neither of them were really ready for those parts, but they tried," explained Rose.

Irene's eyes narrowed. "And what about *him*?" she asked, referring to Matthew.

"Matthew was forced to become the leader, ill-equipped though he is to deal with it." Moving to the stove, Rose took up the kettle and then began to pour the steaming water over the tea strainer. "Do you know what the worst part of a leader's job is?" asked Rose.

Irene said nothing.

"They take the blame," said Rose, answering her own question. "Without making excuses, they accept the blame for whatever happens, whether it's really their fault or not. Leaders don't take credit for success—they give that to those they lead—and when things go wrong, they accept responsibility for any and all mistakes.

"Your father did that in the past. He was an excellent scapegoat, even for the Queen. But he also had a remarkable ability to inspire trust in people. His charisma, and your mother, kept him from being completely ostracized for all the tough decisions he had to undertake. Unfortunately, Matthew didn't inherit that from him, and your mother is gone," finished Rose somberly.

Feeling uncertain, Irene spoke up, "I don't know what you think I'm supposed to do, but I'm not going to forgive him just because you think—"

"I am only sharing my experience, Irene," said Rose, cutting her off once again. "What you choose to do with it is entirely up to you." Then she motioned toward the cupboard. "If you'll get the cups and saucers, we can serve the tea now."

***

As Irene and Rose returned to the room and everyone began sorting through the latest shock, Karen ducked out and went to find Matthew. It would have been a simple task for any mage normally, but the house was divided by a number of separate privacy wards that shielded both the house as a whole and individual rooms within it, preventing her from spotting him with her magesight.

He wasn't in his bedroom—a room he had been sharing with her—nor was he in the hall. She didn't think he would have gone into any of the other rooms, so the best option was the workshop behind the house. As soon as she stepped outdoors, the scope of her magesight expanded and she knew then that he wasn't outside, meaning he had almost certainly gone into the workshop.

It was a safe bet in most circumstances, since it had always been his preferred place to think, and she wasn't disappointed this time. Opening the door and stepping in, she found him standing at the drafting table, a large, blank sheet of parchment stretched out in front of him. There was a pen in his hand, hovering above the page as though he might start writing or sketching at any moment, but it didn't move.

His eyes stared through the page, blank and devoid of purpose.

"What are you doing?" she asked mildly.

Matthew's voice was numb as he replied, "The only thing I can."

"Which is?"

His eyes darted to her for a moment, then returned to the emptiness before him. "Thinking. Searching for a solution."

Karen moved a little closer, painfully conscious of the tension in the air around him. "You look stuck," she remarked, noting how the muscle in his jaw tensed as he received her words.

"This is always how it starts," he responded coolly, "with a blank page. If I stare at it long enough, something will come to me."

She wanted to touch him, to pull some of the tension out of his shoulders, but she knew better than to try. At moments like this, any contact would only make him push her away. It was a lesson she had learned slowly over time. As rational as he seemed, when Matthew was upset the only way to approach him was slowly, from the sides. He wouldn't talk about what really bothered him. She would have to sneak up on it by getting him to talk about something else. "Is this how you usually begin?" she asked.

He nodded without looking at her. "First I define the problem."

"Tell me."

"My father is going to destroy the world, simply by existing," Matthew muttered.

That was news to her, so she asked him to clarify, keeping her questions neutral, and he did. Speaking dispassionately, he described what he had learned from Rose and how it fit with his own observations. It took several minutes for him to explain it all, and throughout his exposition his voice remained calm, clinical, and devoid of emotion.

Except she knew he wasn't devoid of anything. While she was still learning to interpret the aythar around others, she knew enough to know that the flickering of his aura reflected a disturbance in his heart and mind. When he finished, she offered her own suggestion, "That was a lot to take in, even given the fact that he's not *my* father. I don't think you're going to find an answer by trying to think it over logically."

His aura flashed as he looked at her, and in his features she could see desperate frustration. "What are you saying?" he asked.

"Everyone thinks you're cold and calculating," began Karen, "but whether they realize it or not, you're very creative. This problem requires a creative solution, but creativity doesn't come from logic. That's why you stare at a blank page."

Matthew's brows furrowed as he listened, but he didn't reply.

Karen went on, "Creativity comes from boredom. That's what a blank page represents, boredom. But it won't work for you, not now."

"Why not?" he asked suspiciously.

"Because the last thing you are right now—is bored. You're human. You're blaming yourself for what happened to Moira, to Conall. You know how angry Irene is. You know how shocked and upset everyone in the house is. Your heart and mind are full to the brim with a riot of emotions. The very last thing you could possibly be is bored," said Karen.

"I can't help that," he muttered angrily.

"Yes, you can," she informed him. "Go back in the house and listen. Talk to your family. Answer their questions. Argue with them."

He released the tension suddenly with a long sigh. "That won't help anything. Besides, with only a quick peek I can see the outcome. There's no point in having a conversation when I know it won't solve anything." A tiny drop of ink fell from the pen that had been hovering so long, unused, above the page. Matthew glared at it as though it had betrayed him.

"Idiot," Karen reprimanded softly. "You're so smart, but you don't even understand yourself sometimes. You don't go back in there to solve anything. You go in there and talk to your family to drain the wound. They won't be satisfied until you do, and neither will you. You talk until they can't stand it anymore, until *you* can't stand it anymore—until your heart and soul are so sick of it you can't bear to even think about it. You have to wear your emotions down, wear them out. Once you've done that, you'll be too tired to think. You can go to bed and sleep. *Then,* when you wake up tomorrow, and your mind refuses to look back, *then* you can be bored, *then* your answers will start to form. Right now, you're just wasting time."

He stared at her for a moment, then whispered, "First Irene, now you—today has been full of surprises." Putting the pen away, he took out some sand and blotted the spot on the page before lifting his hand to rub his face, leaving a dark smudge beside one eye. "You're right," he admitted, then started toward the door.

Karen moved to block his path, holding out her arms. "Advice doesn't come cheap. You have to pay for what you get."

With little resignation and a wry smile, he hugged her. "How could I forget that?"

"You'll learn eventually," she told him.

Chapter 34

Chad Grayson sat at his favorite table, tucked away in the back corner of the Muddy Pig. Ordinarily, that was all he needed to be content, but this particular morning he was in a sour, sullen mood. In fact, his mood was a holdover from the previous two days, and the fact that he had a hangover did nothing to help.

Danae stood behind the bar, cleaning cups with her hands, while her mind remained with the hunter. He was the only customer, since it wasn't even yet midday. Technically the tavern wasn't supposed to be open yet, but she had let Chad in, despite her misgivings.

"There's something wrong, Danni," groused Chad, using the name he often called her when 'Danae' somehow became too difficult for him.

"It's called 'morning,'" she replied sourly.

"No, not that," he muttered, scratching his head with both hands while resting his chin on the table in front of him. "Something's really wrong."

"I'm not closing the shutters," she warned. "This place needs to air out while there's plenty of sun, so you'll just have to deal with it."

"It's not that either," he muttered. "Well, that's part of it, but that's not all of it. I think I'm dying."

"You're sobering up," she informed him, tossing her head to get a stray piece of hair out of her eyes. No matter how she tried, some always escaped her ponytail.

Chad looked at her with mournful, red-rimmed eyes. "That's terrible. I shouldn't be getting sober. It's only been two days."

"Three days," she corrected automatically.

"Three days," he agreed with a nod. "But I distinctly remember planning to be drunk for a full week. This is too soon."

"Too bad," she told him. "I'm not giving you anything else until this evening."

His face twisted into a grimace, but then an idea occurred to him. "What about the two bottles I promised the lady in Iverly?"

"Eddard packed those up yesterday," said Danae. "They've already gone with the weekly courier."

"It would probably be better if I delivered them meself," suggested Chad hopefully. "Why not pack up another two and I'll take them with me?"

"Not a chance," she replied. "Eddard is coming back with lunch before we open. I told him to bring extra for you. You'll feel better with some ham and eggs in your belly."

"You're trying to kill me," whined the hunter. A few seconds later, when she hadn't responded, he added, "Won't you kill me, Danni? Please? I'd rather be dead than sober."

She knew he meant it in jest, or at least he pretended to mean it that way, but over the past few days she had learned better. Danae had gotten fairly close to the archer over the years, closer than anyone else, at least. In better times, they had occasionally been lovers, but while she had once wished for more, he had never let her into his heart. Now they were just friends, drinking buddies, and occasionally, when she had too many to exercise better judgment, bedmates.

Since he had returned from whatever dark hell he had been wandering in, his mood had been blacker than pitch, and when he was at his drunkest, he had begged her earnestly to put an end to his life. Seeing Chad like that frightened her, for even at his worst he had never been suicidal.

Keeping her worries to herself, she left the bar and walked over to the table he sat at, ruffling his hair with one hand. It was oily and stiff. "Eat with us when Eddard gets here. If you do that and take a bath, I'll let you have a glass early," she said, relenting out of pity.

His face perked up, sensing an opening. "How about before the bath? I don't think I can handle the water with my head aching like this."

Danae sighed. "Eat first, then I'll think about it."

The front doors banged open, and Eddard was silhouetted in them, with the bright morning sunshine streaming around him. Chad winced at the sudden increase in lighting. Then Eddard announced, "There's a stranger in town, looking for a bowyer."

"There ain't one here!" barked Chad. "Tell him to go to Arundel. Old Mattley will take care of him."

A second figure entered, pushing past Eddard. This one was taller, more muscular, and familiar, even to Chad's somewhat blurry eyesight. "I don't actually need a bowyer, just a bow," said the stranger in a low, resonant voice. "Perhaps you have one to sell."

Chad knew that voice, and a chill ran down his spine. Reaching under the table, he patted Danae's knee to get her attention. "Go out the back," he whispered earnestly. "Go home. Don't come back until…"

The stranger approached the table, a gleam in his eyes that only made the strange tattoos running down his arms seem even stranger. "It's really you, isn't it?" asked Tyrion, his voice full of wonder. "I never thought I'd have the luck to see your face again."

Danae stepped forward protectively, placing herself between the newcomer and Chad's seat. "He's not in any condition to bargain," she informed the stranger. "Your best bet is to go to Arundel."

Tyrion stared at the bartender, his gaze boring into her. Slowly his eyes tracked down, then up again, as he took stock of her—then he smiled. "Your guard dog is pretty, Grayson," he announced. "You should call her off before something bad happens to her."

Chad had risen unsteadily to his feet, and he put a hand on Danae's shoulder. "This ain't your fight, Danni. Go home."

She saw a telltale flicker of steel as Chad pushed her aside, and she knew immediately what he was doing. Going with the flow, she pretended to stumble before seizing a nearby chair and spinning to swing it at the newcomer's head.

For a split second, she saw it all, Chad moving with that uncanny speed he sometimes displayed, a long knife in one hand, and then she was flying. Her body struck the wall with enough force to drive the wind from her lungs, but she didn't slide down. Some unseen force kept her pinned there, her feet not quite able to reach the floor. When her vision cleared, she could see Chad sprawling belly up on top of one of the tables, apparently also caught by the same invisible power.

Tyrion was leaning over him, grinning. "Isn't this a heartwarming reunion?"

"Go fuck yerself!" swore Chad, and then he spat in Tyrion's face—or at least he tried to. Whatever kept him pinned down stopped the spittle mere inches from his lips and it dribbled back down to land on the archer's cheeks.

At that moment, Eddard slammed the chair in his hands down over Tyrion's head, but the only result was a broken chair. The man stared at it in open-mouthed horror.

Unfazed, Tyrion took a moment to address Eddard, "The reason I haven't bothered looking at you, slackwit, isn't because I didn't know you were there, but because I have absolutely no reason to even consider your presence. Get out, and don't even think about bringing others unless you want to turn this bar into a slaughterhouse." Then he looked back at the helpless archer. "The last time we met, you didn't even greet me properly before trying to kill me."

"I don't give two shits what you think you dickless—," Chad's words cut off abruptly as something blocked his nose and mouth.

"At least I had the manners to say hello before killing you," said Tyrion as he watched the hunter's face slowly turn red, then purple.

"Please," begged Danae. "Whatever your quarrel is, please don't kill him."

Tyrion studied her for a moment, as though seeing her for the first time, then walked over to inspect his other captive. "Is this your woman, Master Grayson?" he asked as he reached out and lifted her chin with one finger. When the hunter failed to reply, he glanced back. "Oh, that's right, you're suffocating to death."

Suddenly able to breathe again, Chad drew several great, heaving lungfuls of air. "Leave her out o' this. She's just a barmaid. I hardly know her."

"Then you won't mind if I examine her a little more closely," commented Tyrion, letting his hand drift down from Danae's chin to squeeze her breast. Her head jerked to the side as she tried to escape.

"I said leave her alone!" screamed Chad, causing the table to buckle slightly as he struggled against the shield holding him down.

Tyrion stepped back from Danae, a faint smile creeping across his face as he looked at Chad once again. "I thought so."

"Just kill me, asshole," cursed the hunter. "If that's what you want, I don't give a damn."

Tyrion stopped, becoming utterly still for several seconds as he locked eyes with the hunter who had once tried to assassinate him. "You really want me to, don't you? You truly want to die."

"No!" yelled Danae.

Raising one finger, the former Duke of the Wester Isles sealed Danae's lips, though he left her nose free to breathe. "As much as you might want to think I came here to kill you, Master Grayson, our meeting today is pure happenstance. Not that I wouldn't mind ending your miserable existence, but now that I see your utter despair, I find myself wanting you to live. That's the only way you can suffer, *really* suffer."

Chad found the force holding him down suddenly gone, but before he could leap up from the table, Tyrion's voice warned him, "I hold her life in my hands. Don't test my patience."

The hunter said nothing, staring fiercely at his antagonist with spite-filled eyes.

"Go get your bow, Master Archer, preferably the same one you shot me with, and bring the enchanted arrows as well, however many you have left." Walking over to Danae, Tyrion released her and gently eased her down until her feet touched the floor, then he led her over to an empty table where he sat down and gestured to his lap. "Have a seat," he told her.

Danae stared helplessly at Chad as she slowly sat in Tyrion's lap, flinching slightly as she felt his hand slide around her waist.

"You pus-ridden dog fucker. If you touch her, I'll—" warned Chad.

"I'm already touching her, Master Grayson," replied Tyrion. "Hurry and fetch what I want, and she won't be harmed. Take too long, and I might get *bored*, and you wouldn't want that, trust me."

Chad left, and as soon as he was outside, he began to run for his home. Unfortunately, his body rebelled almost immediately after having been abused for several days. He stumbled and threw up in the street before struggling back to his feet and hurrying on. He ran as much as he could, and jogged when he couldn't, but it took him almost fifteen minutes to reach his small cottage. It took even longer to return, despite his best efforts.

When he got back, he found a small crowd of townsfolk gathered outside with Eddard, talking in hushed voices. "Go back to yer homes," Chad told them. "The man in there will kill the lot of you if a whim strikes him." He didn't wait to argue with them, though.

Carrying his warbow and twelve of the enchanted arrows Mordecai had made him, Chad went back inside the Muddy Pig. His head was pounding with pain, and his only hope was that his death would be swift.

To his great relief, the scene hadn't changed much when he stepped inside. Danae was still sitting in Tyrion's lap, her face rigid and her back stiff. She was still clothed, and he couldn't see any blood or visible wounds. "I brought what you wanted. Let's get this over with," said Chad, placing the bow and enchanted shafts on the table.

Tyrion pushed Danae to her feet. "Leave, little one, and warn those outside not to enter."

She glanced at Chad, desperation and fear written on her face, but he only nodded. "Do as he says," affirmed the archer. She left, reluctantly, and when she was gone, he turned to Tyrion. "How are we going to do this?"

The mage merely laughed. "You really do want to die. I hate to disappoint you, but you aren't that important to me." Tyrion's eyes ranged over Chad's sweat-soaked shirt and haggard features. "You couldn't be more worthless if you tried."

The hunter's eye twitched as he bit back angry words before finally responding, "What do you want then?"

The mage laid one hand across the bow. "This. But before I go, I want to share a few thoughts with you." He lifted one finger, "First, despite my past, I am not the murderous madman you seem to think, though it suits my purposes just fine if you believe so. I never had any intention of hurting the woman." Then he lifted a second finger. "Second, although I'm leaving you alive, don't think it a mercy. After I leave here, I intend to kill several of the people who are most important to you."

Chad started to leap to his feet, but found himself abruptly pinned to the floor, his mouth sealed shut. Tyrion stood and looked down on him. "I'm telling you this because I want you to feel helpless. I want you to understand the depth of your worthlessness. That's my payment to you for trying to kill me. What's more, I'm not going to kill them because of you. I'm going to kill them because it's important to me. Meeting you here was pure luck. I couldn't care less whether you continue breathing or not. That's how insignificant you are."

The curses brewing behind Chad's closed lips were foul enough to strip the varnish from furniture, but he couldn't utter a word as Tyrion turned his back and walked away.

CHAPTER 35

Gary the android, Karen's nominal father, stood across the workshop from the stool Matthew sat upon. One of the things Matthew liked about his fiancée's artificial father was that he could quite easily stand by silently for hours at a time without the need to talk. Matt had been brooding for over an hour with no ideas to speak of, and it came as a shock when Gary suddenly broke the silence, "I have a question."

"Good luck," said Matthew dryly. "I haven't had much success coming up with answers."

"When you were talking with your family last night, you left out the most obvious course of action. I presume you decided it would be too difficult for them to face. Is that the case?" asked Gary.

Matthew grimaced, then rubbed at his forehead. "You and Rose are the only two to have noticed that—so far."

"Then it has already occurred to you," stated the android. "If your father's existence will destroy everything, the most straightforward solution is to eliminate that existence."

Matt nodded. "It sounds simple when you say it like that, but it would be easier for me to break the world than it would be to erase him."

"You mean using the Fool's Tesseract?" asked Gary.

"Of course," answered Matthew.

"If you set it properly you could create a singularity that might swallow him when you released it, but that would…"

"Destroy the world as well," finished Matthew. "And anything less than that would do absolutely nothing. No explosion, no matter how powerful, would do anything to him."

"Have you considered a stasis field, like the one you used to save Karen?"

"We think of aythar as magic," said Matthew, "but it has rules. The amount of power inside my dad at the moment would require an even greater amount of power to contain it."

"It sounds as though only a kung fu master could defeat him," said the android, punctuating his remark with a chuckle.

Matthew stared at him in confusion. "A what?"

Gary's mouth opened for a second, then he responded, "Ahh. I guess you didn't see many movies while you were in our world."

Matthew shook his head.

"Kung fu was a martial art practiced by some in our world, but what I was referring to was the philosophy that was espoused in many films. The idea being that a weaker opponent could defeat a stronger one simply by using his own power against him. Of course, in reality that was only true up to a certain point, but—"

"Shhh!" snapped Matthew, his brows knitting together in concentration. After a moment he went to the drafting board and took out the pen and a bottle of ink and began to sketch.

Gary watched him silently for half an hour before speaking again. "That looks somewhat similar to the design of the Fool's Tesseract."

"No, it isn't like it at all. Let me think," responded Matt waspishly. He continued to draw, making strange notes at the edges of the page. Eventually, he ran out of room, and he marked the sides of his drawing with arrows to indicate continuations of the pattern. Twenty minutes later, he took the page down and started anew, using a ruler to keep his lines straight this time.

It took him more than two hours to finish his revised version, and even that seemed to make him unhappy. In the end he stared at the draft as though he wanted to burn it to ash. "This won't work," he muttered. "I'd need a lifetime to create it."

"Pardon me," said Gary, who had remained silently beside him the entire time without complaint.

"Yes?"

"How long do we have? Do you have an estimate?" asked the machine.

Matthew gave him a despairing look. "Oddly, that's the only thing I know with precision. Sixteen days. Everything I see gets blurry and indistinct the closer to the sixteenth day I try to look, so I'm nearly blind when I try to pick out details of the day itself."

"And that won't be enough time to make this?" asked Gary with mild disbelief in his voice. He gestured to the drafting board. "It looks fairly simple."

He sighed. "That's a single cell, an individual building block. There would need to be an almost unthinkable number of others linked together with it."

"Oh."

"Not only that," Matt continued, "but they'd also need to be unimaginably small. There's no way I could inscribe an object that small, even once, much less billions of times over."

"What exactly is it supposed to do?" asked Gary.

A scratching at the workshop door distracted Matthew for a moment, but he ignored it, recognizing the sound as Humphrey begging to be let in. Instead he began to explain his idea to Gary in great detail, even though there were several large gaps in his plan. Over time he had come to trust the android's ability to grasp the bigger picture. Unlike humans, who often became overwhelmed with obvious flaws, the machine had the ability to consider things dispassionately, even if they might be otherwise impossible to achieve.

"It's a shame your world doesn't have the technology mine had," said Gary after a while. "Most of your problems are of repetition and miniaturization, although I must admit the tiny scale you need for this would have given us pause."

Matthew felt a thrill down his spine and sat up straight. "What about ANSIS? It can build things at the atomic level, right?"

Gary shook his head sadly. "It's gone, remember? I'm fairly certain your father eliminated it. If there were any remnants, they either self-deactivated or fled this dimension. That is aside from the fact that it would be difficult, if not impossible, to create an agreement. To make matters worse, if you did get its assistance you would also be simultaneously removing the one major obstacle to it taking control of this world."

Matt slumped again. Another scratch came at the door, followed by the sound of the latch lifting. Myra stepped in, followed by a joyful Humphrey, happy to at last be allowed in.

"Hey!" exclaimed Matthew. "Don't let him in! I'm trying to work." It was too late, however, and he found himself staring down at Humphrey, who was now pawing his leg. The dog's tail wagged with unfounded enthusiasm. Despite himself, he reached down and began scratching behind one of Humphrey's ears. "At least you aren't mad at me," he muttered. "Although I have no idea why you're so happy to see me."

"It's because you ignore him," stated Myra. "Everyone else pays so much attention to him it wears him out. He enjoys the quiet around you." As if to emphasize her point, Humphrey promptly curled up at Matthew's feet and laid his head between his paws.

"Huh," said Matthew. "That explains why he's always trying to get in here. He's looking for a place to relax." Then he glanced at Gary. "Do you suppose the same thing applies to Karen?"

The android rubbed his chin in an artificial human gesture to indicate he was thinking. "That may be true. Our world had much less face-to-face interaction. She may find your neglect attractive."

Myra covered her face with one hand. "Every time I start to respect your intelligence, you say something so stupid it makes me question it."

"Whose?" asked Matthew, pointing at first Gary and then himself. "His or mine?"

"Yours," said Myra instantly. "Gary at least has the excuse of not being human."

The android frowned. "I think I'm offended."

"That makes two of us," agreed Matt. "I'm trying to work. Did you just come to insult us or was there another purpose to your interruption?" he asked her.

She studied him for a moment. "Actually, you've hit a block. I doubt you'll get anything else done today." Then she frowned. "Your shields have gotten better. I'm having trouble reading anything beyond your general mood."

"You did tell us to practice," reminded Matt.

Myra flinched slightly. "That was Moira who said that." Recovering her composure, she went on, "It's time for dinner."

"Just ask Alyssa to bring me something later. No one wants to see me anyway," said Matthew. Reaching down, he stroked Humphrey's head once more. "Except this fleabag."

"Suit yourself," said Myra, and without argument, she turned and left. Gary went with her. He didn't need to eat, but he seemed to enjoy the company to be found at the dinner table.

The door had closed before Matthew could protest. "Hey! Take Humphrey with you!" Looking down at the dog, he let out a long sigh. He got down from the stool and sat on the floor to pet the contented animal. "I guess you can stay a while."

After spending a few minutes with Humphrey, he went and locked the workshop door, sealing it with a quick spell, then he returned to the drafting table, pulling a stool over to it so he could sit while he stared at his design. The dog got up and shifted position so he could lie close to Matt's feet.

Staring at the design didn't provide much inspiration, and after a while he began to drowse. Putting his head on his arms, he rested on the table and let his eyes close. *Just a few minutes...*

A loud banging on the door brought him abruptly awake. From the lack of light coming in the window, he realized he must have slept for more than an hour. "Who is it?" he yelled grumpily, though he assumed it was Alyssa with his food.

"Open the door!" roared an angry female voice from outside. It was Irene.

"I'm busy," he called back, but a rumble from his empty belly made him rethink. "Did you bring food?"

"No. If you want food you can come get it yourself," she snapped back from the other side of the door. "Why are you avoiding me?"

Already irritated by his sudden awakening, Matthew let his contrariness answer for him, "I'm not avoiding you. We talked plenty last night."

"*You* talked. *They* talked. *We* didn't talk. Open the door!" she insisted.

"I'm busy. We can talk later," replied Matthew. "It won't solve anything anyway. What's done is done."

Her response was a low growling that grew louder by the second, and despite himself Matthew found himself smirking as he imagined her face on the other side of the door—until the door shattered, exploding inward. Fortunately, the low-grade personal shield he kept around himself was enough to keep the flinders from impaling him. Irene stood in the open doorway, her red face just as he had pictured it. She was the very image of fury incarnate, and for a moment she reminded him of their mother.

"What the hell, Rennie? That was a perfectly good door!" he declared, more shocked than angry.

"A good door knows when to open!" she shot back.

"Get out!" he yelled, his own blood beginning to boil now. "This is my place. I won't have you throwing a tantrum in it."

"Tantrum?" she questioned, her voice dropping dangerously low. "Is that what you think this is? This shop is more important to you than your family, isn't it? Very well, I'll show you a tantrum!" Snatching up a rune-inscribed metal cube from the work table, she hurled it at him, forgetting the power of her dragon-bond-enhanced muscles.

Matthew saw it coming, but failed utterly to dodge it. Luckily he had already reinforced his shield by that time; otherwise it might have cracked his skull. For a moment a thought crossed his mind, *Why didn't I see that coming?* Then he was forced to attempt to dodge once more as she threw a second random piece of apparatus at him. Again, his precognitive sense failed to warn him.

"Stop! You're going to wreck the shop!" he yelled.

"The shop be damned!" she howled. "I'm trying to forgive you!" Then her eyes fell on a crate of enchanted odds and ends he had made over the years.

Matthew saw the direction of her glance and reacted without thinking. "No!" he yelled, while throwing a battering ram of pure force in her direction. It slammed into Irene with the power of a charging bull and sent her hurtling back out the doorway and into the night.

He felt a cold chill wash over him. *Oh no! I've killed her!* Rushing outside, he used his magesight to locate her, which turned out to be fairly easy. She rose from a copse of small trees like an avenging ghost, her aythar blazing like a bonfire.

"Now, Rennie, take it easy," he cautioned her. "Let's not go overboard."

"Easy? I'll show you easy," she warned, and raising her fist, she uprooted a large oak. The massive tree rose in the air before sweeping down at him like a giant club.

Being unable to predict her attacks left Matthew feeling uneasy, but he had prepared for many contingencies over the years. Having once lost a hand had made him cautious, but he had been determined to turn his loss into an advantage. Lifting his metal hand, he spoke a word of command, and a powerful shield sprang into existence around him.

Unlike a personal shield, or any shield he created directly, this one was structured through an enchantment built into the hand itself, so he didn't need to worry about feedback should it break. Not that it would; the nature of the enchantment made it far stronger than anything he could create spontaneously.

The force of the tree hammered him, and his shield, downward several feet into the ground, creating a hemisphere-shaped depression in the hard mountain soil. Matt created a temporary shield within the enchanted one to provide support, then dismissed the one that his hand controlled, allowing him to let the tree drop until it settled to the ground. At the same time, he collapsed into the depression beneath it.

Irene ran up moments later. "Matt? Are you alright? Oh, no!" She was panicked as she sought to find out if her brother was still alive. With a gesture, she lifted the tree and flung it aside, and her first sight was of him lying unconscious in the compressed earth. "No, no, no," she moaned. "Please, this can't be happening!"

Dropping to her knees, she crawled down the sloping earth to her brother and began rapidly checking him for injuries. Of course, there were none, which her magesight quickly revealed. His heart was beating, his skin intact, and there were no broken bones. Her eyes narrowed with suspicion when one of his popped open to stare back at her.

"You thought I was dead, didn't you?" he asked with a sly grin, though he immediately regretted it. Irene's eyes went wide and began to water.

"You asshole!" she cried, angry tears on her cheeks. "I thought I killed you!"

"Then maybe don't drop a tree on my head next time," he advised.

She glared at him. "How can you be such a jerk? I just wanted to tell you I understood, that I'd forgiven you."

Matthew chuckled. "If this is how you forgive someone, I pity your future husband."

"You're about to be my *late*-brother," she growled, getting to her feet and pulling out her wand. With a word, it expanded to the size of a staff and she used it to assist her as she climbed out of the hole.

Relaxing, he sank back to the ground, enjoying the cool feel of the earth. "If it helps any, I agree with you."

She looked down on him from the rim. "About what?"

"About me," he said quietly, staring up at her.

Irene climbed back down and offered her hand, dragging him to his feet when he took it. "Stop blaming yourself," she said. Then looking at him sideways, she added, "That's my job." She helped him out of the depression, and then with a word she collapsed her staff back down to its more compact wand size.

Matthew froze, a strange look on his face.

"What?" asked Irene.

"What size was your staff originally?" he asked. "Was it a wand that you make larger, or a staff that you make smaller?" Before she could answer, he shook his head, as though trying to clear it. "Never mind. It doesn't matter. The principle is the same either way."

"What are you getting at?"

"Can you show me the enchantment you used?" he asked, ignoring her question. Taking her hand once more, he led her back toward the workshop and its now missing door. "I want to see exactly how you did it."

CHAPTER 36

I stood on what appeared to be a vast lake reflecting the sky above me. When I stared into the distance, the clouds would race by, but whenever I looked up they froze in place, as though time was standing still. Beneath my feet, the water turned out to be a deception, for the surface I stood on wasn't truly reflecting the sky; it was transparent, a window that held me suspended above a vast and mysterious world.

My head felt as though it had been turned inside out. The world I saw was broken into facets, as though it was encased within a colossal gem, yet when I studied the various facets, they showed me different scenes, some familiar, some so foreign to my experience as to be alien.

And within it all, I felt a heartbeat, much like the voice of the earth I had long ago become accustomed to. Yet this rhythmic thrumming was different. I knew it in a way that was intuitive—the knowledge was something I possessed, had always possessed, but had only now become aware of. It was my heartbeat, my existence. It was the lifeblood of the universe flowing through my veins.

The pain, which had once been so overwhelming, was a faint echo on the edge of my experience. Realizing that made me afraid, for I knew it should be closer, more painful. Without pain, there could be no life. *Am I dying?* I wondered.

No, you're growing, responded the other, the god that wanted to pass on. *When the pain vanishes, you will be complete. A new world will be born, and your dream will begin.*

Cracks were forming in the diamond that held the universe. Soon it would crumble. *It's dying!* I cried with my voice that had no sound. *I'm dying!*

No, came the answer, *that is me. I am crumbling, but you will rise from the fragments like a phoenix from the ashes of my body.*

Like a bolt of lightning, the memory of my family tore through me, and I stared down once more, finding them within the crumbling gem. I saw them, eating, arguing, laughing. Rose was with them, and when I focused my attention on her, I became her. I saw through her eyes, felt their love with her heart, and comprehended them through the lens that was her mind.

And what a mind it was. The landscape of her soul was hauntingly beautiful and stunningly tragic. Meticulously ordered, the pieces and memories of her life were arranged in such a way that I could easily see the links between them. In some ways it reminded me of the perfect crystalline memories I had inherited through the loshti, but unlike those memories, these were painted and colored by her painfully human heart.

Her childhood was there, her father, and her mother who I had never known. She had been brilliant, even as a child, and her precocious intellect had utterly captivated the parents who were already predisposed to love her. Rose had grown to womanhood with a far better understanding of the games and politics of life than those who had raised her.

She might have become jaded and cynical if it hadn't been for the appearance of Dorian Thornbear in her life. He stood out among her memories, a pure and simple being who had restored her faith in the future, simply by existing. Beside him was a man I hardly recognized, a man with sharp features and a face that set my teeth on edge almost immediately. I could tell just by looking at him that he was arrogant, overconfident, even prideful.

He was also perceptive, with eyes that saw too much. The knowledge in his eyes was unsettling and the memory of him seemed to stare back at me, as though he were judging me somehow. His memory aged before me, and I could see a keen mind behind those eyes, one that was slowly becoming wiser.

There was a woman beside him, and I recognized her immediately. *Penny!* That was when I finally understood what I was seeing: myself, filtered through the lens of Rose's memory and careful discernment.

For a moment I was lost in her recollections, her love, and her observations of the people around her: her family and mine. It was humbling to see the depth of her devotion to those people, and even more humbling to be so intimately aware of how she perceived me.

She had seen my faults, my vanity, and even my evil, but had judged them to be of less importance than my compassion, my own struggle to provide for not just those I loved, but for those I had never known, the people of Lothion.

Fighting against the tides of memory, I rose to the surface of her mind, to see where her current thoughts were going. And there I found my death.

It wasn't something concrete or easily visualized. Rose had no idea how it would be accomplished, but she was guiding those around her, giving gentle nudges when necessary, or timely advice when it was warranted. She was doing what she had done for me during most of my previous life, working behind the scenes to make my goals come to fruition.

But whose goal is she assisting? I wondered. *Ah, now I see it.* She was helping my son.

I turned my attention to Matthew, and once again, I fell into a strange new world. Through his eyes I saw myself again, this time differently, but I didn't allow myself to become distracted as I had before. I needed to understand his goal. *He's trying to kill me, and it's tearing his heart to pieces.*

I could feel his sadness and pain, and more particularly, I could see the method he was pursuing, though it was far from complete. I wasn't sure if it could possibly succeed. At the very least it would require my willing participation. None of the tricks he had in mind would work, certainly not now that I had seen the landscape of his mind.

Desperately I wanted to communicate with him, but my thoughts were invisible to his perception. I tried moving his memories, or altering his ideas, but that failed as well. The mental structures within him were like indestructible stone to my will. I could change nothing.

You're only torturing yourself, came the voice of the old god, the one I was to replace. *Come away from them. Look at something else for a while.*

My view dissolved and I found my mind spinning through the world until it found something else familiar to latch onto. Tyrion. *I don't want to see him,* I complained.

He's more interesting, said the voice. *What is he doing now?*

Despite myself, I found myself studying the man. Tyrion was leaning over a table somewhere—Arundel, I realized. A tiny silver stylus was in his hand, and with it he was etching runes onto strangely shaped arrowheads. With my interest piqued, I descended into the man whom I had come to loathe, examining his thoughts as he worked.

I understood why the arrowheads were so odd now. He had fused bodkin points meant for penetrating armor to heavy irons spheres. The points were being enchanted to pierce, something I had done many times, and the spheres were made to contain a reservoir of aythar, much like my old favorite, the iron bomb. *No, they are iron bombs.* Tyrion had planned the enchantment to enable the arrows to pierce deeply and then detonate inside their target.

But there was still something missing, something Tyrion didn't know, and he was aware of the gap in his knowledge. *He wants the enchantment Brigid used on her chain.*

Without it his plan won't work, said the voice of the old god, whispering in my ear, *but he'll find another way.*

Studying Tyrion's mind once more, I found his goal: my family. The simmering pain within the man would find an outlet. Moira was his conscious target, but deeper down his murderous intent would spill over onto all of them.

If only Brigid was there to divert him, suggested the voice. And then she was.

Did I do that? I asked, surprised.

There was a smile in the elder god's voice. *It appears so.*

I didn't want that to happen!

Just watch...

***

The design Tyrion was working on was incomplete, and no matter how he searched his memories he had no recollection of how Brigid had created the enchantment that made her chain such a deadly weapon. Apparently he, or rather his predecessor, hadn't given it much thought and had never thought to inquire.

That was regrettable, for the enchantment on Brigid's chain had been one-of-a-kind. Aside from enhancing the weapon's durability and sharpness, it had caused the chain to shed foreign aythar the way a duck's feathers shed water. It had been keyed to Brigid herself, such that only her magic could move it, a necessary feature to keep such a weapon from becoming the focal point of a struggle of wills when used against another mage.

He could already make the arrows functionally lethal in the manner he desired, but once his enemy was alerted to his attack they might easily divert his following shots. "Damn it. Why didn't I ever ask?"

A sudden flare of aythar behind him made him spin in place, dropping into a crouch and activating his shield tattoos. "Ask what, Father?" asked a coarse yet feminine voice.

Tyrion stared at the woman before him, his eyes widening with shock before narrowing in suspicion. It wasn't possible. He had been delirious before. Yet the figure in front of him was that of his daughter, Brigid. Just as she had been in life, she smelled faintly of blood, wore no clothing, and was obviously in need of a bath. Much like a cat, his daughter had never had much use for either clothing or soap and water.

His first thought was that she was an illusion, but his magesight confirmed that she was physically very real, and her aythar was exactly as he remembered. Had Moira done something to his mind? Only she—or someone who possessed his memories, such as Mordecai—would even be able to create such a realistic copy of his daughter.

"Who are you?" he asked warily.

"Exactly who you think I am," she replied.

Without warning, he attacked, feinting left and then slicing at her torso from the right with his armblade. The stroke was stopped by an enchanted chain that whipped around her body like a serpent. He stared into her eyes, unable to believe what he was seeing. "You're dead."

"You didn't attack me last time," she noted. "When I helped get you back on your feet."

"That was real?" he asked, questioning his own sanity as much as the woman in front of him.

"It seemed real," she replied. "As far as I know I should be dead, but here I am."

"This makes no sense," he muttered. Then a thought occurred to him. "Dampen your power! There's a mage in this town. He'll sense you from a mile away if you keep flaunting your aythar that way."

She arched one brow beneath ragged bangs. "And you're *afraid* of a single mage?"

"I'm not here to fight, or to be seen," he responded, relaxing slightly as she did as he asked. He frowned a moment later, though, as he noted a shift in the position of the mage in question.

The range of Tyrion's magesight was greater than most, so he had been able to observe the Lord of Arundel from a distance while keeping his own power tightly wrapped up, but the Baron was on the move now, heading for his position in the bowyer's workshop. A second later, the other mage's presence vanished.

"He's a Prathion?" asked Brigid with faint surprise. "Didn't we kill them all?"

"Human," remarked Tyrion. "He's a descendant of my breeding project."

"And he's hunting us?" said Brigid, her lip curling into a wicked grin. "I haven't had this much fun in…" she paused. "How long has it been since I died?"

"A little over two thousand years," answered Tyrion. "If you're even real." He began rolling up the oilskin that the arrowheads were laid out on, packing them away. "We're leaving."

"You're going to run?" asked Brigid in disbelief.

"I'm not here to wipe out the few human mages left," Tyrion explained. "There are few enough as it is. I have no quarrel with this one."

His daughter remained immobile. "What of the She'Har? Did we succeed?"

He froze for a moment, considering his answer, then replied, "Mostly."

"Mostly?"

"The Illeniel survived. That's how I'm still here. I became an Elder. Lyralliantha survived as well," he told her.

Brigid scowled. "Is that what you're working on, a means to kill them?"

Tyrion stopped, his mind going back to his conversation with the peasant girl. *"Fix your story,"* she had told him. His main goal had been to eliminate Moira, but now that seemed small. She did need killing, there was no doubt of that, but was that *all* he should be trying to accomplish? He hadn't questioned his creator's purposes, but they seemed contrary to what he had truly wanted, the extinction of the She'Har.

Had he gone soft? Had two millennia as a tree turned the original Tyrion against humanity? What would happen in the future, if mankind and She'Har tried to coexist?

There were several people on his kill list—Mordecai, Rose, and Moira—but was that really all he wanted?

No.

"Yes," he replied, his conviction resolving even as he answered. "That's exactly what they're for. In fact, I need to know how you created the enchantment on your chain."

His daughter nodded. "I didn't do it alone. Layla helped me."

"Layla?" He had never expected that answer. The slave-mage had been one of his most ardent followers, practically worshipping him, and while she had been cunning, she hadn't been particularly intelligent or creative. She had just been one of thousand of human slaves born with the Prathion gift. *The Prathion gift,* he repeated silently to himself, *of course.* He put the oilskin back down on the table. There was no need to run. Everything he needed was here.

CHAPTER 37

George Prathion, the Baron of Arundel, woke suddenly and found himself sitting upright in bed. He had been having a wonderful dream, one he wished he could go back to, although it was already fading from his mind, replaced by a strange sense of foreboding. What had awakened him?

As the fog cleared from his mind, he saw it, a flash of aythar in the village nearby. He wasn't expecting any visitors, nor did he recognize the aythar. Since he had met every human mage in Lothion already, that meant the stranger was probably one of the She'Har, or possibly one of the strange magic users that had recently begun crossing over the dimensional divide.

Focusing his attention, he detected a second mage with the first, though this one was dim and hard to see. It only took him a second to recognize Tyrion, however. *Why is he trying to hide his presence?* George wondered.

Then he remembered that Tyrion was a wanted man. The message had arrived from the capital just two days earlier. George's heart sped up as adrenaline brought him fully awake. Almost reflexively, he cloaked himself in a veil that would make him invisible to magesight, but he knew they had already seen him. From what he had heard, Tyrion's range was greater than his own.

And there's no way I can handle him alone, much less with another mage helping him, thought George. His sister, Elaine, along with most of the Illeniel family, had gone to wherever Lancaster was these days. The only person he could think of that might possibly be able to handle Tyrion was Gareth Gaelyn, and that notable was in Albamarl.

George dressed quickly, then left his room. As he went, he modified the veil that covered him, rendering himself almost completely invisible to normal sight as well as magesight. For convenience, he left a small opening so he could see. He could close that later, when he was close enough for normal visibility to matter. For now, he simply wanted to leave his manor without alerting the servants.

Confronting Tyrion directly was not a wise option. He could only hope the man had no ill intentions toward the people of Arundel. What he could do—what Prathions did best—was get closer and find out what the man was doing here. Once he knew that, he would know better what course of action to take.

Slipping out a side door, he walked around the house and found the paved road that led toward the village. Although Arundel wasn't as large Washbrook and Castle Cameron, it was more spread out, so it took him a good ten minutes to get into the village proper. By then he had identified the building Tyrion was in, which was Mattley's shop and home. The old bowyer usually did a lot of business, but not at this time of night.

As he got closer, George fought the urge to peek. The veil that protected him from magesight also left him blind in that regard, so he was limited to the small amount of normal light that entered his peephole in order to see. Consequently, he couldn't be certain of Tyrion or the other mage's current location, not without revealing himself.

Since it was nighttime, there wasn't much light, but he only needed a little to avoid tripping. He just wanted to get close enough to listen in to their conversation. Carefully, he crept toward Mattley's front door, modifying his veil once again to ensure no stray sounds could betray his approach. *When a Prathion doesn't wish to be found, they aren't,* he told himself with a grin.

The faint moonlight vanished, as what seemed to be fog filled the streets. Without his magesight, he couldn't tell if it was magical, but it had appeared too quickly to be normal. Then he felt cold metal pressing against his throat, causing him to nearly jump out of his skin. "Release your veil and remain still, if you want to live," warned a woman's deep voice.

George froze, and then he felt the sharp metal begin cutting into his skin. It seemed to be everywhere, not just at his throat, but wrapping around his entire body. Fighting down panic, he released his veil, and his magesight revealed the full depth of his plight. An enchanted chain of razor-sharp links was wrapped around him, lightly touching his body in places, and hovering mere inches away in others. He could be torn apart at the merest whim of whoever was controlling it.

Tyrion was standing in the doorway of the bowyer's house, watching him with interest. "I think she likes you. You're only bleeding in a couple of places."

Brigid gave her father a dirty look as she walked around her captive. Tyrion knew how she felt about most men. As she stepped in front of the hapless mage, she noted a strange furtiveness to his eyes as he saw her. His features wavered between shock, fear, and fascination. His gaze kept returning to her breasts. "You should let me kill him, Father," she announced. "Look at his eyes. He's defective, like Ian."

Two thousand years prior, her brother Ian had been the worst of her siblings: violent, crude, and most despicable of all, a rapist. Tyrion laughed at her remark. "He's probably never seen a naked woman before, Brigid. The people of this time wear clothes at all times."

George tore his gaze away from the savage woman in front of him and fixed it on Tyrion. He *had* seen a woman's breasts before, one night when a drunken barmaid decided to tease him, but he had never seen anything like Brigid's total, feral nudity. "What do you want?" he asked, hoping his voice sounded firm, because inwardly he was a riot of fear and near-panic.

"I want your help," said Tyrion.

"I c—can't do that," stammered George. "Y—you're w—wanted by the Queen."

Brigid moved closer, licking her lips, and George caught his first whiff of her unwashed body. He wrinkled his nose involuntarily, but when her words reached his ears, a chill raced down his spine. "I hoped you would say that."

"You should reconsider," suggested Tyrion.

"What do you want me t—to do, exactly?" asked George.

Tyrion smiled. "Nothing serious. I merely want your help finishing an enchantment. Do that for me and I'll leave you in peace—in one piece, to be precise."

***

Lynaralla knelt in the large front courtyard of Castle Cameron, staring at hands that were covered in blood, not her own. Her cheeks were wet with tears and a black despair gripped her heart as she looked across the field. In front of her was her sister, Irene, already dead, her blonde hair dyed crimson.

She was shocked from her grief by a thunderclap that shook the ground, and when she glanced up she saw Conall's broken body flying by. It was still in one piece, but only barely; his torso had been mostly bisected by a magical blade. A blade wielded by the man she had once called her father.

Twenty feet to her left, she saw Matthew futilely struggling to contain the enchantment he had created, an enchantment that was rapidly devolving, spiraling out of control. Irene's death had ruined it, and Lynaralla knew his effort was doomed to failure.

Not that it mattered. It had been their last hope. Even if he somehow salvaged it, they would all be dead in less than a day. The world was ending.

Boots stopped in front of her, but she was powerless to fight. She had sacrificed herself to absorb the feedback when Irene had been slain, causing the enchantment to fail. "You've killed us all," she murmured bitterly.

"Even if I believed you, I wouldn't care. All that matters is that I kill *you*. You're the last," said Tyrion.

Anger surged through her, and Lynaralla's head jerked upward. She glared at her murderous sire. "Damn you! Damn yo—"

Her words cut off with a sickening gurgle as Tyrion's armblade entered her midsection and came up, slicing through her belly, lungs, and shoulder. Her last vision was of Matthew, watching her with desperation on his face, impotent to stop the horror.

Lynaralla woke with a gasp, still feeling the searing pain in her chest. She struggled to breathe, her mouth gaping as she tried and failed to draw in air. Her body was convinced she had died, but after a minute of panic her muscles finally relaxed and she was finally able to draw quick, short breaths.

She was alive. This was Irene's bedroom, and Irene was sleeping beside her, snoring loudly enough to wake the dead, which perhaps she had. Despite herself, Lynaralla reached over and touched Irene's chest above her heart, reassuring herself that her sister's body was whole and uninjured.

What was that? she wondered. She had never had such a vivid dream before. Was it a manifestation of her gift? Had she seen the future? Lynaralla closed her eyes and corrected herself, *A possible future.* But despite all her reason, she was afraid. It had been too real.

The snoring stopped, and one of Irene's eyes eased open. "Lynn?"

"Yes," answered Lynaralla, controlling her voice carefully. "It's me."

"Why are you awake?" mumbled Irene. "It's still dark."

"I had a dream. You should go back to sleep," said Lynaralla.

Sensing something, Irene sat up as well, sloughing off the heavy quilt. She reached out and touched her sister's forehead, feeling the cold sweat there. "Are you sick?"

"No," replied Lynaralla, using one hand to pull Irene's away.

Ever stubborn, Irene didn't give up so easily, and she caught the She'Har woman's hand in her own. "You're shaking. What sort of dream was it?" Her sister was obviously upset, which troubled her more than it would have in almost anyone else. Lynaralla was always calm, so much so that many often misunderstood the She'Har woman, thinking she had no emotions at all, but Irene knew better.

"I don't want to talk about it."

"It was a premonition, wasn't it?" asked Irene.

Lynaralla nodded.

"But you'll tell Matthew, won't you?"

"He needs to know, so he can adjust his plans," replied Lynaralla.

Irene's jaw tensed. "You're as dumb as he is sometimes. He doesn't need any more secrets. The weight of them is too much. If you want to help him, share this with me. Share it with all of us, so he doesn't feel as if he has to take the blame for whatever terrible choices the future is forcing on him. Do you understand?"

"Irene, I don't think you want to hear this one," said the young She'Har woman.

Irene chuckled. "Why? Do I die in it?"

Her sister said nothing at all.

"So what?" said Irene. "We're all going to die if we don't get this right. Tell me what happens so you can sleep. Tomorrow we'll tell the others together." Sliding closer, she slipped one arm around her sister's shoulder and squeezed, and after a moment, Lynaralla relaxed slightly.

Reluctantly, Lynaralla shared her vision with Irene, relaying the horror she had seen. Being nearly incapable of dissembling, the She'Har woman explained her vision with all the horrific details, stopping only at the end, when Tyrion had been standing in front of her.

Irene prodded her. "So he's standing there looking down on you… what happened then?"

Knowing her death would affect Irene more than hearing of her own, Lynaralla improvised, "And then I lived happily ever after."

Irene stared at her in the dark for a few seconds before asking, "Lynn, was that a joke?"

Lynaralla sighed. "Was it any good?"

Irene began to laugh darkly. "Actually, yes. I think your sense of humor is improving." The two young women lay back down after that, but neither of them found sleep for a long time.

***

The next day, after breakfast was finished and everyone was still in the same room, Irene made the announcement. "Lynn had a premonition last night."

Sitting at the head of the table, Rose glanced at Lynaralla, reading the young woman's face. "It must have been fairly bad. Tell us the details."

More composed than the previous night, the silver-haired She'Har did just that, reciting the events she had witnessed. This time she included her own death as well, without the attempt at humor. The faces of those around her registered varying degrees of shock and dismay, except for Matthew's. He stared past her into the distance, his countenance so still and unmoving that his face almost seemed to be made of stone.

Cyhan was the first to speak. "What about the others? Did you see Alyssa or Gram in your vision?"

Lynaralla shook her head, but Rose spoke quickly to cut off a reply, "That doesn't help much, Sir Cyhan. She's told us what she saw, and its enough to know we'll all die. Even if they were spared at that moment, we'll all be dying soon after it."

Matthew broke his silence. "Actually, this is good news."

Karen was sitting close by, and she elbowed him. "How is that good news?"

"It means we figured out a solution, and that we had time to implement it," he responded. "That's a relief in itself."

"But we failed," protested Conall.

Matthew shook his head. "It's one possible future, and while it might currently be the *most* likely, it won't be now that we can prepare for it. Of course, we could still fail, but it probably won't be in that exact manner." He looked intently at Lynaralla. "Your dream started at a point *after* things started to go wrong, but you probably had some memory of it in your vision. Can you describe exactly what you think happened?"

"I think it was Irene's death that ruined it. She and I, and perhaps Conall too—we were assisting you. In the vision I was stunned because I absorbed the feedback after Irene was killed. I *think* Conall went to defend us then. I'm not entirely certain, though. That's just my feeling," answered Lynaralla.

"Four of us," muttered Matt. "That fits with one of my ideas, although it hadn't occurred to me that it would be those four. It makes sense, though. I was already thinking we should do it in the castle courtyard, but I guess that wasn't such a good plan. We'll have to pick a different spot."

"Why there?" asked Irene.

Rose smiled. "It's the logical choice. It's defensible and the castle shield enchantment should make it impossible for anyone to get in or out."

"I'd had some doubts," admitted Matt. "Even though the castle shield was strong enough to keep out the Shining Gods, I don't think it will be enough to hold Dad anymore."

Conall and Irene looked at each other, confused. Then Conall asked, "Why would it need to hold him in?"

Matthew froze, realizing he had said too much, but Rose saved him. "We haven't had a way to communicate with him directly. Given his erratic behavior lately it would seem wise to find a way to keep him in place long enough to explain things."

"Oh," said Conall. Irene looked less certain, but she held her tongue.

Chapter 38

Old Mattley was a strong man, though his back was bent with age and his joints were swollen from long, hard use. Though he was in his seventies, he still had the vigor of a much younger man, but he was beginning to think of retiring. His eyes were no longer sharp, and the pain in his back made his work more difficult. Unfortunately, he had no heir or apprentice to leave his business to.

His oldest son had moved away, preferring the life of a farmer to that of a bowyer. Mattley's first and only apprentice had become a journeyman and set up shop in Malvern more than twenty years prior. From what Mattley knew, Gedwin had done well and become a master some ten years after that.

Those thoughts brought a sigh to his lips as Mattley stopped his wagon behind his home. It was laden with a fresh supply of yew and ash from which he would make bowstaves, though it would be many months before the wood had dried sufficiently for such use. This load would supply him next year, just as last year's timber would provide him with material for the current year.

Stepping down from the driver's seat, he started to pull back the canvas that covered the wagon bed. He needed to move the wood to the drying racks in his shed before taking his rest for the evening. A stiff pain running down the left side of his neck to his waist reminded him that this would probably be the last wood he ever bought.

He didn't need money. His trade had earned him a modest amount of wealth over the years, but since his wife's death six years past he had no reason to look forward to retiring. His craft was all that had sustained him since then, and without it he doubted he would have cause to live too many more years.

After unloading, he went to the back door, and it was then that he realized something was wrong. The lock was broken. The old man froze, listening to see if anyone might be inside, but he heard nothing. Not that he could trust his ears anymore. Kneeling down, he was grateful that his knees hadn't suffered as his back had. The heavy iron lock lay in the dirt, but it hadn't been broken, picked, or forced in any ordinary manner. The metal clasp had been sheared into two pieces, cut cleanly, as though the tough iron was as soft as butter. "I'll be damned," muttered the old man.

Reaching down to his waist, he unsheathed the hunting knife there before gently opening the door and stepping into his house. Mattley was afraid the robber might be there, but while he still feared death, it didn't have quite the grip on him that it had when he was younger. He didn't bother removing his boots as he entered, something that would have angered his wife, but he figured her ghost would forgive him this one time, considering the circumstances.

The back door he came through opened directly into his kitchen, and there he saw a man seated at the table, lifting a cup to his lips. In the dim light, he couldn't identify the figure. "Who are you, sittin' at my table as though you owned the house?"

"It's me, Mattley," returned a familiar voice. "Relax. They're gone."

"Grayson?" queried the old man. "Who's gone? What the hell are you doing in my kitchen?" Mattley sheathed his knife and went back to the door to remove his boots. There was no sense in giving his late-wife any more things to scold him about when he finally met her again someday. Then he returned to the kitchen and lit the oil lamp.

Chad Grayson was a terrible sight to see. The archer's face was red and puffy, not from a fight, but from excessive drinking. The man looked ill. Then Mattley's eyes went to the table, which bore burn marks and large dents, as though someone had used it as a bench for metalwork. Mattley's brows wrinkled in irritation. The table was something he had made for Clara decades before, a sentimental treasure from happier days. "Did you do this to my table?" he demanded.

"No," said Chad flatly. "That would be the bastard that came before me."

"And you thought coming here and getting drunk in my house would make me feel better?" growled the old bowyer.

Chad shook his head. "I'm not gettin' drunk. I'm gettin' sober. This is just a tonic to ease me along. The asshole who broke in here came to see me first, and I'm right pissed about it. He stole my bow."

Mattley glared at him. "If you want another, you should've come in the morning. Who's the fellow that did this?"

"Tyrion Illeniel, unless I miss my guess," Chad informed him.

"Am I supposed to recognize the name?"

The hunter gave a dark chuckle. "He's a wizard, and until recently was a nobleman. You won't have any luck getting justice by going to the magister."

Mattley was tired, annoyed, and angry. "Then get out so I can clean up this mess. I'm too old to deal with you right now."

"I still need a bow, Mattley. Haven't I always been one of your best customers?" asked Chad.

The old man glared at him. "Twenty years ago, before I stopped selling to you. Do you honestly have the nerve to say that in front of me?"

Chad screwed the lid on to his flask and put it away. "I need a bow and I don't have a lot of time. I can pay whatever you ask."

Mattley scratched his head, tired and frustrated. Many years before he had been friends with a much younger Chad Grayson, when the man had been shining with talent, but his opinion had changed since then. Once he had learned of Grayson's work as an assassin, he had refused to sell to him, and though the archer seemed more respectable these days, he didn't trust him. "I have several hunting bows that are nearly done," he offered.

Chad shook his head. "I need a warbow."

The bowyer's face hardened. "I don't make those anymore, and if I did, I would only sell them to someone I trust. That ain't you. Go to Albamarl; I'm sure you can find someone there that wants your gold and doesn't care what you do with it."

The difference between a hunting bow and a warbow was primarily one of size and draw weight. The heaviest of hunting bows usually had a draw under eighty to ninety pounds, and sometimes as little as forty, but warbows started at a hundred pounds and could even exceed a hundred and fifty in some cases. The reason was simple: A warbow was meant to pierce armor. It used heavier arrows with bodkin points and required tremendous power to generate the force needed to penetrate chain and sometimes plate.

Chad tapped the marred table. "I'm hunting the man that did this."

Mattley's eyes locked onto his. "As angry as that makes me, it's no call for killin' someone. Go home."

"I know you don't approve of some of the things I did back in the day," began Chad, "but times have changed. I'm sick of blood. That's why I drink so much, but this is important—"

"And yet you just admitted you're going to murder someone," interrupted Mattley.

"He's going to hurt a lot of people if I don't stop him!" declared Chad angrily.

"Two wrongs don't make a right," insisted the bowyer. "Whatever that man does is on his head, but whatever you do with a bow I make rests on my shoulders as well. I won't do it." A knock from the front door distracted both of them, and the crafter held up a hand as he went to check the door. Cautious, he called out before opening it, "Who is it?"

"George Prathion. Open up," came the answer.

Mattley pulled the latch and let the baron in immediately, bowing at the waist. "Milord!"

"That's enough, Master Mattley," said George. "Raise your head. I came to give you an explanation for what happened here while you were gone." As the young nobleman came in, his eyes went to the other man. His magesight had already informed him that someone else was with the bowyer, but he hadn't paid too much attention since it wasn't a mage, now his eyes recognized the face before him. "Master Grayson! How are you here?"

The hunter didn't rise, much less bow, but he did lift one hand to his brow as though tipping a hat, even though he had already removed it. "I'm here for a bow," he answered neutrally.

George jumped straight into his news. "Tyrion was here."

"That's what I was just telling this crotchety old man," replied Chad, before asking, "Did you see him?"

"Worse," admitted George, who then began to relay his story, keeping mainly to the facts. He glossed over the amount of sheer terror his encounter had caused him, and he tried to make his own capture seem a little less foolish, with limited success. "I sent a message to the Queen, but I thought I should come and explain what happened to Master Mattley, since he wasn't here."

"What about Matthew, or your sister, Elaine?" asked the hunter. "Do they know?"

George shook his head. "I don't have a way to contact them. Castle Cameron is empty and they've been gone for months."

"I think they've gathered at Mordecai's home in the mountains," Chad informed him, going on to briefly share his own recent experience bringing Rose and Carissa back. At the end he added, "Tyrion is looking for them. He stole my bow and some of the enchanted arrows I had."

The young Baron of Arundel's eyes dipped toward the floor. "I know. He forced me to help him."

"What did he need from you?" asked the hunter. "And who was the woman you said was with him?"

"He called her Brigid," answered George. "I think she was his daughter. They wanted my help with an enchantment for some arrowheads." He pointed at the table. "The scorch marks are from when he heated the metal to fuse the points with his own additions."

Chad frowned. "His daughter? You said she had dark hair. Lynaralla and the other She'Har have silver."

George shrugged. "She looked human." Then he added, "What's even more strange—she vanished midway through the ordeal. I never saw her leave or use any magic. One minute she was with us, watching everything, and the next she was gone."

"What sort of enchantment was it, that he needed your help?" asked Chad.

George grimaced before answering, "It was a combination of things. The arrowheads can pierce mage shields, even enchanted ones, and Tyrion added an explosive. There won't be much left of anyone he hits with one of them. The part he needed me for was something new, an enchantment to prevent another wizard from touching the arrows with magic."

The hunter rubbed his chin. "Which means…"

"…any mage he fires one at won't be able to defend himself easily," finished George.

In a reverent voice, Old Mattley spoke up, "My Lord, Master Grayson here was asking me to make him a bow. From what I'm hearing, is that something you want me to do?"

George straightened, reassuming his authority. "The man we've been talking about is an outlaw, Master Mattley. He threatened the Queen and escaped from custody in Albamarl. If Master Grayson needs a bow, then I think we had best get him one."

Mattley dipped his head. "As you wish, milord." Then he looked to Chad. "Tell me what you need."

Chad smiled. "I want the strongest bow you can make, two hundred pounds if you have a stave capable of it."

The old bowyer seemed confused. "I doubt you could draw it, and even if you could you wouldn't be able to hold it long enough to aim."

Rising from his chair, Chad walked over to the hearth, which was still cold, and lifted the iron poker from its stand nearby. Putting both hands on the iron, he bent it between them, eliciting a long whistle from George and a scowl from Mattley. "Trust me," said Chad. "I can draw whatever you can make."

"You didn't have to ruin a perfectly good andiron to prove it," complained the bowyer. "I'm adding that to the price."

George chuckled, while Chad drew out a small purse and began counting out gold crowns. He placed ten on the table. "That ought to cover it." Then he looked at George. "Can you enchant more of those arrowheads?"

"It would take days if you want them to explode," answered George. "It takes a while to store up enough power for that. But I can do the other enchantments."

Chad addressed the bowyer, "How long will it take you?"

Mattley scratched his beard. "I've got several pieces that are ready for shaping, but the finish work will take a week."

"It doesn't have to look pretty," said the hunter. "You can skip the polishing and whatnot. It just needs to be functional."

"Two days," replied the bowyer.

The hunter nodded, then reached for a bag at his feet, from which he withdrew a long oilskin. After unwrapping it, he revealed a bundle of heavy shafts, already fletched and tipped with bodkin points—war arrows. "Tyrion took the enchanted arrows I had. Can you work with these?" he asked.

The young baron nodded as he counted the arrows. There were at least sixty on the table. "I can probably do most of these in two days."

Chad grinned, his eyes full of malice. "One should be enough, but I'll take as many as you can make. I'm heading to Albamarl. If I take the World Road, I should be able to get back before you finish."

George looked at him strangely. "I've already warned the Queen. Do you think Tyrion is heading back there?"

"I need to find my dragon."

CHAPTER 39

Matthew and Gary were standing in the large meadow, downhill from the main house, when Myra found them. Stretched out on the ground between them was a square grid roughly eight-feet-wide. It was made of copper wires, which were arranged in a mesh that created squares roughly an eighth of an inch on each side. The entire structure glowed with aythar, and Myra's magesight could make out tiny runes etched along the thin wires.

"Is this what you've been working on for the past two days?" she asked.

Her brother nodded. "It's still too small. Each side will need to be at least this big *after* it is shrunk down. I'm just preparing to get rid of the copper so I can test the size-change enchantment."

Myra was confused. "Copper? Didn't Irene say she used wax?"

"Yes," agreed Matt. "But it wasn't strong enough for such a fine structure. It kept bending and breaking. The copper was strong enough, although it will take a lot more heat to melt it out."

"Then what will you do?" she asked.

Matthew lifted his hands, folding them and turning them to mime the shape of a cube. "If I can create one side that is sound and responds properly, I can create others. Six together will create a cube that can have its size adjusted however we like. If that works—well, then we just have to make a lot more of them."

"How many?"

Her brother stared off into the distance for a minute while doing numbers in his head. He answered, "Two-hundred and twenty-eight altogether. That will make the cube roughly a hundred yards on each side, before we shrink it down." He pointed at the copper mesh. "That will make the individual squares about three-thousandths of an inch on a side after it has been reduced."

She arched one brow. "Are you sure that's small enough?" she asked wryly.

If Matthew noticed her sarcasm, he didn't show it, for he replied seriously, "I'm not sure. I'd like them to be smaller—much smaller—but this size is the best I think we can manage. Even making this much of an allowance, I still don't know how we can possibly finish it in time."

Myra nodded along, although she was still unclear about much of what he was saying. "So, you need a faster way to create the sections…"

"Not just that," said Matt. "We don't have enough copper either. Not to do it this way. I've already figured out a solution for that problem, though. If four mages operate in unison, they can create tiny, stable subsections of the enchantment without using a physical substrate. Unfortunately, that will almost certainly take much longer than using the copper and etching the runes onto it." He let out a long sigh. "It feels like no matter what I come up with, the problem just gets larger and larger."

Gary spoke up then, "If we had ANSIS helping us, we could do it easily, but it's already gone. Nor would it likely wish to listen to us."

"How could it help with an enchantment?" wondered Myra.

Happy to explain, Gary launched into the topic. "Well, as you know, ANSIS is as close to programmable matter as the people of my world were able to make. Consequently, it could construct a structure like this from whatever material was nearby. It transforms the material into nanomachines that can then make more of themselves, and as they grow they can create whatever structure is desired. In this case—"

Matthew interrupted, "Myra, did you come out here for a reason? I'm sure you didn't come to listen to us drone on about this."

Her eyes went back to him. "Actually, yes. It occurred to me that there was something important I left out when I explained what happened to Moira." A cloud passed over Matthew's features, but he said nothing, so she continued, "I was in contact with her when she fought Tyrion, and she learned something interesting before she died."

"What was it?" asked Matt, his eyes drilling into her with intense interest now.

"He isn't the real Tyrion," she answered. "We all thought he had transformed back into human form, but he hasn't. The original Tyrion is still on Wester Isle with Lyralliantha. The one we've been talking to here in Lothion is a copy. In fact, he's the second copy."

"Second? How many are there?" probed Matthew.

"There's only one that I know of," said Myra. "The first one was a krytek that Tyrion created, but Mordecai nearly killed that one when he escaped. Apparently, it returned to the isle and reported its memories before dying. The one here now is actually a She'Har created by Lyralliantha and given all of his memories."

Her brother scratched his head, thinking for a moment. "Wait, this doesn't make sense. I thought only the Centyr could create spell-minds, or spell-twins. That's what this is, isn't it?"

Myra shook her head. "Not exactly. The method they've used isn't nearly as perfect. The first one was essentially just a short-term human body given a copy of his memories. Imagine if you were born as an adult, with no memories of your own, and then you were given a loshti that contained all the memories of who you were supposed to be. You'd have the same body and memories as the original, but your personality could diverge significantly."

"Hmmm."

"What's worse is that the newest version of him is a copy of a copy, and it's been imprinted on yet another living body," added Myra.

Matthew frowned. "I'm not sure I see the problem."

"Remember what we told you about Centyr spell-twins?" asked Myra. "One of the reasons they're dangerous, aside from the ethical problems, is that no copy is absolutely perfect. Errors accumulate with every generation of copying, making the resulting personality unstable. The Centyr method is vastly superior to what Tyrion has done, so there's no telling how it has affected this second-generation twin."

"What about She'Har children, like Lynn?" asked Matthew. "Aren't they essentially the same thing? They're born as adults and implanted with a basic set of knowledge to allow them to function."

"I don't think so," replied Myra. "For one, the She'Har children are all identical, physically speaking. They use a template for the flesh that doesn't have any of the unique differences that ordinary humans have. Their template is designed for a calm, stable personality, and the knowledge they implant is very neutral, without any emotional intensity. What Tyrion has done is create a copy of his original physical body. His intent was to reproduce his personality that way, but that means his twin could be very emotionally unstable. Add to that the fact that he's implanted it with intense memories that contain every sort of emotion and an awful lot of violence, and it's a recipe for madness. That's without even considering the errors created by their relatively crude method of copying those memories."

After a moment, Matthew asked, "Something just occurred to me. Is this new Tyrion an archmage?"

Myra smiled faintly. "That's the only good news. They weren't able to recreate that ability. The current Tyrion we've been dealing with is essentially just an Illeniel She'Har with the knowledge and battle experience of the original man. He's got Tyrion's strength and skill, but not his power as an archmage. The only thing he gained is the ability to spellweave."

"And the Illeniel gift," said Matthew darkly. "That could be worse for us than all the rest combined."

Gary spoke up, "Why is that?"

"Because it means I can't predict what he'll do," answered Matt. "I didn't realize it until recently, but my ability to judge future events is severely limited whenever it pertains to someone else with the same ability. I found that out when Irene and I had our little quarrel."

"Which means we have a potential madman on the loose, and your ability to foretell his actions is practically useless," noted Myra. Then her eyes widened. "That applies to Lyralliantha too, doesn't it?"

Matthew nodded. "She probably has no more idea what he may do than we do." They all fell silent after that, and eventually Matthew turned back to his work, but as Myra started to leave he stood up straight, as though an idea had struck him. He called to her, "Myra."

"Yes?" she said, turning back.

"You're essentially a normal Centyr mage now, right? Now that you've taken Moira's aystrylin you can do anything she could do. Is that correct?" he asked.

She nodded sadly.

"Then you can create spellbeasts," he added.

She nodded once more.

"Is there any limit on how many you can create?"

Myra gave it a moment's thought. "It depends on their complexity and the amount of aythar required."

"Can a spellbeast create another spellbeast, or does it have to be a spell-twin to be able to do that?"

She frowned. "Ordinarily they cannot, but if I included the ability in their creation they could do so. Again, they would be limited by the amount of aythar available to me, and successive generations could never be more complex than the ones that created them."

Her brother jumped into the air, startling her and Gary. He wasn't ordinarily prone to such gestures. "Yes!"

Myra glanced at the copper lattice, then back at him. "Are you thinking…?"

"Yes!" he answered loudly. "Stay right there! I have something I want you to try."

***

After leaving the World Road, Chad didn't enter the capital. Instead he headed east, into the forest. The last time he had been there was months past, when he, Cyhan, and Elaine had been fleeing from Gareth Gaelyn's wrath. At the time he had avoided calling Prissy to him, for the archmage could have detected her from a considerable distance. His last words to her before leaving her had been to make herself at home within the forest.

He should have come back for her long before now, but he had been busy, and to be honest, he'd always considered the dragon to be more of a nuisance. He was a hunter, not a wizard or a knight. The last thing he wanted was some giant lizard following him around. He hadn't been particularly fond of their mental bond either. The archer valued his privacy, and the last thing he wanted was for anyone to see his private thoughts.

"It didn't help that she had the personality of a piece of starched linen either," he groused aloud. "Only thing worse than being married was having her around listening to me think."

He felt a faint presence in the back of his mind. *Then why don't you go back and leave me alone?* It was Priscilla's mental touch.

Making the effort to broadcast his thoughts, he replied, *Where are you?*

Why do you care? she returned, a sullen feeling attached to her thoughts.

I need your help, he sent.

She was definitely sulking, and her next words confirmed it. *That's all I am to you, isn't it? A piece of livestock, or worse, a tool. Go away. I was quite happy here without you.*

Chad found himself grinding his teeth. "Women," he muttered, then added, "Worse, dragons who are also women." Mustering his patience, he sent an apology, *Look, Prissy, I'm sorry. I've been busy.*

He felt her mental shrug. *I heard what you said. You still haven't learned to separate your thoughts and words.*

"Easier said than done," he whispered.

Because you never talk to me, she replied. *We're supposed to be partners, but to you I'm just a nuisance. I only wanted to be your friend.*

The last part of her reply caused his heart to clench, sending an almost physical jolt of pain through him. *I don't deserve friends,* he responded. *It's better for both of us if you keep your feelings out of this.*

You're in pain. Are you wounded? she asked. Chad heard a loud cracking sound as her wings unfurled and whipped down to catch the air, lifting her from the ground. She was somewhere to the north of him.

No, I'm fine! he insisted. *Just ignore that.* A moment later, a shadow passed over the trees and then a gale wind whipped his face as she descended through a gap in the forest. Chad's eyes widened with surprise as he beheld his dragon for the first time in months. "Sweet mother of pigs!" he swore, shocked at her size. "What happened to you? You're huge!"

Priscilla arched her neck proudly. She wasn't quite the size of Moira's Cassandra, or Matthew's Zephyr, but she was close. "I've grown," she purred.

Spitting on the ground, the hunter slapped his hip. "What the fuck have you been eatin'? Cows?"

The dragon turned her head, looking off to one side. "Deer mostly," she replied. "Not that it matters to you."

"Deer?" exclaimed Chad, his mouth agape. "More likely pigs! You could swallow a boar with that mouth!"

"A few boars too," she huffed, insulted. "And a bear, though I don't recommend it."

"Ye look like a fat, scaly sow with wings," observed the hunter. "Didn't you do anything besides eat while you were here?"

Priscilla uttered a low growl, and small flames flickered from the sides of her jaws. "I'm not fat, I'm big boned. This is all muscle—mostly. What did you expect me to do out here in the wilderness? There's nothing to do but eat and sleep. I thought I'd die of boredom waiting for you to return."

"Don't blame this one me," Chad shot back. "You could've flown home. I never expected you to wait here for months."

She glared at him angrily. "Have you forgotten how the bond works? I'm practically a slave. Your last words were to wait here, and here I am! I couldn't leave if I wanted to."

He stared back at her, aghast. "Now wait a minute," he started, but his words tapered off. He did in fact remember something they had told him regarding her obeying his commands, but he hadn't expected it to be such a literal thing. Shaking his head, he changed directions. "Never mind. From now on, don't take anything I say as an order unless I say, 'that's an order.' Got it?"

Her eyes narrowed. "Clarify that for me."

"Act like a regular person," he said, exasperated. "If you don't like somethin' I say, tell me to fuck off, like anyone else would. Only treat it as an absolute if I make it a command."

The dragon sat back on her haunches, somewhat mollified by his words. "Very well then."

Chad nodded. "Good, let's go then. Are you big enough to carry me now? We need to get back to Washbrook."

"Fuck off," said Priscilla, relishing the words.

The archer stared at her for a moment, surprised, then replied, "Alright, I guess I asked for that. Now show me how to climb on."

Priscilla snorted, sending small gouts of flame from her nostrils. "Go to hell," she answered, but she lowered her chest and stretched out one forelimb to allow him to climb up.

Chad grinned as he began scaling her side. "Yer enjoyin' this, aren't you?"

"I've never been fond of your swearing," said Priscilla, "but I find it's growing on me now."

He settled in at the base of her neck, just forward of her wing joints. "It's liberatin', isn't it?" Drawing a deep breath, he enjoyed the view, while simultaneously bracing himself inwardly. He hadn't been in the air enough to be comfortable with the experience yet. Despite himself, he clutched at her neck as she began beating her wings to take off.

"It is," she answered, the wind tearing her words away as she said them. "You miserable sack of shit."

Holding on tightly, Chad agreed, "That's the spirit. Keep it up and I might start to take a shine to you."

Priscilla smiled inwardly. "Don't start acting too sweet or I'll dump you in midair," she warned jokingly. But inside she was remembering his previous words, *'I don't deserve friends.'* She hadn't liked the sound of that, but she hoped that in time, she could convince him otherwise.

Chapter 40

Tyrion watched the ocean roll by endlessly beneath him as he rode the massive dormon toward the Wester Isle. Until recently it had been his dukedom, although in reality it was his creator who ruled it. The Gulf of Garulon was behind him now, and soon he expected the island to come into view.

After finishing the arrows and releasing the Baron of Arundel, he had traveled for several miles before sending a small, spellwoven message to summon the beast he rode. Waiting for it to arrive had taken most of a day, during which time he had constructed his first teleportation circle and practiced with the bow.

His first attempt to draw it had been a surprise. Apparently, Chad Grayson was a lot stronger than he looked, for Tyrion failed completely. He had been forced to use his power to increase his physical strength before he could test the weapon. Thankfully, there had been no one to see his first shots. He had only used a bow a few times in the past, and those experiences hadn't prepared him for the difficulty of using a weapon with such a powerful draw weight. He consoled himself with he fact that he didn't have to be very accurate. He quite literally only needed to hit the broad side of a barn, or to be more specific, a tree.

After practicing for a while, he had grown bored—or at least he had thought himself bored—the flight itself was even worse. But he had a sense of purpose, and that in itself was worthwhile. Since his creation, he had sorely felt the lack. His creator had never lacked for one, but he had lost it over the millennia as he had survived, living as the enemy. "A traitor to himself," murmured Tyrion.

He had been ill at ease since his birth, first having to come to terms with the fact that he wasn't even the person he believed himself to be, and then with the fact that his former self had adopted a new philosophy. But that was behind him now.

The little girl had been right; he needed to 'fix the story.' Meeting Brigid twice had only driven that point home. She had said openly what the voice in the back of his mind had been telling him from the beginning.

He still didn't understand where she had come from. She wasn't a She'Har or a krytek, he knew that for certain, so he didn't think she was a copy like he was. Her sudden appearances and disappearances were even more mysterious. If he hadn't known better, he might have believed it to be the work of some divine power.

A faint, grey shadow on the horizon announced the presence of Wester Isle in the distance. His journey was almost done. Another hour passed before the dormon finally set down gently on the shore of the island, where two krytek waited on him.

This was the tricky part, for he had returned without explanation, and one of the guardians said as much. "Why have you returned?"

Sliding down from his mount, Tyrion tied the quiver of arrows to his belt and held up the bow for them to examine. "I have news for the Elders. The alliance has been betrayed. This weapon is proof."

"Explain," ordered the krytek, a large catlike beast with terrifyingly large claws. Its companion, a shambling giant humanoid, remained mute.

"I'll explain it to the Elders directly. Stand aside," commanded Tyrion, projecting authority.

There was a pause as they considered his words. If they had even the slightest suspicions, the fight would begin now, for his creator was exceedingly careful about allowing anyone into close proximity.

Fortunately, there weren't many krytek left on the island. Tyrion the Elder had been using nearly his entire capacity to produce soldiers to sniff out ANSIS in the human kingdoms, leaving only a few to guard the grove itself. Even if it came to a fight, he was fairly certain of his success in any combat that might arise. The biggest danger was that an alarm might wake the Elders, and they could potentially disable him before he could get close enough to achieve his goal.

The krytek stepped aside to allow him to pass, falling in behind him as he started the trek inland. Tyrion smiled quietly to himself. Things were proceeding much as he had hoped. His heart beat faster as they began the long walk, not from the mild exertion, but rather because his blood was rising. He felt more alive than at any other time since he had been brought forth in this accursed world.

Another hour of walking brought him at last into the new grove, where Tyrion, Lyralliantha, and two new Elders grew. All of them would be dormant, of course. New trees weren't able to speed up their thought processes to match that of a human for many years after they had taken root. Tyrion and Lyralliantha could, but since they weren't expecting him they wouldn't have taken the trouble of doing so.

The krytek following him stopped at the edge of the grove, more than two hundred yards from the Elder Tyrion's colossal trunk. He walked forward alone, stopping only when he was thirty yards from the base. The krytek would be expecting him to go all the way, since he would have to make physical contact before slipping into a trance to contact his creator. Hopefully they wouldn't react to him stopping early.

Setting one end of the bow stave on the ground, he took out the string and bent to slip one loop over the bottom string nock. Then he straightened and put one leg in front of it, using his body to bend the limbs until the other loop could reach the top nock. With the bow strung, he held it in front of himself, anticipating what he was about to do.

What is that? came a powerful mental voice, causing him to flinch.

Evidence of the humans' betrayal, answered Tyrion, fighting to keep his thoughts calm. *You surprised me. I thought I would have to awaken you.*

Tyrion the Elder responded, *The krytek awoke me as soon as you were spotted, since you were unexpected. What is this betrayal you speak of?*

I'll show you, he told the Elder, then he brought out an arrow and nocked it, angling his body as though he would shoot at an outcropping of rock at the far edge of the grove.

Explain first, ordered the Elder Tyrion, but it was too late. Enhancing his strength, Tyrion the Younger pulled the bow into a full draw, then turned at the last moment and loosed the arrow directly at the base of his creator's trunk. The arrow flew toward its target, and though the Elder She'Har created a powerful shield the arrow tore through it, hardly slowing.

His aim was slightly off, but the metal point still found a home in the thick bark before releasing a powerful explosion. The mental scream that resulted was almost as jarring as the concussive force that knocked him off his feet.

He was blown backward, then rolled, the taste of iron filling his mouth—the jarring had caused him to inadvertently bite his tongue. A razor-sharp lash of power whipped by over his head, coming from one of the krytek, who were only now trying to stop him. Coming back up to his feet, he grinned, the blood in his mouth staining his teeth red. He was alive, more alive than he had felt since his creation. "Yes!" he screamed, jubilant as the adrenaline sent his heart rate soaring.

He dodged another attack as he left his bow on the ground and activated his tattoos. Then he charged toward the krytek. They seemed to be slightly off balance as Tyrion the Elder's scream of pain continued, filling their minds, but Tyrion the avenger found the sound of mental anguish to be almost comforting as he methodically cut them apart with brutal efficiency.

They were too few, and he was too strong. A minute later he returned to where he had left the bow. It was time to finish the job. He examined the result of his first attack. A massive divot of shattered wood fully seven feet across marred the side of the Father-tree's trunk. It was not enough to put the great tree in danger of falling, but it was a colossal wound nonetheless. One or two more would be enough to seal its fate. But first he needed to deal with the Mother-tree.

Lyralliantha was waking, and her strength would be a threat to him. Tyrion the Elder was still in shock, so he turned and aimed his next arrow at the source of his life. This time he braced himself to prevent being thrown back by the shockwave, and he watched the explosion with delighted fascination.

No! came Tyrion the Elder's horrified mental call as Lyralliantha's smaller trunk collapsed. Being smaller, her girth wasn't sufficient to withstand the damage and her graceful limbs seemed to flow through the air with exquisite slowness as she fell.

He sensed power gathering and managed to dodge before a powerful hammer of force slammed into the ground where he had been standing. The Father-tree was recovering from his pain. Running sideways, Tyrion the Younger dropped several arrows as he tried to nock another, but he wasn't too worried. He was enjoying himself, and he only needed one to win the fight.

A sweeping blade of deadly force cut across the ground. It was far too large to dodge and too powerful to block, so instead he channeled power into his muscles and leapt skyward. Drawing the bow as he ascended, he did his best to aim and loosed as he reached the apex of his jump. If he missed, he might not survive long enough to try again.

The Father-tree sent a focused lance of power at him while he was in the air, and he had no way to avoid it. Though it wasn't a spellweave, its power was so great that it overwhelmed his shield tattoos and shattered his defense. The world went black as the feedback slammed into his mind, leaving him nearly senseless as he fell. A single roaring sound punctuated the numbness of his awareness as he crashed down: the explosion of his arrow, though whether it had hit its mark he didn't know.

Something snapped in his shoulder when he came down, but he ignored the pain and kept rolling after landing. Temporarily blind, both physically and magically, he had no way of knowing if more attacks were coming. His body felt something heavy landing nearby, sensing it in a visceral manner as the deep vibrations thrummed through his chest.

A few seconds later his eyes cleared, and he saw that his arrow had landed, but not in the best place. It had struck the Father-tree some ten feet higher, carving out another massive hole in the trunk but not in a place that would bring it down. The bow was nowhere to be seen, having fallen somewhere out of sight. His quiver was empty, but several of the arrows were scattered around between him and Tyrion the Elder. Running forward, he narrowly avoided yet another attack that slammed into the ground behind him, throwing dirt into the air. Worse, he hadn't sensed it; his magesight was still nonfunctional. Only luck had spared him.

His first instinct was to use his power to snatch up one of the arrows and propel it directly, but even the thought sent a sharp pain rocketing through his skull. Changing the direction of his run again, he dodged yet another attack, but he knew his death was close. The realization thrilled him. Death would be almost as welcome as victory.

Stopping suddenly, he snatched up one of the fallen arrows. The only option left to him was to drive it home by hand. That meant he wouldn't live to complete the rest of his plan, but he was at peace with that.

Tyrion the Elder must have sensed his suicidal desperation, for before he could charge again, a massive battering ram of force struck the earth in front of him. Only the delay caused by his injuries had prevented him from being crushed beneath it. A loud crack followed the attack, and his eyes went wide as he saw the Father-tree's trunk snap. In his weakened state, Tyrion the Elder had fallen victim to his own power. The force the Elder had put into his last attack had overstrained the damaged timber supporting his weight.

Tyrion the Younger grinned as he watched the great tree fall. Laughing quietly to himself, he staggered about, stumbling across the torn earth as he searched for his lost bow. Gradually his magesight returned, though his headache seemed to grow greater as his ability returned.

He found the bow in a clump of bushes, and with that in hand he began collecting the arrows that had fallen from his quiver during the fight. Apparently, archers weren't meant to be moving the way he had. The execution of his plan had been almost comical. Success had only come because his attack had been unanticipated.

There were more than enough arrows to finish the saplings, but when he attempted to draw the warbow he found his strength to be insufficient. The bow might as well be made of iron, for it stubbornly refused to bend, nor was he able to use his power to grant himself the strength necessary. With a sigh he sat down, leaning his back against the fallen trunk of his creator.

Patience, he told himself. He had already slain the few krytek on the island, and the still immature Elders of the new Illeniel Grove wouldn't be able to waken and threaten him for years yet. He was safe. He only needed to recover his strength, heal his wounds, and finish his work once he was ready.

There was no need to rush. Resting his eyes, he searched inwardly, examining his collarbone. It had cracked close to his right shoulder but hadn't broken completely. Once he could use his power again, he would restore it. For now, a nap was the order of the day.

Opening the pouch at his waist, he activated the spellweave built into it and withdrew one of the calmuth stored within. The fruit of the Mother-tree would nourish him better than almost any other food, as well as keeping the seed-mind in his skull dormant. Once he was feeling better, he would have to search the area where Lyralliantha had fallen and see how many more pieces of the vital fruit he could find. With her death, he was on limited time. Eventually he would run out and be forced to kill himself to prevent becoming like his creator.

He had enough to last a few more weeks if he stretched his supply, eating only one piece every five or six days, and he only needed enough to last until he had finished fixing his 'story.' First the saplings, and then Lynaralla—then he would be done. The She'Har would be no more.

Tyrion drifted into a dream, one where was Brigid was looking down on him. *"You've done well, Father,"* she told him.

Chapter 41

Matthew and Myra stood together, their dragons Zephyr and Cassandra behind them as they looked out over the mile-wide field that stood in front of Castle Cameron. Their hands were linked, a matter of practicality to ease the transfer of power and information between them. A stranger might have thought them the closest of siblings, something that had been both true and false when Moira was alive.

While the two of them had been close in a deep sense, Matthew's prickly nature had never allowed him to show it with such visible displays. Now that she was gone, and he was here beside her twin, he felt some regret over that, but even then, he kept such thoughts suppressed. The work came first. Always.

Before them was the first section of copper that he had painstakingly created, but with their magesight they could see a growing lattice of golden aythar growing out from it in all directions. Its growth was so smooth and natural that it reminded Matthew of a crystal, like rock candy appearing in a heavy syrup.

But it was anything but easy. In his mind he kept the template clearly displayed, while the dragons fed their power to him and his sister. What came to him was redirected to her as well, and from the plan in his mind she created an endless swarm of tiny spellbeasts, feeding them on the enormous power coursing through her.

As time ran on, her nerves began to burn, a warning that she was nearing her limit. Burnout could destroy a mage's ability to manipulate aythar, or it could even kill them outright. To avoid that, she created a complex spell-mind—something like a spell-twin but not quite as complex—to handle the task. She had positioned the spell-mind within the flow between her and Matthew, letting it take the power he was channeling and effectively halving her load.

Half an hour later, the burning started again, and she created a second spell-mind to handle the power coming from Cassandra, taking herself almost, but not quite, out of the flow. Somewhat able to rest, she took the opportunity to examine her brother. Matthew was still channeling his half of the power from Zephyr, passing it into her construct, and while his strength had always been greater than her own, she worried he might be ignoring his own internal warning signs.

Yet he still appeared fine. The only evidence of the strain was a trickle of sweat running down his brow. She looked deeper, studying him through the link, and decided he was still safe, so she didn't interfere. She kept a close watch regardless, for she knew his stubborn nature. If he started pushing his limits, she was prepared to take over. His mind was open, and given their current link she could force him to do whatever was needed to protect him.

Matt's eyes narrowed as that thought crossed her mind, and he gave her a warning look. *Don't. This is more important than either of us. It must be finished.*

It will be, she answered. *But I won't let you kill yourself doing it.*

You can't do it without me, he returned. *It needs the Illeniel gift, and I'm the only one who understands this working.*

There are others with the gift, and your knowledge can be managed, she replied. *Trust me.*

Through the link, he caught the meaning of her plan, and after a moment he nodded. *Alright, but not yet. Wait until I'm tired.*

She agreed and continued monitoring him. Incredibly, he kept it up for another hour before she felt the burning pain creeping through him that indicated he was reaching his limit. Myra created a small independent spellbeast then, in the form of a bird, to carry her message back to the others. A few minutes later Irene, Conall, and Lynaralla arrived.

Myra created a construct based on Matthew's plan and filled it with the template he was holding in his mind, then gently encouraged him to step back, mentally, while Irene took his place in their working. It was delicate work, but in the span of a few minutes she had Irene channeling her power, while her Matthew-construct managed Irene's gift. It was a complex balancing act of different gifts and the workload of pushing so much power into so many spellbeasts.

In this way they continued for hours, and when Irene was too exhausted to continue, Conall took her place. Both of the younger Illeniels lasted for impressive amounts of time before Lynaralla took her turn. She lasted slightly less than half the time they had, but when she could take it no longer, Matthew was ready to take his place once more, channeling the seemingly endless aythar of the dragons into the rapidly growing enchantment.

The work lasted through the day and late into the night before the colossal working was complete, an enormous lattice cube that was a hundred yards long on each side, glittering like gold to those with magesight. When it was finally complete, Matthew lay down in the long grass, utterly exhausted since his had been the last turn. Irene sat beside him, while Conall was sleeping a few feet away on his other side.

"You do the honors, Rennie," he told her, breathing heavily. "This part was purely from your inspiration."

With a faint smile, Irene spoke the final word to transform their new creation, *"Asmollen."* Silently, the massive enchantment shrank over a period of minutes, until it was less than ten feet on each side, a glittering cube whose weave was so fine it couldn't be discerned with eyes or magesight. It was an anticlimactic end to their long labor, though Irene couldn't help but admire the beauty of the shimmering gold walls. Stretching out, Irene made herself comfortable next to her brothers.

Karen walked over to them. She and Elaine had been watching off and on over the course of the day. "That was incredible."

"I still wish you would have let us help," observed Elaine. "Maybe you wouldn't be so worn down."

Unable to muster the strength to reply, Matthew merely waved a hand, as if trying to push her remarks away.

"It had to be them," said Myra, still relatively unfatigued since her creations had been handling most of her work since the early part of the day. "The Illeniel gift was the essential ingredient."

"You were able to help," noted Elaine, "and you don't have it." She hadn't understood Matthew's explanation the day before, and her frustration showed in her voice.

Karen had understood, though she was still unable to help. "Myra was the project manager," she supplied.

"The what?" asked Elaine, once again baffled by the otherworlder's strange use of words.

Frowning, Karen tried again, "Like a factor, or maybe a head chef…"

"It was Matthew's recipe. He would be the head chef. You're not making any sense," argued Elaine.

Karen took a deep breath. They'd had the same conversation with small variations several times over the course of the day. "Nevermind." Suppressing her irritation, she focused on their exhausted friends. "Ready to go home? Alyssa's cooking has reached a new level of excellence, though I think it's gone cold by now." She nudged Conall with the toe of her boot. "Wake up."

Conall cracked one eye, then closed it again. "Go on without me. I couldn't move even if you set me on fire."

"That could be arranged," commented Elaine with a wicked curve to her lips.

"I have an idea," said Karen. Kneeling down, she put her hand on the young man's chest and vanished, taking him with her. A minute later she reappeared, rubbing at her knees, which were apparently sore.

"Are you hurt?" asked Irene. "What happened?"

"I teleported him to his bed," explained Karen ruefully. "Which worked out fine for him, but I forgot to account for my positioning." Matthew began chuckling quietly.

"What do you mean?" said Irene, confused.

"He was on the bed, but I was several feet off the floor, so I landed hard," clarified Karen.

Irene winced. "Ahh. Sounds painful." Together, she and Lynaralla helped Matthew to his feet and Karen took them and Myra back in a single jump.

***

The sun had almost reached the horizon, bathing the field Priscilla was landing in with sullen rays of gold. Chad ignored the spectacle of beauty and clambered down from her back almost as soon as her feet had touched earth. He was glad to be on solid ground once more. "I'm never going to get used to that," he grumbled.

"Flying?" asked the dragon. "It seems perfectly natural to me."

"Nothin' natural about it," groused the hunter. "If I'd been meant to fly, I'd have been born with wings."

"You weren't born with hooves, yet you ride a horse to increase your speed. I was born with wings; what's so different about borrowing my back to get someplace quickly?" suggested Priscilla.

Chad glared at his companion. "For one, if I fall off a horse I won't plummet to my death, and for another—"

She interrupted him, "People die falling off of horses all the time."

He ran a hand across his face in exasperation. "Most of the time they don't die. If I slip off your back, I'm not getting back up again. As I was sayin'—"

"I wouldn't let you fall," insisted Priscilla, interrupting again. "And if you did somehow manage to be that clumsy, I'd catch you. I'd like to see a horse do that!"

The archer swore silently under his breath for several seconds until he found the patience to continue, "*As I was saying,* before you interrupted, I'm not too partial to horses either."

That brought the dragon up short, but after a moment's consideration she replied, "Oh. Well, I don't have an opinion on that, since they're too small for me to ride, but they look delicious."

"What?"

"You heard me," she declared. "Don't make me repeat myself."

"Did you eat any horses while you were on your own?" he asked worriedly.

Turning her head away from him, she replied, "No."

"Have you ever eaten a horse, perhaps some other time?" added the hunter.

Pretending to groom one of her claws, she answered, "Not yet."

"Prissy!" he snapped.

"You said you weren't partial to them. I thought you'd understand," she whined, before adding, "So much for honesty."

Squaring his shoulders, Chad spoke sternly, "Listen, under no circumstances, are you to *ever* eat a horse, and that's an or…" He stopped himself before making it a command. "You know what, screw that. Just know that I don't want you eating them, and if I ever *catch* you eating someone's horse, I'll whip that fat scaly ass of yours into next week."

She smiled inwardly at his wording. Truth be told, she didn't care too much about trying horseflesh, though she also had no objection to it. She just wanted to draw him out of the dark place he kept retreating into whenever the silence lasted too long. To that end she responded, "How?"

"How what?" he asked sourly.

"Exactly how are you going to 'whip my scaly ass?' I'm fairly certain you're not big enough," she replied.

The hunter swore for several minutes, practicing his art, before turning away. "I don't have time to argue with yer crazy ass," he announced. "I'm going into town. I need to find someone intelligent to talk to."

Prissy grinned as she watched him go, calling after him, "Avoid mirrors, then!"

Entering Arundel, Chad headed straight for the bowyer's shop. He passed a few of the townsfolk on his way, some of whom knew him, but when they saw the stern expression on his face, they decided against greeting him. That was fine with Chad, though. He'd been without drink for two days, and his nerves felt like they'd been scraped raw. Arguing with Priscilla all the way from Albamarl hadn't helped either.

Mattley didn't open the door. "Go away," answered the old man. "I'm done with you. The bow is with the Baron, so there's no need for you to come here anymore."

"I need to pay you for it," said Chad reasonably.

"Didn't do it for you," said the old man through the door. "I did it for the Baron. If you want to pay me back make sure your shadow doesn't cross my threshold again."

Despite his gruff exterior, Chad was still hurt by the words. He hadn't realized how deep the old man's resentment was. With a sigh, he reached into his purse. "I'll just leave it on the step."

"Keep your gold. If the Baron thinks I need paying, he can do it. Just go," insisted Mattley.

Frowning, Chad asked, "Where is he?"

"Not here. Probably at the manor," said the bowyer.

Without a word, Chad left. Some days the world seemed to be full of assholes. Deep down, though, he knew better. Mattley had always been a decent man. Ruminating over the many burned bridges in his life, he headed for the manor house. "Everyone's an asshole to a murderin' bastard," he muttered under his breath.

The walk to George Prathion's manor house was less than twenty minutes from the bowyer's place. Unlike Mordecai's land, Arundel wasn't delineated by walls and a fortress. The town had no wall to speak of, and the Baron's home was merely a private manor outside of the town proper. In past wars between Gododdin and Lothion, Arundel had been destroyed several times, until they had simply given up trying to rebuild a significant defense. Since the Barony had previously been under the protection of first Lancaster and now Cameron, their plan in the event of war was simply to abandon the town and retreat to Washbrook or Lancaster. That being the case, it didn't make sense to build fortifications that might aid an invader.

Of course, in recent years things had changed. One of the entrances to the World Road was located close to the town, bringing an influx of trade and commerce. The World Road entrances were all guarded by fortresses of their own, but serious consideration had been given of late to enhancing the protection of Arundel, for the town was growing quickly.

None of this mattered to Chad, though. He was more concerned whether he would have any difficulty getting in to see the young Baron. That turned out to be a non-issue, however, for as soon as he approached the front of the house, one of the two guards went inside to inform George of his arrival, while the other opened the door and directed him to wait in the parlor. It seemed the Baron had been anxiously awaiting his return.

Sure enough, George appeared after only a handful of minutes. "Master Grayson!" he greeted the hunter. "Good news! I've finished the arrows in less time than I expected. The bow is here as well."

The young man's enthusiasm set Chad's teeth on edge. In the past George hadn't shown much ambition—something about being in the shadow of his older sister had made him approach life with seeming indifference, if not downright disinterest—but since his father's death that had changed. Becoming a Lord of the Realm had given him a sense of agency, and also proved to be less exciting than the young lord had anticipated.

"That's great," said the hunter. "I'll just take them and be on my way then."

George looked disappointed. "Don't you think you need my help?"

Chad grimaced. The last thing he wanted was to drag someone else into his troubles. "Nope," he said flatly.

"That bow won't be enough. He'll kill you if you try," said the young man.

The archer was keenly aware of that fact, but he was prepared to accept the risk. He didn't have much to lose anyway. George was an entirely different matter. He had a future. "Only if he sees me coming."

"He can sense you with his magesight," said George, "long before you're within range of him."

"Tell me something I don't know," replied the hunter dryly.

"A Prathion is the ideal partner for what you have in mind," continued George. "No one finds a Prathion that doesn't want to be found," he added, repeating the family motto.

"There's a lot more to hunting than not being seen, boy," Chad said, rebuking him. "I've been hunting men since long before you were born. Trust me, you don't want to get mixed up in this. I've heard Mort's stories about Tyrion's past, and from what he said this bastard's fought and killed every kind of wizard you care to name, including a fair share of Prathions. I'll do this my way and if things go south, well, at least I won't have your death on my head as well."

Undeterred, George asked, "How do you plan to do it then?"

Chad had already given that a lot of thought and had resigned himself to the inevitable. "A lot of waiting I imagine, years if necessary. I'll pick a city with a lot of people, wherever I hear he's heading. Eventually he'll wander into my sights." That was a half lie, since he had a fair idea where Tyrion might be heading next already.

"What if I already know where he's heading?" suggested the young Baron.

"And how would you know that?"

George smiled knowingly. "I finally got a letter from my sister yesterday."

Chad waited.

"Mordecai set up pairs of enchanted message boxes with various nobles around the kingdom. She finally used one to send me a letter. Elaine is with Matthew and the others at their hidden home in the mountains," said George.

Keeping his voice flat and his expression bland, Chad replied, "And what does that have to do with me?"

George went on, "Lynaralla had a vision. Matthew is planning some sort of grand enchantment to cure his father, but she saw Tyrion killing them all in the middle of it. Elaine warned me to stay away, but they're trying to figure out some sort of scheme to accomplish their goal and keep Tyrion from killing them all in the process."

Damn everything, Chad swore to himself. Now he'd never be able to keep the boy out of it. "You should listen to your sister," he told the Baron.

"You need to know where they're going to be when they attempt it," said George, a challenge in his voice.

Chad stared at the sideboard, where several bottles of wine were silently calling to him. He needed a drink so bad that it made his teeth hurt. He forced his eyes back to the young man. "What makes you think I'm planning to help them?"

"Aren't you?"

The hunter shook his head. "I'm done with people. All I care about is killing one man, just one more, and then the world can go to hell without me."

George walked to the sideboard and poured himself a glass of wine, then turned back. "I don't believe it." Then he glanced at the glass in his hand. "Would you like me to pour you one?"

Yes! screamed Chad's inner voice, but with some effort, he reined it in. "No, thank you." There would be time and wine enough to drown himself afterward.

"I'm going there whether you want to help them or not," said George, speaking plainly. "I just have a feeling I could be of more help to you. We could work separately, to act as a sort of backup plan."

"The boy's gotten scary smart," remarked Chad, referring to Matthew. "And he can see the future. What makes you think anything we could do would help?"

George took a sip and put his glass down on a small table beside his chair. "Well, for starters, Lynaralla's vision would indicate that Tyrion manages to surprise him somehow, at least in one version of the future, so he could conceivably do it again in whatever the actual future turns out to be. What did you say a minute ago? 'He's killed every kind of wizard.' You are about as far from a wizard as anyone could imagine. Maybe you'll come up with something he doesn't expect. Tyrion must have some way of gaining information about what they're doing, but I doubt he knows what *we're* doing. If that's the case, we might be the deciding factor."

Despite himself, Chad was impressed by the young lord's words. George had clearly spent some time and serious thought on the subject. That was a surprise. He'd never imagined George being serious about anything. With a sigh, the hunter answered, "Fine. You've convinced me. You talk like a man, so I'll treat you as one, but don't cry to me later if you come to regret this."

The young Baron grinned.

"And don't argue with me. I'm in charge. We'll do things my way, which usually means it'll be boring or uncomfortable, probably both. Pack up your things. We need to go." The hunter studied George's face, gauging the impact of his words.

The Baron's face lit with surprise. "Already? They're not planning to use this enchantment for another week still."

"A hunter knows the land he hunts," pronounced Chad sagely. "You show me the place and we'll take our time sizing it up. The earlier the better. If Tyrion's got some way of knowing where it will be, he may show up early, in which case the one who is already hidden and waiting will have the advantage. I want to pick our spot and be in it early tomorrow morning."

"I haven't even showed you the arrows yet," complained George. "I did more than you asked. And we haven't talked about how we'll stay hidden."

Chad snorted. "I assume you can keep him from finding us with his magic sniffer, but I'll teach *you* how to hide. There's more to it than not bein' seen."

George rose from his seat again with a look of long-suffering. “Just hang on a minute.” Then he left the room, but after several minutes he returned, his arms full. He carried with him a massive bow and an oilskin within which the arrows were wrapped. Pointing at the bow, he remarked, “I hope you can string that thing. I tried and nearly lost the skin from my fingers.”

The archer chuckled. “You don’t string it until you’re about to use it. It’ll lose its power if you string it early and leave it strung.” Then he studied the bow. As expected, it was thick and heavy, and despite Mattley’s previous statements, it was well finished, though it was entirely lacking in decorations or embellishments. Chad approved. It was as it should be, a thing of pure function. He looked forward to testing it later.

The arrows looked much as he had left them, though they were now covered in arcane scribblings that made little sense to him. He noticed that six of them were different; their fletchings had been dyed red. “What’s this?” he asked, holding one up.

George had been waiting for the question and he leaned forward with enthusiasm. “I told you it would take time and energy to make them explode, so when I was almost done, I spent my extra time with those. Those are like the others. They can’t be touched with magic, aside from my own, but there won’t be much left of whatever you hit with them.” He held up a hand to forestall the hunter’s impending interruption. “I added something else, in case we get separated, or something happens to me. There’s a second enchantment to hide them from magesight. They look like ordinary arrows to a wizard, unless he’s close enough to see the runes.”

“That won’t be much help,” noted Chad. “I’ve been told the dragon-bond makes me show up pretty clearly all on my own.”

George reached into his pocked and pulled out a gold ring. “That’s what this is for.”

“A ring of invisibility?” asked Chad.

“I wish,” said George. “I didn’t have time for that. Making something permanently invisible is more difficult than you realize. Making something that will make something *else* invisible is nearly impossible. Otherwise you wouldn’t need me, but this is the next best thing.”

“What does it do?”

George slipped the ring onto his finger. “Easier just to show you.”

For a moment Chad thought the young man had vanished, then his eyes caught something moving in front of him and they focused on what only seemed to be empty air. He could see George's shape then, though his eyes fought to see him properly and the moment he let his gaze drift he lost sight of the young mage again. Helpfully, George waved at him and the motion enabled him to focus on the Baron once more.

"It's like camouflage," explained George. "I'm not actually invisible, but the enchantment causes the wearer to blend in with whatever is behind them. Obviously moving spoils the effect, but as long as you remain still you'll be almost impossible to spot."

Chad stared at him, amazed, until finally he spotted something he could see clearly. "Your eyes," observed the hunter. "Now that I know what to look for, I can see them." The effect was unsettling to say the least. Whenever his perception lost its grip on the strangely colored man in front of him, it appeared, as though there were a pair of disembodied eyes floating in front of him.

George shrugged, revealing himself once more. "I tried covering them too, but it does really strange things to your vision. This works for magesight too, though you can't see that, you'll have to trust me. At any kind of real distance you're as good as invisible, you just have to be careful not too move too much."

"Let me try it," said the hunter, and after George handed him the ring he tried it for a moment before slipping it into his pocket. "You're my new best friend, George," he announced. "And I'm keeping this, by the way. Even after this is all over."

The young mage waved a hand in dismissal. "I made it for you. It's not like I need it after all. With a little more time I can make one for your dragon too."

"We won't need it," said Chad, cutting him off. "She won't be there."

I heard that! came Prissy's mental voice in his mind.

"Get out of my head!" growled the hunter loudly. George gave him a strange look, and he was forced to explain what he had meant. Meanwhile Prissy continued communicating, *Then learn to separate what you project from your internal dialogue. It's not my fault you think so loudly.*

Ignoring her commentary, he returned to the previous conversation. "She's too big to hide. The place you mentioned is a wide field. There won't be enough cover."

"I can make all of us invisible," said George confidently.

"For a week?" asked Chad. "I've heard it takes more effort the more you try to cover."

"A week?" said George, aghast. "I doubt I can cover just myself for even a fraction of that."

"Then you'd better start on a ring for yourself," said the hunter. "We'll be waiting the entire week, just to watch the place. If someone else plans to set up an ambush there, we'll know about it."

George swallowed unhappily. He was already beginning to regret his decision.

Chapter 42

Tyrion spent days scouring the island, making sure there were no hidden saplings. He had come too far to be undone by something so simple. He found none, but he looked again just to be certain. Though he found nothing, he didn't consider it time wasted since he needed to recover before facing another battle anyway. He also spent his time thinking.

Since he had prepared a teleportation circle near Arundel he could get back quickly, but that didn't solve his biggest problem. He needed information. To ensure the complete eradication of the She'Har he had to find Lynaralla, preferably when she was alone or vulnerable. It wasn't that he was afraid of losing a fight, or even dying, but his goal had to come first. Otherwise he would just be a failure, like his progenitor.

Even more confusing, he found no sign of Brigid when he awoke. He might have started to doubt his sanity, but his wounds had been dressed and roughly bandaged, presumably by his mysterious and half-wild daughter. How was she alive, and how did she keep disappearing?

In the end he could make no reasonable conclusions, so he kept to practical matters. Taking an inventory, he still had most of the arrows he had brought, once he had gathered up those that had fallen out of the quiver. The bow was still usable, though he was keenly aware of how miserable his marksmanship had been. Still it was something.

And… that was it. He had no friends or allies.

Gareth Gaelyn might be willing to help him, but his main goal was eliminating Moira. Tyrion wasn't sure if it was worth pretending to gain the man's assistance. Then again, perhaps he only needed to pretend long enough to gain access to new information. The archmage would surely know more about what had been happening in Lothion than he did.

Collecting his things, he created a circle to take him back to Arundel. He was on borrowed time, after all. The circle took him to a spot close to the town, which he planned to avoid. He would make his way to the

World Road and use it to get back to the capital where he could find Gareth, but before he had taken more than a few steps a familiar figure appeared before him.

Cold fear shot through his spine, causing him to activate his shield tattoos before he could even register what he was sensing. The man—no, the She'Har—standing before him was intimately familiar, the figure of countless nightmares. It was Thillmarius.

A true Prathion, Thillmarius had ebony skin, golden eyes, and gold hair. In the present time he stood out much more than even the Illeniel She'Har. The She'Har held up a hand, indicating he had peaceful intentions. "Relax, I'm here to help you," he said in flawless Erollith, further cementing his identity.

Tyrion found that hard to believe, especially since one of his last actions had been to betray and murder his former slave master. "You're dead," he said warily.

"That's true," said the She'Har. "But I'm not entirely who you think. Perhaps I should have chosen a different identity. I thought a familiar face would help. Is this better?"

As Tyrion watched, the stranger's face and coloring shifted, becoming yet someone else he remembered. He tightened his shield as he was confronted with an even more frightening person from his predecessor's past, Ceylendor, the Centyr lore-warden. He tightened his shield even more, acutely aware that he didn't have the option of seeking the mind of stone to protect himself. "Who are you?" he asked tensely.

"At the moment I'm Ceylendor, but not precisely," said the stranger. "You might think of me as God, though the answer is more complicated than that. I'm here to help you fix your story."

Those words brought back the memory of the little girl immediately. "You were the girl too?"

"I'm everyone," said the stranger. "Or rather, you're all part of my dream, but lately I've been taking a more active role."

"I've gone mad," muttered Tyrion, but he didn't really believe it. He spoke merely to fill time while he considered his options. His first instinct was to kill the stranger, to strike without warning, but something warned him the man was too dangerous for such a solution.

"You're not crazy," said Ceylendor. "I know what you want, and I can help you get it."

Tyrion studied him carefully, noting how the stranger's aythar had changed. It perfectly matched that of the face he wore, as though he had actually become the people he imitated. Was he really a

Prathion? Only they could manage such a thing, and even then, only the most skilled of them could do so. He'd seen no sign that either George or Elaine possessed such skill. "The question is what do you want?" said Tyrion.

"Your success will give me what I want," said the stranger. "Matthew and the others are plotting something that will ruin everything I've worked for, but they need Lynaralla to accomplish it. Helping you will stop that and make your dream come true at the same time."

Tyrion's eyes narrowed. "Why should I believe you?"

Ceylendor smiled, showing white teeth between green lips. "Knowledge is power, and I have a lot of power. Let me explain…"

Tyrion listened for the better part of an hour, and despite his cynicism he found himself shocked by what the stranger revealed. The man knew him better than he knew himself, and while his claims were outlandish, they were backed up by facts that were difficult to ignore. After he had finished summarizing, Tyrion still had one important question.

"Why do you need me?" he asked.

"I can't do it myself," said Ceylendor. "Even this small conversation is incredibly difficult for me. Until recently it was impossible, but as Mordecai gains strength, I grow weaker. As I weaken, my ability to act in a conscious way grows stronger. The best way to describe it is that I'm waking up. However, even if the process was more advanced, I still couldn't go to the place where they are planning to undo my work. If I did, a confrontation would occur, between me and my successor. In order to win such a conflict, I would be forced to take the power I've given him, invalidating the very thing I'm trying to achieve. Does that make sense?"

"Not at all," replied Tyrion.

"All you need to realize is that I can't interfere directly, but for a short time I can provide others who will help you."

"Like Brigid," said Tyrion. "Was that really you?"

The Centyr shook his head. "Only as much as you could say that you're me. I can bring back anyone you need, but only for as long as I keep my attention on them. The moment my mind wavers or I drift off to sleep again, they'll vanish. The dream is particularly tenacious when it comes to maintaining itself."

"The dream?"

"What you think of as reality. The simplest explanation is that it's my subconscious self, but it cares nothing for my desires. In a sense, I'm at war with myself, and I've chosen you as my champion."

Tyrion's expression grew sour. "I am no one's champion. You have manipulated me thus far; don't expect me to thank you for it. I'll accept your help now only because I seek to use you."

Ceylendor smirked slightly, then looked away. "As expected. May I suggest those I think could help you most?"

"No," said Tyrion flatly. "You'll provide only those I ask for."

"You speak boldly for someone addressing God," said the stranger.

"You are no god," countered Tyrion, "only a coward shielded by too much power for anyone to gainsay him. Rather than face your responsibility you seek to run from it, to hand it to someone else."

There was no anger in the stranger's voice when he replied, "You dare?"

"I know you because I have been you, in my own way," declared Tyrion. "I despise your weakness, but I will use you anyway."

Ceylendor's face remained neutral. "Very well. Speak as you wish. It means nothing to me. Who would you have me summon?"

Tyrion smiled.

***

Sweat was dripping down George's face as he sat in the long grass beside the hunter. He couldn't remember ever being quite so thoroughly miserable, but it was clear that the archer wasn't worried about his comfort.

"We've been here for days," whined George. "No one has come. Don't you think we've wasted our time?"

"He's been here already," said Chad. "I don't think he spotted us, though."

"Really?" asked George, stupefied. "How do you know?"

"We're still breathing," said the hunter. "You should go ahead and congratulate yourself. Your mother would be proud," added Chad sarcastically.

George's lips thinned at the harsh words. He'd gotten used to Chad's remarks over the past few days, but the hunter always found new ways to get to him. "It wouldn't hurt you to be a little nicer," he said with some bitterness. "Like my mother."

"If I was your mother, you'd never have made it to adulthood," said Chad. "I think you're a fucking moron." He smiled sweetly then. "But I mean that in a 'nice' way."

"How could that be—nevermind," George responded. He was beginning to learn. Instead he returned to his original question. "What makes you think he's been here?"

"Because the bastard isn't stupid. You said his range is greater than yours. I expect he got as close as he could and moved away when he didn't spot us. He's expecting an ambush."

"Then we might as well have stayed at my estate," argued George. "At least we'd have been comfortable. From what you've said, we accomplished nothing."

Chad gave him a look that spoke volumes. The chief topic of those volumes seemed to run somewhere along the lines that he'd never seen anyone dumber in his life. "Every time I start to respect you just a little bit, you say something like that."

George didn't rise to the bait. He merely glared sullenly back at his tormentor.

"For one, we know that no one else has come here," explained Chad. "That relieves us of one major worry. For another, we know that our prey isn't foolish. They're aware this might be a trap. That makes a big difference in how we'll react when the big day arrives."

"How so?" asked George. "Aren't you just going to shoot him when he shows up?"

"They," corrected the archer. "He won't come alone. He won't be the first to appear, either. Hunting men isn't like hunting deer, boy. They're much more dangerous, especially this one. One wrong move and you wind up the hunted instead of the hunter. He'll begin with a smaller attack, hoping to spring whatever surprise Matthew has in store for him. He might even plan a second attack before revealing himself. Whoever has the last trick up their sleeve will be the winner. That's why we'll wait."

"How long do we wait?"

"Until someone loses. If that's Tyrion, fine. I'll just make sure he doesn't get out alive. If that's Matthew and the others, I'll be the dagger in the back that puts and end to our mutual enemy," said Chad.

George was shocked. "What if he kills them while we're sitting here, playing it safe?"

"We aren't playing house, boy," bit back the hunter. "We're betting our lives. Hopefully we'll be able to tell who the loser is before it gets that far, but there's no guarantees in this game. People are going to die. If that pisses you off, fine. I really don't give a shit, because I'll probably be dead before this is all over anyway. If you don't like it you can spit on my grave. But until I'm dead, I plan on doing my best to make sure I kill that fucker first."

"If he tries to hurt them, I'm not going to sit still and wait," warned George, his face serious.

"That's exactly why you'll be over there," said Chad, pointing at the opposite side of the field. "So you can't fuck things up for me. If you jump in and I think it's the right time, I'll help you, but I don't expect that much luck. More likely you'll just get yourself killed."

Chad opened his pack and pulled out a waterskin. He took a long drink before continuing, "My advice to you is to wait until you see me start. If things look good, you might be able to do some good. If not, you should use those magic powers of yours to vanish and start running. Either way, I'll probably be dead."

That brought George up short. "Dead?"

The hunter shrugged, then spread his hands outward, indicating the wide field they were in. "This isn't the best place for a sniper. What do you think will happen once I reveal myself? Hopefully Tyrion will be dead, but there's a fair chance whoever is with him won't be. Once they spot me they'll bring the hammer down."

Stubborn as ever, George refused to give in. "That won't happen. We're not alone. I'm sure Matthew has something planned."

Chad took another drink, wishing for perhaps the hundredth time that it was something better than water. "Don't count on other people's plans, boy. It never works out. If you really want to help, wait until I start, then do something big. Create a big enough distraction and I might be able to keep shooting long enough to kill more of them. Hell, maybe I'll even survive."

George remained quiet for a while, thinking. Then he asked, "Is that what you really think?"

Chad looked up from the grass, his eyes meeting the young Baron's and holding his gaze. The look in them chilled George to the core. "No. Starting a shooting match in the middle of an open field with no proper defenses is the most foolish thing I've ever done in a life full of foolish decisions. If I had any interest in living, I wouldn't be here."

CHAPTER 43

A cool breeze drifted across the field, though in comparison to the mountains it was almost warm. Gram looked around at the others. He was in the last group to have come with Karen, and although it had taken her less than a span of minutes to carry everyone there, using multiple trips, Matthew and Irene were already getting ready.

It was happening too quickly.

Gram looked at his mother. "I don't like your plan," he told her. "At least let me stand beside you. If something goes wrong, I can stop it."

Rose gave him a calm glance. "It won't work if you do that. My life has to genuinely be in danger."

"Then let one of the others do it," he countered. "There's no reason it has to be you. If he would come for you then he most certainly would come for one of his own children."

His mother raised one brow. "And if it went wrong? Of everyone here, I'm the most expendable. This thing they've created needs all four of them."

"Moira," said Gram, ignoring his inner shame.

"You mean Myra," corrected Rose.

"Whatever," he growled. "She's not needed for it to work and she's one of his children."

"He's right," said Myra, listening from behind them.

Rose glanced back at her. "Shush, girl. If things become as dangerous as Lynaralla foresaw, you'll be needed to defend them. This is the only thing I can do. Let me do it."

Sir Cyhan was standing a few feet away, fully armored and with a heavy crossbow in his hands. Alyssa stood next to him, likewise armored and carrying the enchanted spear she favored. Forgoing the use of the crank, the veteran warrior set the steel bow using only his gauntleted hands before placing a quarrel in place. "I don't like it either, Gram," he announced. "But it was your mother's idea and Matthew agreed to it. Together they're smarter than the rest of us put together. I don't see an alternative."

Gram felt a tremor of fear run through him. Desperate he turned back to his mother. "Let someone else do it," he begged. He gestured to Cyhan. "Give it to me."

The older knight looked at him cynically. "Don't be a fool. No one here believes you could do it." He let his eyes roam across the others. "Certainly, none of them could. Besides, if it goes wrong and she dies, who else could bear the blame?"

Alyssa spoke up, "Let me."

Sir Cyhan laughed darkly. "Do you want your future husband to hate you? Would you be the woman who killed his mother?"

Rose glared at the massive knight. "You're not helping. No one is dying. At least not from this. He'll come."

Karen was biting her lip. "But how? I can travel anywhere in the world with a thought, but even I couldn't stop a crossbow bolt with that little warning."

"He can, and he will," said Rose confidently. "He's already done as much three times before. Once for me, once for Matthew, and again when Myra was thinking of killing herself. I won't pretend to understand how, but I know he *can*."

Matthew addressed them from the background. "We're ready."

"Where do you want me to stand?" asked Rose calmly.

"Over there," said Matt, pointing to a spot about twenty yards distant before gesturing to Cyhan in the other direction. "If he stands over there, it will put the device squarely between you."

Even Elaine was nervous, though none of them could see her. Her voice emerged from what seemed to be empty air. "Are you sure he can't sense it?" she asked.

"Can you?" asked Matthew.

"No," answered Elaine immediately. "But even if he doesn't detect the trap, he might not appear where you want him to."

"Anywhere in this twenty-yard spread will work," said Matt. "Though the middle of it would be best. I don't think it will matter, though."

"Why do you say that?" asked Karen.

"Because I think he'll want to do this," said Matthew, absently rubbing the back of his metal fist against his tunic, as though he might polish its perfect enchanted metal. It was a sign of his nervousness. "If he can discover something like one of us being in danger, I think he'll also be able to figure out what we're doing. If he shows up in the wrong place, I'll try to explain it to him."

"If you get too close to him you'll die," announced Myra. "I don't think he can control the power. That's why he hasn't come back to us."

"Enough," said Rose. "Let's get this over with." She spoke with her usual confidence and authority, but inwardly she worried that she would lose her nerve. She folded her hands in front of her to prevent them from shaking visibly.

Karen disappeared, taking Elaine with her to wait at their chosen vantage point, while Matthew, Irene, Conall, and Lynaralla moved apart to their assigned positions at the corners of an unmarked square, thirty yards apart. All of them strengthened their shields. Once they were ready, Cyhan lifted his crossbow, sighting carefully along it at Rose's chest. He had practiced carefully over the past few days to ensure he could strike true. The heavy bolt would not miss, and if things did not go as planned, he would at least make sure that Rose did not suffer as she died. It would pierce her heart and end her life with as little pain as possible.

Gram and Alyssa stood over a hundred yards distant, too far away to intervene, as the big man's finger hovered over the trigger. The tension in the young knight was palpable as he watched. Alyssa's hand was on his arm, but it did little to ease the strain of his muscles as he fought against himself and his own urge to stop the proceedings. "I can't watch this," argued Gram, his eyes fixed on the scene. "I've changed my mind." He took a step, beginning to move forward.

Alyssa's hand was firm. "Trust her…" The words were only half out of her mouth before a sharp clack rang out as the crossbow fired, and then everything happened at once.

Two men's voices rang out, screaming in fear and denial. One was Gram's, but the other came from a newcomer. Beside Gram and Alyssa stood a man with a massive frame, easily the size of Sir Cyhan or Gram himself. The stranger was clad in full-plate armor and carried a great sword that Gram knew instantly, for it was his own. The enameled breastplate bore the arms of the Thornbear family.

All of this registered in a moment of blinding pain, for a pillar of black flame had appeared on the field, standing precisely between Rose and Sir Cyhan. The heat it radiated was not heat at all, but a searing pain that dropped Gram, Cyhan, Alyssa, and the newcomer to the ground, writhing in agony as they began to die.

Only the four wizards remained upright, barely. Matthew and the others were protected by the strongest shields they could create, but even that was not enough, and one by one they fell to their knees as they struggled to complete their task.

***

At the edge of time, in a place that wasn't a place, I watched the crystal that held the universe slowly crumble, and I was helpless to stop it. My pain was gone now, and even my emotions were largely numb. Nothing mattered.

Sleep was what I wanted, the blissful release of dreams, where I could forget this life and all that had gone wrong with it. I fought to stay awake, for I knew what sleep would mean, though with each passing moment it seemed less important to me.

A bell rang, a tiny chime within my awareness that rose in pitch as it went on. I failed to understand it at first, but eventually my mind began to pay attention. The vast diamond world before me sprang into focus, and I realized the sound I was hearing was coming from a point inside it.

Rose.

In an instant, I saw her, standing on an open field, as death crept toward her. If I approached, it would likely kill her, but if I did nothing her death was certain. My family was there, watching with strange expectation, so I borrowed a small slice of eternity and searched their thoughts and memories. In them I found hope. My son had done it; he had found the answer. A small feeling of pride ran through me, washing away the sadness that accompanied the knowledge that I would never be able to tell him or the others how proud I was of them.

There was one small problem with their plan. Rose was too close, and with nothing to protect her my presence would turn her to ash. I had a solution, however, and as gently as I could, I twisted the space around her, sending her to safety.

That taken care of, I appeared, compressing myself down to a size that could stand on the field where they wanted me. I fought to contain my power, and largely succeeded, but it was still too much for them to survive for long.

In a timeless moment I looked on my loved ones, and tears of fire ran down my cheeks to see the pain I caused them. I wanted to speak, to tell them how much I loved them, but I feared the sound would destroy them, so I remained mute. Besides which, my time was far too compressed; they couldn't understand me, and if I allowed myself to remain for more than a few seconds my mere presence would be their deaths.

One presence was strange, though. Standing beside Gram and Alyssa was my old friend, Dorian Thornbear. *Why is he here?* Had I done that? Was he my final farewell to Rose? I had no knowledge of such a thing, and it seemed cruel. He would surely vanish as soon as I did, but then again, perhaps he would last long enough to give his own family a proper farewell.

As I eased my grasp on time, it began to flow slowly, like syrup. The crossbow bolt that they had used to summon me vanished into dust before it could reach me, and then golden walls began to grow up around me, sealing me into another dimension, a place where I could no longer threaten them.

As the golden cube solidified and became complete, I couldn't help but admire it. My children had created something beyond belief, an enchantment that could annihilate even a true god, so long as he kept himself still enough for it to work. *They did well, Penny,* I told myself, wondering if she could hear me.

And then it activated.

***

Almost as soon as it had started, the pain was gone, leaving Gram gasping with relief. Raising his head from the ground, he assessed the situation. A shining gold cube stood between the four wizards, who were now locked rigidly in place, their arms outstretched as they poured themselves into their work.

Gram could see Sir Cyhan was struggling to his knees, the crossbow on the ground beside him, but Rose was nowhere to be seen. That alarmed him, but he needed to get on his feet before he could do anything. Turning to one side, he looked at the woman beside him. "Alyssa, are you…" He failed to complete the sentence though, as something hard slammed into the side of his head, knocking him sideways with enough force to cause his vision to go black for a second.

When it returned, it came with the sound of steel ringing against steel. He must have lost consciousness, for he was already halfway to his feet, Alyssa's strong arms beneath his as she lifted him up. "We have to help him!" she shouted.

"Help who?" asked Gram, still rattled as his eyes began to focus once more.

"My father," she replied, stepping away from him and lifting her spear. Then she added, "He's losing." Her voice was tinged with disbelief.

Gram understood when he took in the scene before them. Two armored knights were battling close by, blades flashing in the sun. One was Sir Cyhan, wielding one of the sun-swords Mordecai had created many years before, while the other was the newcomer, bearing what appeared to be Rose's Thorn. It was impossible.

"I'm hallucinating," muttered Gram, looking down at himself. He still wore his armor, the armor that was a part of the sword Matthew had remade. Speaking the command word, he summoned the weapon itself and it appeared in his hands, an exact match for the sword the stranger held—with one exception. His sword had a massive ruby set in its hilt, his father's heart, and it was pulsing with red light in a way that he had never seen. The light thrummed with a fast and steady beat, as though it had come to life.

With a strange sense of wonder, Gram touched it with one hand, and even through his armor he could feel its heat. Numb with shock, he looked up at the man who was steadily beating his way through Sir Cyhan's defenses. "Father?"

CHAPTER 44

Cyhan fought in a way he hadn't experienced in years—for his life. There was no room for thought or strategy, for his foe was faster than thought, stronger than strategy. Cyhan knew him intimately, for they had been friends, and sometimes enemies, in the past.

He had been the better during their last great confrontation, only to lose because Dorian was willing to sacrifice himself for victory. But that was no longer the case. Cyhan was older now, and the pains from a lifetime of violence were set in his bones. Despite the dragon-bond, Dorian was stronger, Dorian was quicker, and his swordsmanship was just as it had always been, a thing of perfection.

Cyhan couldn't see his old friend's face because of their helmets, but he knew what it must look like, for he could feel the rage in his enemy's sword as it broke through his guard, again and again. Even when his counters met it perfectly, Dorian drove through them, slamming Cyhan's own blade into his armor.

As always, Cyhan improvised, but on an open field he had few options and Dorian anticipated every feint and ploy, turning them against him. Cyhan was losing, and though he was clad in enchanted armor, he knew it would fail against the power of Dorian's strikes if one were allowed to connect without being robbed of some of its force.

Cyhan had been in thousands of sword battles, but he felt something new. He was afraid, for now, unlike the past, he wanted to live. The reason for that will to live was charging in to help him, as Alyssa brought her spear in line to drive Dorian away from her father.

Her form was flawless as she performed a lunge thrust with the spear, aiming at Dorian's hip, where the point could find purchase and deliver its power without slipping away, but it failed regardless of her skill. Dorian's knees bent, allowing him to use his breastplate to deflect the deadly thrust while his sword continued on, uninterrupted until it slammed into Cyhan's shoulder, tearing through the metal and cutting deeply into the flesh beneath.

Without hesitation, Dorian whipped the blade back and spun in reverse more quickly than even Alyssa could anticipate, as he drove the pommel of the great sword into the face of her helm. Stunned, she fell backward, and even as she fell, she saw death coming for her. The sword had gone up and was sweeping down again in a powerful full strike that would cut her in two if its effect on Cyhan's armor was anything to judge by.

It was stopped by an identical blade, when Gram's Thorn interposed itself. Both blades went downward under the force of Dorian's blow, until they hovered in the air just above Alyssa's neck. "Stop!" screamed Gram.

"You were dead the moment you tried to protect a man threatening my wife," came Dorian's voice, its sound hollow and metallic from inside the helm he wore. And then Thorn swept up in a backswing that threatened to take Gram's head from his shoulders.

A storm of steel and sparks erupted as the two metal-clad titans began to fight in earnest. Alyssa rolled away, fascinated and amazed at what she was witnessing, but she had little time for reflection. Her father was down, and his blood was running out to soak the ground. She had to find a way to staunch the flow before he bled to death.

Gram and Dorian's battle raged with unbridled ferocity as they went at each other, whipping the twin great swords through the air with a speed and lightness that made them seem more like rapiers than the six-foot steel weapons they actually were. Up and down they went, stomping across the dry grass, their swords connecting repeatedly, high and low, their bodies a blur of motion too fast to decipher with eyes alone.

Gram fought with a combination of technique and the subconscious battle intuition Cyhan had taught him, while his father attacked with grace and the perfect form he had attained through a lifetime of drilling at his art. Alyssa glanced up at them from her desperate work, but even her expert eyes couldn't divine which of the two had the upper hand.

Gram wanted to speak, to call out to the man he had missed for so long, but Dorian's blade was too deadly to ignore. If his focus wavered for even an instant, it would have his life's blood. He wanted to believe his armor could stop it, but he had already seen what it could do to even enchanted plate. Instead he silenced his mind and let his body speak for him, deflecting strikes that contained the unrestrained force of a novice within the perfect movement of master.

From the corner of his eye, he saw Alyssa tending to her father and he was grateful for the distraction. If she had tried to interfere with the fight, he doubted he could save her from the consequences. The man he fought seemed like a demon clad in steel, unstoppable and unyielding.

Somewhere deep down, Gram found himself enjoying it. It was the fight he had always imagined, if he had ever had the chance to fight his teacher in his prime. During his training he had always gotten the impression that his father was somehow subtly inferior to Cyhan, but now he knew the truth. His father was a paragon of war, one that was pushing him to his very limits. On a different battlefield, he thought he might be able to find an easier course, but here, on the flat and empty field north of the Glenmae River, it was all he could do to survive.

Dorian's sword slowed as he recovered from a strike. It was almost an imperceptible change, but it invited Gram to take the initiative. It was a trap, Gram could see that clearly, wrapped in the silence of his mind, but he took it anyway. Stepping in, he pretended to fall for it, but at the last instant he released his left hand from the hilt of Thorn, and while using his right to avert the deadly consequences of his deliberate mistake, he slammed his open palm into Dorian's breastplate, driving him back several feet.

In the brief space that afforded him, he shouted at his opponent, "Stop! I'm your son!"

"Lies," cried his father. "My son is yet a child." Sword at the ready, Dorian stepped forward to engage once more.

This time Gram retreated, skipping backward. "It's been years! I've grown. It's me, Gram!" The words cost him some of his focus, and he barely avoided yet another lethal swing. Clenching his jaw, he brought Thorn up again. "Fine. If you don't believe me, I'll prove it on your bones." He let the words slip away, and after dodging the next strike he pivoted back toward his father, taking the offensive for the first time.

Their swords rang out in a discordant symphony of violence as Gram attacked with a series of blows that pressed the big man back. An observer would have thought him possessed by the spirit of fury, but inside his steel armor Gram was wrapped in emptiness, his mind and body in a place where thought did not exist. There was nothing in him but the purity of motion.

Incredibly, Dorian began to take the defensive. Alyssa watched them from her father's side, while she held a tourniquet she had devised after removing some of his armor. Her warrior's gaze could read the flow of battle and she began to see doubt in Dorian's movements.

Where before she had feared for Gram's life, now she began to fear he would destroy his own sire, for there was no mercy or consideration in Gram's fighting. He no longer fought to protect, or even to win. He fought to kill. She cursed her own clumsiness as her fingers fumbled to tie the knot on the tourniquet.

Gram's sword was a blinding flurry of steel as he drove his father back, but while his attacks seemed mindless, they were anything but. With each strike, Dorian's responses were forced further out of line, until at last he had no way to defend. Gram's blade whipped across, down, and then back up in a backswing that would take Dorian beneath his right arm and end at his left shoulder.

Alyssa saw the set-up for the final blow a few seconds before it came, and she screamed out to him, "Gram, stop! Let him finish thinking!"

Inside his shell of emptiness, Gram heard her and faltered. In that fraction of a second, Dorian recovered, and leaping forward, he slammed the hilt of his sword into the younger man's face, sending him tumbling to the earth. Stunned, he stared up at his father as the sword that was a twin of his own rose toward the sky.

Alyssa had finished tying off the tourniquet, and quick as light she was up and running. In her heart, she knew it was too late. She couldn't stop it, but neither could she control herself. *If he dies, he won't die alone.*

Before her eyes, Gram's armor vanished, leaving him bare and vulnerable as he looked up at the man who had been nothing but a memory. Diving forward, she threw herself over Gram as the blade came down.

The stroke ended abruptly, and then Dorian's sword withdrew, rising again at the ready. From his position he could end both of them before they could move. "Remove your helm," he barked, speaking to Alyssa. "Let me see your face."

Long seconds passed as she worked at the straps before her helm came off. Dorian's eyes went wide when he saw her face and the tight braid of hair on the back of her head. "A woman? Who are you?"

Her eyes met his, blinking away tears, but there was no fear on her face. "The one who loves your son more than her own life."

Dorian looked from her to Gram, and then his arms seemed to lose strength, letting the sword sag to the ground. "Is this true?"

"My name is Gram Thornbear," answered Gram. "Son of Dorian Thornbear and Rose Hightower. I was named in memory of my grandfather, by *you*, if you truly are Dorian Thornbear."

"My son was a child," said Dorian, confusion in his voice.

"You've been gone for many years—Father," said Gram. "You died holding up a stone monolith to save us."

Dorian shook his head, as though trying to clear it, then lifted his sword, pointing at Cyhan. "Why?" he asked.

"My father did that at Lady Rose's order," answered Alyssa. "In order to summon Mordecai. We had to do it to stop the end of the world."

"Your father?"

"Sir Cyhan, who was once your friend," she explained.

"Cyhan had a daughter?" said Dorian incredulously, then his eyes went to Gram's face, growing wet. "And you…?"

"We plan to be wed," said Gram. "If the world doesn't end first."

Thrusting his sword into the earth, Dorian removed his helm, letting them see his face. It was red, covered in sweat, and full of raw emotion. Bending over, he offered his hand to first Alyssa and then Gram, helping them to their feet. Then he indicated the four wizards standing locked in place. "Who are they?"

"Mordecai's children," said Gram. "We're all grown now."

"And what of Carissa?" asked Dorian, his voice thick. "Is my daughter well?"

***

Tyrion smiled as the fight came to its end. "That went well, though I could have hoped for more blood."

He stood less than two hundred yards from the scene. Beside him were Layla, Brigid, Ryan, Blake, and Piper. Aside from Layla, all of them were his children, dead for more than two thousand years. He had wanted Emma as well, but the god had refused, claiming that an archmage might ruin things. He would also have liked having Abby at his side, but given their last parting he couldn't trust her.

Two millennia before, he had trained his children as killers, and those beside him were the ones he trusted most, for their battle intelligence and efficiency. He almost felt bad for his enemy. Mordecai's children had no chance, even if it weren't for the fact that the best of them were effectively helpless while they worked their enchantment.

Summoning Dorian had been an effective ploy, allowing him to gauge Matthew's plan and defenses. It was obvious that his remaining allies, Karen and Elaine, were in hiding, probably close by. The two of them and the sad collection of enhanced warriors that stood recovering on the field would offer little challenge.

"Should we advance?" asked Blake. "We can see they're weak."

Ryan, ever cautious, shook his head. "That didn't draw them out fully. We know there's two mages in hiding and we've yet to see any sign of the dragons."

Tyrion rubbed his chin, then sent his power into the ground, creating a lattice-work of lines that spread outward to cover the entire field. Four points stood out immediately, three mages and a fourth who wasn't a mage but had more aythar than normal. "He couldn't hide the dragons," he intoned. "He must have left them at considerable distance and then timed their departure to surprise us."

"Are you sure of that?" asked Ryan.

Tyrion shook his head. "No, but it's what I would have done. The one in charge of them is at least as smart as you are." He motioned to his left and right, selecting Blake and Piper. "Strike out, separately, right and left. There are three mages and another, probably similar to the warriors you've seen fighting. Two are Prathions. You know how to deal with those."

The two set out while Brigid glared at him. "Father," she growled.

"Silence," he snapped. "Trust me. I'm saving the best for last."

CHAPTER 45

Karen and Elaine stood together, watching as the battle between Gram and the newcomer finished. They were hidden by a veil that blocked magesight as well as most visible light. Their view came from a tiny window in the veil that Elaine had provided.

"I should go help Cyhan," suggested Karen. "His wound looks serious."

Elaine shook her head. "This is too important for that. Alyssa stopped the bleeding. We don't reveal ourselves until a real threat appears."

"A real threat?" asked Karen incredulously, gesticulating with her arms. "What do you call that steel-clad monster? He nearly took Gram down! Who is he anyway?"

Elaine shrugged. "I'm not sure, but his breastplate has the Thornbear arms on it. Whoever he is, they seem to have made peace. We're waiting for the real villain to show himself. That's why they're out there with a bullseye on them, to draw out the enemy."

Then they felt a pulse of aythar from the ground itself. "What was that?" said Karen.

Elaine's face was marked with worry. "We've been marked. They know where we are."

"I can fix that pretty easily," remarked Karen, trying to hide the nervousness in her voice.

"I'm going to drop the veil for a moment so we can examine the field better," said Elaine. "After I put it back up, move us." True to her words, the veil vanished and both women's magesight began to function normally. They immediately noticed two figures running south, one heading toward them and the other crossing the other side of the field. Both were radiating incredibly powerful aythar and seemed to be protected by strong shields.

Elaine's mouth went dry, and beside her she heard Karen whisper, "Holy shit."

The veil sprang back into place and Elaine looked at Karen. "Are you ready?"

"No, wait," said Karen. "Which one was Tyrion?"

"I'm not sure," Elaine answered. "Both were on par with Irene or Conall. We'll have to take them one at a time." Her hands were clenched on the handles of her enchanted whips. "Move us just ahead and to one side of the closer one, then teleport yourself to the other side. I'll drop the veil and we'll hit him from both directions."

Karen's lips were pressed into a tight line as she nodded agreement. A second later, she moved them and then teleported away. The moment she left the protection of Elaine's veil, she was confused, for she was unable to see. The field was entirely obscured by a heavy mist laced with aythar, one she couldn't pierce with either eyes or magesight. A tremor started in her legs as she moved forward while strengthening her shield. Unable to see, she wasn't sure which direction her opponent might come from and she didn't dare attack carelessly for fear of hitting Elaine. The ground beneath her feet was pulsing intermittently. *He knows where I am,* she realized only a second before a blade of aythar swept through the mist toward her chest.

She would have died then, but a sudden blast of force swept the ground beneath her feet, sending both Karen and her assailant to the ground. A line of fire followed, snapping out of the mist to wrap around the tattooed man's arm. It sizzled there for a moment, unable to penetrate the shield that covered him, and then he was up and moving again, lost to Karen's sight.

Terrified, she got hastily to her feet, unsure what to do. To her right she heard the sound of fighting and she started toward it, although her every instinct screamed at her to run. Run and never look back. "Elaine!" she screamed, not caring how stupid it might be to reveal herself.

A brilliant line of actinic light shot through the mist, narrowly missing her head and a second later she heard a sickening, wet 'crunch'. Panicked, Karen did the only thing she could think of, sending out a wide burst of aythar to clear the mist around her, and as the air cleared temporarily she saw a scene that would forever haunt her dreams.

One of Elaine's silver whip handles was rolling toward her, accompanied by several small objects that she only belatedly realized were fingers. Elaine herself was on the ground, several feet farther away, missing both legs. "It's time, Karen," yelled her friend. "Go get…" Her words were left unfinished as the tattooed man emerged beside her and casually cut Elaine's head from her shoulders.

Time seemed to freeze then, as Karen stared at the one who had taken Elaine's life. He looked back at her with empty eyes, like death itself. She could see no emotion in him, no malice or anger. He moved toward her without wasting time, uncaring for anything but finishing his next opponent. It was then that she understood, time hadn't frozen—only she had.

For the second time in less than a span of seconds, Karen found death coming for her, and she was powerless to move, gripped by a terror greater than any she had ever known. She was screaming inside her head, *move, move, I have to move,* but nothing worked.

A massive shadow appeared in the mist, and before the tattooed demon could reach her a giant of a man slammed into him, knocking him sideways. Dorian Thornbear roared as he followed his opponent, sweeping his great sword across in a swing meant to cut his foe in two.

The tattooed wizard reacted immediately, and rather than retreat he stepped in, catching the hilt of Thorn with one hand and preventing Dorian from bringing the sword down. Karen could see his aythar blazing along his arm as he stayed the mighty warrior's blow with ease, while his second arm prepared to sweep across and return the favor.

But Dorian wasn't finished yet. Jerking backward, he fell onto his back and brought his heels up to strike the wizard in the belly, launching his surprised opponent skyward. The tattooed mage spun lazily through the air, a look of surprise on his face, and as he fell back to earth Dorian rolled to his feet and waited, sword at the ready.

The mage crossed his armblades in front of himself, to block the strike, but Dorian's sword cut through them both and continued on to slice through the man's face, shoulders, and torso.

"Confidence is good to a point," said the big man. "But too much will kill you." Dorian stared down at Elaine's body for a moment, though whether his expression was sad or not, Karen couldn't tell, for his face was hidden by steel. Then he turned to her. "Whatever it was she wanted you to do, now is the time."

Karen watched him, still in shock. "S—she died because of me," she stammered.

"Fear undoes the best of men. Bravery is getting up and doing what needs doing anyway," answered the warrior. "Don't live in shame for what you might have done. Get up and make her sacrifice worthwhile."

With a sudden jerk, Karen managed an awkward nod, and with a thought, she was gone.

***

Across the field, George was running. He had concealed himself initially in the same way Chad had, relying solely on his enchanted ring, but once the two mages had appeared it had become obvious that the enemy knew where they were hidden and one of them had headed directly for the archer. That hadn't been part of the plan.

He had no time to think or plan, so he simply reacted. He had to draw the enemy away from the hunter. Leaping to his feet, he ran directly toward the mage, who he belatedly realized was a woman. She was short but lean, with long, brown hair, and though she looked very little like the woman he had met with Tyrion previously, she reminded him of her somehow.

She was also radiating enough power to frighten him down to his toes. Nothing good would come of facing her head-on. *Then why am I running straight toward her?* he thought. *Right, I'm a decoy. Attack and withdraw.* Drawing on his power, he sent a quick stroke of lightning toward her.

The girl—for she surely seemed much younger—whipped her head toward him, spotting him with her eyes for the first time. And then she did something that made his jaw drop. With perfect timing, her hand reached out and swatted the lightning away, as though it was nothing more than an annoying insect. Her lips curled lazily into a half-smile and her feet changed direction, darting toward him.

"Shit," yelped George, and then he turned and ran for all he was worth, instinctively wrapping himself in a cloak of invisibility that covered everything but his eyes. Beneath him the ground pulsed suddenly, and without consciously knowing why, he dodged to the left. A wide beam of crackling power passed by, barely missing him. The size of the beam was deceptive, for ordinarily an attack that wide couldn't have broken his shield, but he felt the magnitude of power behind it and knew otherwise.

Sweat broke out on his forehead as he began running a zig-zag pattern. As he went, the ground continued to pulse, and then his conscious brain caught up with what his subconscious had already figured out. She was tracking his movements through the contact of his feet with the ground. How the woman managed that piece of magic, while running and simultaneously trying to kill him, he had no idea, but he'd be damned before he stopped to ask her. *Shoot her, shoot her, please by all the gods, Chad, shoot her!* he chanted mentally as he ran.

At that point a magical fog appeared, blocking both his vision and his magesight, and George wanted to scream in frustration. The ground continued to pulse, which told him she was still tracking him at the same time, while he was effectively blind. It was so unfair he wanted to pull his hair out, and he could taste his own death in his mouth.

"How are you doing all this?" he yelled, unable to help himself. His answer came in the form of a series of slender beams that cut through the mist spaced less than a foot apart. Only one hit him, but it shattered his veil, his shield, and went on to burn a deceptively small hole through his belly. George stared down at in horror, feeling nothing but a faint tingling in his stomach.

Ignoring the pounding in his head brought on by the destruction of his shield, he ran on. A slender figure passed him in the mist, and he turned, realizing Alyssa had just gone past. Stopping in spite of himself, he called out to her, "Run! She'll kill us both!"

Of course, she ignored his warning. No one listened to him; they never did. Unable to see, George did the only thing he could think of. Dropping to his knees, he closed his eyes and created a dozen duplicates of the female knight, sending them charging through the mist alongside her, or at least where he thought she was. The pain of using his power in spite of the feedback he had so recently experienced sent pain shooting through his skull.

Piper was ready when Alyssa appeared. She already knew that only one of her attackers was real, though she couldn't be sure which. Undaunted, she bent her knees slightly, anchoring herself and creating a barrier of earth in front of herself. Her eyes widened in surprise as the spear came through both the earthen wall and pierced her enchanted shield, cutting a deep groove along her side.

Pain was an old friend, though. Snarling, she ripped the ground up around her, shaping it into a whirling tornado of wind and dirt that destroyed the illusions and sent Alyssa flying across the field. It destroyed the magical fog, but she didn't need it anymore, as she stalked across the open ground toward her fallen foe.

But as the mist vanished, Gram spotted her and charged in her direction. Rather than maintain the whirlwind, Piper dismissed it, and lifting her hand, she caught him directly with her power. She lifted the young knight from the ground to struggle helplessly in the air.

Not far away, George watched helplessly. Blood ran from his nose as he tried to focus his power, to do something, anything. Ten feet in the air he could see Gram's armor beginning to collapse inward as the tattooed mage slowly crushed him with nothing more than her will. Then he saw something that gave him new hope.

Directly behind the she-demon appeared two of his friends, Karen and Myra.

Piper reacted near instantly, turning and sending an unfocused blast of power to keep her new enemies off balance, but Karen blocked it, though she fell to her knees at the shock of the blow. Piper centered her power to strike again, but then a strange feeling washed over her. Her body began to relax and her aythar faded.

She found herself staring into the endless black pools of Myra's eyes; she could feel the other woman in her mind. "What are you doing?" she mumbled. "Are you Centyr? Where are your spellbeasts?"

"You've never met one like me," said Myra gently. "*You* are my spellbeast now."

***

Tyrion was still watching events unfold while slowly crossing the field of battle. Layla kept them under a veil, and while Ryan was content to observe, Brigid was growing ever more impatient. It particularly annoyed her as Layla restricted their view to help avoid detection.

"It's almost over, Father," complained Brigid. "Why won't you let me fight?" Her expression showed frustration and a sense of betrayal.

"It's far from over," he answered. "The dragons haven't arrived yet."

Her eyes were beacons of hatred as she glared back at him. "This battle isn't over until *I* am satisfied. If there are no foes left to fight, I'll satisfy myself with your blood instead."

He knew it was a bluff. Brigid's loyalty to him bordered on insanity, but the challenge in her voice angered him. His hand snapped out with the speed of a striking snake, catching her throat in his grip. "Do you still think you're a match for me?"

She turned her face up to look at him, and rather than fear or anger, there was something else in her gaze, something that made his stomach churn with disgust. Desire. "No, but I am willing to die for the joy of that defeat."

Brigid was broken. Deep inside, something had gone wrong with her mind long ago. Tyrion knew it, her siblings knew it, but none of them had dared confront her regarding the matter. They all had their own demons to deal with. Tyrion fought the urge to strike her down, but he knew it wouldn't help. His daughter would welcome it. Her lust for battle was founded upon a darker desire. She fought to find someone who could master her in violence, and what lay behind that sickened him.

Swallowing the bile that rose in his throat, he shoved her away and turned his attention back to the battle. "You'll fight when I order it," was all he could say. Then he addressed the others, "The dragons will probably show up before we can get into position. Although they can't use aythar themselves, their bodies are imbued with vast amounts of it. Direct magical attacks rarely work with them, so try to stick to physical attacks.

Layla, when you reveal us, I want you to target the mages dealing with the enchantment. Kill the She'Har first. Nothing else matters," he finished.

"Which type is she?" asked Layla.

"Illeniel," answered Tyrion. "The others are human. You won't have any trouble picking her out from them. Ryan, you're to buy us time with the dragons."

"And me?" asked Brigid eagerly.

He smiled. "Do as you please. Kill everyone else. This is my gift to you."

"Even if we kill the first targets, they substantially outnumber us," observed Ryan. "With the dragons we aren't likely to survive."

"You're already dead," said Tyrion, putting his hand on Ryan's shoulder. "And I should have died long ago. I never intended to make it out of this alive." Of all his children, Ryan was one of the few he felt close to, though he doubted the younger man knew it. He wanted to tell him, to tell all of them, but the words wouldn't come. They couldn't. He had never been a true father to any of them. Wherever they might go when they disappeared again, Tyrion was certain he didn't deserve their forgiveness, or anyone else's.

A new presence appeared beside them, Ceylendor, materializing from nothing. "What are you doing?" demanded the god masquerading as the long-dead lore-warden. "They've almost completed their work. Everything is pointless if you don't stop them."

Tyrion glanced sideways at the god with a visible sneer on his lips. "Your goal means nothing to me. I'll proceed as I see fit. If that fails to stop them from destroying Mordecai, so be it."

"I could take back my gifts," said Ceylendor, letting his eyes roam across Layla and the others.

"Do it," said Tyrion, his voice uncaring.

"Neither of us would gain what we desire," warned the god.

Tyrion chuckled. "You wouldn't. I'm willing to take my chances without your help."

Ceylendor's eyes narrowed. "Hurry. If you fail me, I'll see to it that you suffer as no mortal ever has." Then he was gone.

Tyrion ignored the threat and continued his slow but steady pace across the battlefield. "You already did that," he muttered to the empty air.

CHAPTER 46

Myra, Karen, Gram, Alyssa, and George retreated back toward the golden cube, taking Myra's new ally, Piper, with them. George's balance was off, so Gram and Alyssa stayed close to him on either side to prevent a fall, but even they couldn't protect him from the pain when he spotted Elaine's ruined body.

She was his last living relative, or had been, his older sister, and the person he had been compared against and found lacking for most of his life. Elaine had been willful, overbearing, and had sometimes complained too much, but he had loved her dearly. It was in that moment, as he stared at her blood-soaked and dismembered remains that he realized just how much she had meant to him. And now it was too late.

"It was my fault," said Karen, her voice thick with guilt. "I was a coward when she needed me most."

George had already fallen to his knees, but Dorian walked toward them. "Were you the one that cut her down?" asked the big knight.

Karen shook her head. "No, but—"

Dorian's eyes turned to Gram as he cut her off, for his message was meant for more than just her. "You reward the fallen by living. Give them your gratitude, not your guilt, or you make their loss meaningless."

George looked up, his face twisted by grief, his cheeks streaked by dirt and tears. "Are you sure about that?" he asked, his voice shaking with anger.

"Better than most," said Dorian, "for I'm one of them."

"We need to move," said Myra. "We're too far from what we're guarding."

"Leave me," said George, his voice empty, devoid of hope.

Alyssa put a hand on his shoulder. "We can't protect you here. It's too far from where we'll be."

Karen spoke up then. "I'll take them both back to the house." And with as much respect as she could manage for her fallen friend, she used her power to gather up the pieces of Elaine's body and then she touched George. The two of them vanished.

The others began walking once more as wingbeats filled the air. At the same time, they saw four dark shapes approaching from the horizon. The dragons had arrived. "We should have brought them with us at the beginning," said Myra. "Matthew made a mistake having them come later. We overestimated Tyrion's ability. She might still be with us—"

Alyssa broke in, "You should remember what Dorian just said. And we don't know that it's over."

They waited in silence. Matthew, Irene, Conall, and Lynaralla were almost done. The dragons were less than a minute away. Victory, sad as it was, considering their purpose, was almost at hand. Myra spoke up as they watched the dragons descending, "I think it's too late for him to stop us now."

Alyssa was watching Myra as she spoke, and then her eyes widened in shock and dismay as Myra's body fell apart. Head, torso, parts of her arms and legs, they all separated and dropped toward the ground as Tyrion's armblades ripped through her, once, then twice. Piper stood a short distance away and collapsed, a puppet with her strings cut.

Everything happened at once, for the enemy was among them. As fast as Alyssa was, she barely avoided Tyrion's follow up, bending her body back and to the side as his armblade swept by. Above them the dragons roared with rage, but as they began to descend fieldstones flew up from the ground, slamming into their heads and wings, sending them into disarray. Ryan was standing farther back, behind his father, and he lifted his metal arm to the sky. The stones didn't fall after hitting their targets, but instead began to whizz through the air in wide circles before returning to smash into the dragons once again at blinding speed.

Dorian and Gram leapt to attack Tyrion, but their blades were both stopped by a strange chain of razor links as Brigid stepped forward.

Behind them all, a tall woman ran toward the golden cube. Layla was naked, and nearly as feral as Brigid herself, and in her hands was an enchanted short sword crafted of some strange wood rather than metal. Passing Irene, she went for the far corner, where Lynaralla stood locked in concentration.

Somehow, Sir Cyhan had gotten ahead of her, and he moved to block her path, though it was a miracle he was even conscious. With barely a moment's hesitation, Layla dodged to one side and drove her wooden sword in through his wounded shoulder, where the armor had been removed. The massive knight fell, but when she started to run again, she was brought up short, for his good hand was wrapped around her ankle. She raised her weapon again to finish him, since it was obvious to her that he wasn't dying quickly enough.

"No!" screamed Alyssa, running toward them, though she knew once again she wouldn't be in time. Her feet left the ground as Tyrion's power caught her, flinging her into the air as he laughed mercilessly. Dorian and Gram were being driven back as Brigid toyed with them, using her chain rather than simply killing them outright with her power.

Layla's sword came down almost slowly, as she carefully set the point in one of the eye slits in Sir Cyhan's helm. Then she rammed it home. His legs began to jerk spasmodically, continuing to move even though he was already dead, but his gauntleted fist released her ankle. She turned to run on, but before she finished the first step, a massive arrow ripped through her chest and continued on into the distance.

Tyrion's laugh stopped as he saw the bloody hole in Layla's back. With no arrow to be seen, it puzzled him, and before he could react, he felt a strange pain rip through his own chest. He stared down at the blood pouring from the wound, but his mind was darkening already, for his heart had been destroyed. Without making a sound, he collapsed slowly to the ground.

Ryan fell next, as he began to redirect his stones to meet the unexpected attack. The first arrow took him slightly too low to kill him instantly, tearing through his stomach, but the second went through his neck.

Chad Grayson stood some fifty yards away, a massive bow in his hands, though his form was strangely difficult to see, even as he moved. He had loosed four shafts in almost as many seconds, and he shifted now to bring down the last enemy, Brigid.

But four seconds had been just enough time for her to register what was happening and plan appropriately. Her power lashed out in a broad wave, sending Gram and Dorian tumbling away as she caught the wind and whipped it into a screaming wall around her. Chad's shots tore into the wind and vanished without visible effect.

She was bereft of allies, but that hardly bothered Brigid. She had enjoyed her short game with the warriors, but in the end, it had been little more than an amusement. Myra was dead. Aside from the dragons, there was little that could threaten her, and she feared nothing. Stretching out her will, she began catching the soil around her with the wind, and a maelstrom of dirt, sand, and rocks quickly formed.

Enjoying the use of her power, she began to push the storm outward, increasing its size. With no stronger mage to oppose her, she would scour the flesh from their bones and then take her time killing the dragons. Not for a moment did she doubt her ability to do so.

***

Inside my golden prison, I was cut off from the outside world, and though my annihilation was close, I felt strangely at peace. My cage pulsed with power, my children's aythar, as they filled the framework with the magic that would tear my body, my soul, and even my mind into a near infinity of pieces, scattering them across the boundless reaches of reality.

I was almost impatient for it. For I had nothing to do while I waited, other than reflect on a million choices I could have made differently. I could see a thousand things I might have done differently, ways that might have led to a better outcome.

Minutes passed, while I had no idea what occurred outside, but I could tell the time was almost upon me, for I could see the golden cage filling to completion. As it finished, billions of planes of dimensional force appeared, stretching out to cross the space in the center. When they connected at the center, a tiny fraction of a second later, my life would be done, along with all my regrets.

But time stubbornly refused to help me. As the enchantment raced to its conclusion, it slowed to a crawl. A voice spoke to me, a voice that was simultaneously everywhere and nowhere, for it existed in every dimension and none of them. *You cannot do this.*

Then stop me, I replied. When it didn't answer, I went on, *You can't, can you? They've beaten you.*

This is pointless, said the dreamer's voice. *Even if they remove you, I will find another.*

Will you? I asked, both curious and smug at the same time. *How long did it take you to nudge the Illeniels enough to create Tyrion? How long before ANSIS came to start your war? How long before I was born and cursed to accept the seed of Thillmarius' hatred? You need an archmage with the Illeniel gift, one that has been tricked into accepting the destruction of the void. Do you think you can do that again?*

I can, responded the dreaming god.

It will take half an eternity, I replied. *My children will have lived and become dust before you manage it, along with a thousand generations of their descendants, if not more.*

Then I will punish them, said the dreamer angrily. *Once you are gone I will torment them such that even Tyrion's life will seem to have been a blessing.*

You won't, I said confidently. *It took you ages to arrange that misery. Once I'm gone your power will return and with it you'll be dragged down once more, to sleep your endless sleep. It will be a long time before you find enough will and consciousness to begin your plots again.*

Please, begged the dreamer. *I'll give you anything you want.*

What could you possibly give me that would be worth my children's future?

Your life! I can reset this, return you to the way you were, the god answered.

The way I was before the void took root in my heart? I asked, suddenly curious.

No. The way you were just after that. If you're careful you can live a long life, longer than any man has before. Even if you last a thousand years it will be better than forcing me to start anew, said the god.

I could last much longer than that, I warned. *Don't underestimate me.*

Even so, it will be better. You cannot imagine how long it took to create you.

I pondered that idea for a time, while the planes of dimensional force continued to slowly stretch toward me.

Hurry, said the god. *Time is still moving. I cannot stop it completely!*

Then I have an answer for you, I said.

Chapter 47

Karen appeared outside the mountainside cottage with George and carefully eased Elaine's remains onto the grass. The vegetation seemed uncommonly vibrant in contrast to Elaine's pale, blood-streaked skin. She sat there with George for several minutes, her arms around his shoulders. He didn't move or speak, nor did his shoulders move to indicate he was crying. He was simply *there,* his heart as empty and lifeless as his sister's body.

She looked up in surprise when two figures emerged from the house, Lady Rose and Myra. "How are you here?" she nearly shouted, her question meant equally for both of them. She had last seen Rose in the clearing, miles from where they were now, and she had taken Myra there to assist the others only a short time previously.

Rose answered first, "I have no idea, though I suppose it must have been Mordecai's doing. One minute I was there, trying to keep still, the next I was here."

Myra appeared embarrassed. "It was at Matthew's insistence. He didn't want me to go personally. The one you took with you was a spell-twin." Then her eyes took in what was on the ground beside Karen and George. Rose caught her shoulders as Myra stumbled.

"What happened?" asked Rose, her voice commanding.

Karen felt guilty answering. Even the simple act of trying to keep her voice calm while she recited what she had witnessed felt like a betrayal of her friend. Both George and Myra remained silent while she recounted what had happened, but Rose's body seemed to grow tenser.

When she finished, Rose asked, "Who was the man who you said saved you?"

"The one that appeared at the beginning, when Sir Cyhan fired the crossbow. He fought with Cyhan and nearly killed him. Then he fought with Gram and Alyssa. They had already made peace when he helped me," explained Karen. Then she added, "He had Gram's symbol on his breastplate."

"Symbol?" asked Myra, slightly confused.

But Rose had already understood. "You mean his arms, the heraldic device that Gram has on his shield?"

Karen nodded. "Yes."

Rose's voice was taut as she phrased her next question. "Did they say who he was? Did Gram recognize him?"

"No, they didn't say his name," said Karen, "but Gram called him his father. That part didn't make sense, though. I thought Gram's dad had passed on or something. Isn't he your husband?"

"Take me there," ordered Rose, stepping forward and grabbing Karen's wrist in an iron grip. When the younger woman hesitated, she snapped, "Now!"

Before they could go, Carissa stepped out behind them. She had been listening from inside the door. "Wait. Take me too."

Reflexively, Rose started to respond, "It's too dang…"

"The world might be ending," said Carissa. "And I can't even remember his face."

Rose already agreed; in fact, she had stopped her words before Carissa had even begun to speak. She nodded to Carissa and then looked back at Karen. "Take us both—please."

***

Matthew's mind was clear in a way that only ever came to him when he was working on something that required all of his attention. The enchantment he had crafted was a thing of unbelievable complexity, but at its smallest level it was a repeating pattern, a pattern he understood. Most of the energy required for it had been invested during its creation, otherwise they would never have had time to use it when his father appeared.

Theoretically, like most use-activated enchantments, virtually all of the aythar could have been put into it during creation, so that the user would only need trigger it with a thought or word, but he hadn't had the time to perfect and polish his design. The edges of the cube didn't match up properly, which made the construct more like six separate enchantments, with twelve incongruous interfaces where each side met the others.

Given another year he might have found a way to match everything perfectly, probably with the help of more of Myra's ever-useful spellbeasts, but lacking that there had only been one solution. He and the others, Lynaralla, Irene, and Conall, would serve as living conduits, acting as the mortar that would hold the cube together. Since there were twelve interfaces, each of them would manage three. The four of them were linked mind-to-mind, giving Matt absolute control of their gifts, since he was the only one that truly understood the workings of the enchantment and they would need perfect coordination to balance the immense forces stored within the matrix.

Despite his pretense at confidence, he had been wracked by doubts, and when the black pillar of flame had appeared, he had felt a moment of pure panic. Deep down he knew their effort would fail; it had to fail. The theory was sound, but even though the others all seemed to think that dimensional planes were something that could effortlessly separate and divide people or matter, he knew it wasn't that simple. Transporting something, even through a dimensional interface, required energy. The amount was relatively small compared to the size or mass of the thing moved, but it wasn't insignificant.

The thing that appeared between them, his father, was a mass of aythar and negative void energy so dense that it defied description. The cage that they had prepared contained several celiors worth of aythar, but if it didn't meet the minimum amount required by the almost immeasurable thing that stood between them, the cage would fail.

The consequences of that would be so immediate and catastrophic that Matt figured he probably wouldn't even have time to appreciate his own death. Neither would the rest of the world, in all likelihood. Their universe would probably last longer, perhaps a day or two, and then it and the other dimensions would discover a similar fate.

No pressure.

Reaching out through the link, Matthew assumed control of his siblings, becoming a being with four minds, four brains—four perspectives. As one, they uttered the words to bring the golden cage to life, and almost as quickly things began to spin out of control.

It was too much for them.

Lynaralla's emittance, the amount of aythar she could reliably channel, was too low to handle three sides. The effort would burn her to ash within a span of seconds. Conall and Irene were both strong enough, but were slightly out of balance, and the pressure that created made Lynaralla's problem even worse. To stop the impending collapse, he shifted one of Lynaralla's sides to Conall.

That postponed the immediate risk of failure as Lynaralla's load dropped beneath what she could handle, but it created an imbalance in the structure, and a harmonic resonance began to grow that would eventually shake the cube—and by extension, *them*—apart. To balance it he needed to shift control of a fourth side to either Irene or himself.

Irene was strong enough, but she was in the wrong position. Conall was directly opposite Matt, along a diagonal, so the best option was for him to take it. With a thought, he shifted one of Irene's sides to himself and the resonance faded. Now he and Conall each had four, Lynaralla held two, close to her limit, and Irene had two, which was an easy task for her.

Minutes passed as the construct stabilized and the final activation energy, supplied by the four Illeniel mages, filled in the gaps. It was going to work, and with that realization Matthew felt a wave of guilt sweep over him. They were killing their father, and some of them hadn't known what he was asking them to do.

Irene's thoughts rose from the depths of their communal mind, *We're not stupid.*

Even I figured it out, said Conall. *We're family. Don't try to take all the blame. We're all in this with you.*

Lynaralla's response was the equivalent of a mental nod.

Matthew's face tightened as he felt their support. He had been stupid. Remembering his father's favorite motto, he felt tears forming in his eyes—in their eyes. *I love you Dad, but stupid dies today.*

At the same time, the pain of their efforts began to grow. He and Conall probably wouldn't be good for much for a few days afterward; Lynaralla too, in all probability. With a final surge, the enchantment was complete. He felt a burning pain shoot through him, and then the world went black.

All four of them collapsed, and the link between their minds dissolved. The golden cube was gone, and there was no sign of the black pillar of flame that had been at its center. Matthew and Lynaralla were unconscious, and Conall was nearly so. Irene felt her cheeks begin to sting as she lifted her head from the ground.

The sky was almost dark as a towering brown maelstrom of earth and wind roared nearby, and Irene realized the stinging was because its edge was almost upon her. In the center of the storm, her magesight revealed a powerful wizard, one as strong as Tyrion or one of her siblings, but she didn't recognize the aythar.

At the same time, she became aware of the others around her. Gram, Alyssa, Chad, Karen, Rose, and even Carissa were there, along with another, a man she didn't recognize, though he was too big to forget.

They knelt, close to the ground, trying to shield themselves and one another from the scouring wind. Meanwhile, above them, the dragons were tumbling through the sky, driven by currents of air too powerful for even their wings to counter.

Conall started to pass her, an aythar shield forming over his armor, but Irene put a hand on his arm. "This is too much. You're half-dead already."

Frustrated by the truth, Conall met her eyes. "We have to do something. She'll kill all of us otherwise."

"Shield the others," she told him. "I've still got some fight in me."

Conall nodded and used his power to drag Matt and Lynaralla's bodies closer, then joined the others, kneeling beside them as he formed a shallow hemisphere of force above their heads.

Irene faced the storm, then slipped one hand into her skirt pocket and withdrew what appeared to be a small stylus. She spoke a word and it grew, becoming a full staff in her hands. She placed the butt of the staff against the ground to brace herself, and then she reached out to the wind with her power.

For a moment, nothing happened, but then the winds began to slow noticeably, and the storm began to exhibit strange currents and eddies as parts of it slowed and others sped up. At the center of the storm, Brigid snarled and redoubled her efforts. She already had the advantage and she knew it. It was harder to stop a storm than to start one, and yet, as the seconds ticked past her grip on the wind began to slip.

Outside the storm, Irene stood, implacable. Her will was inexorable, for she had her father's power and her mother's stubbornness. She fought the heavens, pitting herself against the incredible momentum of the air itself, and even with Brigid urging it on, she wrestled it to a standstill.

Abruptly, Brigid stopped, releasing her grip on the air. For a long moment the world seemed to hold its breath, and then the sand and soil that had been suspended began to fall, spreading outward and covering the entire valley in a choking cloud of soil and churning air. The sun vanished, obscured by the dust, and everywhere there was darkness. Then she began to run.

Irene's magesight saw her coming, but she wasn't afraid. She had already proven her mastery. Lifting her staff, she pointed one end toward the woman she couldn't yet see and unleashed a channeled blast of pure destruction. Though Brigid dodged to one side, it still struck her, skimming across her enchanted shield and knocking her sideways. But she didn't stop. Rolling back to her feet, she came on anyway.

Irene sent several more blasts at her opponent, but none managed to stop her. She felt a seed of doubt creep into her heart as the strange and feral mage got ever closer. *How can her shield be so strong when I was able to overpower her storm?* she wondered.

A strange feeling swept over her, and Irene ducked to one side as a razor-sharp chain swept through the air where her head had been a second before. She couldn't see or feel it with her magesight, and if her eyes hadn't seen the shadow as it passed over her, she wouldn't have known why she had ducked.

Then Brigid was upon her, and in the dim light Irene saw why her attacks had been useless, for Brigid's body was covered in a tattooed enchantment. She leapt at Irene like a wild animal, arms outstretched, but instead of claws, her arms were sheathed in pure destructive power.

Irene dropped her staff and did the only thing she could; she brought up both her palms and sent a broad shockwave of power forth, blasting Brigid backward to give her some space. In the dark part of her mind, beneath conscious thought, her brain was calculating, and the answers it was giving her weren't good. Her enemy was very nearly as strong as she was, and her body was covered in tattooed enchantments. That meant there was very little chance Irene's magic could break her defense directly.

At the same time, Brigid's blade-like arms were also enhanced by her tattoos, making them quite capable of cutting through Irene's simple shields. In fact, her shields were a liability, for if they were broken, Irene's ability to continue would be destroyed. She dropped them and dodged to the left as another unseen attack from the chain threatened to put an abrupt end to her.

She was essentially fighting two opponents, and she didn't have much of a chance against either of them. The chain kept coming, completely ignoring her attempts to wrangle it with her power, while Brigid was rapidly approaching from behind. She'd have been dead already if it weren't for the strange sixth sense that kept warning her of unexpected attacks.

Fear found her then, and it felt as though her insides were trying to escape by themselves. But despite it, or maybe because of it, Irene refused to give up. To avoid both attacks, she formed a spear-shaped cone of power beneath her feet and then drove herself downward, letting the ground itself serve as her shield.

She knew it was a foolish move, but it had been her only option. A mage as powerful as Brigid could simply wait above, using her power and the mass of the earth itself to smother her, but that would be a slow process, and Irene was betting that the insane woman wouldn't want to wait.

Robbed of her prey, Brigid let forth a guttural growl of frustration, and then in her eagerness for the kill, she began to user her power to rip the earth apart so she could dig down to reach her tenacious enemy. She discovered her mistake too late, as Irene sent her power upward to encase her body, dragging her down into the torn soil.

A fierce tug of war ensued, as the two women's wills battled for supremacy. Brigid fought to lift herself back up, while Irene pulled her down, threatening to bury her in the ground. Eventually a stalemate was reached, with only Brigid's head and shoulders above the ground, while the rest of her body was trapped by the ground and Irene's power. She couldn't free herself, and Irene's strength threatened to crush her if she didn't continue to resist its iron grip.

Meanwhile, Irene was twenty feet down, holding her breath and painfully aware of the fact that she didn't have long to live. She needed to crush Brigid quickly, for she was running out of air, but no matter how she pressed, the insane wizardess above her refused to give up.

A ray of hope shone in Irene's heart as she felt Brigid's will seem to weaken, but then she discovered why. Through the soil she felt the chain moving, inching toward her as Brigid directed it to worm its way deeper. Whether the chain would reach her first or she blacked out from lack of air was an open question, but it was clear she had lost.

But that didn't mean she would quit trying. Irene prepared to reverse her efforts. A sudden change in the direction of her power would send Brigid skyward and allow her to free herself from the ground.

Hold her, Rennie. Just a minute longer!

It was Conall. He had released his shield over the others, and though his power was exhausted, he still had his sword. Irene could feel him above her as he ran across the torn ground. Brigid's chain reversed itself, struggling to reach the surface in time to defend her, but it was too late. Brigid fought to turn her own power against Conall as well, but Irene kept her pinned, smothering the wild woman's aythar with her own.

And then Conall was there, and his golden blade struck the raven-haired woman's head from her shoulders. It was over.

Irene's heart was pounding by the time she broke free and could draw breath again. Resting on the dirty ground, she looked at Conall and then realized they were alone. "Where is everyone?"

Conall smiled back, then let his head fall forward to rest between his knees. "Karen took them to the house, although Gram and his father put up a lot of argument. I thought you had her at first," he said. "But that girl was worse than Tyrion." After a second, he gave her an apologetic look. "You were still stronger though, Rennie."

She shook her head. "That wasn't what mattered. She probably could have killed me or you, but that's the difference, isn't it? She wasn't fighting just me. She was fighting *us*."

Her brother blushed, embarrassed. "I didn't do much. It was all you."

"You did enough," she countered.

Chapter 48

Dorian was pacing back and forth, full of pent-up frustration, and Gram and Alyssa weren't much better. Watching them, Rose felt sure they would wear out the floor. "Would you stop it?" she complained.

Karen had left a minute before, and when she returned with Irene and Conall in tow, everyone finally relaxed. As soon as the tension faded, Dorian's attention turned to the young woman who had been staring at him the entire time. Carissa had been standing off to one side of the room, as though afraid to approach, but her eyes had never left his face.

Gram and Alyssa had been studying Dorian as well, each for their own reasons, and Rose watched them all. No one knew what to say, and all of them seemed to be waiting for someone else to speak first.

Reading the room, Myra took Karen's hand while glancing at Irene and Conall. "Let's give them some space." Alyssa rose to leave with them, but Karen shook her head.

Rose put a hand on Alyssa's arm. "You should stay. You're family, remember?"

While Rose reassured her future daughter-in-law of her place, Carissa hesitantly approached Dorian, though she kept looking at Gram. She seemed to draw confidence from her brother, as though she was afraid of the stranger in the room. "My name is Carissa," she said tentatively, feeling stupid as she realized how ridiculous the words were.

"I know," said Dorian, his voice husky. "I can't believe how beautiful you are. When I last saw you, you were so small." He lifted his arms to mime cradling a baby, and then his reserve broke and he began to weep. Unsure what to do with himself, Dorian stood alone as he wept, afraid to reach out, but he couldn't control his tears.

Gram gave his sister a nudge and Carissa stepped forward and hugged her father. She wasn't crying, for she hardly knew him, and nothing felt real. Dorian looked up and opened one arm toward Gram, who was standing close by with wet eyes. "Come here, Gram."

The three of them embraced and as Gram sobbed, Carissa's eyes began to water. In fact, there were no dry eyes in the room by then, and Rose pulled Alyssa to her as they watched Dorian with his children. After a minute or two had passed, Gram and Carissa separated from him, and Rose could stand it no longer.

She was in his arms and everyone was crying again. "I missed you so much!" she sobbed, completely losing her usual composure.

"I'm so sorry," said Dorian, repeating the phrase over and over. "I shouldn't have left you."

Lifting her head, Rose kissed him to stop the stream of apologies. "It wasn't your fault," she said gently, before moving on to kiss his cheeks, his chin, and his nose. She held his face in her hands and stared at his features, as though trying to burn them into her mind.

And then Dorian's eyes unfocused and his lids began to droop. "I feel so sleepy," he muttered.

Gram noticed something else entirely. "He's fading!"

Rose looked down in alarm and saw what Gram had seen. Dorian's lower body had become translucent. "What? No!"

Opening his eyes again, Dorian forced his attention back to them. "I don't think I can stay." Rushing his words, he looked at each of them, beginning with Alyssa. "I'm grateful for you. Take care of my boy." Then he addressed Carissa, "Forgive me for not being there. You're more than I ever expected." To Gram he said, "I'm proud of you, son. Take care of them."

His last words were to her, "I love you, Rose. You did better than I ever could have."

She clung to him. "That's not true. Don't go. I need you here. I love…" But he vanished completely as she finished, "…you." Rose's scream echoed through the house, a cry of anguish that tore at the hearts of everyone who heard it.

She wasn't alone, though. They all had grief to deal with, they had all lost loved ones, whether a sister, a father, or as in Rose's case, both the men she had loved.

***

I stood in the courtyard of Castle Cameron. The black keep I had created loomed over me, drinking the sun and shimmering in odd places. It had cooled since its creation, though it still needed considerable work before it would be ready for occupation.

I probably wouldn't be the one to occupy it. My son, Conall, was the Count di' Cameron now. Given the Queen's reversal, she would likely be willing to restore my title, but I couldn't imagine taking on that mantle again, not without Penny. Time had passed, and for a while the entire world had been against me. Trying to reclaim my place here felt wrong. I couldn't forget, I couldn't pretend nothing had happened.

I wandered aimlessly for a short time, unsure of what to do with myself. The castle felt empty and abandoned, like me. I wanted out, for I knew my family was waiting for me, but none of the teleportation circles worked. The ones in the transfer house had been deliberately ruined, and when I tried creating a new one that would take me to my workshop by the mountain cottage, it failed. The shield enchantment around the castle was active, so there was no way in or out, at least not until I could find the controls.

The secret control room inside the keep was gone, a necessity when I had rebuilt the place. My plan had been to restore it to its former location once the interior was ready, but that time hadn't come yet. Still, someone had turned on the shield, which meant they had relinked the key somewhere.

I began searching the outer buildings. It had to be in one of them. *Actually, it doesn't,* my inner voice reminded me, but I ignored it. If it wasn't inside, then I was trapped. Who knew how long I would have to wait before someone came to inspect the place.

A fresh thought came to me, and I tried making a circle to my old home in Albamarl. That didn't work either, meaning the circle there had also been defaced. Frustrated, I stared at the shimmering wall of force that covered the castle and began to think destructive thoughts, but after a moment I took a deep breath. I was kidding myself, for I was far too weak to even consider such a thing.

The dreamer had stripped me of most of the power that had accumulated within me, leaving me feeling decidedly fragile. My aythar would recover, given rest, and I could still feel the dark hunger hovering at the edge of my awareness. I would have to be careful in the future, for now I knew where that craving led.

It took me half an hour to find the control pedestal, which turned out to be in a small shed that for some reason I checked last. I felt stupid. I should have known it would be in a temporary structure rather than one of the more permanent buildings.

Once the shield was down, I looked at the sky, wondering if I dared try to fly. I still had the skill, but I wasn't sure if I had the energy. I had to get home, but trekking through the mountains would take days. For the first time I regretted not having given myself a dragon.

The bond would have interfered with my abilities as an archmage, which was my main reason for not having done so, but it would have been nice to have an easy source of power. *Or just a ride,* I told myself mentally.

"They still think I'm dead," I said aloud. Worse, they thought they had killed me. My children must be filled with a whole host of dark emotions, from guilt to regret.

Since I didn't have any realistic options, I took the gate that led into Washbrook, using a tiny bit of power to disguise my features. Almost everyone knew me there, and the last thing I wanted was to cause a ruckus. Aside from my family, I didn't really care if anyone ever found out I was still alive.

I was tired and hungry, so I went to the Muddy Pig. The place turned out to be full of people all talking nervously about the events of the day. The sky had gone dark earlier, and the town had been coated with a heavy layer of dirt and dust when a cloud of dirty air had settled over it. It had cleared up pretty quickly, but the townsfolk were worried. They had lived in the shadow of Castle Cameron too long, and they knew the work of wizardry when they saw it. The current debate was between those who thought they should use the basement shelter and those who thought they should consider evacuating the town entirely.

I didn't know what had happened, having been isolated by the golden prison, so I had no idea what to tell them. Instead I maintained my disguise and made my way to the bar to find a seat. Since I appeared to be a stranger, I received a lot of suspicious looks from the locals, but I was happy to accept that rather than make myself known.

"Danae," I called, catching the barmaid's attention.

She stared at me quizzically but came over to me, nonetheless. "Do I know you?" she asked.

Realizing my mistake, I answered, "No. Can I get some beer and whatever you have in the kitchen?"

"The kitchen is closed right now," she responded. "How did you know my name?"

"Just a guess," I replied. "A friend of mine comes here, Chad Grayson. He spoke of you."

Her demeanor shifted from wary to worried. "Have you seen him?"

I shook my head. "Not for some time."

Something must have caught her attention, for she looked at me carefully. "Are you sure we haven't met? Your voice sounds familiar."

"This is my first time here," I lied.

Danae frowned. "You sound like a local, though your words are a bit too polished." When I didn't do anything but shrug, she finally gave up. "I have some cold cuts and cheese you can have," she told me. "Wait a minute."

I ate in silence after she brought the food, washing it down with the beer she gave me in a small wooden cup. I was halfway through it before it occurred to me that I didn't have any money. Glancing up, I saw Danae's eyes on me.

She understood immediately. "Broke?" When I nodded, she sighed. "I thought as much."

I waved my hands. "I have money, just not with me. If you can wait…"

"Forget it," she said. "I've heard it all. I could tell by what you were wearing when you came in. Consider it a favor to your friend."

It hadn't occurred to me how shabbily I was dressed. I had returned naked, but I currently wore a somewhat used robe I had found discarded in the castle bailey. It had a number of holes in the cloth and had obviously seen better days, much like myself. After finishing my food, I sat uncomfortably for a while, wondering what I should do. Being penniless, I didn't feel right asking for a place to sleep, but I was still loath to reveal my identity.

It was about then that the front door opened and a familiar figure stepped in, Chad Grayson. I watched as he made his way to the bar—or tried to. Danae didn't bother walking around; she hopped over the counter and ran toward him. I thought she was going to hug him, but she stopped at the last second and slapped him so hard I thought his cheek might come off.

"I thought you might be dead!" she snapped, and while some of the crowd began to chuckle, it was obvious that she wasn't putting on a show. Danae was as angry as I had ever seen her. I wondered what he might have done to piss off the normally easygoing barkeep.

Unsure what to say, Chad asked her, "Can I get a drink?"

She started to slap him again, but this time he caught her wrist and after a brief but awkward struggle she wound up embracing him. I couldn't look away, fascinated by the sight, for I had never seen this side of the rough hunter. Chad's neck bowed and he rested his chin on her shoulder. "It's over," he said simply. "I killed the bastard."

Danae started struggling again, fighting his embrace so she could punish him some more. When he refused to let go, she relaxed. "Jackass. Who cares about that? He could have killed you."

The scene went on for a while, and I forced my eyes back to the bar, though there really wasn't anything to look at. Then I heard her tell him, "One of your friends is here."

Sure enough, he was looking at me, and as our eyes met, I saw him frown, suspicion showing in his expression. Chad's hand was close to the knife at his waist when he walked over. "And who might you be?" he asked.

"An old drinking buddy," I answered. "You probably don't remember me, especially not looking like…" I stopped talking since he had drawn his knife and was holding it below the edge of the bar, barely a half-inch from my midsection.

"I can smell lies," he growled softly, "and you stink of them. Try something else before I lose my patience."

Whether he meant that figuratively or whether the dragon-bond had truly given him such an ability, I didn't know, and I wasn't about to ask. I might have laughed at the situation if I hadn't believed him. *Wouldn't that be ironic?* I thought. *To survive everything and wind up stabbed to death by one of my closest friends.* The enchanted blade I had given him could go straight through my shield, and I didn't feel like fighting.

Instead I said the first thing that entered my mind, the truest and deepest reason I had for living. "I have children," I told him, "and I really am your friend."

His face changed, and the knife vanished. Chad recognized my voice, but there was still uncertainty in him. "Mort?" he asked softly.

I put a finger to my lips. "There's an illusion disguising me."

Chad looked away in disgust and since he didn't yet have a drink, he took the tankard of a man standing nearby at the bar, downing it in a single long draught. The other man looked angry for a moment, but once he realized who had taken his beer, he changed his mind about taking offense and moved away. Chad glared at me. "I'm so fucking sick of magic." Then he asked, "If you're alive, why aren't you at home? Everyone back there was losing their minds when I left."

"You've seen them?" I demanded. "Are they alright? How did you get here?" The questions began tumbling out of me faster than I could talk.

He held up his hands to try and slow me down. "Yours are fine. Cyhan and Elaine are dead. Dorian showed up somehow, and now they're all upset about him as well as you. George and Alyssa are all kinds of fucked up and Rose is just as bad. It's like you and Dorian died on the same day."

"Why did you come here?" I asked. "You should be with them."

His drink had finally arrived, a glass of McDaniel's finest, and he downed it quickly. With a grimace that had nothing to do with the whiskey, he answered, "I had my reasons." Changing the subject, he returned to his previous question. "The real question is why are *you* here?"

"I'm too tired to fly and none of the circles are working," I explained. "What happened to Elaine and Cyhan?"

A refill had arrived, but Chad shoved it toward me. "Drink this. You'll need it."

I wasn't in the mood to drink, but I did as he asked rather than argue. Once the burn subsided, I did find the tension in my shoulders easing. I refused a second one, and he finally got down to relaying what he had seen. His story took a while, even though he kept his words to a minimum. He said almost nothing about his time in Iverly, aside from mentioning that he had found Rose there. Instead he focused on his meeting with George and their eventual ambush.

"The boy nearly got himself killed, but he saved my ass," said Chad. "They put some sort of fog in the air, which kept me from seeing a lot of what happened. When George saw what they did to Elaine, it just broke him.

"It cleared up for a while after that, but I waited. I knew that son of a bitch wasn't finished." Chad paused and took another drink under Danae's watchful eye. "Even though I was watching, it happened so fast it took me a few seconds to realize what was happening. That bastard came out of nowhere and he cut Myra apart faster than you could blink."

It came out so casually that I almost choked. "He what?"

He put up his hands. "Slow down. She's fine. I found out afterward that it wasn't really her, just another trick your kids threw together." Chad made a sour face. "Fucking magic. I wish Cyhan had been as lucky.

"Everything went to shit after that. The dragons were coming down, and one of 'em was smashing rocks into their snouts. That crazy bitch George met went after Gram and Alyssa, I think. There was too much going on to see everything that was happening. Another woman went straight for the ones who had you trapped in that box, but Cyhan got in her way.

"He was already half-dead, but she took him the rest of the way..." His voice cracked suddenly, and he put his head down. When he spoke again, I couldn't see his face. "I should have been faster. It should have been me. The big man had something to live for, me—I don't even deserve to be here."

What could I say to that? "He wasn't exactly a man of virtue either," I put in.

Chad looked up. His eyes were red and swollen, his face made ugly by grief. "He was a man of honor at least, and he didn't kill half as many as I have. At least the men he killed knew it was him. Three-quarters of the ones I've done in didn't even know they were about to die, much less who did it. And what did they tell the widows? 'Hey, Ted died this morning. He was really brave, just sittin' there, then some asshole put an arrow through his throat.'"

Danae's eyes met mine. Neither of us knew what to say. After a while I broke the silence, "What are you going to do now?"

Chad gave me a sick smile. "Drink myself to death if I can steal the cellar key from that wench over there," he answered, glancing at Danae.

"I'll be damned before you do!" she snapped back. I thought it was a casual phrase at first, but she leaned forward and grabbed the front of his shirt before leaning in to plant an embarrassingly sloppy kiss on his lips. Whistles went up from some of the patrons around the room.

The hunter sat back when she released him, then looked around the room before looking back at her. "I thought we were keeping that between friends," he said quietly. "Everyone in the room saw that."

"Like I give a damn," she spat back.

Chad sighed. "You're still young, lass. You've got your whole life ahead of you. You don't—"

"I'm over forty, you ass!" she snapped back.

He looked confused for a moment, probably because she had been in her late twenties when he had first met her. "There's no way," he began.

"I've spent my best years watching this godforsaken bar," she added. "Watching you and every other drunk in town come through the doors. So, don't give me any of your shit about my age or what I'll do with my life." When he started to reply, she held up a finger. "From now on you drink with me or you don't drink at all, understand?"

"I'm not givin' it up, not even for you," he argued.

"I don't expect you to," she snarled back. "But you'll do it on my terms." They argued back and forth for several minutes, and I wondered if I was watching the beginning of a serious relationship or the start of a war. I wasn't sure if Danae would be able to overcome his desire for self-destruction, but she seemed to be determined to try.

A thought came to me as they began to wind down. "Hey," I interrupted. "It might be too soon to say this, but Cyhan told me something a few years ago."

"About what?" asked Chad, still glaring at the woman across from him.

"About Alyssa," I said. "He told me that if anything ever happened to him, he hoped you would look out for her, like a father would."

I had Chad's attention then. "Bullshit," he swore. "That big bastard refused to put more than three words in a sentence, and you expect me to believe some horseshit like that?"

I shrugged, hoping his earlier remark about smelling lies wasn't true.

"If anyone, he'd have picked you for something like that," said Chad. "You're the father. He trusted you, not some half-drunk assassin."

"I've got more than enough children to worry about already," I said bluntly. "He knew I'd do whatever I could for her, but I think he wanted you because you understand her better."

"What the fuck do I know about girls?" exclaimed the hunter. "I know how they eat, piss, and..." He stopped suddenly as he caught Danae's stare burning into his forehead. "Anyway, the point is I don't have a thing to offer her. Not to mention she's already grown."

"She'll be married soon," I reminded him. "And you know who her mother-in-law will be. She doesn't have any family of her own. Who'll stick up for her if she and Rose come to odds?" It was a cheap shot, and I hoped Rose never caught wind that I'd said it, but it did the trick.

Chad nodded. "That's true. I'm the only one in this whole fuckin' kingdom willing to stand up to that bi—"

I coughed and gave him a stern look. "Remember who you're drinking with. I won't listen to words like that about her."

His eyes widened for a brief moment, then he closed his mouth. After a second he remarked, "So the rumors are true then?"

"Probably not the ones *you* heard," I said, backtracking. "But there's a grain of truth there."

He let out a low whistle. "You are a brave man. I knew you were suicidal, but this is a whole new level of insanity. You need to get back so you can start planning your funeral."

Uncomfortable, I tried to downplay things. "Nothing's happened, and besides my children are willing to accept it."

"*Your* kids, maybe," shot back Chad. "Did you forget her oxcart-sized son? He's a walking natural disaster! He killed a mountain lion when he was just a kid—with his bare hands, and that was before you gave him a godsdamned dragon!"

"Gram's pretty level-headed."

"He just watched his teacher get murdered," pointed out Chad. "And then he got to meet his Daddy, who's been dead all these years. Trust me, that boy isn't in a good place right now. If you walk into that house and kiss his Momma not five minutes after he saw her locking lips with Dorian..." He sat back and threw up his hands dramatically. "I'll say something nice at your wake."

"You don't know any nice words," I said dryly.

Chad thought about that for a moment before agreeing, "True. Well, I'll drink some of McDaniel's finest and piss on your grave then."

"You're supposed to pour a drink on the grave," I corrected him.

"Fuck that," he shot back. "I'm not wasting good whiskey on a dead fool."

I couldn't help but laugh at that, and Danae and Chad both joined me. Then I said, "I have no intention of going there and doing something like that. I just need to let everyone know I'm alright." Something occurred to me then. "How'd you get here so fast?"

"Karen took me to Arundel. I left Prissy there. She flew me back from there," he answered. "If you don't want to wait here, you should let her fly you back."

I was already on my feet, heading for the door.

"She's a couple miles east of town," he shouted at my back. "If she says anything about having to stay there, tell her I didn't make it a damn order. She'll know we talked."

CHAPTER 49

I walked the last mile to the house, leaving Prissy to find the other dragons. It wasn't that I thought my arrival would be any less noticeable. The house was full of wizards, and if any one of them wasn't in a bedroom with a privacy ward, they'd see me coming almost as soon as I saw them.

Sure enough, Irene and Conall met me half a mile from the front door, nearly running in their haste to get to me. It was a relief just to see they were well and whole, but I couldn't help but count their arms and legs as soon as they were close enough. Conall seemed to be exhausted, so Irene outpaced him, hiking her skirts and gamboling down the rocky slope like a crazed mountain goat. She slammed into me so hard we both went down, and only our mutual powers kept us from rolling down the mountain.

She had been so mature through all the turmoil of the last year that it had been easy to forget just how young she was, but none of her maturity was in evidence now. "Dad! How are you alive? Is it really you? Are you hurt? Did I hurt you?" Tears ran down her cheeks almost as quickly as the questions tumbled out of her mouth. At the same time, she nearly tore the robe off my back checking me for blood or bruises.

I hugged her and fought back my own tears. There'd be plenty of that after I got to the house, and I needed to pace myself. "For once I'm coming home without a scratch on me," I told her, patting one cheek and ruffling her hair. Ordinarily that would have earned me a scowl, but her hair was already a wild rat's nest from whatever she had done earlier. "As for how I'm alive, I'll explain that later when everyone's together. For now, let's just say I got a second chance."

Her face darkened. "Then we did all that for nothing?"

Thinking of Elaine and Cyhan, I hurriedly shook my head. "No. If it hadn't been for what you did, I wouldn't be here."

Conall had reached us by then, and he dropped to his knees. His head was lowered, as though he was afraid to look at me. "I'm so sorry, Father."

Struggling with my sudden onslaught of survivor's guilt, it took me a moment to realize what was wrong with him. It wasn't the recent deaths that he was apologizing for, but rather his choice of sides when I had been at odds with the Queen. Untangling myself, I crawled over to him and gave him a hug. "You did the right thing, Conall. It would have been much worse for the entire family if you had deserted the Crown. Most of all, I'm proud of you for standing up for your principles. Don't ever be ashamed of that."

Irene had her own opinions, I could see that on her face, but she chose to change the subject instead, "He saved everyone today. It was Conall who killed the wizard that almost finished us all off."

Her brother frowned, shaking his head. "Don't listen to her," he protested. "I didn't do anything. Rennie did it all. Rennie ripped the storm right out of her hands and nearly shoved it down the enemy's throat."

Irene opened her mouth to argue, then changed her mind. "Well, I suppose that's true. But she would have killed me if you hadn't done what you did."

I listened to them argue for several minutes, enjoying their banter. Watching them, a sense of gratitude washed over me, and I found my eyes beginning to water. To stave off my emotions I stood and dusted my knees. "Let's go," I told them. "Do the others know I'm here yet?"

"George and Myra do," answered Conall. "We were together in the main room when we spotted you. I don't know if they told anyone else."

"She stayed with him," added Irene. "He shouldn't be alone."

Myra stepped out the door when we got close, her expression unreadable. The closer I got, the more she frowned. When I was only ten feet away, she held up a hand. "Stop."

I stopped.

She looked at Conall and Irene. "Move away from him. I know you've already talked, but I need to be sure before we let him inside."

Irene grabbed my arm. "It's really him, Myra. I would know."

"No, Rennie, you wouldn't," countered Myra. "I could create a copy that would fool you. *I am* that sort of copy." Then she stared at me again. "He's shielding his mind."

"I always have," I said, feeling nervous.

"Not like this," she replied. "You were never this good before. Let me see."

"Stop it, Myra," ordered Conall. "You're being rude."

A second figure emerged from the doorway, my oldest son, Matthew. "She's right," he said. "We don't know for sure what he is. *He* might not even know."

"Or he could be completely genuine, like Dorian was," argued Irene. Then her face paled.

"It's really me," I said. "And I'm not going to vanish."

"How did you know about that?" asked Matt, his curiosity so cool and calculating that it chilled me for a second.

"Chad told me about what happened," I answered. *And I saw it a few times before,* I thought to myself, but this wasn't the time to try and explain that.

"Drop your shields and let her examine you," ordered Matthew. Then he glanced at Myra and after a few seconds she nodded, almost imperceptibly.

But Irene noticed. "What did you tell her?" she challenged her brother.

"Don't worry about it," said Matthew, his posture tense.

Irene stepped forward, until she was almost nose-to-nose with her oldest brother. "You told her to kill him if she doesn't think he's real, didn't you?" Her eyes swept across to take in Myra as well. "Or maybe you'd do it? You probably told her to stop Conall and me from interfering." Irene's aythar was humming as she spoke, growing stronger by the moment. The look on her face was dangerous.

Eager to stop the impending fight, I held up my hands. "It's alright. I want to be sure too. If I'm not actually me then I don't want to be here." I'd been keeping shields around my body and particularly my mind for so long that it took a deliberate effort on my part to drop them, but I did. Almost immediately, I felt Myra's presence within my head.

Minutes passed while she skillfully rummaged through my memories. I was aware of some of what she saw, but not everything—she was too quick. Myra studied my present thoughts as well as those of the recent past, and she looked at other things I hadn't even been aware of before, parts of myself that I had no words to describe. As time passed, I began to worry. It was taking too long. Was I really myself? Or had I been through too much for her to recognize me?

"He's—different," said Myra at last, and when the others began to tense up, she quickly added, "but it's him." Then she answered their questions in the most demonstrable way possible: she hugged me. "Sorry for doubting you."

Irene let out a loud sigh, and Conall, still exhausted, sat down. "I thought my heart was going to give out," he complained. Glaring up and Matthew and Myra, he added, "Don't do that to me."

My attention was on Matthew as Myra finally released me. "What?" he asked, and I opened my arms. He gave a long-suffering sigh. "I knew it."

"I just came back from the dead," I remarked. "Doesn't that deserve a hug?"

"Again," said Matt, putting special emphasis on the word. "This isn't the first time."

Conall threw his arms around me once more. "I'm here for you, Dad."

Irene began laughing. "At least someone loves you." She joined in a moment later, along with Myra. Matthew watched us with an expression of annoyance on his face.

After we had all disengaged, I glanced at him again, lifting my arms. Rolling his eyes, Matt *allowed* me to embrace him, though he began pushing me away after a brief time. *He probably counted the seconds,* I thought wryly.

I felt a fresh wave of trepidation as we went inside the house, and seeing George's despondent features filled me with yet more guilt. My life had been full of similar moments. How many people had paid for my mistakes? Over the years George's entire family had paid the price for mine—his mother, father, and now his sister as well. And what had it gotten him? An empty title and worthless thanks from people like me.

"You survived," he said quietly, giving me a weak smile.

...And she didn't, I finished internally. I wished he hated me. It would have been easier, but I could see in his eyes that he was actually glad for me, despite his own sorrow. If anything, he probably felt guilty for his mixed emotions. *Damn it.*

One thing I had learned from a lifetime of ruining people's lives, however, was that they didn't appreciate hearing about how guilty you felt about it. They wanted to feel like it had meant something, or at the very least that you were grateful for their sacrifice. The last thing they wanted was an apology.

"Your sister was incredible," said Karen, coming in from the hallway. "I didn't always get along with her, but I've never seen anyone so brave. I wouldn't be here if it wasn't for her. I wish it had been..."

I gave her a warning with my eyes and Karen stopped. I had to admire her intelligence. She was learning faster than I had in her circumstances. Then George said something that made my heart ache, "Elaine was a hundred times better than me. After Dad died, I was all she had left, but I couldn't do anything. Now it's just me."

Crouching down in front of his chair, I met his eyes. "I know this sounds trite, but you're part of our family too. Even though it feels like it, you aren't alone." Then, for no other reason than the fact that I'm stupid and still hadn't learned how to act appropriately, I leaned in to whisper in his ear, "Plus, I have three unmarried daughters."

George uttered a sad laugh and Irene gasped. Somehow, she had managed to hear me. "Dad!" she snapped, giving me a look of pure spite. "This isn't the time for jokes." She hovered beside him protectively.

The last Prathion looked up at her and gave a smile that was almost sincere. "I don't mind. It was sort of comforting—and funny."

"How was *that* funny?" said Irene.

"Where's Gram?" I asked, though that wasn't precisely what I wanted to know.

"In Alyssa's room with her," answered Myra, not fooled in the least. "Carissa and her mother are in Rose's room. They were all a little shaken after seeing Dorian." The look on her face was both sympathetic and a warning to me.

Leaving them in the main room, I headed down the hall, where I encountered Lynn on her way to see what all the commotion was about. She stared at me for a moment, then put her arms around me. It was a rare gesture of emotion from the She'Har girl, though unlike my oldest son, such things didn't embarrass her. When she let go of me I could see she was full of questions, but she didn't ask them. She just continued on into the den, confident that I would answer them later.

Sometimes she seems like a child, other times I wish I had half her maturity, I observed, walking onward. I stopped in front of Alyssa's door, but then moved on. I wasn't fooling anyone, least of all myself, but when I came to Rose's door I hesitated.

Like all the bedrooms, it was protected by a privacy ward, so I couldn't see what was happening inside. Listening for a moment, I heard faint sounds. It wasn't crying, but Carissa and her mother were having a quiet conversation. The first big round of tears had probably finished before I got home, though there would surely be more to come.

And there I stood, listening in the hall, an intruder, trespassing on their family's privacy. My knuckles hovered in front of the wooden door, but after a moment my hand dropped down to hang uselessly at my side. Turning away, I went back to the front room.

All eyes were on me. "I know you all have a lot of questions, but I'm tired. I think I'm going to sleep for a while."

A chorus of encouragement answered me, urging me to rest. So I went back to my own bedroom, the one I had once shared with Penny. It felt like it had been years since I had been there. As I closed the door, my hand hovered over the lock. I wanted privacy, but it felt like a betrayal to shut them out. Finally, I left it. If anyone needed me, they could come in and wake me.

Stripping off my borrowed clothing, I went to the adjoining chamber and took a short bath. I wasn't very dirty. In fact, I had reappeared utterly clean, but wearing the discarded robe had left me feeling in need of a cleansing. Then I climbed into the bed and pretended to sleep.

I was very tired, but not sleepy. It was emotional exhaustion, and all I really desired was to be alone. Thinking on it, I decided that was probably why everyone had already split into separate rooms before I arrived home, and why they hadn't been impatient for answers.

At the moment, all I wanted was to see Rose, which made me feel guilty all over again.

***

Hours later, I woke at the sound of the door opening. Although the room was dark, my magesight told me it was Rose. She closed it and then my ears heard a distinctive 'click' as she locked it behind her.

I had been sleeping on my side, and my back was toward her as she stopped beside the bed. "Mort? Are you awake?" she asked, her voice almost a whisper.

What should I say? Why was she here? Those and a dozen other questions ran through my mind, but in the end, I chose the easy course and pretended to be asleep. Then I felt her pull the covers back and the bed shifted as she settled onto it, easing in to lie next to me. Her breath tickled the back of my neck as she scooted closer and wrapped her right arm around my waist.

She wore only a simple shift, and I was naked, but for once my conscience was clear of dirty thoughts. My heart was in a different place, one full of guilt and regret, and at the moment a measure of panic.

A quarter of an hour passed, and I began to think she had fallen asleep, until I heard her voice in my ear. "I know you're awake."

I stayed quiet. That was the mistake so many pretend sleepers made, they answered a question, giving themselves away. I was too good for that. Rose's palm pressed against my chest. "Your heart is beating too fast," she told me.

Stupid heart, I thought. It never did what I wanted it to, in more ways than one.

"Do you understand how glad I am that you're not dead?" she asked. "That I wasn't a party to your death?"

Despite my best intentions, I nodded. Sleeping people moved sometimes.

"You don't have to tell me what happened. There will be time for that tomorrow, but you should have come to see me when you got back. Why didn't you?"

I didn't dare turn to look at her. "I couldn't."

"Why not?"

I said nothing.

"You heard about Dorian's return," she said simply. It wasn't a question.

Of course, I had. I had seen him before the cage sealed me away. I knew not only how it had happened, but also what must have happened later. He had been my best friend, but he had been Rose's husband, her one true love. His brief visit would have torn the wound in her heart wide open and then rubbed salt in it. "It was because of me," I said at last. "They wanted to use him against us."

I felt her smile in the dark. "They tried, but after he and Gram sorted it out, he did just the opposite. He stopped one of them from killing Karen."

It felt good to hear that, and yet it caused me a faint twinge of jealousy. I had loved Dorian like a brother, and given the opportunity I'd have gladly taken his place. But it also hurt. He had always been better than me. Not smarter, not more powerful, not even more handsome, but he'd been perfect. He hadn't compromised, he'd been nearly incapable of lying, and his honor had been without fault. In comparison, I was none of those things. The best that could be said of me was that I was sly, or perhaps clever, but the truth was darker. I was deceitful, petty, vengeful, and worst of all, selfish.

My only redeeming quality was my role as a father. I had done a decent job there, but I owed much of the credit to Penny.

I hadn't said anything in quite some time, but Rose, in spite of her lack of magic, could read my mind. "You're worried I've changed my mind after seeing him again. Or perhaps you think you don't deserve happiness."

"Something like that," I admitted.

"I've had similar thoughts," she replied. "But fortunately, I'm smarter than you."

I started to turn over, to remind her who had lost our last game of chess, but her arm tightened, holding me still. "Don't roll over," she said. "I don't want you poking me with that thing…" After a long pause, she added, "…yet."

Regardless of the situation, I hadn't been thinking of that—a first for me.

"I never told you that Penny came to me," she said suddenly, changing the subject.

"What?"

"It happened when we were lost on that strange beach," she explained. "You fell asleep and she took your place. We talked about a lot—the past, the present, the children, and you."

The tension in my back reached new heights, so much so that my kidneys began to feel as though someone had punched them.

"I promised to take care of you, and them," she told me. Her voice was firm when she continued, "I keep my promises, Mort."

"What about…?"

"Most of them already know, or have some idea," she said, stopping me mid-question.

Self-restraint flew out the window, and I rolled over. Our faces were less than an inch apart and in the dim light we studied each other for a moment before I pressed my lips to hers. The fire that kindled grew rapidly, until I thought it would burn me to death, but like a moth to the flame, I couldn't control my desire to get closer to the light. When my hands started to roam, tugging at the edges of the gown she wore, Rose stopped me.

"I can't," she told me. "Not tonight. Despite what I said, today was a shock." The beast inside me roared in disappointment, which she probably saw in my eyes, though I didn't utter a sound. "I need some time," she added.

We lay together and I held her for a while, enjoying our closeness, but even that proved to be too much for me. I rolled back over and she held me instead, claiming it was easier to sleep without a dagger in her back.

I pretended not to know what she was talking about, though I couldn't help but chuckle a little. Somehow Rose fell asleep, though I didn't; not that I minded. My body was frustrated, but I was happy for the first time in at least a year.

A few hours later, Rose quietly got up. Moving like a ghost, she left my room and returned to her own. Over the course of the next week, she returned frequently to hold me in the warm dark, but we remained apart in the most intimate sense.

The week after that she began staying longer, until one night I woke to find myself in the jaws of a hungry beast. It had been a long time since I had been so pleasantly imperiled, and from that night on we took turns at being both the hunter and the hunted.

EPILOGUE

Rose and I kept our private matters, well, private, and if anyone noticed our odd glances or nighttime visitations, they didn't mention it. With the worst of my problems behind me, life settled down, but it wasn't easy. After all the explanations, I—and more importantly—everyone else, had to deal with the consequences. Other than Chad, no one left my house for a full two weeks.

In part, it was for comfort. All of them were tired, grief-stricken, or traumatized, and everyone handled it differently. The only common denominator was that they sought solace in the presence of their fellow survivors.

George had it the worst, I think. Myra, and especially Irene, spent a lot of time with him. Irene and George hadn't really known each other well before then, but they seemed to find a lot of common ground in the weeks that followed. I was glad to see it and didn't think much about it.

My survival removed a great weight from Matthew's shoulders, and for a while he was more social than Conall, who was still dealing with some guilt over his choices. In time, however, they both returned to their usual selves, with Matt spending most of his time alone and Conall becoming more relaxed and open.

Something about meeting his father changed Gram, and he spent more time with Carissa afterward, though they had little in common. Meanwhile Rose decided to take up cooking and asked Alyssa to teach her, using it as an opportunity to become closer with her future daughter-in-law. To be honest, the results were mixed. I trusted Lynaralla in the kitchen more than I did Rose. My She'Har daughter might do something outrageous like trying to serve rat, but she had gotten to the point that you knew the rat would at least be properly done, rather than raw or burnt.

Lynaralla turned out to be the most pressing problem. When we finally learned the news of what had happened on the Wester Isle, she informed us that she only had a few weeks left. Being a She'Har 'child' meant she required calmuth, the fruit of the mother-tree, to retain her human form. The supply we had in stasis would run out, and once that happened, she would begin to take root about a week later.

The news hit me like a slap in the face, and the others were just as unhappy about it. Irene and Karen were particularly upset. Unfortunately, the only solution I knew of was the barbaric procedure Tyrion had created thousands of years before, burning out the seed-mind and leaving his victims with irreparable brain damage.

That was obviously unacceptable, so neither I nor Matthew mentioned it. Instead, he and Lynn talked it over and she decided to take root in a place that would at least benefit everyone. Matthew was already working on plans to restore the dimensional boundaries that kept our world neatly divided into two separate demi-planes. Lynaralla's choice to take root made that much easier, as she chose to plant herself in the spot where Kion had been, serving as the gatekeeper that maintained the dimensional enchantment.

It would still be the work of a lifetime to find and repair all the damage that had been done to the dimensional boundaries, but at least it wouldn't degrade any further while Matthew and the others worked on it. Needless to say, Irene was unhappy with the choice, especially once it was revealed that Lynn would be dormant for ten years or more after the transformation before she could be expected to be able to converse with people again.

It was like losing someone else, and we were all still tender from the deaths of Elaine, Cyhan, and Moira.

Before she left, we held separate memorials for those we had lost. Without a proper body, we had Moira's at the mountain cottage, since no one outside of our small group of family and friends would have understood. As far as the world knew, Moira was still alive.

George took Elaine's remains back to Arundel and we had a private service for her there, while Alyssa decided to bury her father in the private Cameron graveyard at Castle Cameron. Gram had decided to live there and take service with the new Count di' Cameron. Since Rose had lost the title of Lady Hightower, their family no longer had much to their name in the way of lands.

It was a year later when Gram and Alyssa finally made their vows. Chad took his role seriously, standing in for Cyhan during the ceremony (and offering Gram a few token threats if he ever made Alyssa unhappy). Rose was rather displeased when she learned that Cyhan had appointed the hunter to be her godfather, even if it didn't have much legal weight, and I made a point of not mentioning that it had actually been my idea.

It was the first large event to be held at Castle Cameron, even though the keep itself was still a work in progress. The shining black stone I had built it from proved to be exceptionally difficult to work with, making it a nightmare for the masons and carpenters who had to fit it with doors and other necessities. Conall nearly worked himself to death assisting them until Matthew suggested he provide the craftsmen with enchanted chisels and other tools to help them cut and shape the stone.

Not long after that, Matthew and Karen were wed, primarily because she became pregnant and they could no longer hide their relationship. It wasn't that they didn't love each other, but neither of them had been particularly interested in making it official in the public's eyes.

Ariadne, the Queen of Lothion, gave birth to a daughter, and while there were plenty of rumors regarding who the father might have been, the official story was that it had been her late-husband's. The child had dark hair, unlike Ariadne or her purported father Leomund, and as she grew older, I couldn't help but note her resemblance to Brigid. I had no doubts about who her sire really was.

Rose and Carissa moved back to her house in the capital, and by coincidence I decided I would move to the old Illeniel house there. With Tyrion gone it was mine again, and I developed an uncharacteristic interest in the center of Lothion's political life. In reality it was to be closer to Rose of course, and we made quite a production of secret meetings and trysts, behaving like people half our age.

Carissa probably would have caught us, but not long after that she met the son of the Viscount Ledair, from Iverly. She and her grandmother moved there before long, and eventually she married into Gododdin's nobility. After that Rose and I didn't bother much with the pretense; we took turns living at one another's homes and the servants knew better than to talk.

Lady Rose returned to Lothion's social circles, much to the dismay of those who had formerly defamed her. With the Queen's open support for both of us, and the groundwork Moira had done previously, changing the minds of Lothion's most powerful nobles, no one dared do more than whisper. In fact, Rose seemed to relish the rumors, turning her infamy into yet another bartering tool in political circles as she gained a reputation for being untouchable.

A big surprise came to me when Irene announced that she would be marrying George Prathion, for I had been utterly clueless. I had known she was spending more time in Arundel, which was growing into a prosperous city, but I hadn't understood why. She had always claimed to be involved in this or that charitable project, and I had believed her. Needless to say, Rose had known about their relationship long before I did, and she shook her head in disbelief at my ignorance.

"I'd have told you, if I'd known you were that oblivious," she told me when the letter came. "How can you be so obtuse?"

Never one to accept my failings without making a joke, I winked at her and then cast my eyes lower, staring at what I lovingly referred to as her 'charms.' "I was distracted," I said, using my most frequent excuse.

Her response was a stern look that was no more serious than my remark. "No dessert for you after dinner, sir, since you can't behave like a gentleman."

I genuinely hoped she meant the pie she had put in the oven earlier. She was still continuing her efforts at cooking, and lately that had been baking. I had pleaded with her to let the servants handle the kitchen, but she insisted on dabbling, much to my stomach's dismay. Too stupid to keep my mouth shut, I asked, "You mean the mince pie—right?"

Her eyes simmered with annoyance when she saw the hopeful look on my face. "I meant exactly what I said," she retorted coolly, "and you *will* be trying the mince pie."

In the end I had the pie, and I did such a good job of praising it that she forgave me. It wasn't actually too hard to pretend, for she had improved considerably.

After Irene's marriage, she and our other children began to put pressure on us to end our sinful ways and make our own relationship official, which we eventually did, creating another big stir in Lothion's social circles.

The decade that followed was a busy one, for everyone else. Rose continued to dabble in politics, but I stayed resolutely out of things. The Queen's daughter, Mariana, grew into an interesting woman, precocious and unpredictable. She delighted her mother and proved to be both intelligent and talented in magic as well as politics. At Ariadne's request I spent a considerable amount of time with the girl, mentoring her in the magic she had inherited and providing her with some of the lessons I had learned in life, but she likely profited most from the things Rose taught her.

Rose and I enjoyed her autumn years, for there were plenty of grandchildren. Gram and Alyssa gave us three, and Carissa produced five. Conall had married a niece of the Duke of Cantley, and he and

Irene had two children each, while Matthew stopped with his first. He was too careful and too taken with his various projects to bother with more, though I harassed him about it continually. Myra never married, having come to the conclusion that the Centyr gift would end with her, and while I wanted to argue the point, I had a genuine fear of what a child with her sort of power might be like.

With advancing age, I began to worry about Rose, but her health remained strong. Great-grandchildren were beginning to appear, enriching our days and giving us plenty of reasons to travel. It was one of the best periods of my life, especially since I wasn't personally responsible for any of them. My only job was to show up now and then to teach them bad things, and nobody dared to try and stop me. People think normal adolescents are bad, but quite a number of my great-grandchildren were mages, and I delighted in encouraging them to do things that earned me the ire of their parents.

Say what you will. I call it justice.

Things took a darker turn for me in Rose's ninety-second year. Her health began to decline precipitously, and there was no longer much I could do about it with normal wizardry. A shadow fell over my heart and I spent my days contemplating how I would endure without her. I became desperate enough to consider drastic options, such as enlisting Gareth Gaelyn's aid to create a new body for her or tempting fate by touching the void magic that still dwelled in my soul.

She refused everything, and as her days drew to a close, I abandoned my pride to beg her incessantly. I was desperate to find a way to save her, but she adamantly defied me, no matter how wild my tantrums became. "I've lived long enough," she told me, patting my hand with hers.

It looked smaller than I remembered, wrinkled and weak. Mine seemed old too, but it was a lie. I had altered my appearance over the years to match hers, but inside I was still young. The light touch of her fingers brought fresh tears to my eyes. "You could live longer," I said, trying again to convince her.

She shook her head. "I love you, Mordecai, but there's someone waiting for me. It wouldn't be right for me to ask for more time. I'm ready to see him again."

But there's no one waiting for me, I wanted to yell. Penny wasn't really dead, she was still trapped in limbo, in some strange corner of my heart. Rose's passing would create a second scar as great as the one I had from losing her. I couldn't imagine how I would survive it. I didn't want to.

"I still talk to her sometimes," said Rose. "She loves hearing about the children."

"What?" I couldn't believe her words. She had to be hallucinating.

Reaching out, she pulled my head down and kissed my cheek. "I'm sorry for not telling you. She thought it better that way."

"Penny did?" I could barely get the words out.

Rose nodded. "Remember when Dorian came back? She thought it might be like that. She didn't want to reopen old wounds. She wanted you to be happy."

My breath came in gasps as I cried. "How many times?" I finally managed to say.

"Every few years," she answered. "Whenever you got sad or started reminiscing about the past. She would wake me up in the middle of the night and we would talk about things."

"And how did she feel?" I asked.

Rose closed her eyes. "Happy—and sad too. She hated missing everything. She tried to hide it, but I knew her too well for her to fool me. Time has been different for her. She still looks the same. I think she's only lived a month in all the years we've been together." Rose's voice began to drift, as though she was dreaming. "I can see him, Mordecai."

"Tell him he's going to have to wait longer," I cried.

She smiled at my outburst and opened her eyes again, focusing on my face. "I know what you're thinking. You told me before. The world is just a dream. There's no one waiting. But that's not true. This is my dream too, and Dorian is waiting for me. Someday you and Penny will meet us there."

"No," I said, denying everything. "This isn't fair. You can't leave. Who's going to keep Penny company when she comes? She'll be lonely. Haven't you thought about that?" I could hardly see Rose's face anymore with all the tears in my eyes.

"I love you, Mort, but I'm tired. Let me sleep," said Rose, letting her eyes drift closed once more.

She slept then, while I watched her, but she never woke again. It was hours before she drew her last breath. I cried the entire time, and when I knew she was gone I gave up my attempts to be quiet and screamed my sorrow at the walls.

As Rose had predicted, I survived her passing, though my food no longer had any taste to it. The world was grey, as though it had all turned to ash. I moved back to the old mountain cottage. It had been empty for a number of years, for after Matthew and Karen's child finished coming of age they had moved out. They were still married, but saw each other only occasionally, for he was continually busy with his work, and Karen had developed a wide range of interests and contacts all over the world.

Soon after, Myra came to join me. She claimed to be lonely, but I knew it was because she was worried. She refused to let me mope too much, though she still failed to reawaken my joy for life. I started cooking again, something I hadn't done much of since the years when Penny and I had raised our children there.

Mariana had been Queen for a number of years by then, putting to an end any doubts left regarding whether a woman could rule. At that point few of the people had ever lived under any monarch but a queen. Her skill at governance, along with the presence of the World Road, gradually led to Lothion holding sway over both Gododdin and Dunbar, and the empire she founded ushered in a golden age.

A few years after Myra came to live with me, Conall died, though he was still young for a wizard. Ever wild, he broke his neck while hunting. How he managed that when I had reminded him so many times to keep himself shielded at all times was a mystery to me. His death sent me into an even darker depression, until I think even Myra grew tired of dealing with me.

A decade later, when Irene lost George to yet another stupid accident, she decided to move in, and coincidentally, Myra moved out. She had her reasons, but they were lies. I was a burden, and it was Irene's turn to shoulder it. I told Irene as much, which resulted in an argument of epic proportions. She was still dealing with her own grief, which made my self-pity particularly offensive.

We tore up a few trees during that fight and a few more during the ones that followed it, and strangely, I began to feel a little better each time. I didn't fight with Rennie often. I was civilized most of the time, and she was as sweet as a lamb, the perfect daughter, but when she let her hair down, the wildlife usually decided it was time to migrate to another mountain for a while. Honestly, I enjoyed those fights, and the years between them. She was a lot like her mother.

Myra visited now and then, and I think she was surprised that Irene had somehow gotten me to smile again, when she had had such poor luck at it. I explained it to her by saying I'd had no choice. "After all, you don't think her husband died of natural causes, do you?"

Myra told me in no uncertain terms that my joke was in very poor taste, but I was pretty sure her sense of humor had simply atrophied with old age.

Penny enjoyed seeing them as well, and as time went on, I got to hear a number of stories about her sudden visits when I was sleeping. Like Rose, they didn't tell me about it for a long time, but Irene was stubborn, and she eventually told me the truth. I began to leave letters on my bedside table at night, and occasionally I found a reply, written with Penny's distinctively terrible penmanship.

I took up gardening, raising roses and other flowers, and I started leaving fresh flowers with my letters, along with food and other treats. They were almost always left untouched, but every few months I would find that someone had eaten the food and there would be a new letter where mine had been. Those were bittersweet moments for me.

A few times I woke to discover an entire meal laid out, reminding me of the old days. It felt as though if I waited, she might walk in through the door, to chide me for letting the food grow cold. But of course, she didn't. I enjoyed the meal and tried not to let my tears spoil it.

The decades passed by and the new empire of Lothion showed no signs of weakening. After all, its Queen was a wizard as well and would very likely be on the throne for a long time. Mariana was a political genius, with a mind that would have given Rose a close race. She had a conscience, which I attributed to her time with me when she was younger, yet she was also utterly ruthless when the need arose, which I figured had something to do with her father.

I knew it was a personal conceit, though. Ariadne had taught her daughter well, and Rose had helped to hone the Queen's political acumen. But I liked to think I'd had some small part in her success.

In my second century, Matthew finally got lonely and decided to live with me. As before, Irene found an excuse to leave, confirming my suspicions. My children were taking turns making sure Dad didn't get depressed and do something stupid. I was sad to see Irene go, and had my doubts about living with my son, but we got on like two happy bachelors.

There were no more fights, and while the house grew persistently dirtier, neither of us cared. On a few occasions I found signs that someone had been cleaning during the night and a letter from Penny confirmed that I had better do something about the state of affairs or suffer the consequences. I laughed it off, figuring I'd wait a few more days before doing some serious cleaning.

What could she do to me anyway?

I woke up the next morning in a bed covered with wet mud, along with another letter promising it would be poison ivy the next time. The empty bucket that had transported the mud sat in the middle of the room, a stark warning.

So, we got busy cleaning, and Matthew finally confessed that it had been Penny who had organized my caretakers since Rose's death. She had actually sent them letters years before Rose died, and she had met each of them on various occasions. I probably should have felt betrayed, but I didn't.

I went to my room and cried behind the safety of the privacy ward for over an hour.

My son and I worked hard, devising new enchantments that helped to usher in a new age of magic as great as the one that had come over twelve hundred years past. There were a lot more wizards now, though they were comparatively young.

Somewhere in my fourth century, Mariana was assassinated and the empire she had built began to fall apart. I steadfastly refused to participate in saving it, being rather disgusted with the animal that took her place. My children stayed out of it too, but a number of my grandchildren, great-grandchildren, and great-great-grandchildren and so on died in the wars that followed.

The dragons I had given out became pieces in the game of power between nations. I should have seen that coming, but while Mariana had ruled it had never been an issue. Matthew and I hid the remaining eggs deep within the earth where I hoped they would never be found.

It was around then that I began to give serious thought to the fact that my children were going to die. They were starting to show their age, and I was still just as I had always been. The thought of losing them horrified me, reminding me once more what a curse my immortality had become.

I spent considerable time brooding over it, and I was determined not to see it happen, though at the same time I couldn't bear to bring the world to an end. As messy as it was, it was full of people who deserved to live, and quite a few of them were my grandchildren of various generations.

My deal with the dreaming god had been clear. I could live as long as I wished, but to escape I had to use the power hidden in the dark scar on my soul. Doing so would start the process all over again, causing me to accumulate power until my existence ripped his dream apart and I fell asleep to create a new one.

I wasn't even five hundred years old yet and it was beginning to get unbearable, but I felt I owed it to the children of the world to give them a future. The dreamer was a coward, and in the words of a wise man I had once known, *Fuck that.* Chad would have been proud.

So, I devised a new plan. I created a stasis box to hold me, along with a few modifications at Matthew's request. I would wait out the millennia, until everything that could possibly happen had happened. It was cheating, sure, but I didn't give a damn.

We placed the box in a chamber built beneath Lynaralla's roots. Matthew, Irene, and Myra each had a talisman that would not only release me, but would summon me to their sides when used. They were masterpieces of enchanting, something I couldn't have imagined creating in my younger days, but we had advanced the craft considerably since then. I also included a timer in the box itself that would shut it off every hundred years, so I could check on the progress of the world myself.

I waited a while before using it, as every year my children begged me not to go, but eventually I could stand it no longer. We said our goodbyes and I laid down to rest.

They dragged me back repeatedly over the next century. A couple of times because of a genuine emergency, but usually just because they missed me. We would visit for a few weeks, and then I'd return to my slumber in stasis.

When the day came that I was summoned by a stranger, it caught me off guard. Almost a hundred years had passed, and my children were long gone. The feeling of despair and loneliness that came upon me then nearly overwhelmed me, and the hapless ruler who had inherited one of their talismans never realized how close he came to precipitating the end of everything.

I kept my emotions under control and helped him, then went back to my tiny home under the tree. Feeling bad for Lynaralla, I spent a few years talking to her, a conversation that seemed like days to her, then I put myself back to sleep. This time I changed the timer to run for a thousand years, realizing it had been a mistake to set it for only a hundred. I had no interest in seeing the world anymore.

I was summoned a dozen times in that period, and it got rather tiresome. By then I was a creature of legend, and often the holder of the talisman thought its purpose was only a myth. At some point most of the wizards had gotten themselves killed again and the world was once again in a dark age with little magic.

Thankfully, the talismans were lost in the long run, and the next person to bring me back was some sort of scholar who found one hidden in a tomb. Irritated, I didn't feel very bad about scaring him half to death. A little miffed, I returned and changed the timer to an interval of five thousand years and hoped no one else would find a talisman. My goal was to wake up and find nothing worth continuing for, so I could put an end to it all.

No one interrupted me, a first, even though I had set my timer for the longest period yet. When I emerged, I found that the area around Lynaralla's tree had become a desert. She still seemed healthy, probably because her roots went down so deep, she wasn't reliant on the rain. We had another long conversation, and she shared some of what she had seen with me. I was disappointed to learn that civilization was doing just fine.

Returning to my box, I repeated the process several times. It was beginning to dawn on me that history might turn out to be much longer than I had imagined. After four cycles of five thousand years apiece, someone found one of my talismans again. This time it turned out to be some sort of weird demon worshipper.

While talking to him I learned that somewhere along the line someone had indeed created demons, or something nearly indistinguishable from such. The man who had called me thought I was an archdevil of some sort and was suffering under the delusion that he had bound me with whatever nonsensical incantation he had recited while activating the talisman.

I gave him the benefit of the doubt. It was possible he had a benign purpose. Maybe he was willing to endanger his imaginary afterlife to help someone in need. Sadly, that was not the case, and when we emerged from the cave he had summoned me to, I saw the body of the child he had sacrificed during his rituals. I wound up escorting him back to the cave and dropping the ceiling on his head. Humans could be so disappointing.

Another five thousand years and I received a shock. Lynaralla's tree was gone, only the roots remained, dry and withered. Thirty thousand years was a long time, even for a She'Har elder. I grieved again, for she had been my last child, my only remaining companion.

I was truly alone now.

Turning off the timer, I returned to my stasis. There was no reason to wake again. I was done with it all.

Ages passed into eons, and eons became mere pebbles in the riverbed of time. Unknown to me, the world I had once lived upon burned, consumed by a sun that had grown red and swollen. Yet the husk of that world survived, becoming a cold, dark rock that persisted even after the sun itself burned out.

Unaware of anything, I floated down the empty river of eternity, until even matter itself began to die of old age, evaporating into nothing. The stasis box failed, and I emerged to find myself in a cold, dark void. There were no stars, no air, no light. My body died shortly thereafter, but even physical death wouldn't release me.

Reaching inside myself, I found the darkness and light and brought them together. In that empty place, it took a long time to draw enough power from the dissipating universe to accomplish my goal, but I did it anyway. As I ascended to godhood once more, there came a point when I was close, but not yet asleep, and I was granted a final gift.

Perhaps I granted it to myself, it was hard to say, but in the place that wasn't a place I found Penny looking back at me. "It took you long enough," she said, giving me a smile.

"Are you really here?" I asked, stunned. It had been so long since I had seen her face, I wasn't even certain anymore whether she was the same woman I had loved before. "Penny?"

She took my hand and led me into a green field, full of flowers. "Everyone's waiting for us," she said, giving me a quick kiss.

Turning to survey the place, I realized we were back in the valley where I had been born. It was a dream. It had to be. But I didn't care. They were all there, all the people I had loved. Crying tears of joy, we ran to them.

I slept, and my dream began. The old universe vanished, falling apart as a new one emerged from the remnants.

The story continues in:

Transcendence and Rebellion

Stay up to date with my release by signing up for my newsletter at:

Magebornbooks.com

Books by Michael G. Manning:

Mageborn:
The Blacksmith's Son
The Line of Illeniel
The Archmage Unbound
The God-Stone War
The Final Redemption

Embers of Illeniel (a prequel series):
The Mountains Rise
The Silent Tempest
Betrayer's Bane

Champions of the Dawning Dragons:
Thornbear
Centyr Dominance
Demonhome

The Riven Gates:
Mordecai
The Severed Realm
Transcendence and Rebellion

Standalone Novels:
Thomas

ABOUT THE AUTHOR

Michael Manning was born in Cleveland, Texas and spent his formative years there, reading fantasy and science fiction, concocting home grown experiments in his backyard, and generally avoiding schoolwork.

Eventually he went to college, starting at Sam Houston State University, where his love of beer blossomed and his obsession with playing role-playing games led him to what he calls 'his best year ever' and what most of his family calls 'the lost year'.

Several years and a few crappy jobs later, he decided to pursue college again and was somehow accepted into the University of Houston Honors program (we won't get into the particulars of that miracle). This led to a degree in pharmacy and it followed from there that he wound up with a license to practice said profession.

Unfortunately, Michael was not a very good pharmacist. Being relatively lawless and free spirited were not particularly good traits to possess in a career focused on perfection, patient safety, and the letter-of-the-law. Nevertheless, he persisted and after a stint as a hospital pharmacy manager wound up as a pharmacist working in correctional managed care for the State of Texas.

He gave drugs to prisoners.

After a year or two at UTMB he became bored and taught himself entirely too much about networking, programming, and database design and administration. At first his supervisors warned him (repeatedly) to do his assigned tasks and stop designing programs to help his coworkers do theirs, but eventually they gave up and just let him do whatever he liked since it seemed to be generally working out well for them.

Ten or eleven years later and he got bored with that too. So he wrote a book. We won't talk about where he was when he wrote 'The Blacksmith's Son', but let's just assume he was probably supposed to be doing something else at the time.

Some people liked the book and told other people. Now they won't leave him alone.

After another year or two, he decided to just give up and stop pretending to be a pharmacist/programmer, much to the chagrin of his mother (who had only ever wanted him to grow up to be a doctor and had finally become content with the fact that he had settled on pharmacy instead).

Michael's wife supported his decision, even as she stubbornly refused to believe he would make any money at it. It turned out later that she was just telling him this because she knew that nothing made Michael more contrary than his never ending desire to prove her wrong. Once he was able to prove said fact she promptly admitted her tricky ruse and he has since given up on trying to win.

Today he lives at home with his stubborn wife, teenage twins, a giant moose-poodle, two yorkies, a green-cheeked conure, a massive prehistoric tortoise, and a head full of imaginary people. There are also some fish, but he refuses to talk about them.

www.ingramcontent.com/pod-product-compliance
Lightning Source LLC
Chambersburg PA
CBHW060605310726
48982CB00008B/1240/J

* 9 7 8 1 9 4 3 4 8 1 3 0 9 *